OUT OF TIME - BROKEN GATES

Kenneth Bandoly

First Edition

ISBN: 979-8-9936719-0-1

For all who dream in the stars - may you always reach beyond the horizon, chase the impossible, and find adventure among the cosmos.

If you're holding this book, two things have already happened:

1. I finally shoved my perpetual "someday I'll write a novel" dream onto paper instead of letting it orbit my brain like space junk, and
2. You decided to tag along—so thanks for boarding the Aurora with me.

I've been a card-carrying sci-fi addict since Atari joysticks were the height of ergonomic design. Stars, wormholes, scorched gunmetal hulls—give me all of it. Yet after years of 2 a.m. physics deep dives and a bookcase groaning under dog-eared paperbacks, my story kept slipping through the airlock.

Then one crisp night I dragged the scope to the front yard and zeroed in on Saturn. The rings tilted like a cosmic turntable; its moons looked ready for a weekend camping trip—pack the marshmallows, ignore the vacuum. While I was busy daydreaming interplanetary tailgates, I swung past Saturn toward a fuzzy globular cluster (don't ask which; the coffee was weak and the hour was late). That's when it hit me:

What if humanity's last lifeboat docked long after the party was over?

Boom—Out of Time ignited.

This is my first full-length novel, and writing it felt a lot like space travel: months of silence punctuated by heart-pounding moments where everything shakes and you're positive something's about to explode. The process was humbling, exhilarating, occasionally painful, and—let's be honest—ridiculously fun. Book 2 is already drafted (spoiler: the throttle opens up). Book 1 moves at a deliberate pace because I needed room to build the universe, sketch the tech, and make friends with the characters before the lasers start flying.

I'll confess: one "quick" pause between chapters turned into a full-on week of linguistic procrastination. Instead of writing, I fell down the rabbit hole of building the Belta Lexicon. I pictured rock-hardened miners orbiting the asteroid belt, cut off from mainstream culture and marinating in a bizarre stew of ancestral languages. So I trawled dictionaries I can't even pronounce, mashed roots together, and tried to hear how a true Belter would spit the words through a cracked helmet mic. Was it productive? Debatable. Was it a blast? Absolutely.

I'm the type who bounces between obsessions—woodworking, hobby farming, wood-smoking an entire chicken at midnight—but the itch to write has never left. If you've got your own Big Idea rattling around, consider this permission to chase it. No, don't nuke your day job or sell the house. Just carve out a sliver of time—early mornings, lunch breaks, those weird hours when everyone else is doom-scrolling—and do the thing. Fear is a lousy editor; momentum is your best co-author.

So here's to uncomfortable first steps, to staring at the stars until a story stares back, and to every reader brave enough to turn the page with me. Strap in—light lag is real, the future's messy, and we've got one hell of a jump ahead.

    — Ken

Prologue

Two centuries ago, humanity's footprints clung to the dusty surface of the Moon and the wind-blown plains of Mars as timid promises rather than triumphant declarations. Those early off-world settlements— scarcely more than research outposts and resource stations—were the first attempts to stretch beyond Earth's fragile cradle. At the time, space travel was costly and slow, and the idea of settling distant worlds seemed as quixotic as it did grand.

Yet progress was relentless. In the mid-21st century, a confluence of necessity and ambition reshaped our species' priorities. Climate pressures at home sparked a renaissance of international cooperation. The United Nations, once a diplomatic forum prone to stalemate, became the backbone of a shared mission: secure Earth's biosphere and expand humankind's chances of survival by looking outward. Research grants ballooned, private and public sectors intertwined, and bold engineering concepts gained fast approval. The Artemis and Ares missions—those first tenuous steps to establish permanent Moon and Mars habitats—set the precedent. They put humanity back on the moon. Humanity then quickly proved that people could live off-world with minimal resupply from Earth. Solar power harvested beyond the atmosphere and rudimentary farming in hydroponic domes brought a measure of independence from the old home planet.

Within fifty years, fusion reactors on orbital platforms provided ample energy. With stable power, advanced ion drives and experimental nuclear-thermal propulsion systems began to shrink the solar system. Cargo ships could ferry materials from the asteroid belt; advanced robotics and AI-assisted construction crews assembled habitats from local regolith and ice. Mars, once a horizon of reddish emptiness, hosted sprawling underground communities by the turn of the 22nd century. The Moon served as a bustling logistics hub, a waypoint for every ship venturing out to the resource-rich frontier. Without anyone quite noticing at first, the solar system had become an extension of our economy, politics, and culture.

It was the discovery of stable antimatter production methods—scaling from nanograms to milligrams—that catalyzed the next leap. Scientists had pursued antimatter propulsion for decades, always hampered by astronomical energy costs and perilous containment challenges. By 2150, the Antimatter Stabilization Arrays built in Mercury orbit—where solar energy was abundant—finally yielded consistent, controllable thrust. Suddenly, ships could achieve velocities that had been theoretical dreams on old university chalkboards. A journey to Jupiter's moon Europa, once a three-year round trip, compressed to a matter of months. Saturn's rings, once distant wonders, became tourist attractions for the wealthy, and Titan, with its hydrocarbon-rich atmosphere, was eyed as a major refueling stop.

But near-light-speed travel between systems demanded more than powerful engines. It required mastery of materials science to shield vessels from interstellar dust. It demanded cryogenic life support systems that could operate for decades without failure. It required a profound understanding of physics to minimize and manage relativistic effects that turned time itself into a variable factor in exploration and heat into an enemy.

By the late 23rd century, humanity had built on the shoulders of thousands of engineers, physicists, explorers, and visionaries. Our shipyards orbited the outer planets, crafting sleek vessels designed to approach that ultimate barrier—99% the speed of light. Four-story centrifuge rings provided artificial gravity for long voyages. The delicate dance of balancing mass, radiation shielding, and propulsion outputs defined the blueprint of starships that would dare to reach beyond the Oort Cloud. The crewed starship Aurora, christened in the year 2221, was the culmination of these efforts: a vessel poised to sail not only through our solar system but to the star systems beyond.

And so, two hundred years after our tentative footprints of humanities' return to the Moon, we stood on the brink of interstellar travel—still fragile beings made of water and carbon, but now equipped with the means to challenge the silent darkness between stars. The spark of life that had flickered in Africa's savannas ages ago now glimmered in orbit around Saturn, forged antimatter engines near Mercury, and dreams of the day when we would slip the bonds of our sun's gravity to set course for distant worlds. Humanity had pulled itself from the mud and aimed for the heavens—and in doing so, we finally stood ready to confront the cosmos on something approaching its own terms. Little did we know, our greatest challenge would be ourselves.

1

Tu 23 Nov 2258 Earth Time - Dione Saturn moon Ship Station

T-48 hours to launch

The Orbital Assembly Complex hovered silently against the speckled canvas of space, its intricate framework glittering in the distant sunlight. Docked securely at the station's far rim, the interstellar vessel Aurora, the largest and fastest ship ever constructed, rested like a coiled spring of potential. Beyond the station's spars, Saturn drifted majestically, its pale rings throwing shards of reflected light into the darkness. The ship would soon break free of this cradle of human engineering and hurl itself across unimaginable distances. For the moment the docking clamps still held it close, as if Earth and its extended family refused to let go just yet.

Captain Aveline Morrow drifted gently toward the station's umbilical connector, her magnetic boots engaging with a soft clunk as she reached the docking bay's wide observation ports. The ship's gravity rings were not rotating while still docked, leaving the entire ship still under micro-gravity. They would not rotate until the ship detached to avoid gyroscopic interference with the orbital platform's position. The corridor lights were subdued. Crew members and technicians hurried about with last-minute tasks, holographic images hovering above their forearms from computers strapped on like digital vambraces. Aveline's uniform, crisp and austere with subtly embroidered mission patches, bore no medals or adornments. Recordings, interviews, and last-minute press coverage awaited, but she'd chosen simplicity—a quiet statement that this mission transcended personal accolades. Recordings, interviews, and last-minute press coverage awaited, but she'd chosen simplicity—a quiet statement that this mission transcended personal accolades and focused instead on the crew and their monumental undertaking. Still, no one doubted her authority. Her quiet confidence was earned through years of commanding deep-space survey runs.

Today, that confidence was put to the test. In the docking bay, transparent panels revealed the ship's silhouette: a slender forward hull that flared out like a large pyramid before joining to the rotating habitat ring sections. A large cubic module nestled behind the series of four rotating rings. Behind the cubic module, shielded engine housings bulged outward, forming a spherical section bristling with antennae and radiators. The rearmost portion of the ship was a massive array of container-like attachments that ringed the ship in horizontal columns. Each of these blocky containers were capable of atmospheric entry and would hopefully deploy a rapid setup colonial habitat in virtually any environment. The Antimatter Core Control unit was already online. The Alcubierre field generators—controversial, bleeding-edge tech— had passed every simulation so far. They had to. They would be the crew's lifeline against a universe that did not easily yield to travelers. Captain Morrow admired the external view of her new ship just a moment before entering the umbilical and going inside.

Morrow paused by a console and allowed her wrist computer to submit her authorization code, linking her to the ship and taking control over the vessel. She reviewed the cargo manifests: raw materials, medical supplies, agricultural starter kits, even a few personal mementos allowed to each crewmember listed in terms of mass. There were the stasis pods too, lined up in neat rows within the ship's cargo bay. Hundreds of sleeping colonists already in stasis and currently unaware that in just over a year of their subjective time they would wake up orbiting a distant world none had seen. Assuming everything went according to plan that is. Aveline thought briefly about the long and troublesome list of applicants for this mission. Although she had to sign off on final approval, she was thoroughly grateful she had not had to narrow that list down. The selection committee had done all the hard work there and allowed her to maintain a more high level of oversight. In the end, she had read over the personal files of each and every one of the final selections.

There were decades of work involved in this massive project to ensure the survival of life by spreading humanity to other systems throughout the galaxy. Due to the distance, there would be no return for the star faring travelers. The selection process for the colony was not an easy one. The motivations for people to gamble on a still relatively unknown planet with only a high probability of supporting life 1400 light years away was more often than not indicative of qualities undesirable for such a mission. In the end, a relatively small number of colonists were put in stasis. Not nearly enough to provide a sustainable gene pool for future generations. Instead, it was far easier to carry an entire civilization's worth of people as genetic material. The first generation of colonists birthed on the new world would be birthed in a laboratory. Genetic material was collected from a larger pool of applicants willing to send a piece of themselves on such a mission, while living the rest of their life in Sol. It had been dubbed "The Arc," a lifeboat for humanity.

"Captain, resource verification is complete." A soft voice broke her concentration. She turned to see Marcus Ito, their Communications and Operations Officer, leaning against a railing. His short dark hair framed perceptive eyes that seemed perpetually calm, as though he listened more than he spoke. He held a tablet against his chest, still preferring a more tangible alternative to the popular wrist computers.

"Excellent," she replied. "No surprises?"

Marcus shook his head calmly. "All accounted for, Captain—every kilo of seed stock, every liter of emergency water, every atom of hydrogen and oxygen. Data links are green across the board, and we have clear comms with Earth. We're ready for launch."

Aveline managed a small smile. Communication delays would be measured in centuries on earth as they raced near the speed of light and after acceleration of the ship, return messages would not catch them on the ship. They would be attempting to send their flight data back to earth for as long as they could though. The scientists insisted on it. The crew however, would be on their own. "Good work, Marcus. Let's gather everyone in the central hub. I want a final face-to-face with the core crew before we undock."

Riley Thompson was busy performing a last inspection on the stasis pods. He hummed softly, running a handheld scanner over life-support indicators. Riley was all cheerful grins and bright eyes. Even under these stakes, he radiated reassurance. The ship's physician and morale officer, he had a knack for sensing tension and unraveling it with a well-placed joke or kind words. A few station technicians stood nearby, double-checking the pods' nutrient feeds.

In an adjacently connected pod, Dr. Clara Song examined sealed containers of seeds and algae cultures. She hovered over them protectively, as if they were children about to step into a dangerous playground. Clara had a quiet reverence for life, no matter how small. In her mind, these seeds were the ancestors of entire ecosystems that would one day bloom under an alien sun. Today though, each one was meticulously stored for the journey through the stars, tucked away in their own form of natural stasis just like each one of the future colonists.

"Riley," Clara said, "the hydration feeds are stable, but I'm still concerned about the pH levels if we have to extend stasis for too long."

Riley looked up, meeting her gaze, "We'll be all right. The system's got redundancies. We'll make it work. That's what we do."

In the front of the ship, Navigator Jason Alvarez hunched over his console, his face bathed in the ghostly blue of holographic star charts that shifted continuously, accompanied by intricate mathematical overlays. Jason's eyes were shadowed, a hint of strain in his features that even the station's gentle lighting couldn't hide. He ran calculations over and over. The distance to Kepler-452... roughly 1400 light years... the margin for error... his job was to thread a cosmic needle at unimaginable speeds. One error could mean missing the target star by light-years. He sighed and muttered a half-joke to himself: "Just another casual drive down the cosmic highway, Jase. No pressure."

John Ferris, Chief of Security, stood silently observing from the corridor. He rarely intervened without need, but his presence was constant, reliable, and watchful. His arms were folded across his chest, face grim and steady, his dress uniform was perfection. John had spent hours ensuring every piece of metal was polished to a mirror shine and not even the slightest thread was out of place. He checked his sidearm out of habit, knowing full well there was almost nothing in what lay ahead that a bullet could solve. Still, preparation was comfort and he wore the relic of a sidearm for show as much as anything this day. He'd seen too many close calls during his past assignments. Out here, he'd protect these people—whatever form that protection needed to take.

In the engineering bay, Elena Park meticulously monitored diagnostics on the Alcubierre field projectors, fingers swiftly moving over shimmering holographic controls, whispering status updates under her breath. Her hands moved nimbly over shimmering control surfaces. She was precise and intense. As she worked, she whispered under her breath, "Containment field stable... quantum fluctuations minimal..." This ship was her magnum opus, an engine born of her own dreams and nightmares, and she was determined not to let it fail. She didn't notice Dr. Amir Qureshi standing behind her, observing quietly. Amir, the historian and archaeologist, seemed out of place amidst the hum of machinery. But he was living his dream. He would be witnessing first hand the cultural shifts as humanity separated itself into another branch. For the colony, he would be the link to understanding their place in history when they were so far from its source. While Elena stressed over every minor detail of the engineering that had been purely theoretical until she helped design it, Amir pondered what possibilities there would be for him on Kepler-452b. He decided he would have to suggest an easier name than that before they established the colony. Earth 2.0 was the nickname casually used for a couple centuries, but it would be their planet. Why shouldn't it have a good name that represented them?

A chime echoed through the corridor. Captain Morrow and Marcus stepped onto the bridge. One by one, the crew arrived and gathered near the central holotable. Captain Morrow surveyed them quietly: Marcus, steady and insightful; Elena, fiercely intelligent and intense; Jason, cloaked in sardonic humor; Riley, ever cheerful and perceptive; Clara, protective and nurturing; Amir, reflective and wise; and John, a vigilant sentinel at their threshold. She knew she was lucky to have such a great crew on this mission.

"Alright everyone," Captain Morrow began, her voice steady, "we launch in two days. This is our final all-hands meeting before we board for good. We'll do the photos and interviews shortly. Once we detach from the station, we'll be on our own. I don't need to remind you—this mission is unprecedented. We will push relativistic limits and trust new technologies that no crew has ever relied on. Very soon, we will embark on a journey unlike any other. Greater than the crossing of the Atlantic, far more dangerous than any of histories' intrepid explorers. In only a matter of weeks from our perspective, we will already be in the history books here in Sol. Beyond that, we take with us the hopes of a new beginning for humanity."

She paused, allowing the gravity of her words to sink in. The holotable glowed softly, displaying Aurora's model slowly rotating, each compartment labeled, each subsystem accounted for. Behind her, wide viewports revealed Saturn's majestic rings—silent sentinels witnessing their departure from the cradle of humanity. While the viewports would be covered by thick shielding for the journey, they offered one last tour of the cradle of humanity.

"If there are concerns, voice them now," Morrow continued. "We have the resources to handle minor last-minute adjustments, but once we leave, there's no turning back."

No one spoke immediately. The silence wasn't fear or resignation—it was understanding. They had trained, prepared, weighed the risks. They were ready, willing and committed. It was a hush of acceptance, a calm before the leap.

Aveline nodded, "We finalize loading tomorrow without press or interruptions. After that, each of you gets a day of rest. Write a last message home, if you need. Spend time with each other or find a quiet corner to reflect. Take the time to do whatever you need to do. In two days… this crew, this ship—this is our family and our home from now on."

They dispersed, drifting back to tasks that would soon be finished: calibrating sensors, sending final pre-launch data packets to the base stations on Saturn's moons & Earth, and sealing the last cargo containers. The work had a ritual quality. Soon, they would become travelers cast free of known shores, aiming for a distant star and a planet they had never set eyes upon—until now, just a designation without name and a set of promising spectrographic readings.

As the station's corridors gradually dimmed, signaling the onset of the artificial night cycle, each member of Aurora's crew found solitude. In their private darkness, they quietly grappled with doubts, acknowledged fears, and nurtured cautious hope. In two short days, they would leave behind the warmth of Sol and embrace the vast silence between the stars.

2

Thu 25 Nov 2258 Earth Time - Dione Saturn moon Ship Station
Launch Day

Launch day had arrived, yet the station corridors were calm, hushed —almost reverent. Dione was close to its lowest orbit dipping just below the ecliptic plane. From the station, the distant glimmer of Saturn's rings showed off for the crew. Captain Morrow stood by one of the forward observation windows, watching a last flurry of activity beyond the docking bay. A few maintenance drones zipped back and forth on final checks, their blinking lights reflecting faintly against the hull of the interstellar vessel. Everything looked so peaceful, so orderly —so different from the tumult and roar of old-world rocket launches she'd studied in the historical archives.

Those ancient footage clips fascinated her: the deafening crackle of engines biting into Earth's thick atmosphere, the towering billows of smoke and fire, crews strapped tightly into narrow capsules, hearts pounding, awaiting the violent shove skyward. The moment when pilots clenched their teeth and flex muscles through intense G-forces, wrestling gravity's grip, waiting for the exact second they passed the maximum aerodynamic stress, passing the first major milestone— before climbing to the serene darkness beyond the clouds. That must have been something to experience, though she found it a rather violent image.

Today would be... subtler. No thunder, no roar. Just the quiet unlatching of docking clamps and a gentle push into open space. To Morrow and her crew, the sensation would be little more than a slight shift beneath their feet, if they even felt anything at all. The ship's own artificial gravity, active only in key areas, would smooth it all out. They would simply drift away, leaving this shimmering station behind like a leaf slipping free from a branch.

Morrow sighed softly and turned away from the window. On a console nearby, countdown timers glowed in crisp yellow numerals. Only minutes remained before they untethered. The crew would be at their stations now, securing final readouts, going through last-minute mental and digital checklists. In the cargo bays, stasis pods held their silent passengers, each colonist suspended in engineered stillness. Years of research had refined these suspended animations, but they still had limits. She hoped they wouldn't need to push those limits unnecessarily, but nobody actually knew what they should expect when they arrived.

She made her way through a central corridor that led to the command deck. The lighting was set to a gentle daylight hue, and the hum of the ship's life support systems was a soft lullaby in the background. Approaching the command deck hatch, she could hear faint voices—Marcus's calm instructions over comms, Elena's final whispers to herself as she confirmed engine readouts, and Riley's easy banter meant to keep everyone's nerves in check.

Stepping onto the deck, she found Jason Alvarez already secured at the navigation console. He looked up as she entered, his usual smirk in place. "Captain," he said, nodding. "All star charts verified. Nothing's moved in the last five minutes of cosmic time. Hard to believe."

Morrow returned the nod and took her seat at the command station. John stood at the tactical station just behind her own, arms folded, scanning the status readouts on his displays. Amir hovered near a side console, wearing an expression of thoughtful curiosity rather than worry, and Dr. Clara Song was strapped into a spare seat, idly twisting a small seed vial between her fingers. Marcus was at his comms station, lines of data scrolling before him. Elena tapped controls at the propulsion console, her face set in determination.

"Status, everyone?" Morrow asked quietly.

"Comms nominal," Marcus said. "External hardlines are going dark for separation. Station acknowledges we're ready."

Elena's voice was calm: "Antimatter containment is stable. Alcubierre fields in standby mode. Just a nudge from the maneuvering thrusters will get us clear. Then we can slowly build to cruising speed."

Riley's cheerful tone came through on the overhead channel. He was down near the stasis bay: "Pods stable. Everyone sleeping soundly.

Nothing to do but tuck 'em in and take care of each other."

Aveline smiled at that. "Good. Prepare for clamp release on my mark."

No one braced for impact—no need. This wasn't a rocket's fury. She glanced at the countdown: thirty seconds. Her mind drifted again to the ancient launch sites. Cape Canaveral, Baikonur, Vandenberg— names that once sang with the sonic booms of glory and danger. Compared to those, this was a silent ballet. Gravity here wasn't Earth's heavy hand; the ship's rotating habitats offered a gentle approximation, and the artificial gravity on the bridge and key areas was online at reduced power until they were free of the station. The engines wouldn't roar; they'd whisper. Instead of shattering free from a well of gravity, they were simply sliding out of a gentle embrace.

"Five seconds to release," Marcus said softly, voice steady with practiced calm.

Morrow breathed in. The numbers on the main display dropped: 4...3...2...1.

"Release clamps."

A gentle chime acknowledged her command. On the main forward screen, they saw the station's docking appendage retracting, its mechanical arms folding away. Without fanfare, their ship drifted free. The sensation was almost nonexistent—a slight shift in the background hum. If one were to close their eyes, they might miss it entirely.

"We are free and clear," Jason confirmed. "No relative motion issues. We're drifting on inertia. Ready for thruster burns when you are, Captain."

Morrow tilted her head. "Elena, give us a gentle forward push. Just a whisper."

"Aye, Captain," Elena replied. Her fingers danced over the controls, igniting the forward thrusters. The ship nudged forward, slipping into the black. The orbital station began to shrink behind them on the display, the curve of Saturn and its rings receding, becoming just another celestial ornament.

Riley's voice came over comms again, this time quieter, more sincere: "Well, that was easy. No offense to old chemical rockets, but I'm grateful not to be pressed into my seat like a pancake."

"Don't underestimate what lies ahead," John said, his tone gruff but not unkind. "And don't curse us like that. We're all going to miss pancakes for weeks now."

Morrow keyed the ship's comms, broadcasting inside the ship, to the docking station and the base stations. "Good work everyone. We have clean separation and are leaving the station's perimeter. Preparing for gradual acceleration to cruising velocity. Farewell and wish us luck."

She ended the transmission and released the intercom button. For a moment, the only sound on the command deck was the faint hum of power coursing through the consoles. She ignored the reply that came from some distant command center. Outside the viewport, the station's lights grew dimmer as they drifted away, receding into a star-flecked backdrop.

Morrow keyed open a detailed navigation display. The ship's path spiraled elegantly toward the Sun, Jupiter, their first great partner in this cosmic dance lay just ahead. This mission would weave through gravitational fields like a careful whisper, using physics itself as a stepping stone and gaining velocity by circling through large gravity wells.

She turned her gaze to Jason Alvarez at the navigation console. "Jason, confirm our trajectory to the inner system."

He nodded, his dark humor tempered by focus. "Trajectory confirmed and locked in, Captain."

Jason pushed a 3D rendering of their trajectory to the main display. It showed them slingshotting around Jupiter, passing Earth at high velocity, then diving toward Mercury's orbit. There they would skim the Sun's gravity well. At perihelion, they fire the main engines to complete an Oberth maneuver, using the velocity they gain from the Sun drawing them in and using their own thrust to add the additional velocity necessary to escape its hold and get the boost they would need to begin their journey.

Morrow moved to stand behind him, studying the lines. They had gone over the details for this in simulations thousands of times.

"Good. The old world's pioneers had their rockets. We have gravity and antimatter engines. Let's show the galaxy we know how to dance."

From her station, Elena interjected softly, "I'm keeping a close eye on solar activity as we approach. The magnetic shields and thermal layers will hold, but I'd like to stay on top of any unexpected flares. Even minor spikes in solar radiation would require precise adjustments to the magnetic shielding and thermal controls."

John drifted closer, arms folded. "I'm not worried about radiation. Margins are my concern. The closer we get, the tighter the window for the burn. No room for sloppy work. This is the part I don't like. Riding a giant missile toward a star." He glanced at Jason, who grinned ruefully.

"Don't worry," Jason said. "I plan to be very neat about this, but if I screw up… you'll hardly feel a thing."

Riley's voice crackled in over the comm: "You lot sound like daredevils plotting a stunt. Just remember we have sleeping guests in the hold who might prefer not to be flambéed."

"Understood, Riley," Morrow said, smiling. "We'll keep it tidy."

Marcus chimed in, "Comm arrays are ready. We'll lose direct line with Earth as we sweep below the ecliptic plane, beyond where the relay beacons are set. Our last messages have been sent. From then on, any replies from Earth will take millennia to reach us, if they even do reach us."

Amir, watching the trajectory lines, added in a thoughtful tone, "History in motion. We are enacting a maneuver that future historians —if there are any—might find quite elegant. It's like the great explorers catching the perfect wind."

Clara, seated quietly, pressed the seed vial in her palm as if it were a lucky charm. "They'll grow into gardens under another sun," she said softly. "They'll never know about this moment, but it's the first step of their roots, in a way."

Morrow let their voices settle into silence. She took one last look at the shrinking station behind them. They were leaving behind all the frameworks of home: the trading routes, the comm relays, the familiar beacons of human civilization spread around the solar system. Ahead lay the Sun's gravity well, which they would court and then escape, leaving the cradle of humankind behind forever.

She placed a hand on the back of Jason's chair, steady and confident. "All right, everyone. This is how we begin."

They all knew their parts, and the ship responded in kind, thrusters nudging them onto that subtle, off-ecliptic path. In the quiet darkness, far from the roar of old rockets, this new breed of explorers prepared to claim the stars with a delicate, deliberate glide into the unknown. This first leg of the trip would span weeks, during which the external feed of Earth expanded, then gradually diminished, replaced by a view of the entire solar system that none of the crew could resist watching. It would be their last view of Sol, soon just one among billions upon billions of distant sparkling dots in unfamiliar skies.

3

21 Days after launch.

They were falling toward the Sun, though it hardly felt like it. Weeks had passed since the ship drifted away from the station and slipped into its elliptical dive. The crew noticed the subtle shift in the hue of cabin light—Clara claimed it was her imagination, but Marcus assured her it was a minuscule recalibration of interior illumination to match their changing proximity to Sol. Outside, through reinforced observation ports and external sensor feeds, the Sun's brightness intensified subtly yet insistently—a constant reminder that they were venturing closer to Sol's formidable gravity well.

Captain Morrow stood on the command deck once more. Though the acceleration was gradual and delicately balanced, she felt the tension in her limbs. It wasn't physical—this wasn't the crushing thrust of old rockets—but a psychological weight, anticipation building toward the Oberth maneuver that would determine their momentum for the rest of the journey. If they timed their burn perfectly at perihelion, they would gain that precious extra speed to fling them outward, beyond the boundaries of the familiar solar neighborhood. If they botched it, they'd waste fuel and might have to settle for a slower departure, complicating their entire mission timeline.

At her side, Marcus Ito worked quietly, fingers dancing over console interfaces. He monitored solar wind readings, sensor feeds, and the ship's comm system—now largely silent. The silence from Earth was expected; even the messages sent in these last moments would not return for centuries, if at all. Marcus had come to accept that the crew, and the colonists sleeping below, were now the only humans he would likely ever see again.

Across the deck, Jason Alvarez studied the navigation display with an intensity that temporarily banished his usual sardonic humor. The bright digital star of Sol dominated the center of his board. Threading this gravitational needle demanded concentration. The Sun was not malevolent, but neither was it kind. It was simply a fact of nature—unyielding, indifferent. Elena Park perched beside him, her hands folded in her lap, gaze flicking between the engine readouts and the solar data. She could do nothing until they reached perihelion, and that waiting—hanging between inaction and the need for precision—gnawed at her nerves.

Down in the lower habitat ring, John Ferris completed a final sweep of the ship's compartments. The crew's personal effects were stowed, emergency gear double-checked. Security was nominal. There would be no pirates or interlopers here—just physics and silence. He preferred it that way. Still, he wanted to be sure they were ready for anything. He passed a viewport and paused, observing the subtle increase in brightness. Even here, he could sense it. They were swinging in close, like a comet racing toward perihelion. It was beautiful and dangerous.

In the med bay, Riley Thompson checked on the stasis pods through a set of remote monitors. The colonists, obliviously floated in their time-suspended dreams. He couldn't help but envy them a little. While he and the rest of the crew felt the anxious hum of approaching destiny, the sleepers were at peace. "One advantage to being out cold," he murmured. He tapped a status screen, then flipped through biosigns—everyone stable. Good. He wouldn't have to worry about medical emergencies for now.

Near the hydroponics modules, Clara misted a row of seedlings. The plants did not care about orbital mechanics. They responded only to water, light, and nutrient balance. Here in the gentle confines of their small ecosystem, life persisted, quietly honest. Clara hummed softly—a lullaby to herself as much as to the plants.

Amir drifted through a corridor, occasionally stopping to record a few notes on his handheld device. He had decided to journal the journey. Someone had to. "Approaching perihelion," he wrote, "we stand at a threshold. The star that once defined the boundaries of human civilization is about to give us its final gift—a gravitational nudge that will send us into the great beyond." He imagined future readers, maybe centuries down the line, discovering this record. Would they understand the courage and uncertainty? Would they smile at how reverently the crew approached a maneuver that might become routine for future travelers?

Back on the command deck, Morrow watched her crew through discreet camera feeds. It was comforting to see them all in their places, each fulfilling their role with quiet competence. This was what being a captain meant: trusting that her people would excel, even at the edge of everything they'd known.

"Marcus," she said softly, "what's the latest on solar weather?"

He glanced up, scanning the data. "Steady. Low flare risk, moderate solar wind. A slight uptick in charged particles, but well within our shielding parameters."

She nodded. That was one less worry. "Jason, how's our approach vector?"

"Locked in," he replied, voice subdued but sure. "We'll hit perihelion right on schedule. Elena's got the engine sequences primed, and we have full redundancy on the timing relays."

Elena turned in her seat, meeting the captain's gaze. "Everything's running stable, Captain. We won't waste a drop of antimatter. Once we reach closest approach, I fire the engines at the peak of our velocity. That should give us the best boost." Her eyes shone with a quiet intensity.

"Good," Aveline said. She studied the main display where the Sun blazed in digital representation. They were still distant by any conventional measure—tens of millions of kilometers of vacuum between them and the star—but in cosmic terms, they were daringly close. As they glided along their curved path, the notion of subtlety or gentleness in this maneuver vanished. It was an intricate ballet, gravity as the silent partner, and time as the conductor.

She imagined what a future historian might say: They approached Sol with reverence and cunning, using its gravity to fling themselves outward, to break free of the solar system's long gravitational leash. In another era, the Sun had been worshipped, feared, revered. Today, it was an engine of opportunity. They would ride its influence to the edge of interstellar space and beyond.

Outside the hull, countless particles of solar wind streamed past. The heat shields managed the incoming radiation with ease—this close pass had been planned meticulously. On the bridge, no one raised their voice. They were past the stage of dramatic speeches. All that remained was to trust their planning, execute their burn, and accept the fate they were carving into the fabric of space.

Morrow took a quiet breath and placed a hand on the back of Elena's chair, just as she had done weeks ago. "Steady as she goes," she said, voice gentle. "We'll do this right."

A day later, perihelion approached like the silent toll of a distant bell. The star's light pressed upon the hull with a radiance that monitors translated into subtle thermal shifts. Inside, the crew moved with focused calm. Each knew their part: Elena at the propulsion controls, Jason double-checking navigational lock-ins, Marcus monitoring solar data, John quietly surveying safety readouts, Riley and Clara ensuring the stasis pods and life-support systems remained stable, and Amir compiling notes with academic reverence. Captain Morrow stood central, hands clasped behind her back, her gaze fixed on the holo-display as if it were a temple altar.

"Approaching perihelion in three minutes," Jason reported, his voice clipped and steady.

Elena's display bloomed with readiness indicators. Engines prepped, antimatter flow stable, Alcubierre generators warm but dormant. This would be their last great dance with the Sun, a final whisper of home before they leapt into the long night.

Aveline touched a control to broadcast ship-wide: "All hands, stand by for engine burn." Her tone held a calm gravity. "We're at the threshold now. After this, we leave the solar system behind at unprecedented speed." She paused, her voice softening. "For the colonists and for us, this moment marks the true beginning of our journey. Steady on."

In the med bay, Riley placed a gentle hand on a stasis pod's exterior. He murmured to the sleeping colonist inside, "You've no idea what's happening, but trust us. We've got this."

Clara, perched by her seedlings, gave a hopeful nod to no one in particular. The plants would soon be fed by distant starlight, their lineage carried further from Earth than any vine or leaf had ever known.

Amir flicked through his notes. The metaphor was too perfect—using the Sun's gravity as a catapult, throwing themselves into interstellar space. He typed a line: We bent the knee at our star's feet, then rose with its blessing.

"Ten seconds to burn," Marcus said quietly, eyes on the readings. Solar wind steady, thermal load nominal, radiation within limits.

"Engine sequences nominal," Elena confirmed. "We're green across the board."

Aveline inhaled, heart calm. "Do it."

At perihelion, the ship ignited its antimatter engines. The thrust was subtle but insistent, a carefully timed exhalation of power. No roar, no shaking—just a readout showing velocity climbing in neat increments. The Oberth effect worked its magic. They were already moving fast relative to the Sun; burning fuel at this closest approach multiplied their gains. The ship rode that momentum like a surfer catching a perfect wave.

Jason watched the numbers surge. "Velocity increasing. We're on target, Captain."

Outside, the star's brilliance began to recede as their path curved upward, out of the ecliptic plane, carrying them away from the crowded lanes of the inner system and the familiar orbits of planets and habitats. They angled above the flat swirl of cosmic dust and worlds, heading into quieter seas. Their star's domain would soon shrink behind them.

"Engine burn complete," Elena announced softly, quiet pride clear beneath her professional composure. "We got the boost we wanted."

John nodded to himself, tension easing from his shoulders. They'd done the delicate bit. No alarms, no radiation spikes beyond protocol. Quiet competence, the hallmark of this crew.

Marcus typed commands, reorienting sensors. "We're clearing the plane now, moving above the usual dust disk. Fewer micrometeorites here, less clutter. Just clear space."

Aveline pressed her hands gently into the armrests of her seat. "Good. Let's set course for Kepler-452." The name hung in the air like a distant promise. They were no longer bound to Sol. Their star of origin had served its purpose, given them a cosmic push. Now, they sailed free.

Elena took a breath, preparing for the next step. "Captain, the Alcubierre field generators are standing by. Shall I engage the protective warp bubble?"

Aveline glanced at Jason. He gave a slight nod—charts and trajectories confirmed, nothing unexpected ahead. Marcus signaled no unusual solar flares or large debris fields. Riley and Clara had no medical or life-support concerns. Amir watched, eyes bright, as if waiting to record history's turning page.

"Yes," Morrow affirmed, voice steady and decisive, "bring the Alcubierre field online. Engage the bubble."

Elena's fingers danced over holographic keys. The generators hummed softly, a frequency felt more than heard. Space around the ship began to distort subtly, a careful, engineered manipulation of spacetime. Not an FTL jump—yet—but a controlled, protective shell that would shield them from interstellar dust and hydrogen atoms that might smash into them at near-light speeds. It was their shield, their buffer, a crucial step before pushing to the velocities that would compress their journey into a manageable timeline.

On the main display, the star-field wavered as the bubble stabilized. Marcus checked the sensors. "Spacetime gradient stable. The bubble's integrity is at one hundred percent."

Elena allowed herself a thin smile. "Field is good. We're safe to accelerate towards near-light speed now."

Aveline tapped a sequence on her chair's console. "Begin incremental acceleration. Let's climb toward our cruising speed slowly. We have time."

Time, indeed. They had a year, give or take, in their own frame of reference, to reach Kepler-452, though millennia would pass back at Sol. As they pressed on, the Sun's bright pinpoint would eventually fade behind them, lost in the tapestry of stars, just another distant spark in the universe. In that future sky, Earth and Sol would be gone from sight, preserved only in their memories, their archives, and in Amir's careful words.

Riley's voice came through the internal comms, light and warm: "Congratulations, crew. We've officially left the neighborhood."

Laughter rippled softly across channels. Aveline felt a knot in her chest loosen. They were doing it. Actually doing it. The mission was fully underway, with all the complexity and calm daring they'd rehearsed. Now, as the engines purred and the Alcubierre field guided them like a protective bubble through the cosmic dark, they were free to reach for near-light speed and then beyond, forging into a realm no human had ever touched.

They had claimed the stars not with a roar, but a whisper. Above the familiar plane of planets, in the serene stillness of interstellar space, they set their course straight and true. The voyage to Kepler-452 had truly commenced.

4

After navigating their way out of the solar system, the crew of the Aurora drifted through the quiet darkness of space, one day merging gently into the next. Inside the ship's rotating habitat ring, there was no sunrise or sunset—just the subtle shifts in cabin lighting that marked the passage of time. The crew had settled into comfortable routines: a few hours at their stations, routine system checks, personal projects, exercise sessions in the centrifuge loop, and finally, communal meals.

It was mealtime now, and the galley—a compact space with a central table and a small kitchenette—had become something like a hearth in an ancient home over the last couple months. Warm lighting, muted colors, and the soft hum of life support systems gave it a welcoming air. The crew gathered slowly, drifting in from their respective corners of the ship. They wore casual shipboard attire: zip-up jumpsuits or lightweight shirts and pants. The crisp uniforms reserved for docking procedures and special occasions seemed long forgotten now. The closest thing to a uniform were the matching utility suits they wore when the work called for it.

Clara stood at the galley's small prep station, her back turned to the table as she arranged bright green leaves and small, delicate fruits on a ceramic plate. She was humming quietly, face lit with anticipation. For weeks, she had nurtured the seeds and seedlings in the hydroponics bay—tiny carriers of Earth's botanical legacy. Under controlled light and nutrient-rich water, they had grown steadily. Now the first edible harvest was ready: a handful of cherry-sized tomatoes, crisp lettuce, and something that approximated strawberries. They were pale and smaller than Earth's standard variety, but their scent had teased her senses every time she tended to them.

Tonight, it was her turn to handle meal prep. While the ship carried ample rations—dehydrated meals, protein pastes, and synthetic nutrient bars—fresh produce was a luxury. Clara's pride shone through as she arranged the greens and fruits into a vibrant salad. She'd paired them with carefully rationed olive oil and a touch of powdered balsamic vinegar she had just rehydrated. Nothing fancy by Earth standards, but here on the ship it was a feast.

Riley Thompson leaned against the wall, arms crossed, a broad grin on his face as he watched Clara work. "I'm telling you, I can smell that from here," he said, feigning a dramatic sniff. "My nose might be playing tricks, but it's telling me that's going to be delicious."

Clara cast him a warm smile over her shoulder. "Your nose is correct. It might not be quite the flavors we remember, but it's definitely fresh."

Morrow entered and took her seat at the table. She was relaxed, her posture less formal than usual. "Clara, I don't recall ever being this excited about lettuce in my life." There was a small ripple of laughter through the galley.

Jason joined them next, sliding into his chair. His mood had stabilized over the past weeks; the relentless tension he'd carried at the start had eased into something more manageable. He still cracked the occasional dark joke, but tonight he just looked quietly expectant. "If these strawberries taste even half as good as I remember, I'll be impressed," he said dryly, tapping the table. "Keeping expectations low —just in case."

From the other side of the room, Amir approached with a slow stride, as if appreciating the scene from a historian's perspective. "This will be one for the journal," he remarked, voice gentle. "The first fresh produce from Clara's hydroponics on this mission. A culinary milestone." He took his place, folding his hands on the table.

Marcus and John arrived together, having come from a round of routine inspections. Marcus, calm as ever, settled into a seat and raised an eyebrow at the display of greenery. "Now there's a sight that beats powdered spinach." John nodded in silent agreement, though a faint smile tugged at the corner of his mouth. He said nothing, but his eyes flicked to Clara with genuine gratitude.

Elena Park was last, a smudge of lubricant or something like it on her left sleeve where she'd been tinkering with something in engineering. She gave Clara a nod of respect. "We can stabilize a spaceship near light speed, and still nothing compares to the magic of growing plants in space." Her words carried a mix of engineering awe and philosophical wonder.

Clara carried the first platter to the table. Meals were typically portioned at the table, as the small prep station could quickly become crowded, even for their modest-sized crew. She portioned out small servings for each crew member, a careful equanimity in how she distributed leaves and fruit. "I know it's not exactly a five-course meal," she said gently, "but I hope it reminds you a little of home. Honestly, I'm thrilled the seedlings gave us anything this soon—the conditions were… experimental."

Riley took a bite first, ever the adventurous one. His eyebrows shot up. "Crisp! Sweet!" he announced, giving Clara a thumbs-up. "It's like —well, it's like a real strawberry, just a bit milder." He popped another in his mouth, savoring it slowly.

Jason tried a leaf of lettuce and gave a small nod. "Not bad. Actually… quite good." He ate another piece, looking pleasantly surprised. The tension around his eyes softened.

Marcus chewed thoughtfully. "The flavors are subtle, but honest. Definitely beats rehydrated greens." He raised his cup—filled with recycled and purified water, though it felt like a toast nonetheless. "To Clara—and her green thumb."

A small chorus of agreement rose from the table. Amir was scribbling notes on his tablet. "A taste of Earth, in the void of space. Historians and archaeologists will find poetry in this, I'm sure."

Clara blushed faintly at the praise. "I'm glad you like it. I've been worried they wouldn't flourish with lighting conditions that don't exactly match sunlight—at least not the Sun we knew. They need to grow under… starlight I suppose. The lamps and nutrients seem to be doing their job."

John, who had been quiet, offered a single, sincere word: "Thanks." It carried weight coming from him, a soldier turned protector, grateful for this little reminder of what they were all working toward.

Elena picked up a strawberry, examining it thoughtfully as if assessing an engine component. She bit down and hummed softly. "Nice." Relaxing into her seat, she continued, "I can't wait until we scale this up—imagine harvesting a variety of fruits and vegetables regularly. It would make the voyage feel a bit less… distant."

Morrow watched her crew as they enjoyed the meal. Their voices overlapped, gentle and unhurried. The ship's computer managed the engines and the Alcubierre field, quietly guarding them from cosmic hazards. Here at the table, they were free to be themselves, to remember Earth not as an unreachable memory but as a legacy they carried forward in seeds, stories, and camaraderie.

They talked about how the plants might evolve over time in zero-g conditions, what new flavors might emerge, and whether cooking experiments could push the limited seasoning packets to new heights. Riley promised to concoct some kind of "space salsa" if Clara could produce enough tomatoes and peppers later on. Marcus volunteered to help, joking he'd trade language lessons for cooking tips. Elena wondered if gentle vibrations or music would help the plants grow better. Amir proposed an experiment, while Jason teased that maybe the plants needed a good, sarcastic joke or two.

In the quiet hum of the ship, far from any star, the crew found a moment of normalcy—a simple meal shared among friends. This was how they lived now, and in these moments, the idea of journeying across the galaxy to distant worlds seemed just a little less daunting. Each fresh bite reminded them that, wherever they went, they carried the essence of Earth with them: in their laughter, their shared hopes, and in the green, living heart of new growth sprouting in the dark.

As dinner wrapped up and the crew began dispersing, a pleasant contentment lingered in the galley's recycled air. Plates and utensils still cluttered the small table, but no one seemed inclined to rush off. They were all, for once, a bit too comfortable—at least until Captain Morrow stood, gave a subtle nod of gratitude to Clara and the team, and announced she would review some overnight reports. One by one, people drifted away: Riley promising to return with some musical suggestions, Jason heading to the observatory deck for his habitual star-gazing, Amir still scribbling notes as he made for his cabin, and John moving quietly along on his usual security rounds.

Clara stacked a few plates and shot a look across the table. "I'll deal with these, no problem. But I might need a hand if we're to keep this place from turning into a compost heap."

Marcus, leaning back in his seat, raised a hand in mock surrender. "I'm at your service." He glanced around at the lingering crew. Elena was also still seated, flipping a fork between her fingers thoughtfully. Clara looked between them and gave a small smile. "If you two want to tackle the dishes, I'll head back to the hydroponics bay and tidy up. Sound good?"

It was a gentle nudge—subtle, but unmistakable. Clara's eyes twinkled as she stepped away, leaving Elena and Marcus alone at the table. For a few moments, neither spoke. Outside their small circle of light, the ship hummed softly, and the occasional soft hiss of circulating air reminded them of their cozy isolation.

Elena broke the silence first, chuckling softly. "We've been on this ship for months, and I'm still not entirely sure how I ended up on dish duty."

Marcus shrugged and began to gather utensils. "Natural order of teamwork, right? One day you're plotting gravitational maneuvers, the next day you're scrubbing plates."

She smirked. "I'd still rather wash dishes at near-light speed than back home, crammed into some tiny apartment kitchen. Here at least I have a view of the stars—abstract as it is on the monitors."

They stood side by side at the small cleaning station. Elena activated the sonic rinsers, carefully placing plates inside the unit. Marcus wiped down the table surfaces with a sanitized cloth, leaning in just enough that Elena caught a whiff of his subtle, clean scent. Space travel didn't encourage heavy colognes or perfumes, so every personal scent was always personal and familiar.

"So," Marcus said, placing the last of the cups into the rinser's holding slot, "you've been tweaking the Alcubierre adjustments lately. Everything stable?"

She nodded, eyes on the rinsing cycle as tiny vibrations shook debris off the plates. "Stable and steady. We're more or less on autopilot now. The ship's systems are good at alerting us if something drifts out of spec. Honestly, I've had less to do these last couple weeks than I did prepping for launch."

Marcus leaned a hip against the counter, watching her profile. "I remember you said you were worried you'd feel useless once we were cruising. How's that panning out?"

Elena tipped her head slightly, meeting his gaze. "Not as bad as I feared. I've been thinking of new optimization models for when we do decelerate. Also tinkering with some ideas on how to reduce micro-vibration in the habitat ring. It's subtle stuff—nothing critical—but it keeps me busy."

He smiled, a small, genuine curve of his lips. "I find it funny that we're racing through space at near-light speed and you're concerned about micro-vibrations. Perfectionist much?"

"Guilty." She laughed, a quiet, throaty sound. "I can't help it. Just who I am."

They stood close now, the galley feeling more intimate with every sentence exchanged. Outside these walls, the universe stretched unfathomably, but here, it was just two people and the hum of machinery.

"You know," Marcus said softly, "we're going to be out here a long time. I mean, we've accepted that, right? A year by our clocks is nothing to scoff at when it comes to daily routines."

"True," Elena murmured, drying her hands. "And as we get further, we'll have even fewer ties to what we knew. I suppose that gives us a kind of… freedom?"

Marcus nodded. "Exactly. Freedom to define our own norms, our own way of living. Relationships. Friendships." His gaze held hers for a moment. "We're not just a crew. We're all the human family we've got now."

Elena swallowed, aware that this was a moment of significance. Marcus's tone had shifted, warmer and more personal. She felt a subtle warmth spreading through her chest, a gentle nervousness that was surprisingly welcome in the sterile environment. "It's funny," she said, lightly, "I was never much of a joiner on Earth. I preferred engines and math to people. But now…" She gestured vaguely. "Now we're all in this tin can hurdling through space, and suddenly I'm glad we're not just colleagues."

"Yeah," Marcus agreed, stepping just a fraction closer. He reached out, brushing an imaginary speck off her shoulder and investigating the stain on her sleeve, a gentle gesture that brought them within each other's personal space. "I think we've got a chance here to… well, to get to know each other in ways we never would have back home."

Elena felt a slight flutter in her stomach at his touch. It was a minimal contact, but in the vast emptiness of space, human closeness meant more. She tilted her head, eyes steady on his. "What do you think that looks like?" she asked quietly, her voice almost a whisper, half-playful and half-sincere.

He let his hand drop. "Maybe it looks like sharing a meal every now and then, just the two of us. Maybe it's talking about something other than engines and navigation arrays, if we can even think of something else to talk about. Learning each other's stories. Maybe it's you showing me the difference between a badly tuned vibration damper and a well-tuned one, and me explaining obscure language patterns nobody's used in centuries. Working out together in the gym perhaps." He grinned, eyes warm. "We have a lot of time, Elena. I'd like to spend some of it getting closer to you."

A subtle blush stained her cheeks. She hadn't blushed in ages, but here she was, in the middle of a spaceship, blushing like a teenager. "I'd like that too," she admitted, softly.

They stood there, hands still slightly damp from dishwater and sonic rinsers, the aroma of that freshly picked produce and rehydrated vinegar barely lingering in the air as the sterile scent of sanitizing wipes and fluids began to take over. Beyond the hull, stars raced by as distorted points of light. The ship's AI quietly oversaw their journey, alert and watchful of every sensor and function of the ship, but content to leave them to their moment.

Elena took a half-step closer, leveling her eyes with his. "I've got maintenance on the hydroponic pumps tomorrow. Maybe afterward we could… talk? Just us?"

Marcus's smile widened warmly. "You can count on it."

A comfortable silence settled between them. The dishes were done, but neither felt like moving away. In that lingering pause, new possibilities took root—small seeds of connection, ready to grow in the fertile, timeless soil of a life lived between the stars.

5

Along the gently curving corridor of the third habitat ring, John moved with quiet purpose. He passed through patches of soft, indirect lighting and the steady hum of life-support systems. A tool pouch hung loosely over one shoulder, half-unzipped to reveal an orderly array of multi-tools, spare filter cartridges, and a compact diagnostic scanner. His daily routine had become a series of small, practical gestures: checking filters that ensured breathable air, verifying maintenance bots were still busily rolling along their tracks to sweep corridors or polish the deck plates, making note of any squeaks or rattles that might need oiling. This ring was almost entirely dedicated to the hydroponics systems and required frequent filter checks. He prided himself on order, on ensuring that if something did break, he'd know before it became a problem.

In another life, back in Sol, he'd served as a guard, a soldier, leading security teams escorting hazardous shipments across dangerous stretches of space. There, his job had often meant bracing for violence, sleepless nights in fortified outposts, and the constant awareness that a threat could materialize at any moment. Here, the threats were quieter, more subtle: micrometeoroid impacts, radiation leaks, system malfunctions. None of which demanded his old skill with a sidearm. He didn't mind. This quiet life was a gift, and he'd take filter checks over firefights any day.

He stopped outside the hydroponics bay main entrance, tapping his scanner against the door's control panel. Everything read nominal, as usual. Still, he listened for any unusual hum. Nothing but the gentle whoosh of nutrient solution pumps and air circulation. Satisfied, he turned just as Clara rounded the bend in the corridor, returning from tidying up in the galley.

"Evening," he said, adjusting the strap of his tool pouch. He stepped aside so she could access the hatch. She smiled gently, as warm and welcoming as the seedlings she tended.

"Hi John," Clara responded. She picked up a small bin with a few clippings and nutrient packs, ready to return to another bay. "Back to my children," she joked, nodding toward the bin. "Got to make sure they're tucked in."

John half-smiled. He appreciated her humor and the easy gentleness she brought with her. "Need a hand?" he asked, the words quiet, tentative. He wasn't always good at initiating conversation, and certainly not at expressing his feelings. But something about Clara's kindness made it simpler.

She tilted her head, pleasantly surprised. "I'd appreciate that, if you have time. I just need to reorganize a few trays and check some drip lines."

"Sure." He sounded more casual than he felt. Any excuse to stay in her orbit a bit longer was welcome. It beat trudging around alone looking for problems that didn't exist.

Inside the hydroponics bay, bright grow-lights washed the compact rows of leafy greens, vines, and shoots in a soothing light temperature. The scent of damp earth—synthetic, but close enough—filled the air. For John, it was a welcome departure from the metallic tang of machinery. He helped Clara with a tray of seedlings, easing it onto a higher shelf. She pointed out how the roots dangled in carefully oxygenated nutrient solution, ensuring optimal growth.

"I'm amazed at how well they're doing," he said quietly. He wasn't one for long speeches, so he chose his words carefully. "You've made something alive and thriving out here in the middle of nowhere. Feels… comforting."

Clara paused, looking over at him. "They remind me that we come from a place rich with life," she said. "We're carrying a spark of Earth's abundance with us. Even if we never see Earth again, it's not gone, not as long as we nurture these little pockets of green."

John lifted a hand to brush a stray leaf that had broken off and landed on a sensor panel. Gently, he removed it to place in a compost bin. He admired how Clara treated these plants not just as resources, but almost as companions. "I never cared much about plants before," he admitted. "Guess I never had time to notice them. They weren't around much on ships and stations and well… Life was… busy in a different way."

She met his gaze, sensing the weight behind his words. Her voice softened. "Busy how? I mean, if you're comfortable sharing."

He shrugged, evaluating the drip line with his handheld scanner, observing density readings to check for any potential clogs or buildup. "Had rough jobs back in Sol. Always on guard, always expecting trouble. I never saw things grow, not like this. I mostly saw things break, get damaged, or... end." He didn't need to elaborate. The sadness in his eyes spoke of old scars and hard memories.

Clara nodded, placing a gentle hand on his forearm. The gesture was light, but it anchored him in the moment. "I'm sorry," she said simply, and he believed it. Her sympathy wasn't forced or pitying, it was genuine understanding. "But you're here now," she continued. "And out here, we have a chance to shape something kinder, better. That's what this expedition is about, isn't it? Building a new world, a new life. A fresh start with a blank canvas."

He looked down at her hand on his arm, her skin warm against the cool fabric of his sleeve. He was still getting used to such casual contact. In his old life, any touch was guarded, suspicious and rarely came without controversy. Here, it conveyed trust and empathy. "I never thought I'd find that," he murmured quietly. "A life without threats lurking around every corner."

Clara squeezed gently, then let go, returning to check a sensor node. She smiled over her shoulder at him. "We all came for our own reasons. Me, I wanted to see new ecosystems, help them thrive. You wanted peace, right? We ended up on the same ship, heading into the deep unknown, hoping for something better."

John moved to the next bay of sprouts, a variety of beans that would be ready for harvest soon. He tested a drip line clamp, then wiped a bit of condensation from a panel. As he worked, his posture relaxed. The tension in his shoulders eased, and the lines around his eyes softened. He realized he was enjoying this: just quietly helping her maintain the delicate ecosystem they'd brought with them.

"It's strange," he admitted softly, "you handle these plants like precious treasure. I suppose they really are, in a way." He chuckled softly, a rare sound from him. "I feel like that too now. They're our little green lifeline out here."

Clara placed a nutrient pack into its slot and looked at him. "They are. Not just food, but a reminder that life adapts and thrives, given a chance. We're giving these seeds that chance." Her voice carried a warmth that seemed to settle over them, as comforting as the grow-lights overhead.

He nodded, taking in the scene—her careful movements, the rustle of leaves from the fans that imitated a gentle breeze, the gentle hum of pumps. This was so far from the life he once knew, and he was grateful. Maybe, he thought, this is what he needed all along: not just distance from a violent past, but proximity to something gentle and nurturing. Someone gentle and nurturing.

Finishing up, Clara turned and smiled at him, a real smile that made her eyes crinkle at the corners. "Thanks for the help, John. Really. It means a lot to me that you're interested."

His response was quiet but heartfelt. "Thanks for showing me a different side of all this." He motioned to the plants. "And for caring about every leaf and root. It's… nice."

She reached out, hesitant, her hand hovering as though waiting for permission. He shifted subtly closer, bridging the small gap until her fingers brushed gently against his sleeve. He met her halfway, moving a fraction so her fingers brushed his sleeve once more. It was a small, shared moment—a gentle bond forming in the midst of stars and silence. They stood quietly, two souls carrying their separate histories, hopes, and vulnerabilities forward into a shared future they could shape together. In the soft, comforting glow of the hydroponics bay, John found solace not only in Clara's gentle presence but also in what they were building together, leaf by tender leaf, moment by quiet moment.

6

After leaving the galley and finishing his quiet reflection time on the observatory deck, Jason made his way down a gently curving corridor. He absently brushed his fingertips along the softly illuminated wall panels, as though seeking a comforting rhythm to match his drifting thoughts. The ship's hum was ever-present, a subtle reminder of the engineered environment that sustained them all. Jason didn't know if he found it comforting or unnerving—both, maybe.

Riley spotted him approaching and stepped casually into Jason's path, arms loosely crossed, leaning comfortably against the gentle curve of the corridor. Riley's bright smile and easy posture contrasted with Jason's distant look. He'd been meaning to talk to Jason again, to check in and try to bring some perspective to whatever weighed on the Navigator's mind.

"Hey, Starman," Riley said, using a nickname he wanted to test out. He grinned, open and friendly, but not pushy. "Taking the late shift stroll, I see."

Jason stopped, raising an eyebrow. "Starman," he echoed dryly. "That's new. Trying out your stand-up routine in zero-g, Thompson?"

Riley gave an exaggerated shrug. "Gotta keep the humor flowing. Without Earth's gravity, puns tend to float away if you don't anchor 'em." He patted the curved wall. "What's up? You looked pretty deep in thought back at the galley."

Jason crossed his arms. Usually, he'd sling a sarcastic remark Riley's way and brush past this kind of small talk. But tonight, maybe he was tired of bottling it up. "Just thinking about all this," he admitted after a pause. "The distance, the time involved, the responsibility… standard existential-crisis-at-midnight kind of stuff."

Riley softened his grin into something gentler, stepping closer but not too close. He'd learned to give Jason some space. "Wanna talk about it?" he offered, voice quieter. "We're all on this ship together, Jase. You don't have to carry the whole thing alone."

Jason's jaw tightened a fraction. He glanced down the corridor, as if ensuring no one else was listening. "I'm the Navigator," he said finally. "One slip in my calculations, one tiny misalignment, and we shoot past Kepler-452 at a hundredth of a degree off course. We'd be as good as lost. Everyone depends on me not to screw up."

Riley nodded, not dismissing the seriousness. "That's true, you've got a lot on your plate. But you haven't slipped up once, Jase. You're constantly double- and triple-checking star charts. Elena and Morrow trust you. I trust you." He reached out, gently patting Jason on the shoulder. "You're allowed to feel the weight of it, though. Being responsible doesn't mean you don't get to have doubts."

Jason let out a low breath, something between a sigh and a quiet laugh. "Doubts, huh? Try waking up at 0300 with your heart pounding because you realize just how far we are from Earth. It's not just the navigation. It's the whole… concept. We're headed 1,400 light-years from home, give or take… and yes, I caught the irony in that. Sure, it'll only be about a year of ship time, but Earth is… gone. Not literally, I mean, it's still there, but centuries and centuries out of sync already. Everyone we knew? Dust. Civilization changed beyond recognition."

Riley inclined his head, empathy in his eyes. "I know," he said softly. "It's hard to wrap your head around. I think about that too sometimes. My sister's grandkids will be ancient history by the time we arrive. When I dwell on it too long, I get this tight feeling in my chest. I'm a physician and I'm going to be from a time far enough back I might have studied myself when we get there."

Jason studied Riley's face. He hadn't realized others might share that same gut-clench of fear and sadness. "You feel it too?"

Riley nodded. "We're on a one-way mission. The reason I stay cheerful—and maybe crack too many jokes—isn't because I'm immune. It's because if I didn't, I'd be screaming inside. Humor's my coping mechanism."

A wry grin tugged at Jason's mouth. "I thought it was just your personality. You know, perpetual sunshine."

Riley chuckled, happy to see Jason easing into the banter. "Sunshine's a limited resource out here, friend—if I had any extra, Clara would have me tied up in the hydroponics bay. Nah, I'm just as human as you. We all are. When I see you all moody, I get it. We're all carrying something heavy."

Jason relaxed a fraction, uncrossing his arms. "Thanks. It's weird, but it helps to know you're also faking it 'til you make it."

"Fake it 'til you make it: the official slogan of the far-flung star explorer," Riley teased. Then his voice grew more thoughtful. "It's not just you. Clara's nurturing plants to feel connected, Elena tinkers with engines to feel useful, John's trying to find peace in maintenance routines. We all have ways to handle the void."

Jason mulled that over. "Amir's busy writing everything down as if we'll be studied by historians. Marcus is learning more obscure languages. Morrow's... well, Morrow. Cool and composed, but she's hitting the gym pretty hard these days. I guess we've all got something we're wrestling with." He paused, inhaling slowly. "I keep this image in my head: the star charts, the trajectory lines. They're neat, predictable. If I follow them exactly, I can deliver us right to Kepler-452. That's my anchor. But the rest—understanding we'll never see Earth again, or how to cope with what's waiting out there—scares the hell out of me."

Riley nodded, pressing his hand against Jason's shoulder again, this time leaving it there a moment longer, a reassuring weight. "You're allowed to be scared. It's a huge thing we're doing, bigger than anything humans have done before. Don't let it paralyze you, though. You're not alone in this."

Jason looked into Riley's steady, understanding eyes. He felt something lighten inside him, as if by sharing this fear, it lost some of its power. "Thanks, man," he said softly. "I don't say this often, but... I appreciate your stupid jokes and relentless optimism."

Riley grinned, relieved. "I knew you secretly loved my jokes. Just wait until I break out the space puns—they're out of this world."

Jason rolled his eyes, a genuine smile creeping onto his face despite himself. "Don't push your luck."

$$7$$

John left the hydroponics bay feeling lighter than when he'd entered, Clara's warmth having quietly softened some internal knot. Still, he had tasks to complete before sleep. He passed through a series of hatches, tapping his diagnostic scanner absently against a panel here, conduit there, verifying green lights and stable readings.

Soon, he stood before engineering, aft of the hab-rings. Here the hum thickened, layered with the cool bite of recycled air and the faint tang of metallic lubricants—and something subtler: Elena's voice murmuring to herself. The hatch slid open, admitting him.

Elena stood half-immersed in a tight service bay, a holographic interface projected at eye level. She was scrolling through engine performance logs, her brow knit in intense concentration. The Alcubierre field generators and antimatter engines were stable and automated now, but Elena's attention had not waned in the slightest. It was as if the lack of emergencies made her double down on perfection. She ran simulation after simulation, searching for micro-improvements no one else would have noticed or cared about.

John cleared his throat. "Evening," he said, voice subdued. He didn't want to startle her.

Elena glanced back over her shoulder. "John," she said curtly, acknowledging him but not moving away from her console. Her tone wasn't hostile, just clipped and focused.

He stepped closer, glancing around. Everything seemed in order—no loose panels, no stray cables. He eyed a smudge of lubricant on her sleeve. She was always elbow-deep in the guts of the ship, even when diagnostics showed perfection. "Making your usual rounds?" Elena asked, flicking through another set of diagnostics.

"Yeah," John replied. "Filters are good. Maintenance bots did their sweep. Thought I'd check in here, make sure nothing's out of place."

"Nothing's out of place," Elena said, deadpan. She reached up and tightened a clamp on a conduit that looked perfectly fine to John.

A silence settled between them, broken only by the soft hum of the machinery. John considered his next words. He'd seen her intensity turn sharper lately, as if the constant perfectionism was now grating at the edges of her well-being. He wanted to show concern—maybe offer the same warmth that Clara had shown him. He was no natural comedian. Still, he tried.

"Everything's running smoothly," he said quietly. "Might be okay to… ease off a bit. Don't want you to burn out." He managed a slight grin, trying to frame it as a gentle joke, a pun on her propulsion tuning obsession.

Elena froze mid-adjustment, then turned slowly to face him. Her eyebrows arched. "'Burn out'? That's the line you're going with?" Her voice was flat, and whatever humor he had hoped would spark between them fizzled in the stale air.

John cleared his throat, feeling heat creep up his neck. "I mean— we're stable. Maybe you don't have to push so hard." He realized too late that his tone had become defensive, as if he were apologizing for even trying.

Elena sighed and stepped out of the service bay, folding her arms. "Look, John—I appreciate you doing your rounds, I really do. But I'm not pushing hard for fun. I'm making sure that when we decelerate, we do it efficiently. Any small inefficiency we fix now could save us significant fuel and time," she said, her tone implying far more than mere numbers.

He nodded, attempting to maintain calm. "I know. You're good at what you do. Best we've got. I'm just…" he paused, searching for words that wouldn't irritate her. "I'm saying you've been at it nonstop for weeks. Everyone else is starting to find some sort of balance out here."

"Balance?" She let the word hang in the charged space between them. "John, I'm an engineer. I solve problems, optimize systems. That's how I contribute. That's my balance." Her voice was even, but not warm.

John ran a hand through his hair, frustration tightening his jaw. He wanted to tell her she'd proven herself enough already, but the words jammed in his throat, stifled by caution. The calm he'd felt earlier was slipping away. "All right," he said simply, not wanting to escalate. He'd tried to nudge her gently, but it had misfired. Maybe she needed time, or maybe it was just a bad moment.

He checked a nearby panel, feigning another task just to break the tension. The readings were perfect. Of course they were—Elena wouldn't have it any other way. He turned back, meeting her gaze. "If you need anything, let me know. Otherwise, I'll get out of your way."

Elena pressed her lips together, as if considering a softer response, but her shoulders remained tense. "I'm fine," she said at last, tone neutral. "Thanks for checking in."

"Sure," John replied, stepping toward the hatch. "Goodnight, Elena."

He left engineering feeling a mix of awkwardness and regret, shoulders slightly hunched. Perhaps it was just the close quarters, the endless days, and the silent press of infinite darkness. Not every interaction would be smooth and comforting. Not every attempt at humor would land. They were all still learning how to coexist in this cramped world they'd built, and sometimes the gears would grind.

Behind him, Elena turned back to her console, brow furrowed as she input new parameters. Under other circumstances, maybe his attempt at humor would've drawn a smile. But tonight, in these tight corridors with no place else to go, even well-meant words could feel like friction against worn metal.

8

Hours after the awkward tension in engineering and the quiet understanding reached by Jason and Riley, Marcus wandered a deserted section of the habitat ring. He'd finished logging comm diagnostics and triple-checking the onboard data stores. Everything was stable—had been stable for weeks now—and there was precious little in the way of new signals to parse or languages to decode. At times, Marcus wondered how many hours he could spend reorganizing the ship's internal library before he went stir-crazy.

Amir sat in a small alcove off the main corridor: a recessed workstation with a chair and a pull-down holographic display. He'd claimed this spot early in the voyage as a semi-private "study." The historian's hands skimmed through virtual pages of old Earth texts, cultural archives, and anthropological reports. He was constructing a narrative—an ongoing record of their journey, sure, but also weaving their current experiences into a tapestry of human endeavor. Amir cataloged bits of language the crew used, their daily rites, jokes, complaints, their improvised traditions in the absence of any external cultural input.

Marcus paused at the threshold. "Hey, Amir," he said, tone soft so as not to startle him. "Mind if I join you?"

"Not at all." Amir glanced up, smiling kindly. He pressed his fingertips together. "I could use a break from my own thoughts."

Marcus stepped in, leaning a shoulder against the smooth curve of the wall. "What are you working on now? More journal entries?" He nodded to the translucent text hanging in midair before Amir's eyes.

"Sorting and contextualizing," Amir replied, voice contemplative. "Right now, I'm tracking how our language has shifted since launch."

He paused, thoughtful. "It's subtle, but I've noticed we reference Earth less frequently. Our jokes, slang, even metaphors—they're shifting. I'm trying to capture that process, maybe understand how we're evolving culturally, even here, in isolation."

Marcus let out a quiet, thoughtful hum. "Makes sense. We've been gone for a while, and Earth-time… well, it's probably unimaginable now. We're, what, hundreds of years out of sync at this point, relatively speaking?"

"Yes," Amir confirmed. "From Earth's frame, ages have passed. We've effectively become temporally isolated. We carry Earth within us only in memory and records. Everything else—our customs, routines, relationships—they're starting to grow in the soil of the now."

Marcus folded his arms. He'd noticed that too. Simple Earth references that once flowed easily now felt distant, fuzzy at the edges, like trying to recall a half-forgotten dream. The ship's environment, the crew's personalities, and the constraints of their mission were shaping a new micro-culture. "It's like we're our own tiny civilization," he said, half in awe. "Eight souls and a hold of sleeping colonists. A seed of human society at near-light speed."

Amir nodded, eyes shining with intellectual fervor. "Exactly. And future generations—if we ever have them—will look back at this initial phase as 'the old ways.' The jokes, the tensions, the relationships forming now will become part of our origin mythos."

Marcus smirked. "Origin mythos, huh? I never saw myself as a mythical figure."

"History turns ordinary people into legends over time," Amir said gently. "Imagine what our story might mean centuries from now, if the colony thrives. Or even if we fail—these records will explain how we tried, who we were."

There was a moment of silence as both men contemplated their place in an unfolding narrative that might never return to Earth. Marcus finally broke it. "I guess that's where you come in," he said, tipping his head to the holographic texts. "You're the keeper of the collective memory. Making sure our words and actions have a voice beyond the now."

Amir chuckled softly. "Heavy responsibility, isn't it? The historian among the first interstellar travelers." He paused, becoming more introspective. "I try not to let it go to my head. I'm just recording what I see, what I feel. I'm as flawed and biased as anyone. But maybe that's the beauty: the record won't be perfect. It'll be human."

Marcus considered that. "Human. We use that word like we know exactly what it means, but our concept of human is going to evolve, especially as we set foot in a completely alien star system. What if we find life—or just the faintest traces? How much more will we change? I wonder what 'human' will even mean by the time we set foot on another world."

Amir smiled a small, warm smile. "I like that you're asking these questions. It means we're aware of the journey, not just physically but culturally and psychologically. We've separated from Earth in more ways than one, and every day we redefine who we are."

Marcus reached out and tapped a line of text on the hologram. "Any good quotes in there?" he asked, wanting to see what sort of wisdom Amir had pulled from the crew's daily lives.

"Plenty," Amir said, scrolling through. "Jason's dark humor, Riley's puns, Clara's gentle encouragement, Captain Morrow's measured reassurances, Elena's technical manifestos, John's quiet acknowledgments. They all form a lexicon of this unique world we inhabit. And you—your calm, measured observations, and your interest in language. You translate our silence into understanding."

Marcus felt a flush of gratitude. He often wondered if he truly contributed beyond routine checks and calm steadiness. "I'm glad it counts for something," he said quietly.

"Of course it does," Amir assured him. "You and I, we're observers. We listen, we note, we interpret. That's important, especially now. We have no contact with Earth—our meaning has to come from what we build here. Your role, my role… they matter."

Marcus exhaled, relieved to hear this articulated. "You know, I think I needed to hear that. Sometimes I worry I'm drifting, just doing comm checks that never change, waiting for a signal that won't come."

Amir reached out, gently resting a reassuring hand on Marcus's arm. "We all drift sometimes. That's part of living in this void. But you're helping define who we are, just by engaging, talking, thinking about what this journey means. Your interest in languages, your conversations with everyone—these shape our communal narrative."

They both fell silent, comfortable in each other's presence. Outside, the stars remained distorted by the Alcubierre bubble, the engines humming along, stable and steady. Time passed differently here—conversation, reflection, and subtle shifts in perception all carried a new kind of weight.

Marcus offered a small grin. "Thanks, Amir. For reminding me that this quiet role matters."

The historian smiled back. "Thanks for giving me material to work with. Historians need good conversations as much as records."

Together, they lingered in that small alcove—two quiet observers charting the course of their fledgling society. On a cosmic scale, it was only a fleeting moment. Yet, perhaps centuries from now, their words and thoughts would echo softly through the minds of those who followed, shaping the story of humanity's first uncertain steps into the endless dark.

9

Four months into the voyage, the crew settled into a rhythm. Beyond the hull, stars remained warped by the Alcubierre bubble, offering few signs of progress beyond navigation updates. Inside, time was marked by routine, shared meals, fleeting tensions, and laughter—reminders that they remained human, drifting farther from Sol.

The crew kept time on the ship relative to earth time. Without a star close by and the rotation of a planet to differentiate day from night, the automated lighting on the ship helped to maintain circadian rhythms. The lack of natural light and the patterns the human body evolved around caused for some, a feeling similar to a perpetual jet lag. This and the confinement of the ship caused some mental struggles from time to time. Elena, John and the Captain were often seen working out in the ship's gym.

John was extra fond of the resistance training. He would often spend hours of his day doing different exercises to focus on specific muscle groups each day. There were a couple of machines for this that were designed to work in the artificial gravity or in the weightless environment of microgravity. In the artificial gravity, John didn't feel the need to strap himself into the machines. He would press, move and flex against articulated arms that were designed to use an adjustable resistance of gas filled tanks. By adjusting the compression or vacuum in the tank, John was able to push his limits and strengthen his muscles.

Elena seemed to prefer a stationary bike and rowing type machine. Both would also work without gravity. Every now and then Elena and John would end up working out at the same time. Elena typically worked out with Marcus during his allotted time in the gym. Since

John used the equipment Elena was fond of, he made sure to do so during his own time slot and Elena had no issues with John extending his time into her time slot. While there was still some friction between them, they were professionals after all. Elena even appreciated when John was still in the gym on days she was frustrated. Watching him push himself on the equipment, not just to avoid losing muscle mass and ward off atrophy, John pushed hard to try and improve his strength. Elena respected this and would often challenge herself more when they shared the gym. She knew the contest was only in her head, but always felt better after one of those workouts.

It was just one of those days. Elena's mind wandered as she strapped into the rowing machine, annoyance simmering beneath her calm exterior. Counting strokes to quiet her thoughts, she was startled by John's laughter as he wiped down equipment. Irritation flared instantly.

"What's so funny, Cowboy?"

John, looking up in surprise at her tone shrugged it off and replied, "Oh, I was just wiping down this equipment and I got to thinking. See, I wipe down and sanitize places commonly touched around the ship and things the bots don't reach. Just struck me as funny. Back in the military, all we ever did was drill and clean. Mostly clean. We joked about being the system's deadliest janitors. I used to hate it. Everyday it felt like the higher ups took it as a challenge to find something new for us to clean, or find an issue with something we'd just cleaned so they could have us clean it again."

John shook his head and chuckled again while he scrubbed the machine clean. "I just wanted to be out doing the job I thought I'd signed up for, but that was so little of what we actually did. And it was never as glorious as the recruiter's made it sound either. Anyway… here I am, hurtling through space to a new world we get to make from scratch and what am I doing? The same old shit I've always done. I'm back to an over glorified janitor again… only this time, I don't mind so much." John stopped wiping and looked over at Elena who had stopped rowing and was just staring at him dumbfounded. John shrugged. "Sorry, I didn't mean to disturb or distract you. I appreciate you allowing me to intrude on your time in here. I'll get out of your way." And with that, John gathered the rest of his personal effects and made to leave.

"Hey, Cowboy!" Elena called after him before he left. John turned around and waited.

"You always push yourself like that? Or is that just something you do when I'm in here too? You trying to show off or something?" She asked.

"Always." Was his reply as he left.

Just as he vanished from her view, she realized he hadn't really clarified anything. Was he always pushing himself or always showing off. She let out a frustrated growl and gripped the handle to the rowing machine with white knuckles. Just as she was about to try and rip the cable off the machine with a ferocious workout, she heard John chuckle just past the hatch. On the verge of a furious rage, he stuck his head back around the corner.

"I always expect more of myself than I can give. Fatal flaw I guess," and he disappeared for good that time. Likely headed to the only actual shower aboard the ship.

Elena relaxed her grip and increased the resistance on the machine. For the next half hour, she worked herself harder and harder. Not in competition with the infuriating man on the resistance trainers, just with herself. She cleaned up the equipment and headed out the door to get herself clean as well. She'd worked up quite a sweat.

Elena entered the compact shower pod, noting John was still there, back turned as he scraped water from his skin. She sighed inwardly—privacy was a rare luxury aboard the ship. Turning away, she quickly undressed.

"Good workout?" he asked casually.

"Actually, yes," she replied reluctantly. The space felt uncomfortably intimate with conversation.

Silence returned until curiosity escaped her lips. "Why do you push yourself like that? Seems like you're always punishing yourself."

He hesitated. "I never gave it much thought. I've got goals; being stronger's always helped. But I couldn't tell you why it appeals more than physics or engineering." He chuckled softly. "Didn't always push this hard. I was kind of a nerd as a kid."

Elena caught herself turning slightly towards him, drawn by unexpected vulnerability in his voice. When he slipped out, she turned back, annoyed at herself—but not without acknowledging a thought she wished hadn't surfaced: *He really does have a cute butt.*

She was just about to ask him another question when she heard the flip flop of his sandals and the door opening as John left. Under the hot stream, Elena reflected on her own habits—always pushing herself, competing with shadows and ghosts. John's presence today forced her to confront something uncomfortable: maybe she had more in common with him than she cared to admit.

The next ship morning dawned gently through artificial lights cycling from soft amber to crisp white. Jason awoke early, slipping earbuds in place for his habitual jog to navigation. Marcus had been up even longer, engrossed in comm logs. As they passed in the corridor, exchanging nods, another ordinary day aboard Aurora began.

Marcus preferred the early hours, taking advantage of the quiet bridge to review comm logs or sensor data. Compared to his Mars-Earth communications days, his current duties felt minimal—mostly hardware and systems checks to ensure readiness upon arrival. Stored aboard were comm satellites that would establish global communications for generations to come.

With his duties all but done for the day, he made his way to the galley. It was part of his routine to get some coffee brewing for the rest of the crew as they began to wake. Once again, he passed Jason on his way to the galley and waved as the navigator jogged past. The scent of reconstituted coffee grounds, while nothing like a fresh Earth brew, was still enough to beckon a few bleary-eyed crew mates to gather. Marcus greeted them each as they came in. One by one, they thanked him for the coffee. He sat at a table in the back of the galley where he sipped water from a coffee mug and jotted a few notes in a small leather journal, one of the few physical books to make the journey on the ship. Sometimes he read a book on his tablet. He rather enjoyed having access to the entire literary history of humanity, up until they left that is. He was a sucker for the classics. Today, he was debating on if he should read Asimov's works in release order or chronological order.

By the ship's midday, the habitat rings buzzed with subdued activity. Crew moved between the main deck, where the big holoscreens displayed external readouts, and their specialized workstations scattered throughout the rings. Most crew downtime was filled by scientific experiments planned before departure. Though few scientists had submitted proposals—preferring experiments they could see through personally—the crew still had ample resources to explore their own interests. They'd been provided nearly every book, scientific article, film, and song imaginable. Legal constraints were waived, acknowledging no intellectual property claims could survive the voyage's vast timescale.

10

The crew shuffled into the viewing lounge, snacks floating lazily between hands in the low gravity of the inner hab-ring. Elena took her usual spot near the exit, Jason stretched out comfortably, earbuds loosely around his neck. Marcus teased Riley about her insistence on comedy.

"Seriously, is laughter all you live for?" Riley merely smirked. "Better laughter than existential dread."

Movie nights quickly revealed the crew's tastes. Elena favored fast-paced thrillers, the more tension the better. John predictably enjoyed classic action flicks and gritty westerns. For John, westerns were never just entertainment; they reminded him of simpler moral codes, rugged independence, and freedom from politics—ideals increasingly hard to find in deep space.   Clara surprised everyone by choosing heartwarming romances and feel-good comedies. Jason preferred cerebral sci-fi, claiming he liked spotting navigational inaccuracies. Marcus, somewhat predictably, liked thoughtful documentaries and historical dramas. Riley consistently went for irreverent comedies—the sillier, the better. Captain Morrow rarely revealed preferences openly, though her quiet smiles suggested nostalgia for classic cinema.

"Kung Fu again?" Clara teased, nudging Amir playfully.

Amir sighed dramatically. "Only because the subtleties of existential European cinema were lost on you heathens."

Amir's tastes were indeed surprising—eccentric and eclectic. He regularly challenged the crew to step beyond their comfort zones, sharing films he appreciated from his multicultural studies. Although Amir had perhaps the deepest insight into these influences, most political or cultural nuances in his chosen films were lost on the rest of the crew. After all, almost all movies aboard were produced on Earth, with only a few dozen made on Mars.

Long before humans branched out into space, treaties were signed which prevented any one nation from making claim to the Moon or Mars. This spread to space and the rest of the system after debates for mining claims caused political issues back on Earth. As most of the exploration and business in space was originally provided for by large multinational companies that were the first to become interplanetary, the concepts of patriotism were largely diminished in space.

This was further exaggerated some 150 years prior to mission launch, when the first natural born citizen of Mars came into existence. An instant celebrity as the first human to be born off planet Earth, it was not long before the "spaceborn" were a commonality. Unable to be governed from Earth, every permanent or semi-permanent establishment in space began to claim autonomy. This was especially true at the larger outposts on the moons of Saturn and Jupiter, or the mining colonies in the asteroid belts.

Nationality became a notion of Earthbound and the past. The spaceborn eventually began to band together and affiliate based more on what area of the system they were born, lived and worked. There were three primary cultural divisions for spaceborn; inner system, outer system and belters. The division for inner and outer system was generally considered to be Jupiter's orbit.

The inner system culture was heavily dominated by Earth culture, due to proximity and access to Earth and were thus called Earthers by the rest of the system. The outer system was most heavily centered around the moons of Saturn as they supported the largest populations and largest space stations.

Much of the Outer system was very sparse and dispersed. Small pockets of miners would join together, rarely seeing others outside of their small social bubbles. This area of the solar system became a haven for piracy and crime. The Earthers simply referred to them as Outers or Space Hillbillies, if they referred to them at all. Eventually, the name was shortened to Billies.

As propulsion technology developed further and demand for resources grew, two cultures of Belters emerged. Initially, these were the asteroid miners that operated heavily around Jupiter. Later, this was extended to the asteroids pushing farther out than the Outers. Each developed their own culture and in some cases a dialect that was so difficult for anyone not from there to understand, it was considered by many to be a unique language.

The most popular movies generally came from Hollywood, though there were a few Bollywood films that were popular throughout the system.

"Remember when you tried showing us that Martian indie film?" Marcus chuckled.

Amir raised his brows defensively. "I stand by that choice. It perfectly captured Martian existentialism."

Marcus laughed. "It captured Martian boredom perfectly."

Much to his dismay, the cultural nuances were not very well understood by the crew when Amir started selecting French and other European films. After several unsuccessful attempts with European films nearly resulted in open rebellion, Amir settled into a routine of selecting martial arts films. His popularity at movie night soared—something he found amusingly frustrating. Watching Clara become quietly emotional during romantic scenes had become something John noticed more frequently lately. He wasn't sure what to do about it yet, but it lingered in the back of his mind.

11

Earth Date Tue 18 Feb 3659 01:00:00 GMT

"Alright, people," Captain Morrow's voice echoed through the comm. "Time to hit the brakes."

The entire ship seemed to hold its breath as Elena keyed in the carefully prepared sequences for the Alcubierre field reversal. She had worked with Jason for weeks to ensure her drive parameters and maneuvers kept in proper alignment with the desired trajectory. The ship's computers had done most of the hard work, but with so much extra time on their hands, they both preferred to do things the long way. Calculating out all the variables kept them fresh. Dependence on technology didn't sit well with either of them.

Over the past few days, they had eased off their near-light-speed cruise, gradually shaving off velocity in relatively small, meticulous steps. Although it felt like a few days for the crew, from the perspective of the system they approached, they had been slowly decelerating for many weeks. The nuances of physics and frame of reference were somewhat difficult to grasp, where fractions of light speed and the small incremental changes to velocity were equivalent to the maximum capabilities in the early twenty first century. Now, the time had come for the final deceleration burn, the so-called "warp brake" that would bring them into the Kepler-452 system without slingshotting past it into eternal darkness.

"STB engaged," Elena announced quietly, referring to the spacetime brake of the Alcubierre "warp" drive system. A subtle vibration coursed through the floor panels, more a sense of pressure than any real jolt as the drive condensed space and time into a denser bubble ahead of their trajectory and created a less dense area behind the ship.

Her eyes remained glued to the readouts, lips pursed in concentration. "We're decelerating smoothly, Captain. No anomalies so far."

Now that the warp bubble had shifted from shielding them at relativistic speeds to actively decelerating them, the antimatter drive consumed precious fuel at an alarming rate. The exotic particles and energy being directed through the magnetic field of the drive cone slammed into the curvature of spacetime created by the bubble. The effect caused alarms to sound on Elena's console.

"Adjusting field generators to compensate for the antimatter drive energy," Elena worked feverishly at the controls of her console. A bead of sweat formed on her brow as she and the ship's computer tried to keep up with the changes.

"Sensors indicate we've collected a lot more radiation and energy in the bubble than anticipated, Captain. We're going to put on one hell of a light show when we arrive."

The ship was decelerating rapidly now. If someone had been watching from the Kepler-452 system, the ship would decelerate too fast for humans to survive over the course of several weeks, shooting in from deep space with the glow of a miniature star.

Another alarm sounded and the crew suddenly lurched forward, feeling more of the deceleration instantly. It felt like the deck shifted forward, their stomachs lurched and they were thrown into the consoles they sat or stood behind. Clara, seated without a console for support, nearly flew from her chair. She gripped the seat desperately, legs kicking out in front of her as though dangling from a cliff's edge.

"Inertial dampener malfunction. Artificial gravity system for the forward section encountering thermal issues. Rerouting power to augment from backup conduit." Jason announced.

"Warp geometry stable. Increasing thrust output. Jason, reroute coolant to forward HS32 from Hab1. That should take some of the heat away from there." Elena directed.

"That's going to make things rather toasty back there," Jason replied as his hands moved across the console, redirecting power and coolant systems.

The crew nearly fell backwards when the forward pressure they had felt instantly vanished. Having braced themselves against the force, the sudden loss was almost worse than the sudden onset. Worried about the potential issues this might have caused, Captain Morrow started checking additional systems. Life support looked good and so did the stasis chambers. *Well, at least they wouldn't remember the bumpy ride,* she thought to herself.

Riley, concerned about deep vein damage and the crew's health began looking them over. Clara had managed to position herself back in her seat just in time and managed to avoid more than a few bumps and scrapes. Marcus however, appeared to have blacked out over his console. Riley rushed over to him. Marcus regained consciousness just as Riley reached him and started to get back to his feet. Riley kept him seated on the floor while looking him over to make sure he was ok.

Another alarm chirped on the bridge. "Just a valve sticking, we're good," Jason called as the alarm silenced itself.

"Bleeding off as much of this heat as we can, infrared beam emitters are ineffective now due to the shift in warp bubble... but I'm running out of systems to store it in. We're burning up from the inside here. Coolant loops are reaching capacity here. We're reaching beyond heat saturation in several systems." Jason's voice betrayed his anxiety.

Elena froze in thought. How could she dissipate the heat. If the warp bubble was interfering with the infrared emitters, they could not shed the heat. Thoughts racing in her mind as more alarms chirped and red and yellow lights began to show all over the bridge.

The ship's radiators are tight against the hull to avoid being disintegrated by interstellar dust... they were only designed for in station and station keeping use. They wouldn't be able to handle this much energy. Energy—that's it!

"Jason, send me everything you can."

"Wait, what?" Jason stammered.

"Direct all the heat you can to the thrust system, I'm getting an idea here... If we pass it through the magnetic arrays on the thrust nozzle..." Elena paused briefly.

"Right, we can add an additional plasma conversion to the drive bell's exhaust and vent it with additional thrust," Jason finished her thought.

Elena's hands flew over the console, moving so fast Jason could not keep up with what she was doing. Captain Morrow, who was struggling hard to just let them do their jobs without interference understood the problem entirely though. "But how will you keep it from just slamming back into the hull? I don't fancy plasma burns,"

Elena replied in a staccato as she worked furiously at her console. "I'm reshaping the warp bubble geometry on the fly. If.... I ... can... get... There!!! Ok, I've got the warp bubble prepared to deflect more interference and deflect the plasma toward its shell. With any luck, this just might pass the plasma behind us in our wake."

"And if it doesn't?" Captain Morrow asked.

"Then it either sticks to us and hits when we stop, we fling a massive plasma wave ahead with all the collected radiation—or it doesn't work at all, and we fry." Elena said calmly as she continued working and maintaining the bubble geometry and simultaneously updating the computer on what she was doing so it wouldn't fight her trying to correct it to previous parameters.

"Options?" Captain asked.

"Burn up the ship and break apart, releasing all antimatter in the storage containers while the warp bubble collapses around the ship and with our velocity still being so high, we probably just get ripped apart into our component atoms by stellar dust and blue shift a lot faster than micro meteors would do it otherwise and our atom stream eventually makes its way to the galactic core, unless Andromeda collides with us first." Elena explained in an awkwardly cheerful tone.

"Well aren't you just a bucket of fun today? How sure are you about this? You're making this up as you go?" Captain Morrow asked in an even tone.

Elena spun around sharply. "Captain, I've been making this up as we go—every maneuver, every contingency, since before we left Earth. None of this existed until we did it. There isn't another option—unless you want to arrive extra fast and extra crispy."

Captain Morrow held her gaze. The two women stared into each other's eyes. There was no animosity in it, just a searching for answers. Elena saw the moment Captain Morrow's resolve solidified and with barely a nod between them, she spun back to her station and continued working on the issue.

"Send it, Jase. Send it all now. See the pathway I've opened up there?" Elena was all business, calm and collected.

Captain Morrow hoped Elena's collected appearance was from a confidence in the math and not just in herself, but found it comforting in either case.

"I see it. Rerouting now."

"Ok, plasma flow is routed through the bubble boundary-plasma stream's stable, waste not want not! Take that entropy!" Elena exclaimed.

"Well that's a 'screw you' to the second law of thermodynamics," Jason muttered, shaking his head.

Almost at once, the amber and red lights across the consoles on the bridge began going out or changing to green. The chirps and sounds from each alert silenced and stopped demanding attention. The bridge became quiet, almost too quiet.

"So, let's just hope this isn't the part where it all falls apart and we come apart at the seams," Jason muttered, but in the new silence of the bridge, everyone heard him.

Captain Morrow cleared her throat and shot him a sideways look.

"Sorry Captain. It just, well everything looks good over here, we're green."

Captain Morrow nodded, a flicker of relief passing across her features. "Jason, what's our approach vector looking like?"

Jason, hunched over navigation, poked rapidly at the holo-controls, shifting from his attention where he was assisting Elena. His usual sarcasm tempered by pure focus, he muttered a string of calculations before speaking up. "We're lining up a high-level orbital insertion around the system's outer region. Once we drop further speed, we can pivot for a direct course to Kepler-452b. By the time we enter low orbit, we should be fully synchronized with the planet."

Morrow allowed herself a tight smile. "Good work. Everyone, keep your eyes open. Any more unusual signals or system anomalies—report immediately."

Marcus Ito was already scanning the comm frequencies, searching for even the faintest hint of transmissions. "So far, just cosmic static," he reported softly. "No artificial signals or obvious signs of activity."

Hearing Marcus made Elena jump slightly. Sheepishly she stole a glance around the bridge. She had been so engrossed in the situation, she had flat-out forgotten anyone but her, Jason and the Captain were there.

Standing beside Marcus, Amir watched the swirling planet on the display with quiet awe. "Look at it," he said under his breath, more to himself than anyone else. "A new Earth… or so we once believed. We're about to see for ourselves. Thank you both for keeping us in one piece by the way."

From across the deck, Riley chimed in, his tone half-joking to counter the tense excitement. "I hope they've got better coffee beans on that rock. We might need a fresh supply."

"I think I'd settle for a new pair of shorts," Amir quipped.

A few chuckles rippled through the group, cutting through the hush of anticipation. After so many months (subjectively) in deep space, a shared moment of levity was welcome.

12

A few hours later, the ship had reduced velocity to 0.869c according to the information Jason had placed up on the main holographic display. With the entire crew confined to the Bridge and the small accommodations at the forward cone of the ship, Amir was getting a little bit bored and was feeling confined. Wiping a bit of sweat from his brow, he hopped to ease a bit of tension seeming to collect on the bridge.

"Elena, could you explain to me a little bit about what's going on here? Remember, I studied the past and not physics, so from my perspective this is pretty much all just magic."

Elena gave Amir a thoughtful look, then glanced at her control panel one last time before giving it a brief nod. Happy with the data she was seeing, she turned to face Captain Morrow.

"We're right on schedule, dropping about 0.037c per hour Captain." Elena turned to Amir, "Sure, I can try. What would you like to know?"

"Well, for starters, your galactic speedometer up there is moving kind of slow, but I understand that's just a percentage of a really really big number. And of course all that rollercoaster ride earlier... I think that's the fastest I've ever lost weight in my life by the way, thanks for that new personal best... anyway, I get the gist of what happened, but what's happening now? I don't feel any differently than normal at the moment, but we're stuck here in the nose cone and those numbers are big... magic. How's it work?"

Elena chuckled. "Well, I've heard a magician should never tell their tricks." She winked at him, but continued. "We're actually decelerating at about 3000 meters per second per second. Relative to Kepler-452's perspective anyway."

Riley and Clara who had been listening in both looked shocked.

Riley said, "That's… three hundred g's or more!"

"You just did that in your head?" Clara asked him.

"Well, a few g's can have serious impact on the human body… so I'm not unfamiliar with that, but now I'd really like to know why we weren't all puddles of mush when the inertial dampness cut out earlier."

Elena explained, "They didn't actually cut out. That was just a slight dip in their efficiency. If they had cut out, there wouldn't be much left of us right now. 300g's is not survivable. But, we're not actually pulling 300g's right now. That would also rip this ship apart. Way too much stress for it to handle. The warp bubble is actually doing a lot of the heavy lifting for us there. It offsets a very large portion of that."

Elena stopped and thought for a moment, seeing the puzzled faces trying to figure out what she meant.

John spoke up in the silence. "Think of it like handing off some of our momentum change to the warp bubble. It's all still there, but while we're inside it… we can hand off momentum to the warp bubble from our perspective. It's acting like a giant inertial damper for the entire ship and the inertial dampers inside the ship handle what's left so that we're comfortable. That's why we're stuck here and had to lock down the habitat rings, because you'd feel it rather uncomfortably back there."

Elena's jaw dropped as she stared at John.

"Sorry, did I get that wrong?" He asked.

"Uhh, no. Actually… that was close enough. I mean, it's… well, close enough."

John gave her an acknowledging nod and went back to looking at his console. Elena turned back to look at Amir.

"So, as John just explained, that's why you're here and why it feels normal and how we're all in one piece. Also, why it's a bit warm in here. Even though we're venting the heat as plasma, the thermal systems are still working overtime and we're actually burning though plasma faster than we did for acceleration. Without the warp bubble offloading most of our momentum, we'd need to vent more mass than the ship itself just to slow down. As it stands, we still dump tens of thousands of kilograms of superheated plasma over the course of a day—enough to glow like a tiny star, but not enough to strip us down to the framework!"

"And now the fun part, why we can break the laws of physics and live to tell the tale," Jason chimed in.

Elena rolled her eyes. "We're not actually breaking the laws of physics here… but if it's magic you want, I'm afraid you've got the wrong seats. If you were already in system watching us arrive, you would have had to be watching through a really big telescope for weeks now. We wouldn't have been hard to find though. We'd look like a comet streaking through the sky or maybe a meteor falling through atmosphere would be a better analogy. All that plasma we're dumping out the back is leaving a bright streak so long behind us, the radiation and energy we've collected in the bubble from all the stray hydrogen atoms, exotic particles and space dust along the way didn't all just get pushed around us. Some of it got trapped in the shell of the bubble. We're pushing so much more into it right now, I'd imagine we're glowing like a micro star shooting through the void here."

"So, what happens when we slow down and drop the bubble?" Amir asked.

"Well that's where I come in," Jason answered. "I've got to have us pointed just right, while basically guessing where we are. With the blueshift, even the best sensors can hardly see the star we're going to and in no way see it clearly, but I've got to make real sure we're not pointing at anything important out here when we turn it off."

Elena nodded. "Yes Jase, you're doing a fantastic job over there. Keep it up. We don't want to roast our new planet before we get there."

"Roast?" Clara asked.

"Yeah, so all that energy and radiation's got to go somewhere. Conservation of mass and energy and all that. We're going to put on one heck of a light show when we stop. If there were anyone out there, maybe even as far as Deneb, they would see us flash in their sky like a tiny supernova when we release it all. So, we need to make sure we're not pointing at or too close to anything important."

Amir shook his head slowly. "Serious magic. I'm afraid I don't understand it any better now than I did a minute ago. So that's what happens in about twenty one hours then?"

"That's right. We're kind of pushing it here… if it weren't for the magic, we wouldn't have had enough room to even reach relativistic speeds by now and it would have taken us close to two years to slow from 99% of light speed to just one tenth, .1c," she said as she pointed at the display that showed their target speed and a bar slowly falling towards it. "But, thanks to the magic, as you call it. We can do it all nice and quickly and we won't be too old when we get there to enjoy it."

Jason was shaking his head at his station as he listened. "She might be bragging just a bit there since you boosted her ego and all, but Elena's designs for the warp field and the antimatter chambers blew past anything anyone else has been able to do in applied physics in the more than two centuries since we discovered the math for it. I hate to say it, but it's truly a miracle they even let her on this ship and didn't lock her in a lab to study her brain or something."

Elena smiled. "You know, I think that's the nicest thing you've ever said to me Jase."

"Don't get used to it, and for crying out loud… don't let it go to your head. We can't spare the antimatter to contain an ego that big in a warp field."

13

Earth Date Tue 18 Feb 3659 23:45:00 GMT

Just short of 24 hours after beginning the intense deceleration process, the ship and crew were coasting into the system at about one tenth the speed of light.

"Approaching the 20 AU mark Captain. I'd recommend we drop the bubble and release the radiation to be safe. We're close enough now, I think we can get some visual on the planet." Elena announced with an exhausted tone to her voice.

"Excellent, let's see it first. No point in delaying this any further," Captain Morrow's eagerness was evident.

The displays throughout the bridge shifted, showing multiple sensor and telescope feeds, first of the Kepler-452 system.

John, ever watchful, kept to the sidelines with his hands gripping his console. "Any idea what those smaller planetoids are?" he asked, jerking his head toward the sensor readouts. "Asteroids? Dwarf planets?"

Elena glanced at a secondary display. "We're picking up at least three minor bodies that might qualify as dwarf planets, plus a thick band of rocky debris in an asteroid belt we didn't expect. Our initial data from Earth's telescopes was incomplete; at fourteen hundred light-years away, no wonder we missed a few details."

Zooming in on her own display, Clara gazed at the swirling disc of Kepler-452b. The greens and blues conjured memories of Earth—lush forests, rolling oceans. "If it's anything like our home-world," she said softly, "we have so much to learn. We might even find life. Maybe not sapient, but at least microbial… or maybe more. All that green, there must be an abundance of flora down there!"

"That's exactly why you're here," Morrow answered, catching Clara's eye. "And also why we brought the stasis colonists. To build a future out here, once we confirm it's safe."

A hush fell over the group again as the ship gradually slowed, the engines firing in careful bursts while the reversed Alcubierre field drew them into a stable orbit far above the plane of the system. They watched as the planet's swirling patterns grew more distinct. Clouds formed silvery caps over what seemed to be vast continents, and something like deep azure oceans dominated the lower equatorial latitudes.

"It's beautiful," Jason murmured, forgetting for a moment his usual terse cynicism. "It really is."

From her station, Captain Morrow exhaled. "Alright, enough gawking for now. We're not there yet. Let's get final insertion vectors locked in. Elena, keep an eye on the warp brake. I don't want to overshoot or come in too hot and we don't want to bathe the system in radiation either."

"Yes, Captain," Elena acknowledged. Her fingers moved fluidly across the console, adjusting parameters to guide them through the last phase of deceleration, the computer system almost anticipating her commands.

John looked on, the tension in his stance receding just a bit. "We made it," he said under his breath, though no one replied. It was a statement of relief and a kind of wonder—he never really doubted Elena's engineering skill, but seeing everything work so flawlessly underscored how much they'd gambled on bleeding-edge technology.

A new beep sounded on Marcus's panel. "Picking up a faint energy signature from the far side of the planet," he announced, brow furrowing. "It's probably just a natural phenomenon, but I'm tagging it for follow-up."

Morrow's lips tightened. "Keep it flagged. We'll pass over that region once we reach stable orbit and let me know if you get a better read when it rotates to face us."

With that, the final stage of deceleration commenced. Elena keyed a sequence, and the Alcubierre bubble shifted, easing them into an easy coast and drawing them slightly askew into alignment with Kepler-452b. A wave of inertia pressed lightly against them before fading. Minutes ticked by in a hush, the only sound the subtle hiss of air circulation and the steady thrum of the ships thrusters cycling.

"Ready to release bubble for radiation venting." Elena called out.

"Go, no go report." Captain Morrow ordered.

In turn each station reported "Go" status.

"All sensors and visual arrays shut down and protected." Jason called out. "We are a go for radiation release."

"Releasing now." Elena announced. Her voice tense and focused.

For the first time since beginning the acceleration to near light speed, the protective bubble that worked like magic to make this trip possible, according to Amir anyway, vanished. Shuttered inside the ship and shielded from the outside world, the crew was completely blind to the intense flash of light and radiation that erupted from their position. The blast emitted energy across an enormous range of frequencies, even triggering a faint gravitational ripple. If anyone was around within many light years, their arrival would be very hard to miss as it would register on practically every sensor array and even be visible to the naked eye.

Then, in a single smoothly choreographed maneuver, the ship glided into position, capturing itself in a high orbit roughly 20 AU, or twenty times the distance between Earth and the Sun, relative to Kepler-452's bright star.

"We've arrived in-system," Jason reported, voice taut with excitement. "Orbital insertion confirmed. Estimated two days of final approach maneuvers before we're in a stable low orbit around Kepler-452b, including final deceleration."

A murmur of satisfaction spread. The mood on the command deck was electric—months of travel, centuries passing on Earth, all leading to this. Outside the ship, the planet loomed, a silent sphere of possibility. Inside the ship, a mix of emotions so vast and varied it could never be defined.

Riley turned and grinned broadly at the rest. "We did it, folks. Welcome to our new neighborhood."

Their new neighbor glowed with promise through the displays, a distant oasis in the star-strewn darkness. It would take a few more days of careful maneuvering to see it up close, to truly confirm what secrets it held. But for now, they allowed themselves a moment to bask in triumph—and in the relief that their technology, training, and sheer nerve had carried them safely across light-years of empty space, into orbit around this fabled second Earth.

From the wide forward viewport, Kepler-452b looked every bit the green and blue paradise they'd dreamed about in the centuries since its discovery. Behind the tinted transparisteel, eight sets of eyes took in the swirl of clouds, the hints of landmass, and the dark oceanic stretches that glimmered under the distant star's light. After so many abstract mission briefs and sensor readings, seeing it firsthand carried a weight that nearly stole their breath.

Jason was the first to break the hush. He stood at the navigation console, arms folded, gaze fixed on the planet. "You see that wide expanse of deep blue along the equatorial belt?" he asked, voice uncharacteristically reverent. "That's gotta be one massive ocean. If the maps we have on the holo-display are right, it's bigger than the Pacific on Earth. And the landmasses—" He stopped, as if words failed him. With a mass of just over three and a quarter earths, this planet was huge, but there just wasn't any frame of reference. The holographic displays were the only source of relevance as the images of New Earth were superimposed over a smaller Earth. Jason played with the two spheres, rotating Earth around within Kepler-452b trying to make sense of the vastness of scale they were looking at.

Riley Thompson let out a low whistle, stepping closer to the window. "Gorgeous," he murmured. "Imagine what the beaches must look like. Might finally be able to bust out my Hawaiian shirt." He tried for a teasing tone, hoping to keep the mood light, but his voice shook from excitement.

Elena, still seated at the propulsion console, wore a half-smile that did nothing to hide her amazement. "We traveled light-years and left everything behind for that view," she said quietly. "And it might just be everything we hoped… oxygen, water—actual, real water." Her gaze flickered to Clara, who hovered close by, eyes bright as she studied the planet on her data tablet as she too zoomed and played with images much as John was doing.

Clara was practically glowing. "Preliminary spectrographic sweeps confirm complex organics in the atmosphere. Not just algae or bacteria either—there's a strong chance of full-blown ecosystems down there. I knew the scans from Earth weren't lying, but this is—" She cut herself off with a slight laugh, tears pricking the corners of her eyes. "It's more than I ever let myself believe."

Amir edged closer, adjusting the wide-brimmed glasses perched on his nose. "A new cradle for humanity," he murmured, letting the poetic notion hang in the air. "If the climate's right and there's no lethal pathogens waiting to greet us, we could—"

"Captain?" Marcus Ito's sudden interruption sliced through the atmosphere of wonder. He was at the ops station, frowning at lines of scrolling text on his display. "I'm picking up an anomaly in orbit. Several anomalies, actually."

Captain Morrow stiffened, crossing the deck in swift strides. "Talk to me, Marcus. What are we looking at?"

Before he could reply, the main holo-display flashed. A swirl of faint metallic returns highlighted the near-orbital region around Kepler-452b. At first glance, it looked like random scatter—asteroids, debris clouds, the usual cosmic noise. But then a faint ping repeated itself, artificially regular.

Marcus's brow furrowed. "There's something… metallic in the orbit. Wait… multiple somethings. Sensors are reading symmetrical geometry."

A long pause filled the bridge.

"You're telling me those are… satellites?" Elena breathed.

A stunned silence hit the command deck. Even the gentle hum of life-support felt loud in the hush. Jason blinked rapidly, as if trying to confirm he'd heard correctly. "Wait—what?" he managed. "Satellites? As in, advanced technology… derelict around the planet?"

John Ferris, standing near the rear, ran a hand over the stubble on his chin. "Impossible," he growled under his breath, though he didn't sound entirely convinced. "We were supposed to be the first humans here. The scans from Earth indicated no sign of intelligent life, just the possibility of primitive biospheres."

Captain Morrow exhaled, slow and controlled, though her eyes betrayed her own shock. "Riley," she said quietly, looking to the crew's unofficial morale officer, "Any quick wit to break this tension?"

Riley swallowed. "Right," he replied, forcing a half-grin. "Hey—no big deal, right?" Riley forced a grin. "Just a few lumps of metal. We'll sort it out, folks…" He paused, swallowing. "…Okay, so maybe I don't have a joke for this."

"We're dealing with a genuine mystery," Morrow concluded, composing herself. "Whatever's out there is defying all our expectations of a 'pristine frontier.' We need scans—thorough, wide-spectrum scans, and we need them now."

Elena, hands dancing over controls, pulled up high-resolution sensor arrays. A swirl of data took shape, revealing faint outlines, twisted frameworks. "Captain, these structures… are they… stations?" she asked, almost to herself.

"Looking that way," Marcus answered grimly. "No active transmissions. They're derelict for sure, or close to it. Some are in stable orbits, some drifting in elliptical paths. I'm seeing debris fields, too, as if something big broke apart."

As if on cue, a 3D render blossomed on the main display: irregular hunks of metal swirling around the planet, tethered by gravity but clearly not natural asteroids. Amir raised a trembling hand to his chin, eyes wide. "This changes everything," he whispered.

John stepped forward, the tension in his body like a coiled spring. "Captain, recommend immediate caution. We have no idea what we're dealing with. Could be a war zone leftover, an abandoned colony, or— who knows? We should be on guard. We have no idea who or what is behind any of this and we probably shouldn't go barging in for first contact on an apocalyptic scenario. We don't want to be mistaken for an aggressor and we do not know what defenses may still be active."

"I agree," Morrow said, voice tight. "We'll hold orbit, and run full-spectrum scans. Jason, map a safe perimeter. Elena, keep the warp drive on standby in case we need to bubble. I'm not risking anyone until we understand what's happened here. Jason, give us a 30 degree offset from target. I want a visual but I don't want an aggressive approach."

The swirl of excitement and fear swept through the bridge like a gust of wind in an airtight tomb. They had come looking for a new world untouched by humanity, an untouched paradise. Instead, they had found the remnants of something—someone—who came before.

Clara's voice trembled as realization dawned. "My god… we're not the first ones here."

A hush fell once more, thick with questions. In the face of that silent, drifting evidence of prior inhabitants, they realized this mission was about to become far more complicated than any of them had bargained for.

14

Earth Date: Wednesday 19 Feb 3659 00:15:00 GMT

For twelve hours, the crew had worked feverishly to gather every possible scrap of data about the mysterious orbiting structures. They had used every sensor array, every telescope, every deep-scan protocol on board. The main orbital station, while battered in places, was largely intact and appeared to be the epicenter of the derelict satellites strewn around Kepler-452b's orbit. The closer they got, the more hints of advanced alloys and elegant design patterns emerged, far more sophisticated than anything the crew had learned in Sol's engineering programs.

Having recently returned from a rest break, Marcus, Elena, and Jason were back at their consoles and catching up on the collected data. Captain Morrow took very little rest and had kept awake for nearly 36 hours straight on stimulants.

"It looks to be of human make," Elena kept muttering, tapping at her console. "Or if not human, at least derived from Earth's technology. Look at these shapes—bulkheads that echo our own structural designs… but it's all more advanced, like they had centuries more research."

"Centuries they shouldn't have had," Jason cut in from his navigation station. He focused an external telescope on the station's outer hull, zooming in on faint markings. "That bay door… do you see that? Looks like a docking ring, but it's… different. Compatible with our systems, in principle." He trailed off. "I can't wrap my head around this. It's all so familiar and yet alien."

From the command deck, Captain Morrow folded her arms, eyes never leaving the main display. An incomplete 3D model of the station glowed in the center of the holo-projection, compiled from hours of scanning the portions they were able to observe. Several modules were crumpled or torn, as if impacted by debris or something worse. Yet, a few sections seemed intact, sealed behind thick bulkheads.

"I'm detecting a faint signal," Marcus said, voice hushed in the tense atmosphere. "It appears to be coming from a docking bay airlock, in pulses. Minimal power. Almost like it's on an emergency reserve."

Jason peered over Marcus's shoulder at a stream of code and waveforms, brow furrowed. "You're sure that's a human standard? Or at least Earth-derived?"

"It's extremely close," Marcus replied, pointing at a waveform on his screen. "The digital handshake is old—like something from a pre-antimatter era, but not exactly. It's akin to those short-range comm beacons we used in the outer solar system a hundred years ago. I can't decrypt the data, though. It's too corrupted or incomplete or maybe it's using a form of encryption we don't know. I'm having the ship's AI analyze it now."

A shudder rippled through the gathered crew. Jason ran a hand through his hair, eyes darting between displays. "Someone was here, built all this—then vanished? Or… maybe we're not so alone after all."

Captain Morrow breathed in. "We'll do this cautiously. Elena, see if you can coax any more from that signal. Marcus, keep pinging the station. If it has a computer with basic handshake protocols, it may respond."

"Yes, Captain," they answered, almost in unison.

Marcus approached Captain Morrow quietly, Voice lowered for privacy.

"You should rest, Captain. We're still 12.5 AU out, just data collection. I've got this covered—I'd rather you be fresh when we arrive." I can ease us in cautiously, but there's no sign of life. I promise to wake you at the first hint of any changes to that." Marcus's tone was calm and respectful, but firm.

Captain Morrow gave him a searching look then nodded.

"Jason, plot us an indirect course. Leave us an exit lane that doesn't require maneuvering first. "If we need to haul ass, I want immediate egress available. Alert me if anything changes—anything at all. I'll be resting. Marcus, you've got the bridge."

"Aye Captain. Avoiding the debris will have us on an indirect route anyway, I'll leave you a clear lane."

Marcus nodded at her, his lips drawn tight. "I've got the bridge. Get some rest Captain, this is going to be boring for a while."

True to his words, the next sixteen hours would be boring. Captain Morrow was able to get 12 full hours of rest. Ten hours after Marcus relieved the Captain for rest, he called for another crew rotation to give Elena and Jason time to recover before reaching the 1 AU mark. Captain Morrow relieved Marcus with four hours of travel time remaining. By the 16 hour mark, Elena and Jason had returned to their stations for final approach and deceleration. Captain Morrow held the bridge and Marcus had returned after a 4 hour nap.

"Begin final deceleration and match orbital velocity of the station. Take us in, Jason, let's get some answers directly if we can."

"Bringing up the bubble now," Elena announced. "Bubble stabilizing."

"Thrusters on standby. Ready to fire," Jason said.

"Bubble geometry is stable, ready for thrust."

"Fire thrusters, max burn," Captain Morrow ordered.

"Thrust burn. Calculating two and a half hour burn," Jason announced.

"Marking time." Elena pushed the countdown timer for the thrust duration to the main display.

After the ship had reduced velocity to a manageable speed, Elena dropped the bubble and the ship adjusted course under much lower and survivable forces the inertial dampeners of the artificial gravity system could compensate for. By this time, the rest of the crew had rejoined them on the bridge for the final maneuvers.

They maneuvered in carefully. The great arcs of the station came into full relief through the ship's high-resolution cameras: the labyrinth of modules, trusses, docking ports, and a central core. Most of it was dark, apparently powered down. But near one docking bay, the detected signal was still just a flicker—an airlock control mechanism that still registered a faint charge.

Jason guided the ship's thrusters with almost surgical care, adjusting their heading in micro-increments to line up with the best possible docking approach. The tension on the bridge mounted with each passing moment. The station was large, easily the size of a couple city blocks, but their own vessel was even longer—built to house thousands of colonists, stores, and equipment for planetary settlement. Moving these two colossal masses into a shared orbit without incident demanded full concentration.

"Approach at ten meters per second. I want to see less than ten centimeters per second at final contact," Elena advised, hands dancing over propulsion and antimatter engine adjustments.

Captain Morrow hovered beside Jason, eyes on a secondary readout. "Any sign of reaction from the station?"

Marcus shook his head, frustration etched on his face. "It's just that faint docking bay signal, repeating like a beacon. Could be purely automated. I'm not seeing any other transmissions or remote commands."

Finally, the ship drew into position. Through the forward viewport and on every console screen, the battered station's docking bay loomed, a large, circular portal that glinted faintly with the leftover starlight reflecting off its metal surface. The pulses from the airlock were steady and unchanging, like the fading heartbeat of a once-thriving organism.

Captain Morrow took a breath, her voice hushed but firm. "All hands, prepare for docking. Marcus, coordinate with Elena to assist with any last-minute alignment. Jason—keep that approach speed down once we're within final contact range. We can't afford a scrape or collision, so lets take it extra slow."

"Yes, ma'am," they answered.

Gently, carefully, the giant colony ship edged closer to the silent station. Air currents on the command deck were nonexistent, but everyone felt the intangible hush that heralded a momentous event. The docking clamps began to deploy on the hull's exterior, guided by sensor-laden arms that probed for a matching ring.

Jason's display flashed. "Contact in thirty seconds."

In the observation viewport, the station's docking ring swelled to fill their vision. A hush settled over everyone, the tension thick enough to taste. The faint docking beacon pulsed in the darkness, an echo of technology strangely familiar yet impossibly more advanced than anything from Earth's known timelines.

This was it: the moment they would connect with a relic of another society from eons before they had any right to arrive. There was no telling what they might find on the other side of that airlock, nor how the fragile remains of the station would react to their presence.

They were about to extend a literal bridge into the unknown—

15

Earth Time: Wednesday, 19 Feb 3659, 19:00:00 GMT

Clamps confirmed. Pressure seals were properly aligned. The faint hiss of decompression indicated the integrity retained by the station's ancient airlock, defying centuries of abandonment. There were no protective warp bubbles or advanced shields in play now. The ship's engines idled at station-keeping, allowing the micro-thrusters to maintain the delicate balance between two massive objects in orbit. The ship was as quiet and docile as it had been just before they detached from the space dock around Saturn.

Captain Morrow watched through the forward camera feed as the boarding team assembled at the docking collar. The boarding team consisted of John, Marcus, Elena, and Amir. John carried a portable scanner strapped to one forearm, a vibrosword, and a sidearm on his hip—standard protocol, though nobody expected hostilities. More likely, rather than hostile forces, they'd face malfunctioning machinery or unstable structural elements. He was their front-line caution in the face of unknown hazards.

"Team One," Morrow's voice softly crackled in their helmet comms, "confirm suit integrity before breach. Proceed with the manual override on the station's airlock computer."

"Copy that, Captain," John replied. His tone was clipped and his focus evident. "Marcus. Elena, Amir—double-check your readouts. Suit pressure stable?"

Elena responded with a brisk nod he could see through her visor. "All good. Minimal external radiation, no sign of vacuum breach. I'm patched into the station's docking interface, but it's glitchy. We'll have to coax it open."

"Same here," Marcus confirmed quietly, glancing at his own suit readout. "Vitals steady. Ready when you are."

Behind them, Amir hovered near the back, mag-boots locked to the floor and carrying a data tablet loaded with translator AI and any historical reference files they might need. "Standing by," he added. "Let's see what old ghosts live in here," Amir commented.

They clustered at the hatch. The docking collar of their own ship had extended, magnetically locking to the station's ring. Additional magnetic clamping extended from the ship to hard points on the station to provide additional support. A small mechanical keypad flickered on the far end, with half-dead lights. John slowly moved forward toward the outer door of the station, monitoring the display on his arm as his suit's sensors were continuously scanning for structural weakness. Satisfied, he stepped back and motioned Elena forward. John had been a part of many breaches in his previous lives in the military and private security, but something about this one just felt off. Perhaps it was just the lack of his familiar team for such situations as they were still in stasis. For a brief moment, John wished he had his security detail for this excursion, specifically Hanna and Vogel for this excursion. He didn't expect trouble; otherwise, he would have insisted on waking them and Serena. No time to wake them up though; he would have to make do with this ships crew.

"All yours, Elena," he said tensely.

Elena tapped a sequence on the keypad. Garbled text scrolled past on the tiny screen. Elena cursed under her breath. "It's definitely English-based, but... heavily fragmented. The station's main computers are offline. We're basically dealing with a backup microcontroller designed to power the airlock."

"Can you bypass it?" Marcus asked, shifting his grip on a handheld diagnostic wand.

"Working on it," Elena muttered. A few more movements of her fingers against the holo-keyboard, a rudimentary input function of the holodisplay of her wrist comp, above her left forearm. Then, with a shuddering groan, the airlock hissed. The ancient door hissed open slightly, ground to a stop, then jerked enough to let them squeeze through. They squeezed in, one by one, taking extra caution not to catch any of their suits or gear on the edges of the outer door. Once inside, Elena worked again at her system to get the outer airlock door to shut. Once in place and sealed tight, the whole process repeated itself with the door on the inner side of the air lock. The slight sensation of pressure they would have felt as the chamber was pressurized to one atmosphere was eliminated by the suits they wore. Though thin and tough, the suits did not provide any tactile feedback from their surroundings.

"Airlock cycling, no catastrophic leaks so far." John reported over comms, "Let's move."

One by one, they slipped inside the station. Stale air assaulted their suit sensors—recycled far beyond its intended design. The readouts on the inside of their visors showed elevated CO_2 levels and traces of industrial fumes, likely from decomposing machinery or coolant leaks. It wasn't immediately toxic, but definitely not recommended for breathing.

"I bet it smells like an abandoned factory," Marcus said, imagining the metalic tang as he wrinkled his nose under the visor. "If it had gone fully stale, we'd be seeing more hazardous compounds. Something must've partially cycled it every so often... or at least tried to."

With a final hiss, the station's innermost door slowly unlatched, rust and dust flaked off ancient hinges. Past the threshold, the station's inner corridor stretched away in a dark gloom, lit only by the lights of their suits and the faint emergency strips that reminded Elena of bioluminescence. The general design was eerily familiar: angled metal bulkheads, overhead light panels, handrails along the walls—like a futuristic version of the orbital stations they'd left behind in Sol's system.

"Everyone, check this out," Amir breathed, shining a small flashlight on the wall signage. Bold English letters read: Engineering Section →. Another labeled corridor pointed toward Bio Labs, and a third indicated Command Deck in blocky, practical script.

"Elena, you seeing this?" John asked, somewhat stunned. "Written in plain English."

She approached slowly, her gloved fingers tracing the lettering without touching the surface. "It's like walking into Earth's future. Or... a parallel path that left us behind."

Amir looked as though he was witnessing a holy relic. "All advanced. All neatly structured. It's as if Earth underwent a millennium of design evolution. Could this be of a later expedition that somehow arrived before us, armed with new technology? But how?" He searched their eyes for an answer no one had.

"We can theorize later," John cut in, shoulders tense. "We need to secure the area and see if there are hazards. Let's keep moving." His eyed each branching corridor warily.

Marcus's tone was gentler. "Easy, John. We're not expecting booby traps, right?"

John remained silent, his eyes fixed forward, betraying a flicker of unspoken concern. He simply led the way, stepping carefully over displaced floor panels and scattered debris. With every footstep, their helmet lights cast shifting shadows along the walls, revealing more English signage—some warning labels about radiation, others referencing hallway numbers. Occasionally, a red emergency panel blinked with dim power, hinting at systems valiantly holding on after all this time.

"Atmosphere here is thin but stable," Elena noted. Her sensor readout hovered near the bottom of her faceplate. "No major hull breaches so far, so the station's structure must be intact."

They followed the corridor labeled Command Deck, each new intersection yielding more baffling details. They passed a large window that should have shown stars—but it was covered in some metal shutter or blast shield, locked in place by ancient clamps. There were also occasional scuffs on the walls, blackened streaks that looked suspiciously like scorch marks.

"Signs of a fight, maybe?" Marcus noticed John's taut posture and guessed, "Or just an equipment short?"

"Don't know yet," John muttered. "Stay sharp."

Soon, they reached a broad set of doors bearing bold lettering: COMMAND DECK. A smaller sign to the side flashed a constant caution light: Access Restricted—Authorized Personnel Only. The door itself appeared locked, unresponsive. Elena was unable to find a control panel. Prying loose a maintenance panel next to the door, she was able to connect her wrist computer to what she believed where the controls.

She exhaled in frustration. "It's not budging. The system's offline, or jammed. It's requiring a higher command authorization—like a station master key. We can try a manual override, but it might take time."

Amir peered at the sign, tracing the English letters with his flashlight. "I can't believe how… normal this all feels. Like some advanced Earth station, just… lost here for ages."

John angled himself toward the others, voice low in their shared comm. "We take it slow, methodical. Forcing an override might damage something critical or trigger an alarm or security measure.

Captain Morrow's orders were caution first."

They all shared a glance. The stale air pressed around them, accompanied by a sense of profound unreality—human words on the walls of a station that should not exist, in orbit around a planet humanity had only theorized about until their journey began.

Elena carefully began prying open another side panel, searching for a manual release mechanism. The oppressive hallway's darkness seemed to watch them as they worked. Each breath in the suits a reminder of their solitude within this silent, future-Earth relic. It was a relic teeming with more questions than their team could possibly answer in a single day.

They had come all this way seeking a new frontier—none of them expected this outcome.

16

Earth Time: Wednesday, 19 Feb 3659, 19:23:00 GMT

The station's corridor lay quiet and still around them-a near-silent tomb of stale air and unspoken stories. The overhead lights flickered intermittently in an attempt to respond to their presence, each weak glow reflecting from their helmet visors. Elena knelt beside the sealed Command Deck door, pry-tool in hand, carefully examining the manual release hatch hidden behind a scorched panel. She wiped away dust and grime, quietly murmuring diagnostic readings to herself.

John, standing guard, cast his gaze down both ends of the corridor. Nothing stirred—only the faintest hiss of what might be old ventilation ducts struggling somewhere in the dark. His breath sounded loud in his helmet. His instincts screamed that abandoned spaces rarely stayed benign for long. Something had happened here, and until they knew what, every step could be a hazard.

Marcus hovered a few paces behind Elena, holding a portable work lamp that cast sharp shadows across the battered walls. "Any luck?" he asked, tone deliberately mild to mask his own tension.

Elena let out a soft grunt of frustration. "The station's main control lines must be severed or offline. Without power, the door's locks are jammed in a secure state. There's a manual override, but it's fused shut." She twisted the pry-tool for emphasis, metal scraping on metal. "Might need to cut through some of this plating. Perhaps if I could head to engineering and see if there's a way to restore power…"

"Absolutely not!" John's abrupt and almost harsh tone cut her off. "We stick together and until we know more about what happened here, we are not going to be flipping big switches. The last thing we need is to turn this thing on fully before we even know what we're dealing with."

Marcus drifted in closer, his visor reflecting the blinking red lights from where Elena worked. He ran a scanner along the door's edge, reading structural integrity metrics. "We'd risk damaging the mechanism if we cut blindly," he cautioned, eyes flitting between the readouts. "But if it's our only option…"

John's voice rumbled again through the comm. "Captain, we're at the Command Deck entrance. The manual release seems compromised. We may have to do a controlled breach if we can't find another route."

A brief static crackle, then Morrow's measured tone: "Understood. Do what you must, but proceed carefully. Are there alternative passageways?"

Marcus glanced down the hall. "I see an access corridor branching off from the next junction, could be a backup route."

Elena pursed her lips. "Another path might be easier than prying this main door. There should be multiple entrances… or maybe If we can restore some local power from an auxiliary node, we could unlock the Command Deck from inside the station's sub-systems. No big switches, John. Just a couple of small ones"

John nodded curtly, relieved at the prospect of not forcing a direct breach. "Alright. Team, let's check it out. No point in wrestling with this door if there's a simpler path." He glanced down the hallway, deeper into the gloom. "But stay sharp. We keep our eyes open for anything that'll give us a clue about what happened here too."

They turned away from the sealed entrance, heading for the next junction. The corridor's dormant overhead panels cast harsh shadows along the ceiling as some emergency lights struggled to come online, flickering with half-burned diodes. Some element of the station was trying to respond to their presence and the crew could make out a faint glow marking a pathway deeper into the darkness of the halls. A hush hovered, broken only by the clicks and slaps of their mag-boots on the station's deck plating and the low hiss of air through the suits' filters.

At the next juncture, a battered sign read → AUXILIARY CONTROL in that unsettlingly familiar blocky typeface. Something heavy had impacted the corner of the corridor—debris and broken metal jutted out in a twisted knot of plating. They navigated around it carefully. Flickering hazard indicators projected across the floor from a damaged emitter, painting the hallway in shifting red stripes.

Clara's voice crackled through the comm from the ship. "Boarding team, do you see any signs of life or functional systems yet? The old life-support data suggested partial cycling."

Elena answered as she scanned a small panel mounted on the wall. "There's a faint charge in these lines, yes, but it's ephemeral. Might be solar cells or some emergency generator running at minimal load. Life-support itself appears kaput. The atmosphere's too stale for direct breathing. Whatever was here is long gone and the station has been in standby for a long time."

They advanced in tense silence. Every so often, they passed an open door revealing a side chamber strewn with metallic and plastic crates, broken items, or corroded circuit boards. One chamber displayed rows of bunks—faintly reminiscent of typical Earth ship design—now half-collapsed from disuse, the bedding rotted away. More stark evidence that, whenever this station was inhabited, it was long, long ago.

The corridor ended in a sliding hatch labeled AUXILIARY CONTROL ROOM. Like before, there was no sign of a control panel or way to interact with the door. Marcus removed an access panel. A faint green LED blinked behind dusty plastic, suggesting some minimal power source still clung to life.

"Let me try," Elena said, stepping forward. She pried off the protective cover of the control box and began tapping instructions on the mechanical keys inside, her bulky suit glove making the delicate work challenging. Sparks danced briefly when she made contact with a corroded circuit.

A slow grind of gears followed. The door slid open a mere hand's width—enough for stale air to hiss through, stirring dust motes in the flashlight beams.

Marcus edged closer, shining his lamp inside. The room beyond lay in murky shadows, dark panels and consoles lining the walls. They appeared dead except for a single, flickering display that pulsed faintly green. The floor was a clutter of broken chairs, scattered tablets, and a thin sheet of overhead panel dangled precariously by a few cables.

John and Marcus physically forced the opening wider a few more inches, just enough for the helmets to fit through. John took point, stepping in cautiously, scanning left and right. No immediate movement, no sign of anything but emptiness. Yet the atmosphere was heavy with a sense of trespass, as if they'd entered a sacred tomb.

Amir followed, his breath catching at the sight of large, English-labeled consoles: Main Sub-Systems, Engineering, Comms and a few more that were covered or illegible. It was uncanny, an echo of Earth station architecture, yet advanced in ways he couldn't fully parse. One corner console suddenly illuminated and displayed a string of meaningless data, half the display blacked out.

Then, a flicker on the single working screen: an error message loop, lines of code that flashed in and out. Elena approached it, hooking a portable power module into the console's side port. She tapped a few keys, scowling at the garbled text. The interface was reminiscent of old Earth programming languages… but with subtle, unfamiliar complexities. Through her suit, she connected back to the ship.

"Jason, I'm patching through to a console that seems to be somewhat responsive. Can you work some AI magic here?"

"I see it. Lets see what we can… coming… holy shit… " the comms came in and out, breaking up Jason's transmission.

"Elena, do you copy?"

"Hey Jase, I copy. You were cutting in and out there for a moment, what do you see?"

"It's earth based. Half the code seems to be in Chinese, the other half in English, but it's got the same kernel as the ship. I've got it booting into a diagnostics mode now."

"Reading logs… or trying to," she whispered. "It's—holy… it's referencing system times that are… long after our time. Hundreds of years? More? Hard to say. The formatting is… I just can't make it out. Marcus, does this make sense to you?"

John took up a guard stance near the door, adrenaline pumping. So much of what they saw felt like Earth's legacy and yet impossibly advanced. Something about this station felt alive, despite the ancient abandonment that permeated everything. "Elena, can you find a node controlling the Command Deck lock? Or at least a partial map of how to get there?"

"Working on it," she replied, breath shallow with excitement and nervous energy.

Marcus, light in hand, edged around the perimeter. He crouched beside a toppled chair. The seat padding had decayed, but the frame was an alloy he recognized from advanced Earth starship builds—lightweight, durable. It was the type of material that might have been used in the outer colonies… only improved. He set the chair upright again and exhaled a slow, shaky breath.

"Whatever happened here," Marcus said over the comms, voice subdued, "it's like we're stepping into Earth's far future. Or a breakaway civilization. But we've only been gone—what—barely over a year, ship-time. This is hard to wrap my head around."

Amir approached a dim console labeled Records. The display was cracked, the lens fracture distorting the holographic text. He tapped it gently, but it gave no reaction. "If we could just access one complete file… we'd have answers."

John's eyes flicked from corner to corner, tension radiating in the set of his jaw. This place was too quiet—no hum of a functional station, no chatter, no life. Just these broken echoes of familiarity.

Behind them, the corridor stretched back toward the sealed Command Deck. Ahead, more locked doors likely awaited. The ghosts of Earth's future beckoned, offering neither comfort nor clarity—only unanswered questions in every rusted panel and half-lit console.

And somewhere, in the hush of stale air, the station waited for them to take one step further toward the secrets entombed in its silent halls.

17

Elena hunched over the console, the faint green light illuminating the edge of her visor. Time blurred around them, with stale air seeping through gaps in the corridor behind. John stood guard at the open hatch, scanning back the way they'd come for anything that might be lurking in the shadows. Marcus hovered near Elena, shining his beam where she needed it, a silent pillar of support. Amir moved about the auxiliary control room like a curator in a museum, gently touching bent chairs and cracked screens as though each artifact might whisper the station's story.

"Come on," Elena murmured, fighting with the half-corroded interface. Every keypress she made resulted in scrambled text, fleeting glimpses of file names or timestamps far beyond her comprehension. She felt more like she was coaxing an ancient relic than operating an advanced piece of technology. "Just give me something coherent... a door command, a system map—anything."

Amir paused in front of a second, half-lit panel that had the words SYSTEM DIAGNOSTICS etched above it. Slowly, he tapped an unresponsive touchpad. A mirrored flicker ghosted over the shattered display. "It's locked in some weird loop. I see references to 'Auto-Repair Subsystem B,' but it's all corrupted."

"This place is essentially a floating ruin," John said quietly, keeping his tone level, but his posture was taut. "Wouldn't surprise me if everything critical is shot to hell. The fact that anything responds at all is a miracle."

Marcus offered a half-smile under his helmet. "Glass half full, Ferris. At least the door opened for us." He cast the flashlight around, illuminating torn panels and half-buried debris. "You think they left in a hurry? Or were they forced out?"

No one answered. The question hung thick in the air. The battered state of the station suggested some abrupt, disastrous event… or a drawn-out collapse. Neither possibility was comforting.

Suddenly, Elena's console beeped—a short, sharp chirp that made them all jump. She froze, eyes wide in her visor. "Wait. That's… a partial response from the command module. Something recognized my ping." Her gloved fingers flew over the keys, chasing the fleeting thread of connectivity. "Yes, there's an isolated node with minimal power. Possibly an emergency control or sealed subsystem in the Command Deck area."

A low hiss escaped John's lips. "Could it let us unlock the main door?"

"Maybe," Elena answered, brow furrowed in concentration. "I can see a reference to 'Deck Authorization Node.' Trying to route the command—"

Her words faltered as the console flickered. A burst of static scrolled lines of text too fast to read, then abruptly snapped back to the stand-by screen.

Amir peered over her shoulder, straining to decipher any random snippet. "Looks like a script or a log. Something about 'critical failure… system lockdown…'" He glanced at Elena. "Can you reestablish the connection?"

Elena tapped a few more keys, but the console only responded with dull error codes. She sat back, exhaling in frustration. "It's gone. The link was there for a few seconds, then blinked out." She lifted the portable power module from the console's side port, checking its readout. "This station is too unstable. I can't keep a stable handshake going—there's probably a thousand circuits burned out between here and the command node."

A moment of disheartened silence enveloped them. Then John shifted his stance. "We're losing time," he said, voice calm but urgent. "Captain Morrow's going to want a status update. If we can't open the door from here, maybe we should regroup, bring specialized tools— cut through that main entry if we have to."

Marcus's shoulders slumped. "I was hoping we'd find a simpler solution." He panned the flashlight across the flickering console, as if searching for a hidden button labeled Answer to Everything.

Before anyone could decide, a faint rumble shivered through the deck. It felt like a muffled vibration from somewhere deep in the station's guts. Dust cascaded from the overhead rafters. Amir stumbled, catching himself on a twisted metal brace. "What was that?" he whispered.

Elena froze, scanning her suit's sensor feed. "No sign of an impact from outside. Maybe something internal—could be a structural shift, or a failing support beam."

"Or a system waking up," John said grimly. He toggled his comm. "Captain, we just felt a tremor in here. Not sure what caused it. Might be structural. We're considering extracting."

Morrow's reply came, laced with concern. "Acknowledged. If you can't safely reach the Command Deck, return to the ship. We'll come up with a new approach. We don't want you trapped if the station shifts again."

Elena hesitated, eyes flicking to the dead console. "I almost had a lock on that command node. If I could just find a stable line..." She trailed off. The tremor had rattled not only the station, but also her resolve. The risk was real.

Marcus placed a reassuring hand on her shoulder. "We'll get more gear, more power modules. Maybe we can run a line from our ship's systems if needed." His voice held confidence. "No sense risking your neck when the station could be on the brink of collapse."

Amir exhaled slowly, his disappointment etched in his posture. "We're so close, though. We have to get that door open and see what's on the other side. If there's any log or record of—" He cut himself short, glancing away. The historian in him was desperate for answers, but the realist accepted the danger.

John took a step toward the corridor, posture resolute. "Let's move, people. I'll take point again. Stay alert for more tremors. If we hear anything suspicious, we double-time it back to the docking ring."

The team retraced their path, flashlights slicing through the darkness. The hush was thicker now, charged with the knowledge of how fragile this station truly was. Flickering panels cast odd, dancing shadows that played tricks on their peripheral vision. Each clank of their boots echoed ominously, underscoring just how deserted the place was.

As they neared the T-junction where the battered signs marked Command Deck and Auxiliary Control, the lights overhead blinked in unison again, as if seized by a brief surge of power. For an instant, the corridor was starkly illuminated. Then it all dimmed to near-black, sending a fresh jolt of unease through the group.

"Steady," John murmured, gripping the corridor rail. "Just station ghosts."

Through the tinted visor, Marcus offered a wry, shaky grin. "You had to say 'ghosts,' didn't you?"

They pressed on, the corridor stretching ahead like a silent test. Behind them, that sealed door to the Command Deck remained locked —its secrets firmly intact. Out in the blackness beyond the hull, their ship waited, a beacon of relative safety. But inside these walls, they'd gotten just enough of a taste—enough to sense the echoes of some long-lost future that humankind was never meant to discover in this way.

Another tremor pulsed underfoot, fainter but still unmistakable, urging them forward with renewed haste. They had glimpsed only the first layer of this hidden chapter, and it left them with more questions than answers. If the station was truly failing, how long before it collapsed entirely—and how much time did they have to unlock its mysteries before everything crumbled into dust?

The tension mounted with every step as the team pressed on toward the docking ring, each of them silently preparing for the next revelation this silent frontier might unleash.

18

They reached the docking junction unchallenged, but the station's every creak and rumble seemed louder now, more purposeful. Just as John led the team past a half-collapsed corridor, the deck trembled again—this time with a peculiar, rhythmical pulse, as though a larger system was testing its limbs after a long coma.

"What was that?" Marcus asked, pressing a hand to the wall for balance while his magnetic boots held him in place.

John scowled, glancing back over his shoulder. "Another structural shift?"

Before anyone could answer, a shimmering flicker traced the length of the corridor's dim overhead strips, a crawling wave of faint light, too organized to be random damage. The hiss of stale air whined in their suit speakers, picked up from external microphones in their helmets. Then came a faint, synthesized voice—barely audible in their comm frequencies, as though piggybacking on the station's leftover broadcast systems:

"...Engineering... ...Power... ...Hurry...**"

Amir froze mid-step, his eyes darting. "Did I just... hear something?"

Elena checked her helmet display. "That transmission—it's station-wide but, extremely low power." She turned to John with a stunned expression. "Someone—or something—is calling us to Engineering?"

John's jaw tightened. "That's impossible. We scanned for life signs. There was nothing."

"Could be an AI system," Marcus said, half-wondering if he should be excited or terrified. "I mean, these signs all over the station—

English, advanced tech, consoles and doors with no physical input devices and limited controls. If they were building advanced drives, they might have had advanced AI as well."

A silence pressed on them as they considered that possibility. Captain Morrow's voice broke in over the team frequency, sharp with concern:

"Boarding party, status? We're picking up odd pulses on the station's external hull, like directed energy surges. Is everything okay?"

John quickly relayed what they'd witnessed. On the command deck back in their ship, Morrow weighed the risks: a seemingly defunct station with a possible AI calling them deeper in, a labyrinth of corridors that might collapse at any moment—and crucially, the burning need for answers.

"We can't ignore a direct call for assistance," the Captain concluded after a tense beat. "But keep the exit path clear, John. If something goes wrong, I want you all out of there. Understood?"

A murmur of assent, and the team turned away from the docking ring, retracing steps deeper into the station. Only now, the station seemed to guide them—lights flickered in sequence, leading them around debris-filled passages they hadn't spotted before. Doors that had been locked snapped open with abrupt, mechanical hushes, revealing dim corridors lined with advanced structural plating. Even the floor design had changed, shifting from battered metal grates to smoother alloys reminiscent of Earth's next-gen research labs.

They wound up in a large, dome-shaped chamber dominated by an imposing apparatus that took Elena's breath away at first glance. An antimatter reactor of some kind sat at the center, enclosed by transparent crystalline frameworks that pulsed with faint luminescence. Transparent conduits ran outward in symmetrical branches to ring-shaped modules on the walls. Overhead, an array of intangible holographic interfaces flickered: swirling patterns of symbols and color-coded lines, reminiscent of Earth's engineering displays—but undeniably more advanced, more elegant.

Marcus exhaled, shining his helmet lamp around the perimeter. "It's... an engine room, right? Or something bigger than a simple engine. But look at it—way more compact than our drive."

Elena stepped closer, enthralled. Her boots shuffled on the smooth deck, leaving faint scuff marks in the dust. "I recognize the layout. It's based on my dimensional coupling theories," she whispered. "My designs for next-generation antimatter compression. But this is… it's as if someone took my prototypes and advanced them centuries ahead."

John scanned the room suspiciously, hand hovering near his sidearm. He swept his beam along the walls, noticing patterns that might be vents or integrated sensor arrays—he couldn't tell which. "Captain," he reported over comms, "we've found a reactor core. A large one. Tech level is beyond anything we've seen. Possibly an AI controlling it, or some distributed system."

As if on cue, another low tremor pulsed through the station. The overhead lights flared to life in a wave, each section coming online with a ghostly glow. And in that eerie half-illumination, a faint holographic figure winked into being at the far side of the chamber. Indistinct, shifting, it seemed more like an echo than a person, flickering in and out.

John took a protective step forward, placing himself between the hologram and Elena. "Identify yourself!" he barked, voice echoing. His suit's external speaker carried the words into the stale air.

The figure didn't respond in words. Instead, an authoritative female voice cut into their helmet comms, crackling with digital distortion:

"Initialize… core… power. Stabilize… station."

Marcus's eyes widened. "It wants us to power the station? That's… a big risk. We don't know what systems it'll activate."

A series of symbols swirled in the air near the reactor, bright enough to catch Elena's gaze. They looked suspiciously like a heavily upgraded version of her old engineering interface. Touching one of the holographic icons might feed instructions directly into the reactor console. For a moment, she stood transfixed. "They're instructions… I think," she said quietly. "It's guiding me to re-engage the core safely, lock by lock."

Amir, who had inched closer to a bank of half-sunken consoles, spoke up, voice trembling with excitement. "This is insane. It's as if we're the 'chosen' ones. Like the station was built by Earth's future generation specifically to be… deciphered by us?"

John's scowl deepened. "Or it's a trap. We still don't know if this AI is benevolent, or if it caused whatever catastrophe befell these people." His grip on the sidearm tightened. "Captain, requesting guidance. This could wake a sleeping monster."

Captain Morrow's reply crackled in their ears, the tension evident in her tone. "John, you're right to be cautious, but we need answers—and this station's full power might unlock them. Elena, can you confirm it's safe to bring the reactor online without risking meltdown or a structural collapse?"

Elena's gloved hands hovered over the flickering icons. Despite the advanced tech, she recognized enough of her own design philosophy to guess what each symbol did. "From what I can see, the reactor's in a dormant state. If I re-engage it step by step, it should run an automated systems check first—like a self-test. If there's a breach or a short, it'll shut down."

Marcus exhaled, scanning the suits' environmental data. "The station is barely holding atmosphere. If the AI is leading us here, it could mean it's literally dying and wants us to save it."

"And if it's not that?" John pressed. "If it's trying to lure us into flipping the switch on something worse?"

The channel fell silent. Everyone felt the gravity of the decision. Then Morrow's voice returned, quiet but firm:

"I'm authorizing an attempt to restore power. The need for answers outweighs the risk… for now. Proceed, but stay alert. One sign of danger and you pull the plug."

John tensed but nodded to Elena. "Alright, you heard the Captain. Do it, but carefully." He looked up at the pulsing reactor overhead, suspicion etched in his eyes. "If this thing tries anything hostile—"

Elena stepped up to the shimmering console. Her hands glided over intangible controls, each responding with subtle shifts of color. "Then what, John? We're too low on fuel to go anywhere else. This was a one-way trip… we don't have a lot of options here. And… it's responding," she breathed, half in awe, half in dread. A series of runic shapes glowed across the reactor's surface, like safety checks in progress. The faint thrumming in the deck-plates shifted in pitch, as if an ancient beast were stirring.

A moment later, a resonant hum spread outward from the core, and the overhead lights intensified. Console after console lit up around them, revealing more of the station's advanced architecture. Dust motes swirled in the newly circulating air.

Amir shielded his eyes at the sudden brightness, scanning the walls with renewed curiosity. Screens that had been dark now displayed cryptic readouts in English-based code. "Is this a partial reboot?" he asked, stepping forward with caution.

Marcus's gaze snapped from the screens to Elena. "We have full atmospheric readings spiking. The system's venting or scrubbing the CO_2. Pressure is stabilizing."

John's jaw remained locked in tension, but he kept his weapon holstered. "We've awakened the station," he said under his breath, glancing around warily. "Let's hope it's not the station that ends us."

Above them, the holographic figure flickered back to life, more defined this time. Though its features were still distorted, it raised a translucent hand, as if beckoning. Then, the same voice—clearer, more deliberate—echoed in their comms:

"System power… online. Command Deck… accessible. … Hurry…"

An uneasy thrill rippled through the group. They had their invitation—whether it was salvation or an ambush remained to be seen.

Together, they stood in the heart of an impossible future, the station now awake and watching, and the path to its locked secrets finally beckoning them onward.

19

They moved through the station's corridors with measured urgency—helmets illuminated by the now-active overhead lights, each step resonating through deck plates that no longer felt quite so dead. Power coursed through the veins of this ancient, future-Earth station once more, thanks to Elena's delicate restart of the reactor core. The AI's low, pulsing guidance seemed to ripple in the very walls, ushering them forward. The new life in the station brought a sense of awoken spirits. No longer a derelict ruin, an unrealistic dread of encountering someone occupying the station settled over the crew with unease.

At last, they found themselves outside a set of heavy doors marked with bold, English letters: COMMAND DECK. Unlike before, these doors now hummed with life. Faint bands of light traced their contours, revealing stylized patterns that hinted at a more elegant era of human engineering. The overhead display—a holographic panel of shifting lines—flashed with a waiting prompt.

Elena stepped forward, swallowing a knot of tension. She raised a gloved hand to the panel, her suit's sensors detecting the subtle flows of energy beyond. "It's responding to me," she whispered, more to herself than anyone else. "Like it recognizes my presence."

John, ever at her flank, kept one hand near his weapon, scanning the corridor behind them. "Or it's just following the AI's script," he muttered under his breath. "Stay alert."

Marcus exhaled, drawing up alongside Elena. He placed a steadying hand on her shoulder. "We've come this far. Let's see it through."

Elena hovered her hand over the holographic interface; it pulsed once, then the doors slid aside. The Command Deck doors split open with a whispering slide, revealing a wide chamber bathed in pale white light. Consoles lined the curved walls, each with holographic readouts flickering erratically. At the center, a large, semi-circular control station loomed—its shimmering displays too advanced and too similar to Earth's design for comfort.

Amir gasped. "It's… bigger than I expected. Like some grand control center for an entire colony." He stepped inside slowly, gaze dancing across the darkened screens overhead.

Stepping gingerly forward, Captain Morrow joined them from the station entrance—she had come aboard personally once it was clear the AI intended them to converge here. She cast an experienced eye over the silent consoles. "Everyone, keep your helmets sealed. We don't know the station's integrity."

"Atmosphere's still iffy," Clara's voice came through comms from back on their ship. She was monitoring from a remote station, cross-referencing the station's renewed sensors. "Oxygen levels are rising but the CO_2 scrubbers haven't caught up. Definitely keep your visors locked for now."

"Copy that," Morrow replied. She walked deeper into the command deck, trailing gloved fingertips over a smooth console that lit up under her touch. "John, what are you thinking?"

John, moving systematically around the chamber, thought to himself for a moment before replying. "No immediate signs of structural damage here—just flickering power lines leading into large, holographic panels. Nothing's alive on here, the only immediate threat seems to be the condition of the station. Something about this just makes the hair on my neck stand up though. It doesn't feel right. Maybe I just didn't expect to walk through a coffin today, but I get the impression there was a fight here at some point."

"Why do you say that?"

"The scorch marks on the bulkheads and…" John paused, staring off into space while he gathered his thoughts. "I can't explain it Captain, it just has that feel. Familiar, like how things looked after running a breach and apprehend mission. Light resistance, lots of motion. It's just a feeling."

Captain Morrow considered him for a moment. His gaze appeared to her as if he was lost in memories better forgotten.

In the center, a ghostly silhouette coalesced—another projection of the station's AI. It flickered, half-formed, as though only partially stable. Then the same disembodied voice echoed in their helmet comms:

"Command Deck active… partial data restoration…"

Elena and Amir exchanged a glance, hearts pounding. "AI," Elena spoke carefully, "can you access the colony records? The planet's surface feed? We need to know—what happened down there?"

Static crackled over their link. The silhouette rippled, lines of code dancing across the consoles. Then a series of images materialized on the main holo-display—a sweeping view of Kepler-452b's northern continent stretched out below them, a large city sparkling beneath the planet's sun. As the feed transitioned, they saw a sprawling skyline abruptly fractured by a vast crater at the city's northwest edge. Massive structures lay in rubble. Portions of the city to the southeast still stood tall, hauntingly intact, while others were reduced to cratered wasteland.

"Dear God," Marcus whispered. "It's worse in high resolution than the ship's scans first showed."

The AI's voice hissed:

"Cataclysm event… unknown origin… partial record: high-energy impact…"

A cascade of clipped video logs took over the holographic display:

- Glimpses of frantic colonists rushing through corridors not unlike the ones on the station.

- A few unrecognizable shapes and fiery streaks across a distant sky.

Then, static.

Amir reached up to steady himself against the central console, transfixed by the ghostly scenes. "An orbital bombardment? A meteor strike? This is… I don't know."

Morrow's face hardened. "AI, what was responsible for this? Did you detect foreign vessels? A natural disaster?" Her calm command voice betrayed the tension beneath.

Garbled text scrolled across the surrounding consoles. Bits of code, partially in English, partially in some advanced notation. At last, the AI responded:

"Memory sectors corrupted… external threat or cosmic event—unconfirmed.

Records indicate… significant destructive force. Colony evacuation. No life signs detected. Forced station to minimal stasis. Waited for return."

Silence settled among the team. This was both a revelation and a dead end—partial truths, incomplete information. They could see the devastation but had no certainty of who or what caused it.

John tensed, footsteps echoing as he crossed the deck to one of the side consoles. "So it doesn't know. Perfect. We're still guessing." He leaned in, scanning the flickering text. "Anything else, AI? Survivors? Signs of life?"

"No colony signals. Surface scanning… minimal power sources. Automated or… deserted."

The news hit like a blow. If any humans had survived, they'd long since gone dark. Elena allowed a shaky breath. "But they had the station's technology, advanced drives, who knows what else. Could they have fled the planet entirely?"

The AI flickered again. A new image materialized: a partial blueprint of the city's substructure—some mention of a central data archive. The text under it read: Data Vault: 4,500m depth. Then more static. The voice returned:

"Archive location… may contain full logs. Access planet-side facility."

Riley shook his head in disbelief. "So we have to go down there."

Morrow nodded, though her gaze lingered on the crater footage. "We may not have a choice if we want answers. That was also the plan all along." She gestured to the flickering displays around them. "AI, can you help us repair more of the station? We'll need stable orbit, reliable communications, and a way to get planet-side safely."

Elena spoke up, "We can use the ship's thrusters and power to restore stable orbit. It's lost a bit of altitude without proper station keeping, but if we go easy with it there should be no problems using the ship to maintain stable orbit."

A wave of affirmative pulsed across the console lights. A new holographic panel opened, displaying detailed station schematics—supply bays, repair drones, and the hangar modules brimming with advanced craft. The AI's voice returned, more insistent:

"Station functionality… incomplete. Assistance required… maintenance protocols. Must confirm… system integrity."

Elena's eyes shone at the sight of the shuttle designs. "We saw a hangar deck on the way to engineering, with potential vehicles. Looks like it can give us instructions to bring them online. We could upgrade our drop ship, maybe dock a smaller craft to do recon down there."

John's frown deepened. "I still don't like how this AI is steering everything. It's telling us to fix the station, go planet-side—like it's got its own agenda."

Morrow turned to him, expression thoughtful. "Maybe it does. But if we want the truth—and any chance to salvage what's left of this colony's legacy—this is our best lead. Besides, isn't every one of those things also what we want?" She squared her shoulders. "We'll remain vigilant."

The AI's hologram flickered one more time, its features almost resolving into a face—a faintly human outline—before dissolving into static. Then text scrolled across the central console in large, bold letters:

"Begin Restoration. Recover the Truth. Restore life."

The message lingered on the screens, a directive that felt part command, part plea. Outside, the station's metal bones groaned as newly activated systems continued the slow process of reawakening. Each breath in the stale air reinforced the gravity of the moment. They were inheritors of a grand, broken dream, forced to rebuild this station piece by piece, guided by an AI that only half-remembered how it all fell apart and still had no idea what happened to the original colonists.

Amir, remembering an ancient motion picture from movie nights, muttered, "If that thing says 'red rum,' I'm hauling ass back to Earth if I have to swim there in an EV suit."

John, obviously not missing the reference, shot Amir a sharp look before stifling a chuckle. "That's it—the AI is named Johnny."

Slowly, Captain Morrow placed a hand on the console's edge, turning to face her crew. "You heard it. Let's get to work. We'll coordinate repairs from here, see what the hangar has to offer, and figure out how to reach that archive on the planet." Her voice lowered, the final note for them all to hear:

"If the colony fell to an external threat, that threat could still be out there. We need to be ready for whatever we find. Prioritize life support, energy, and station keeping. Then I want every sensor available online and to find out if there's any sort of system-wide monitoring or anything we can use."

The Command Deck lights dimmed momentarily as though underscoring her words. Then a surge of power stabilized them again, leaving the crew to trade determined glances. The path ahead was steep: reviving a station two centuries more advanced than their wildest tech, unraveling the fate of a colony whose triumph turned to ash, and preparing for a confrontation with a menace that might yet haunt this system.

20

A rhythmic hiss of stale air—and the taste of possibility—followed the team as they spread out across the Command Deck. Captain Morrow called more of the crew over to the station. Panels on every wall fluttered with half-formed holograms, icons flickering in and out of visibility. Some responded to gesture-based commands, while others blinked erratically, as though awaiting a sequence that had been lost to time.

"Should we wake some of the colonists or advanced crew?" John asked.

"Not yet. They are safe on the ship right now, let's get a better confidence rating in the station first," Captain Morrow replied.

She tapped one of the larger displays. It glowed in response, revealing a skeletal map of the station's modules—many were still red, labeled OFFLINE or DAMAGED. Yet others flashed amber, the AI's subtle invitation to start repairs.

"John," she said quietly, scanning the map, "scout the hangar. Take Riley with you. Looks like a med bay next to it, I'm sure he'll want to check that out when you're done in the hangar. We need eyes on those smaller craft, make sure they're stable before we risk stepping onto one of them."

John gave a firm nod, though his expression remained suspicious of the station's every quiver. "On it, Captain. Come on, Thompson."

Riley tapped at his visor, as if a nervous tic was blocked by a forgotten helmet. "Time to see if those fancy shuttle designs are as good as they look." He flicked a quick, reassuring grin at Elena and Amir before following John out of the Command Deck hatch.

With them gone, Morrow shifted her focus to Elena. "Those amber modules—do you think they mark the most urgent repairs?"

Elena studied the interface. "Yes. Looks like the AI wants us to focus on four key areas: Life Support, Engineering, Data Processing, and the Main Dock." Her gaze flicked to another panel, which displayed a swirling schematic of the station's power grid. "I can see multiple short-circuits. Repairing those lines will stabilize station gravity in some sections and improve total output."

Near her, Amir scrolled through columns of text in a complex mixture of English and advanced symbols. "Listen to this," he murmured. "It's referencing secondary and distributed memory banks —like archives scattered in different modules. Possibly backups of colony logs. We might piece together more about what happened… or at least understand how they built all this if we can get enough of the station online."

Elena placed a gloved hand on his shoulder, eyes gleaming with curiosity. "Then let's do it. We split the tasks. I'll tackle engineering fixes with help from the AI. You can coordinate with the station's data subsystems. If we restore even one major memory archive, that could shed real light on the colony's final days."

"That's our best shot," Morrow agreed. She turned to address their ship's comm link. "Clara, do you copy?"

Clara's voice crackled in through the suit's speakers. "Loud and clear, Captain. Systems stable on our end. Minor radiation from the star, but well within expected range and tolerances. We've got partial telemetry linking to the station now—makes it easier to coordinate repairs."

"Excellent," Morrow said. "Stand by to send us resource packs. We're going to need extra spares and specialized tool modules from the cargo hold." She cast a glance at Amir. "And keep analyzing those planetary scans, don't just get lost in those databanks. If we discover a safe zone to land, we'll want to know that soon."

"Understood."

Meanwhile, in the Hangar Deck

Riley held his breath—mostly out of habit—while stepping through a newly powered airlock. He, John, and two station maintenance drones glided into a cavernous hangar bay that was now illuminated by pale overhead lights. It was huge—easily swallowing the docking bay on the colony ship in volume—yet littered with half-buried containers spilling out of the storage and supply bays, twisted metal braces, and an array of unfamiliar spacecraft.

"Look at them," Riley breathed. Each ship perched on elevated platforms or set into open docking ports. From small, angular shuttles to elongated vehicles bristling with advanced weaponry. "They're… they're so sleek."

John swept his weapon-light across the deck, focusing on a fighter-like craft with menacing railgun attachments. "Sleek isn't exactly the word I'd use," he muttered. "Looks like they were gearing up for war."

Riley moved closer to a tall, bipedal machine—some kind of mech-suit with thruster pods on its shoulders. "I've never even seen designs like these," he marveled. "Like exoskeletons with built-in EVA capability." He patted one of its curved metal arms, half-expecting it to jolt to life. "Think these might come in handy if we gotta do some real heavy lifting."

John's response was terse. "Or heavy fighting. That isn't designed for maintenance routines, that's built for defending this station from outside." He stepped around a rack of half-decayed gear, eyes constantly sweeping for any sign of danger. The hangar felt too still, like a vacuum of time sealed away. "Let's see if the AI can boot up a diagnostic. Last thing we need is to board a shuttle that misfires its engines and blasts us into pieces."

Riley nodded, hooking his personal data-link into a small glowing terminal. It responded sluggishly, spitting out lines of partial code. "It's still half asleep," he observed, scanning the readouts. "But it's showing green on a couple of smaller transports. We might be able to power them up with some new fuel cells. The information is so basic. I don't seem to have full access here."

John's guard never lowered. "You do that. I'll check if any of these things have hidden booby traps or power surges. Remember, we found advanced weapon platforms. That means advanced failsafes."

Riley rolled his eyes with a faint grin but said nothing. John's paranoia had kept him alive more than once. No sense arguing when they both knew the risks of rummaging around abandoned tech that was centuries ahead of anything Sol had produced before they left home.

A soft clank echoed from the far corner of the hangar. Both men froze, turning. One of the newly awakened station drones scooted into view—an ovoid chassis on stubby treads, scanning a row of sealed cargo pods. The drone's mechanical arm popped open a latch, rummaging for something inside.

Riley relaxed and let out a laugh under his breath. "Guess even the drones are rummaging. Feels like we're in a living museum."

John approached the drone, noting its advanced sensor arrays. "Or a tomb," he countered. "No telling how long they waited for us."

But Riley only offered a small shrug, half-lost in the wonder of the alien-yet-familiar craft. "Let's hope we don't end up the next exhibit."

On the Command Deck

Amir hovered in front of a main data console, images of the planet's ravaged city looping across half the display. The other half showed threads of station diagnostics: partially decrypted logs with references to the cataclysm that ended the colony. Each snippet ended abruptly, as if cut short by a final, violent moment.

Elena, crouched beneath a flickering console panel, manipulated a set of holographic icons projected from an open module. "Yes—this one leads to the Engineering Grid. If I can just direct full power to the sub-level conduit…"

A gentle hum built in the floor beneath them; a second later, a status bar glowed green. The overhead lights steadied. It felt as if the station finally drew a calm breath after decades of ragged inhalations.

"Great work," Captain Morrow said, arms crossed in studied approval. Then she turned to the AI's small shimmering figure near the center dais. "AI, confirm—have we stabilized life support?"

"Life-support at forty percent efficiency… requires filtration repairs in sub-module D5."

The Captain nodded. "Understood. Priority two. For now, we can move freely in most compartments with suits. We'll fix that last. Our next objective?"

A swirl of text replaced the silhouette. Amir read it, summarizing quickly: "It's recommending we patch a cluster of data units in the station's mid-deck. Maybe it could restore partial memory about the colony's final hours."

Morrow's gaze flicked to Elena, who was climbing to her feet. "Take whatever help you need to keep the power stable. Amir, coordinate with the AI on that data cluster. I want as much recovered as possible before we decide on a planetary landing."

Elena nodded. "We'll be methodical. I'm guessing the bigger secrets are planet-side, but this station must have context we can use. I can also route power lines to the hangar so John and Riley don't have to rig an ad hoc solution for those shuttles."

Captain Morrow stepped back, letting the hum of the active consoles fill the Command Deck. Each beep and flicker reminded her that for all its advanced wonders, this station remained a haunted shell —its colony destroyed, its fate unknown. Whatever cosmic blow had fallen, it left behind technology Earth could barely grasp and a puzzle that threatened to snare them if they weren't careful.

She touched a palm to one of the shimmering interfaces. "AI," she said gently, "you've helped us a great deal already. But we need more clarity. If a threat truly destroyed this colony, our people—our colonists in stasis—could be at risk. Help us piece this story together."

The AI's wavering image hovered, as though it understood the gravity of her words. Then it displayed one final line of text:

"REPAIR... SEARCH... DISCOVER. DANGER LINGERS."

The station's overhead lights flickered, as though in silent agreement, and the hum underfoot grew, a whisper of the unstoppable forces waiting beyond. Morrow's voice immediately echoed through John's helmet.

"John, wake your team. Now."

John froze mid-scan of the hangar's power conduits, confusion slicing through him. Captain Morrow had made it clear she didn't want colonists or additional crew awakened until the station was stable. He wondered what had changed.

He motioned Riley over, toggling his comm. "Captain, confirm? You want me to wake the security detail?"

Morrow's voice held a steady calm that belied underlying urgency. "Yes. Now. We don't know who or what's moving into this system. You've got a security team ready in stasis—get them up. I need more boots on deck."

Riley's eyebrows shot up. "You're sure we can spare the supplies to start waking folks early, Captain? Our food—"

"Clara and Elena will figure out resource balancing," Morrow interjected. "We'll rely more on those, ah... nutrient bars if we have to."

A grimace crossed Riley's face. Their unappetizing "energy bars" were meant as emergency rations—capable of sustaining a person's dietary needs for months, though no one relished the idea. They looked like dull gray bricks, tasted like damp cardboard, and were terrible for morale. But they'd keep you alive.

John, ignoring the banter about supplies, failed to miss the Captain's statement. Something was headed into the system, and they didn't know if it was organic, friend or foe. John snapped a final look at the half-repaired shuttle behind him. "Alright. We'll manage. I'm heading back to the colony ship to handle stasis protocols. Might need a hand with the thaw."

"Riley, go with him," Morrow ordered over the channel. "Elena can keep pushing repairs with Amir. I'll coordinate from the Command Deck and try to glean more about this inbound object."

Riley nodded, stowing the tools he'd been using to patch the hangar's power feeds. "Understood, Captain. We'll get our security folks up and running. No telling what shape they'll be in—waking from stasis can be rough."

John's jaw was set, eyes flicking over the advanced warships in the hangar. "Let's hope they bounce back quick. We're light on manpower."

John and Riley threaded through the station's corridors, which flickered with renewed life thanks to Elena's partial repairs. The docking collar connecting the station and their ship hummed softly, a sign that environmental seals remained stable. A few station drones wheeled by, scanning for further damage—polite, futuristic helpers that once belonged to a colony far more advanced than the reality they left behind at Sol.

21

Stepping back onto their own vessel felt oddly comforting to John. Here, the corridors were narrower, the overhead lights more familiar. The faint hum of antimatter reactors and air recyclers welcomed him like a second skin. The promise of extra security was overshadowed by the question of what was headed in their direction and the knowledge that each awakened crewmember meant more resources consumed. John pushed these thoughts from his mind and focused on the task at hand, forcing a self-discipline the knot in his gut didn't seem to share.

Riley caught the fleeting expression on John's face and noticed him steel himself. "We'll need to ration. The Captain's set aside three months of decent food for the awake crew, but if we double our numbers—"

"—we'll burn through it in half the time," John finished, letting out a weary sigh. "I guess that's where the bars come in." He wrinkled his nose. "Nothing kills morale like those slabs of dried synthetic paste, but we don't have a choice."

They passed through the ship's narrow mid-section toward the stasis bay, a chilled environment lined with sleek pods. Fog curled around the bases of the units, each looking like a human-size egg with a frosty windshield at face level. Some pods were set to longer-term cycles; others were ready for quicker revival. John's security detail fell into the latter group—trained for the possibility they'd be needed first if trouble arose.

Riley approached the nearest console and keyed in the stasis codes. A holographic panel unfurled, reading the occupant's vitals. "Looks like the team is in good shape for reanimation. No medical flags."

"Good," John said. He could see four pods set aside for his people:

Vogel, Han, Serena, and 'Doc' Walters. Each had a broad skillset ranging from weapons and tactics to hacking and battlefield triage. He'd handpicked them before launch, confident they could handle any threat a deep-space colony might face. *Though we never expected to face threats centuries more advanced than us,* he thought wryly.

Riley tapped the final confirmation. The console's lights glowed amber, then green. The four pods began to rotate slowly into a horizontal position. The sounds of pumps and fans added to the white noise unique to this part of the ship. "Reanimation in progress," he announced. "We'll need half an hour for stable revival. Once they're out, we'll do standard checks."

John nodded, arms folded. "Let's hope they adapt fast. The station is crawling with technology we barely grasp, and now there's… something inbound."

With a hiss, the first stasis pod began its thaw cycle, vapors rolling off the smooth, glassy cover. John stepped closer, face softening fractionally. He hadn't seen his squad since the day they'd sealed themselves in, back in Earth orbit. *Feels like yesterday for me, but for them, it was,* he reminded himself.

Riley scanned his medical kit. "We'll keep them on an adjusted diet —mostly nutrient bars—to spare the real food supply. They won't like it, but we can't risk too many mouths on the good stuff. It will also help with the awakening sickness, being closer to what they've been fed through those tubes for the last year."

A fleeting grin tugged at John's lips. "Let them complain. We need more bodies awake right now… or we risk losing everything if trouble arrives." He laid a hand on the closest stasis pod, feeling the subtle vibrations of the warming fluid. *You're needed now, guys. And I'm sorry it has to be this soon.*

While Riley tended to the reanimation protocols, John paced to a small comm station around the corner. Pulling up a hologram display, John flipped through various sensor feeds. Noticing activity on another comm channel, John touched the icon to listen. Captain Morrow's voice crackled through, mid-sentence:

"—no further updates from the station's sensors. The object is still inbound, but the AI's trying to recalibrate the old orbital arrays. We might get better resolution soon."

John replied. "My people will be waking in a few minutes. How's Elena doing on the sensor grid?"

"She and Amir are patching data banks to improve resolution. So far, it's just vague readings—mass estimates, faint energy spikes. Could be a drifting hulk or an automated probe." Morrow paused, then added, "But let's be real, John. All signs say it's under power, which means it's not debris. We made quite the entry, if there was someone or something out here watching… they couldn't have missed us."

John's mouth went dry. "Meaning it's definitely coming here on purpose."

"Yes." Morrow's voice was measured. "Be ready for anything. Even if it's just salvageable tech, we can't be caught off guard."

John lowered his gaze, quickly glancing back to the stasis bay. "We will be, Captain," he promised. "I'll update you once the team's coherent. Let me know if you need anything else while we wait."

"Understood. Stand by."

John looked on as the first of his security detail stepped out of the stasis pod, blinking furiously. Sergeant Serena, a lean, fit woman with cropped black hair, raised a trembling hand to her forehead as if to confirm she was really awake. Around her, the low hiss of the stasis bay's climate-control vents underscored the stillness.

John noted that she certainly looked like she had put on some muscle. The stasis pods completed a course of gene therapy that strengthened bones, increased muscle density, and fortified the cardiovascular system. Essential for surviving the harsh realities of the new planet and its greater gravity. At around twice Earth's gravity, the colonists would not easily survive without the gene therapy. They would likely still require additional mechanical assistance and the use of mech-suits would be commonplace. There was an ample supply of basic versions in the cargo pods.

"Feels like I'm swimming in syrup," Serena muttered, voice raspy. She flexed her fingers in front of her face, testing her motor control. Her eyes darted around, taking in the subdued lights and the silver pods lining the bulkhead. "Didn't think I'd be up so soon."

Across the aisle, Han groaned, stepping carefully out of her pod. She reached for the overhead grab bar but missed by an inch, momentarily unsteady on her feet. "Ugh. That's… new. Didn't realize stasis could scramble my coordination this much." She glanced at John with a slight grimace. "No offense, boss, but I was hoping for a longer nap."

Next to her, Vogel quietly tested her own balance. She was broad-shouldered and calm-eyed, the kind of soldier who let her actions speak for her. "We awake on schedule, or did we just get the short straw?" she asked dryly, her words tinted with a foggy haze.

"You definitely got the short straw," John said, offering a faint, wry smile. "There's a situation. We found a station in orbit—long story, advanced tech, possibly… probably from an old human colony. And now there's something inbound to the system. Could be nothing, could be trouble." He paused, letting them absorb the gist.

Serena exhaled loudly, blinking at Doc, the fourth of the newly awakened team, who was sitting on the edge of his pod rubbing his temples. "Great," he rasped. "Just woke up and already we're dealing with a… what exactly? Alien incursion? Some kinda warship?"

"We're not sure yet," John admitted, crossing his arms. "We've got partial sensor data and an AI system that says 'Danger lingers.' That's enough for Captain Morrow. She wants security up and running."

Han took a moment to stretch her arms, rolling out the stiffness in her shoulders. "And here I thought the plan was to keep us on ice until the new colony was established," she said, half to herself. "Well… guess we adapt."

Vogel offered a grim chuckle. "We always do." She turned, scanning the cramped stasis bay. "So, what's the job? We locking down the station? Defending the ship? Going planet-side?"

"All of the above, eventually," John replied. "Right now, we're in orbit around Kepler-452b, hooking the station's systems back to life. We have limited resources—only so much real food—and we don't want to blow through it. So be prepared to see a lot of those flavorless nutrient bars."

Doc cracked a half-smile, finally getting control of his motor skills enough to stand. "Oof. So we get the worst meal prep of all time, plus potential combat. Perfect. Put me first on the list to go back to sleep."

"We might just do that," John said.

Serena flexed her knees carefully, regaining her balance. Her adapted body felt awkward and stiff. She snorted, wiping sweat from her forehead. "Nah, even those bars beat rotting in a stasis tube while the rest of you get shot up, I guess. I'd rather be awake for all the fun."

John tossed her a small packet of rehydration salts. "Think you'll change your mind after your third ration bar. But yeah, we need more boots on deck—someone who can handle security protocols, respond fast if that incoming contact's hostile."

Their chatter slowed as the group instinctively shifted into training mode. Walters and Han began pulling standard-issue body armor from the storage lockers. Serena powered up a handheld scanner, reading its instructions through half-lidded eyes, stifling yawns between lines. Vogel carefully attached a sidearm's charging pack, her fingers still shaky, but her expression resolute.

"Feels like I'm on autopilot," Han murmured, pressing the uniform's seals. "Brain's hazy, but the muscle memory's there."

John nodded. "Exactly. Let your training handle the basics until the fog clears. We'll do a more thorough briefing once we're sure you're stable."

They exchanged understanding looks—this was part of the job. Stasis might dull their wits temporarily, but discipline, routine, and adrenaline had a way of snapping them back. They'd trained for abrupt awakenings, practiced reorientation drills, memorized procedures in case they ever had to defend the ship with half-clear minds. Now, all that preparation was paying off.

As soon as they were suited up, Serena took a few tentative steps, checking her stride. Doc tapped his visor's comm checks, verifying frequencies and syncing to the team's vital signs. Vogel tested her rifle's power cell, lips pursed in silent concentration. Han paused, giving John a nod of acknowledgment. "Alright, boss. We're up. What's our first move?"

"Riley's in the next compartment," John said. "He'll do quick medical checks to make sure you're all stable enough for duty after the gene therapy. Then we head to the station to see the Captain." He looked over their gear. "We'll likely do a rotation, conducting inventory and maintenance on the station's armory while engineers fix up the critical systems. The inbound contact might be hours, could be days."

Vogel tested a quick pivot, her stance smoothing out. "Good to go." Her voice had regained its crispness—military efficiency creeping back in.

Han, Doc, and Serena all nodded in agreement, each tucking away personal qualms behind professional resolve. The underlying tension was there—the creeping dread of an unknown threat, the knowledge that their resources were limited, and that they might soon be chewing on those dreaded nutrient bars for weeks on end. But for now, the moment demanded action, not worry.

"Then let's move," John said, turning on his heel. "We'll get you processed and armed. Captain Morrow wants a show of strength if this inbound visitor decides to pay us a visit."

Their boots clanked over the deck plating, the ephemeral haze of stasis shedding with every purposeful step. Despite the mental fog still wisping at the edges of their thoughts, the newly awakened security team followed John's lead without complaint—professionals ready to do whatever was necessary to protect their crew in an uncertain new world.

They filed out of the stasis bay in a purposeful march, boots ringing on steel deck plating. Walters rolled his neck to shake off the last of the stasis fog, while Han slowed momentarily to lean against a corridor railing, blinking hard to clear her vision. One by one, they entered a small med station where Riley Thompson waited, arms folded, medical scanner in hand.

"Alright," Riley said, already in professional mode. He gestured to Serena first, who stood with squared shoulders but slightly unfocused eyes. "Let me see how badly the stasis is messing with your vitals."

She stepped forward, letting him press a device to her wrist. A flicker of readouts appeared on a compact holographic screen.

"Heart rate's high," Riley noted, "but that's normal for quick-thaw." He checked pupil response and general motor function. "Try touching your nose with your left hand."

Serena's hand wavered a second, then found her face. "Not as easy as it should be," she grumbled, "but I'll manage."

Riley's lips quirked in sympathy. "Stasis fog wears off in a few hours. Adrenaline helps." He glanced at the others. "If any of you experience dizziness, chest pains, or confusion that doesn't fade, let me know immediately."

Serena moved aside, letting Han step up. "Woke me too early," Han muttered in half-jest as Riley ran a similar check. "Guess that's life on the frontier."

John stayed near the doorway, scanning a holoscreen for updates on the station's status. He spoke quietly to Walters, who leaned on the wall to rest heavy legs. "As soon as you're cleared, we head to the station. The Captain's coordinating with Elena on repairs. We'll be jumping in on that effort initially. Once the station is stable, we've got to inventory its armory and op-check some mechsuits and fast fighters. There's some slick toys in there."

Walters rubbed at the back of his neck. "Got it, boss. Might need a few minutes before I trust my aim." He let out a weary chuckle, gazing at the standard-issue sidearm strapped to his hip.

Vogel, already cleared by Riley, was tightening the seals on her gloves. "Aim might be off, but discipline isn't," she said firmly, giving

Doc a faint nudge with her elbow. "We'll snap back quickly. That's the whole point of the drills."

Han nodded as she finished her check, stepping away from Riley's scanner. "I feel like I've got sand in my brain," she admitted, "but I know the routine." She drew a calming breath. "So, Captain Morrow... She said something's inbound?"

John dipped his head in confirmation. "We've got minimal sensor data. Could be an abandoned craft, some lost orbital debris, or... something else entirely." He paused, letting the silence weigh in. "We're preparing for the worst."

Serena, rolling out her shoulders, shot him a confident look. "We wouldn't be your security detail if we scared easy. I say bring it on."

Riley finished up with Doc, then gave the group a final once-over. "Alright, medically, you're all stable enough for duty. Try to stay hydrated, though. The reanimation process can dehydrate you faster than you think, and we're short on water until we can confirm the station's supply lines."

They exchanged nods, each absorbing a fresh wave of reality: short resources, potential conflict, and a battered, centuries-ahead-of-their-time station waiting to be salvaged. The tension weighed heavily, but in the space of a few minutes, each of them had reconnected with the muscle memory of soldiering, the calm focus that came with training.

<h1 style="text-align:center">22</h1>

"Alright, team," John said, pulling them together at the hallway's junction. "Gear check. We've got sidearms, standard rifles, vibroswords and the station has an arsenal of advanced weaponry we can't fully figure out yet. For now, we stick to what we know. Keep your suits sealed—oxygen levels on the station are iffy."

Vogel gave him a crisp salute, a glimmer of wry humor in her eyes. "Yes, sir. Don't supposin' we reckin' tha fancy bang-birds in the hangar?" As she slid back into the outer belt slang she grew up with, reminding John briefly of the life they left back in Sol.

John exhaled. "Hopen' no. But flyrock gone angry we's puttin' down ya-good… sure' sure kinetic," He shot a side glance at Vogel just in time to see her grimace slightly behind her visor and roll her eyes. His gaze flicked down the corridor, imagining the battered hulls of stealthy looking fighters and railgun-laden ships they'd uncovered. "We'll do what we must."

"All set," Serena affirmed, resting a gloved hand on the butt of her rifle. "Lead on, boss."

They took off down the dimly lit corridor, each step a testament to discipline overriding stasis fatigue. Heads cleared second by second, and by the time they reached the docking collar that connected the colony ship to the station, they moved with something close to a practiced squad formation.

As they stepped aboard the station, the newly awakened security detail fell silent—eyes hardening at the sight of exposed plating, flickering lights, and distant rumblings of a place wrestling itself back to life. The cold hiss of the station's partial atmosphere greeted them like a ragged breath. Over the comm channel, Captain Morrow's voice crackled:

"Good, you're here. We've got movement on sensors—object is closing in faster than we expected. Join me on the Command Deck. We need immediate reaction plans if it proves hostile."

They exchanged glances. Despite lingering mental haze, they recognized the gravity of the situation. No further questions, no complaints—just soldierly acceptance of the role they were called to fill. As one, they marched deeper into the station's corridors, ready for whatever "danger lingers" truly meant. The bit of adrenaline helped clear the mental fog, just as Riley had said it would.

Their footsteps echoed through Kepler-452's lonely outpost, stirring new life into old metal, forging a path to meet the unknown head-on.

The station's corridors loomed before them, lit by intermittent overhead strips that hummed with recovering power. It still felt eerie—like wandering a vast, empty factory from a forgotten future. The newly awakened security team formed up behind John in a practiced wedge: Vogel and 'Doc' Walters on his right, Serena and Han flanking left and rear.

Every so often, the station's AI would turn on a nearby wall panel or floor grid, projecting a small pulse of light that pointed toward the Command Deck. It reminded them of a nervous guide, beckoning them forward. John led the way with calm purpose, though his gut still churned with the uncertainty of what exactly they might be facing.

"Feels... bigger than I expected," Serena muttered, adjusting her rifle's sling.

"It does," Han agreed. "Could be the stasis fog, or maybe the station's interior is... shifting?"

Vogel frowned. "Shifting how? Your eyes playing tricks on you?"

John cut in quietly, "The AI's running partial repairs and reconfiguring corridors. We've seen entire bulkheads realign for easier access. This place is advanced, but half-broken. Don't let your guard down."

They rounded a corner into a wider corridor that ended in a tall, arching hatch labeled Command Deck in blocky, English script. The door's edges pulsed with a faint neon glow, as though responding to their approach.

A hiss, and the hatch slid open. Warm overhead lights greeted them —a stark contrast to the gloom outside. Captain Morrow stood at a central console, leaning over a swirling holographic display. Elena and Amir were flanking her. Riley paced nearby, arms folded, giving side-glances to the newly arrived team. The swirl of tension around them was palpable.

Morrow looked up, eyes steady. "Good timing. You're all cleared for duty?"

"Yes, ma'am," John confirmed. "Still shaking off the last of the stasis, but they're functional."

Vogel nodded sharply. "Ready for orders."

Morrow gestured them closer to the central console. A rotating image of Kepler-452's star system filled the display. A bright ring denoted the planet's orbit, while a smaller, blinking marker glided inward from beyond. Data lines scrolled along the edges: velocity estimates, mass calculations, power readings—contradictory and incomplete.

"This object," Morrow began, voice cool and concise, "is accelerating in our direction. The AI reactivated some of the station's sensors, but we're still mostly in the dark. No definitive shape or composition. Could be an old probe... or something else entirely. It'll reach near-orbit in a matter of hours. We need contingencies. The ship is low on fuel. We've got nowhere else to go and not enough fuel to get there. We didn't get round-trip tickets, so this is what we have. The station has some defenses. While most are offline, it's more than we have on the colony ship... We don't have time to deploy planet-side and that's not a great defensive position anyway. So, we defend this like home. "

Elena tapped a separate panel, flicking up partial weapon readouts. "Station defenses are in tatters. We have a couple of railgun platforms online, but they're not exactly the best compared to the rest of this advanced tech. We can't be sure they'll work right either, no room or time or ability to test them. Laser batteries don't have enough power to come online yet, but are charging up now. We're figuring out which capacitors are shot... I'd estimate we'll get about twenty percent of them functional. Other advanced energy weapons are out. No way to get them online in time. About the only thing we can count on currently is a missile battery. Details are limited, access to the defense inventory is still somewhat restricted, but it appears we have anti-matter missiles as an ultimate backup."

Amir's gaze lingered on a separate hologram, referencing old colony archives. "No mention in the logs about a returning vessel or an automated system that orbits the star and comes home. If it's from the original colonists, we have no record of it I can find."

Riley sidled up to the newly awakened security detail, eyeing their half-foggy expressions. "You folks good for a possible scramble? Or do you need more time to adjust?"

Han straightened. "We'll manage. Got adrenaline to spare."

Serena gave him a tense grin. "Just show us where to stand and point at the target."

John cleared his throat, meeting Morrow's gaze. "Captain, what's our best-case scenario?"

She breathed out, lips pressed. "That it's a lifeless hulk or drone on some automated return with the station coming online, awake from some sort of return home beacon. That, we figure out how to salvage or avoid it entirely."

"And worst case?" Doc asked, keeping his voice neutral.

"Worst case," Morrow said flatly, "it's hostile. Or carries something that can hurt us. And we have minimal means to repel an advanced attack. If the colony here fell to something in this system…" She let the sentence hang.

Elena rubbed a stress cramp at the back of her neck. "We do have those stealth craft and weaponized ships in the hangar. With the AI's help, maybe we can ready at least one for emergency intercept."

John nodded. "I've got a crack security detail—four capable fighters. We can handle small-team infiltration if that's what it comes to as well." He glanced at his people, each of them standing straighter under his words. "But we are limited by numbers. We'll make up for that."

Captain Morrow pivoted, raising a finger for each point as she spoke in a low, determined tone. "Alright then. Here's the plan:

1. Elena, Amir, and the AI will keep feeding us sensor updates. The moment we get a real reading—shape, composition, trajectory changes—we decide our response.

2. John, you and your team remain on standby in the hangar. If we need a boarding party or to operate those advanced ships, you're it. Do what you can to get some of that gear online.

3. Riley, you coordinate medical triage. See what you can do with the medical facilities here first. If you need to, we'll use the ship's medical if the inbound object turns into a firefight. And keep an eye on the newly awakened—if the stasis fog becomes an issue, I need them operational, not groggy.

4. I'll oversee final station repairs and see if we can power up an old defense platform or at least hail the object. If it's listening, we might avoid conflict."

A subdued chorus of "Yes, ma'am" followed. John's squad shot him brief looks, confirming they were in, no matter how heavy the strain. The hum of the station's reawakened systems provided an unsteady backdrop—like an enormous mechanical heartbeat, skipping and restarting on half-fried nerves.

Morrow's final glance swept across them. "Stay alert. We'll know more in a few hours, but that's no time at all in a place this big. If something goes wrong, remember: we'll designate the colony ship as the first fallback position. We can sever the docking collar if needed."

John grimaced at the thought of leaving the station behind, but nodded. "Understood."

"Alright," Morrow said softly, "let's get to it."

They broke apart into groups—John motioning for his team to follow him, Elena rushing to a console to re-check sensor calibrations with the AI's cryptic guidance, Amir poring over logs to glean any hint of returning vessels or hidden threats, and Riley hovering between them, ready to treat the half-awake soldiers if stasis side-effects flared.

In the midst of it all, the station's overhead lighting shimmered again, a subtle reminder that it, too, was still waking from a centuries-long slumber. A hush of anticipation clung to every metal strut and walkway as they braced for the unknown that crept steadily closer, unstoppable in its course toward Kepler-452.

23

The next few hours weighed on everyone like the thick silence before a storm. On the Command Deck, Captain Morrow maintained a tireless watch over the holographic display where the blinking object crept ever closer to Kepler-452's orbit. Despite Elena's constant calibration of the station's battered sensors, the data remained frustratingly vague or nonexistent. The AI offered occasional flashes of insight—small improvements to scanning protocols or energy reallocation to improve resolution—but each time, the image of the inbound contact remained stubbornly elusive.

Down in the depths of the station's hangar module, John and his freshly awakened security team prepared for the worst, half-dreading a scenario in which they'd need to scramble advanced craft they scarcely understood. The newly awakened security team—Vogel, Serena, Han, and 'Doc' Walters—used the lull to orient themselves further, practicing short drills to steady their post-stasis reflexes.

"Pivot!" John barked, as they lined up in a rough circle around a crate of spare parts. At his command, each member spun to a different quadrant, aiming a standard rifle at imaginary targets. Even with the mental fog lingering, they moved with a drilled precision that spoke of countless hours of training. Due to the physical changes in their bodies provided for by gene therapy in stasis, the team went over basic formations and drills to ensure they were at peak performance. The increased muscle and bone density made them feel stiff and awkward at first, but the familiar motions John pushed them through repeatedly brought back familiarity and comfort to the team.

Han lowered her weapon after a three-sixty sweep, breathing a bit heavily. "At least we're not stumbling over our own feet," she muttered.

Serena nodded, rubbing her brow as if trying to push lingering fatigue away. "A few more reps and I won't even notice the headache."

Doc slung his rifle over his shoulder. "We'd better pray if we do scramble these alien warbirds, the controls aren't as tricky as they look." He glanced toward a row of sleek, needle-nosed crafts illuminated by faint overhead spotlights. The station's AI had woken enough systems in the hangar to keep them powered, but it still felt like exploring an ancient temple full of half-understood relics.

John gave him a cautious nod. "Everyone's awake enough now. Let's see what this station has to offer."

John and his team stowed rifles in a rack along the wall and began investigating the craft in the hanger bay. Many of the craft seemed to be lacking some basic controls, which made them impossible to operate. Han suspected there may have been some sort of interface with the pilot's suit or helmet to make up for the lack of displays and controls. Until they found some suits or helmets that were meant to interface with these ships, they would be of no use to anyone.

Of all the craft available, they found only five that seemed possible to operate. Unfortunately, they also appeared to be in the oldest and most battered condition. Scorch marks and carbon deposits streaked the outer hulls. Numbers and markings were faded or hidden under large scrapes, dents, or black stripes resembling burn marks.

They investigated the mech-suits next. Vogel pored over them with a well-trained eye, quickly identifying a number of issues she felt confident could be repaired in time. She was able to get a few of the suits operational, though it appeared once again that many functions had no controls or options for use. The suits would respond to body movements, and weapons triggering through some manual controls on the hand grips made them functional enough for basic use.

Just as Vogel was finishing a bit of testing on the last mech-suit, Riley arrived with a portable med-scanner in one hand and a small container in the other. He surveyed the group with a professional eye. "Vitals?" he asked, voice kept low to maintain the calm.

"Normal enough," Vogel replied, flexing her left arm. "Stasis ache's about gone."

Riley offered Doc the container with a wry smirk. "Got some supplement shots that'll boost your post-stasis metabolism. Sorry, no real meals right now—just these bland nutrient bars and hydration packs." He let out a soft laugh. "If you're lucky, I can rustle up some freeze-dried tea leaves later."

Doc groaned in mock despair but took one of the bars nonetheless. The dull gray slab looked as unappetizing as legend foretold. "Cheers," he said dryly, ripping the wrapper and taking a bite. His grimace spoke volumes.

Riley clapped him on the shoulder. "Better than keeling over, yeah?"

Meanwhile, overhead in the Command Deck, Elena and Amir sifted through partial data logs. The AI's small flickering hologram stood near the center console, lines of code running like a heartbeat monitor. Every few minutes, Elena would mutter, "Try re-routing power here," or "Let's run a test on the gamma-band scans," encouraged by the AI's suggestions.

Amir paused at a console, biting his lip. "The logs still reference a 'planetary defense array' that was once positioned near the station. If we could get that online—even partially—it might give us a clearer picture of what's inbound."

Elena flicked through half a dozen error screens. "It's fused," she said softly. "The event on the planet or whatever orbital bombardments happened must've wrecked that array. The AI says it's beyond repair… for now."

Amir's shoulders slumped. "We're basically blind beyond what the station can see."

Elena only nodded, re-checking the energy readouts. "The AI's trying to spin up a backup sensor ring that circles part of the station. If it can calibrate that, we might get better clarity—just not soon enough."

At the main console, Captain Morrow tapped her gloved fingers on the holographic display. Her gaze fixed on the blinking object as though sheer willpower might force it to reveal itself. The seconds felt slow, each beep of the system clock echoing in the deck's hush.

Over comms, she heard John's voice from the hangar: "Security standing by, Captain. If you need us to move on those advanced fighters, say the word. Otherwise, we'll hold here. We've got a couple ships that may fly and a couple mech-suits that may operate. Without more time, I'm afraid most of this is just no use to us."

"Copy," she answered. "Just stay at the ready for now." A quiet exhale escaped her lips before she reopened a private channel to the colony ship. "Clara, how are resources looking if we need to expand the wake-up schedule?"

Clara's gentle tone replied. "We're managing, but it's tight. The second wave of colonists are weeks from recommended wake-up, and we'd dip heavily into the fresh stores without the bio-labs deployed to the surface to produce food. Even expanding the hydroponics bay over here and focus on algae production, we could quickly outpace demand and the meals won't be much better than the ration bars. The ration bars themselves will only stretch so far without hurting morale, but will sustain us for a little while. The majority of the colonists initial rations are inaccessible until we deploy the pods. Basically, the harder we push and more we deviate from the deployment plan, the worse it will get… but we can manage for a while with maybe six to ten more if we have to. As long as we start deploying colonial settlement pods ASAP that is."

"I understand," Morrow said, glancing sideways at the sensor feed. "But if an actual threat arrives, we might need more specialized support—engineers, pilots, more security. Keep analyzing. We might not have a choice. Evaluate options including putting some back in stasis once they are no longer essential to the immediate threats."

Time pressed onward, each moment an exercise in tension. The inbound contact continued its approach, occasionally changing vector with near-purposeful precision—enough to rattle the nerves of everyone aboard the station. They noted a few course corrections and a strategic approach that ruled out debris or an organic object. As time stretched on, attempts were made to rotate crew through rest cycles. None of them were able to relax enough for sleep with the exception of John's security team. The rest of the crew resorted to using stimulants to remain alert and focused.

At last, a small beep on Morrow's console flared orange. Elena and the little mute AI hologram seemed to swapped glances. A swarm of new sensor data filled the display, partial 3D outlines congealing into something reminiscent of a heavily shielded craft. Its silhouette was jagged, bulky, but the final readout scrolled:

MASS: Unknown - best estimate approximately 1600 metric tons
ENERGY SIG: Low-level, variable
TRAJECTORY: Intercept course w/ Kepler-452b Station orbit
Range 250,000km
ETA: 2 hours (approx.)

A hush fell over the Command Deck. Morrow shifted her stance, eyes cold. "John, do you see that? The latest estimates?"

John's voice, taut with readiness, came back through the overhead speaker. "Yes, Captain. We see it. Looks like we may have to scramble the small craft after all."

Morrow nodded, though no one was able to see it. "Stand by," she said softly. She glanced at the newly awakened security detail's life-signs on a side panel—Han, Serena, Vogel, Doc. All stable, if a little low on rest. "How many craft are ready?"

"Only three, Captain." John replied instantly "They've got limited functionality though. We don't seem to have more than basic controls to any of them."

"That's enough for a show of force. We'll have to rely on what station defenses are available to us for actual defense... hopefully it won't come to that."

She gave a tight smile to Elena and Amir. "Alright. Looks like we're about to find out if history here is truly repeating—or if something else is coming to finish what it started."

Elena turned back to the swirling data with renewed urgency. Amir double-checked an old log reference, trying to see if the shape matched anything from the colony's advanced designs. Meanwhile, the AI pulsed a single ominous line across the main display:

"WARNING: OBJECT UNCLASSIFIED."

In that moment, the station felt more alive than ever—lights steady, systems thrumming, an ancient star-fortress poised on the edge of revelation or annihilation. And at its heart stood a handful of determined souls, forging their own place in this silent war between an old, crumbled legacy and the uncertain future rushing toward them in the dark.

"John, launch small craft for interception."

"Acknowledged, preparing for launch."

John turned and ran for the first craft while he called for Serena and Han to pilot the other two. Climbing in with a quickness only due to discipline, the unfamiliar craft made John feel clumsy. The basic controls were similar enough to the intercept craft he and his crew had piloted back in the outer belt in Sol he was confident in their ability to fly the craft, but they would be clumsy. The lack of training and experience could cause confusion and sluggish responses when quick action was needed. The situation was not ideal.

New data scrolled across the holodisplay on the bridge. Elena called out the changes as fast as she could make sense of the sensor data, "Object is performing some sort of maneuver Captain, it appears to be... Captain, the object is decelerating and appears to be on a course that will pass star side at about 5,000 km."

"John, be advised the object has begun to decelerate and appears to be attempting to match station velocity starside."

"That will be hell to target if we have to look into that star. We aren't familiar with these craft Captain, pre-flight is taking too long. We don't have the acceleration to get there first."

"Understood, do what you can."

Elena gasped suddenly and the symbol on the holodisplays began blinking with an overlayed question mark. "Captain, it's gone."

"What do you mean it's gone?"

"The object, it's just… its gone, we can't see it. There is nothing in the sensor data to even hint that it exists other than a faint ion trail along the path it had been following. It is no longer producing any perceptible energy output"

The tension was palpable. Captain Morrow realized she was holding her breath and it felt as if the station and the universe was as well. "John, stand by. I'd love to have visual on whatever that thing is, but I can't risk you all right now. Remain ready for anything, but let's not make any provocative movements yet."

"Captain, you're going to let that thing get the drop on us?"

"It already has it, John. I'm going with my gut on this one. So far, it's not acting aggressive. If it simply wanted to do us harm, it would have come straight in with an attack, but it appears to be imitating our approach to the station."

"Aknowledged. Standing by Captain." John replied in clipped tone. He then flicked over to a private channel with his team in frustration.

"Vogel, Doc, get suited up in those EVA Mech-suits. Be ready for anything."

Only the thrum of life support and the equipment could be heard on the bridge as the minutes seemed to stretch for hours. Captain Morrow was on the edge of her seat and tense, concentrating hard at the information on her display and her mind frantically analyzing her options. When Elena spoke up, Morrow jumped, startled by the sudden interruption in her focus.

"I've got an ion burst, Captain. Object appears to be making a velocity adjustment. … one extended burn, and several pulses. Captain, the object appears to have possibly stopped in position directly between us and the star. Imaging is difficult, but there appears to be a small cool spot in our direct line of sight with the sun. It's just sitting there, perfectly camouflaged, if it wasn't for the sun behind it, we would never see it."

"You think that's intentional then?"

"Yes Captain. Anything capable of piloting something so stealthy as that object surely must know its limitations and would not show itself so obviously if it wasn't intentional."

"What's the range?"

"That's hard to say Captain. We really don't know anything about it enough to calculate."

"Guess."

"About 1,000 km."

"Open all channels. If that thing tries to communicate on any frequency, I want to hear it."

"Monitoring all Channels, Captain."

John and his team continue to scramble through preflight to get the small craft online and flightworthy. With the large outer bay door open, the three craft were positioned in what amounted to a giant airlock, ready to launch. Vogel and Doc were standing off to the side in large mech-suits. Magnetically held to the deck, they were ready to climb out onto the outer hull of the station.

John was watching the same data feed Elena and Captain Morrow had on the main command deck display. He saw immediately when the object's identification icon turned green positively identifying it as friendly.

24

The deck lights glowed an insistent amber as alarms for scramble readiness sounded throughout the station. John Ferris was strapped inside the cockpit of the small craft, fingers ready to issue the final launch commands when a chorus of overlapping signals flooded the comm.

"Inbound contact establishing link on wide spectrum," Elena called over the open channel. "Captain, we've got an incoming hail. Looks like it's... streaming identification codes using some advanced Earth-based encryption? The AI appears to recognize it."

"Holy shit," Captain Morrow subvocalized to herself. She tapped a holo-panel in front of her on the Command Deck, eyes darting across rows of streaming data. "Patch it through. If it's a trap, we'll know soon enough."

A sharp crackle slid across every frequency the station was monitoring. Then a faint but surprisingly calm human-like voice spoke:

"Attempting to contact whomever has taken occupancy of the colonial space station. I am BETR, chief colonial engineer. I request permission to dock with the station. Please respond."

John froze mid-latch of his harness. "Captain," he said, pressing a private comm link. "Do we keep scrambling or stand down?"

Captain Morrow's answer came a moment later. "Stand by, John. Let's see what they have to say. Keep those birds warm though."

"Acknowledged," John responded, casting a sideways glance at Serena and Han, who were equally caught in the tension of half-readiness. He mouthed the word standby while making a hand gesture to them, and they eased off the controls but kept their craft on, ready to launch at Morrow's command.

On the Command Deck, Captain Morrow fingered the icon for an open channel and replied, "Unidentified craft, this is Captain Morrow, Captain and leader of the Sol Colony Aurora. Please clarify, you claim to be a colonist survivor? An inhabitant of this planet?"

"Greetings Captain Morrow. I am, as far as I know, the last remaining survivor of this colony. Communicating this way is difficult for me, may I come aboard so we may talk in person?

I am BETR: Biological Evolutionary Technological Reconstruction. I have been floating alone for a long time, since the colony was destroyed. I wish to come aboard and exchange information. I apologize if I have alarmed you, I mean no harm. In fact, I possess no means to cause you any harm."

Amir's brow shot up. "A... a what now?"

Captain Morrow exhaled, trading a baffled look with Riley Thompson. "Let's find out." She depressed the comm switch. "Unknown contact, you say you're from the original colony. You have a name?"

A moment's static, then the voice returned, somewhat halting: "I was once human. Now, I am... BETR. Biological Evolutionary Technological Reconstruction. I've been in low-power stasis for close to three centuries. May I approach and dock?"

Morrow gave Elena a quick nod to keep parsing data. "Permission granted. Please be advised we will be taking precautions. Do not make any aggressive actions and come aboard unarmed. We will maintain weapons lock on you at all times and you will be greeted by a security detail. If you truly mean us no harm, you won't mind our caution until we have more answers."

"I completely understand Captain. I mean you or your crew no harm... as long as there are no twitchy fingers, there won't be any issues. You won't have any trouble from me."

"Make your way to the open craft bay. My security team is there ready to escort you in."

Addressing John and his security team directly on a private channel, Captain Morrow relayed her instructions. The three craft launched from the bay to intercept and escort the strange vessel aboard.

Bright lights pulsed green along the hangar's arched ceiling. Serena's cockpit shuddered around her as the craft came to life, infighting thrusters for the first time in centuries. Graphics and icons flared across a holographic HUD—far more intricate than Earth's standard. Over the comm, Serena's voice crackled:

"Systems reading nominal, but everything's labeled in half-broken English. Not sure how to switch from passive to active sensors."

Han eyed a swirling icon. "Try that sphere in the top corner," she guessed. "I see one that might be a scanning suite toggle."

A beep indicated Serena had found it. "Got it. Thanks."

Morrow watched the holo-feed from the fighter bay, frowning. "Alright. Rendezvous with the contact, keep visual if possible. No heroics. We have no idea what it's capable of."

"Understood, Captain," Han's voice came back. "We'll keep it neat."

Vogel hovered nearby, sensors active. "Captain, we have partial visual on the inbound craft: it's smaller than we thought, almost like a single-occupant stealth shuttle. Ion thrusters consistent with advanced Earth-based designs from the station's blueprint archives… but heavily modified."

Amir, scanning an older log, muttered, "So it's not purely alien. Maybe an internal design from the lost colony."

Morrow nodded but stayed silent. Her jaw tightened as she saw the three newly launched craft appeared on external cams, arcing away from the station with flaring engines. The star's glare made everything silhouette-rich—perfect for stealth, terrible for clarity.

Han's fighter soared out, buffeted by faint solar wind. To her left, Serena's craft kept pace. Han took a higher vantage, keeping dispersion between the craft. Up ahead, the small black wedge that was BETR's craft winked in and out of sensor contact, almost ghost-like. They approached cautiously, thrusters on minimal burn.

"Contact in visual range," Serena reported. "Man, that thing is… weird."

Han nodded in her cockpit, heart pounding. "Yeah. Hard to see. The star behind it gives a faint outline. Keep a perimeter. John, you going to open comms?"

John replied, "Working on that now, it's like half the controls are missing on these craft."

He keyed a channel: "Inbound contact, this is Escort One. We're forming up on your flanks. Don't deviate or power any weapons. Clear?"

The new entity's voice replied warmly. "Clear. Thank you. I see your fighter signatures. Preparing to match velocity."

John exhaled, nerves thrumming. One wrong move, and they might blow each other to pieces.

On the station, Captain Morrow leaned over the console. Morrow gave a curt nod. "We'll trust it just enough. Time to meet our new friend face to face."

Vogel and Doc watched out the large bay door of the aircraft launch bay. As the four craft approached for touchdown, Vogel and Doc positioned themselves at the forward nose of the strange craft, which had no canopy or viewports. The ship was dense, black and made from some sort of exotic material.

John addressed his team. "Han, Serena, you heard the Captain. Once that door closes and we get partial atmosphere, get out there and intercept. No chances, if that thing so much as winks at you…"

Han nodded, a motion barely seen through the craft's canopy, eyes still slightly weary from stasis but determined. "Copy. We'll keep it on a tight leash."

Serena cracked her neck. "Better than sitting here twiddling thumbs. Let's see what we're dealing with."

John looked over to Vogel and Walters, who were strapped into advanced EVA mechs—a weird hybrid of exosuit and short-range thruster pack. "You two stand by," John told them. "If anything goes sideways, be ready to react. You're the muscle."

Vogel gave a crisp nod. "Roger that."

Once stationary, the large bay door closed behind them, blocking off the vacuum of space. For a time, there was no motion from any of the craft as the section went through the lengthy process of pressurization. Once the process of pressurization began, John, Serena and Han quickly exited their craft to take up a defensive position in front of the mech-suits. The hum of the craft's engines powering down filled the hangar as John opened the canopy of his craft. He, Serena and Han felt it through their suits more than they heard it, the sound muffled by the air tight suits intended to protect them from the vacuum of space. As soon as the pressurization was complete, Captain Morrow entered through a personal hatch behind them, flanked by Elena and Marcus. A hatch opened on the strange craft and slowly a single being began to exit.

John, wearing only his light armored flight suit, stood just at the front of the formation, his old pistol at the ready. Just behind him stood Serena and Han, with their energy rifles at the ready position. Vogel and Walters—suited in the advanced mech suits—loomed like steel sentinels ready for any betrayal. Captain Morrow walked up to stand next to John, and Han repositioned herself slightly to maintain a clear line of sight to the stranger.

John nervously watched as mechanical legs emerged from the ship, walking down the ship's hatch. He swallowed. This was it: their first face-to-face with a being who claimed to have once been human, had lived 300 years in deep space, and now called itself BETR. Whatever that was.

John gave a clipped nod to his team on their private comms channel. "Alright, we let the Captain do the talking, but it doesn't get past us if anything goes south."

Vogel's mech servos whined as she adjusted her stance. "On your lead."

A slight hiss echoed through the launch bay. Faint lights from the stealth shuttle's interior bled onto the station's deck. Then the figure fully emerged—tall, human-shaped, but with a metallic sheen along half its face and chest with the rest appearing like some form of synthetic skin. Its motions were fluid yet stilted, a strange blend of biological grace and mechanical stiffness.

"Greetings. Am I to assume you are Captain Morrow?"

"I am. We have more than a few questions for you," she said. "But first, give me your name. If you were human, you must have had one."

"I am BETR"

"I doubt that. If you are who you say you are, I'm not calling you that. What was your human name?"

A pause. "Elmo," the voice admitted quietly, with a hint of self-consciousness.

"Elmo?" Morrow repeated, eyebrows nearly climbing off her forehead.

Listening and watching from the Command Deck, Riley let out an incredulous snort. "Well that was unexpected. Seems to have thrown the Captain off a bit." Elena ignored him, staring intently at the feed. Marcus just shook his head in disbelief.

Morrow addressed the inbound contact again. "Alright, Elmo. Listen carefully: We're not exactly comfortable letting you any farther if we don't know your intentions. But you say you have knowledge of the original colony—how do we know we can trust you?"

BETR/Elmo's response came slower, as if carefully chosen: "I understand your fear. But I have been isolated out here for centuries. The colony... it fell. I lived off scraps of advanced technology I helped develop in my prior life. Please, let me come aboard. I can share what I know."

Morrow's gaze flicked back to the silhouette of the stealthy craft that was parked in front of her. She saw no obvious weapon signatures— then again, the stealth systems might hide anything. She took a measured breath. "Fine, you can enter the flight bay for now. But you'll be escorted by two of our security at all times, and you will not attempt access to the rest of the station without explicit authorization. Copy?"

BETR/Elmo's voice sounded oddly relieved. "Acknowledged. It will be nice to sit down and have a discussion with other humans."

John, Serena and Han escorted the entity, Elmo, to the hangar bay's ready room along with Captain Morrow. He triggered the private comms to his team. "Vogel, Doc, you two get out of those mech suits. Leave them out there for now. We're not opening the inner door yet, I want that ship isolated. Get geared up and come relieve Serena and Han so they can get out of flight suits. I want eyes on it at all times. Captain seems ready to show some trust, let's not get in her way… but if that thing so much as flinches the wrong way you protect the Captain. Good?"

Each member of John's security detail clicked their mic in acknowledgment.

25

A hushed tension clung to the crew as John beckoned the mysterious visitor into the flight deck's ready room. Behind the tinted visor of John's helmet, his jaw was set—eyes scanning for any flicker of betrayal in this strange being's movements.

The figure—an uneasy amalgam of synthetic flesh and plating—walked with a mechanical limp, or perhaps just the strain of low-power hibernation for centuries. It was tall and thin, its features sculpted into something that bordered on gaunt. Yet its dark eyes had a spark of life. This was no mindless robot: it seemed, if anything, utterly exhausted from a life spent in the void. Walking into the ready room, the metallic figure paused, glancing about as if in nostalgic wonder—or dismay.

"It's changed since I last saw it," the being murmured, voice a strange echo of both man and machine. "The station." The faint swirl of mechanical undertones laced its words. "Or maybe I'm the one who changed."

John cleared his throat. "Now isn't the time for a tour," he said tersely. "Come on." He led them onward toward a seating section, hand on the hilt of his pistol which was now back in its holster at his side. He made sure it was visible enough to convey caution.

"Your name is… Elmo," Han said from within her flight suit, voice transmitted from speakers on her helmet. Her tone was politely curious, though the barrel of her rifle never strayed far. "Used to be human, you said?"

The figure—BETR—glanced at her, mechanical jaw tensing. "Yes, though that name feels so distant now. Call me what you want." A faint, ironic smile tugged one corner of its mouth. "But not 'Elmo' if you can help it. Wasn't a fan of it even back then."

They approached the seating area allowing BETR and the Captain to sit down facing one another. John and his team kept an alert posture a few paces back to give the illusion of a relaxed environment. The station's overhead lights stabilized, illuminating the metal panels with a cool white glow. A moment later, the doors hissed apart, revealing Elena, Marcus and Riley with Amir waiting behind them. Amir took a seat off to one side, discreetly recording the encounter with a handheld camera rig, a relic for which he seemed attached, to document this extraordinary moment.

Morrow's gaze swept the newcomer from head to toe. She wore a steady, practiced calm that spoke of deep-space commander experience. "So," she said quietly, "I suppose introductions are in order first." She introduced her crew one by one.

BETR's mechanical eyes flicked over her, then the others, apparently reading them with equal wariness. "Thank you Captain. Typically social protocol would mean I'd say 'it's an honor,' but the situation seems too… bleak for that and well, I really don't know who you are anymore than you know me. From my perspective, you're trespassing and from yours, I am and a potential threat."

A pause settled like dust in the air. Riley broke it first, leaning forward, palms half-raised in a friendly gesture. "You said you were out here alone for centuries. Must have been… well, lonely's an understatement. You don't look like any android I've ever seen."

"Because I'm not an android," BETR replied, voice tinged with an odd sympathy for Riley's curiosity. "I was human. Certain… events forced me to adapt. This station's technology—cyberneticus augmeta—kept me alive." It shrugged, the mechanical plates along its collar shifting with a faint whirr. "I'm neither fully synthetic nor biological now. I am Synthorganic."

Elena, who had not yet taken a seat, circled to the side, scanning BETR's form with a portable sensor. "I see overlapping energy signatures. Some standard Earth-based tech. Some I can't even identify." Her brow knitted. "You say you used to be part of this colony. Which generation?"

BETR's expression drew tight. "Third, I believe, from the time of founding. Born about eighty years after the first wave arrived. I helped develop advanced drives, propulsion theories, exotic particle physics. Then it all went to hell." The last sentence dropped with the weight of centuries, as if summoning memories BETR would rather forget.

Captain Morrow folded her arms, glancing between John and the newly arrived being. "We need to know more. We found this station—intact but abandoned. We suspect an external threat or catastrophic event. Which was it?"

BETR nodded slowly, an echo of sorrow crossing its metallic features. "It was both, in a way. A… cataclysm beyond anything we'd prepared for. This station once thrived with thousands of souls. Now, it's… was just an empty shell."

Amir stepped forward gently, clearing his throat. "We have partial logs referencing 'orbital bombardments' and 'evacuation events'. The AI on this station has incomplete memory. We hoped you might fill in the blanks."

At that, BETR's gaze slid to the overhead holo-lights, as though searching for the station's own AI presence. "That old system? It was good at what it did, but we pushed it beyond design limits. I might know more than it, or… less. My mind is not what it was." His voice trembled, as if from some deeply embedded trauma.

Morrow exhaled softly. "Alright. We'll have that conversation soon. First, let's handle safety. No offense, but we have limited trust right now." She gestured at John and the rest of security. "For the moment, you will remain a guarded guest aboard this station. I'll request that you comply with my crew on scans to ensure our safety."

BETR—Elmo—let a wry, sad grin flicker across half a mouth. "I can guess what the scans will show: a battered chassis, leftover organic cells… none of which are a threat to you. The only hazard I pose is knowledge. And knowledge can be dangerous, can't it? That's why I shall be your prisoner now?"

A brief hush followed before Morrow spoke with resolute calm. "Let's not get ahead of ourselves. Riley, run a quick diagnostic. Elena, you monitor. "

Riley stepped forward, his handheld medical scanner poised. Behind him, John Ferris tensed ever so slightly, though vigilance shone in his gaze. Walters and Vogel, no longer in their mech suits, entered the room and took up flanking positions, ready to jump if BETR made any threatening moves. Serena and Han glanced at John. John nodded and they left the room to get out of their cumbersome flight suits.

"Alright, arms out," Riley instructed, conducting a wide scan that glowed around BETR's metal-plated torso. The figure complied silently, letting the beam pass over its limbs. On the scanner's display, an avalanche of data scrolled—some recognized as advanced cybernetic implants, others an enigma of partial organics fused with nanotech and many fully mechanical prosthetics.

"Heart rate… unusual," Riley murmured. "Not exactly human. But stable. No elevated aggression hormones." He checked the atmospheric readouts. "No sign of contaminants introduced into the air."

Elena kept watch on a console feed, verifying that station sensors detected nothing amiss. Finally, she nodded at Morrow. "Looks clear, Captain."

"Then let's talk," Morrow said, gesturing toward his chair. "You're avoiding answers and dancing around the conversation. Let's cast formalities aside and talk. Perhaps it would help if I explain who we are first."

BETR inclined its head with something approaching relief. As they retook their seats, John Ferris listened carefully through the external microphones in his helmet, mind swirling with questions. Deciding he would not be leaving the room, he removed his helmet and hung it from a small hook on his hip intended for keeping it available when not being worn. So many unknowns: Could this being truly be an ally, a relic of the colony? Or was it hiding some deeper agenda?

Captain Morrow studied BETR's stiff posture, the half-mechanical face that spoke of a fusion between humanity and necessity. She didn't press further on the subject of its mind just yet. Instead, she kept her voice controlled, professional, though an undercurrent of sympathy glimmered behind her eyes as she explained their journey for the last year or so and the purpose of their adventure. She explained the surprise when they arrived and made a point of where they originated in time.

Amir, checking his handheld camera rig, stepped beside BETR. "Hope you don't mind," he said gently, indicating the recorder. "I'm documenting what's left of this colony. You're… well, you might be our best window into the past."

BETR's jaw twitched, a ripple of metallic plating echoing the movement. "I don't mind. Memory fades anyway. This might help me remember who I was." It said the last line with a hint of loss, as though the notion of "who I was" stood on the edges of his own mind.

Elena began scanning the immediate environment with the portable sensor. "You mentioned a cataclysm—both an external threat and an internal meltdown. It aligns with some of the partial logs we've found. But we need specifics if we're to avoid the same fate."

BETR gave a hollow nod. "I'll share what I know. Though… my recollection might be patchy."

"So," Morrow began, folding her hands. "Let's start with the basics. You said you were third-generation, about eighty years after the founding. The station logs we've recovered place the founding around… what, 250 years ago, station time? Possibly more. Does that track?"

BETR pursed its metallic lips, the expression half-lost amid fused plating. "The colony was established, I believe, 430 to 440 years ago—depending on whose record you read. Generations became muddled once we started extending lifespans and we had no need to track them in terms of adaptations for this planet. Even the first generation was capable of instantaneous adaptation of their bodies to the new environment. I assume, given your origin, this is the basis behind your generational curiosity. When I was…" it paused, scanning the shadows in its memory, "around thirty, I joined a propulsion research team. That was about 110 years after the colony was founded. We were fairly well established by that point in time and great research was beginning to emerge from… this distant outpost of humanity. I worked to advance the technology behind our exotic energy productions and FTL drives."

Elena's eyes lit with professional curiosity. "That must have been the advanced drive the station seems built around—some next-gen antimatter or hyper-energy model. It's beyond anything Earth has right now…" she paused as reality caught up with her, "or, had when we left anyway. You helped develop it?"

A faint inclination of BETR's head. "I was good with engineering, yes. And it worked. We grew bolder, tested bigger theories—wormhole bridging, early attempts at negative mass experiments. Humanity had FTL travel between systems and a broad reaching galactic economy. But eventually—" It shut its eyes, if they could be called eyes, as though pained by a memory.

Morrow leaned forward, voice gentling. "What happened?"

BETR's response came slowly, like someone picking through the rubble of a ruined home. "First, we began to war within ourselves. Certain factions of society felt oppressed. Others, well absolute power corrupts absolutely. Then, we discovered we weren't alone. There were… signals, faint but unmistakable, from beyond our reach in the galaxy. We thought it might be extraterrestrial. Perhaps we drew attention to ourselves with our experiments." It shook its head, an oddly human gesture for such a mechanical being. "But the researchers

—some said it was a cosmic phenomenon, not an alien force. Others insisted it was an attack. Word from the lower colonies, oh I suppose that wouldn't mean anything to you… Humanity divided the colonies by the galactic plane. Those above were the upper colonies and those below the lower colonies. The majority of our colonies tended to be closer to Sol or in the lower colonies around places like Rigel. For a while, it was just routine updates through the quantum communications, but then some supply ships coming to retrieve energy pods began to bring rumors of something worse. The little rebellious spats had turned into a greater war within humanity. We found ourselves on the fringes and attached to The Empire by default, but we felt no loyalty to any side. We were mostly scientists and researchers. With abundant free energy, it was rather utopian out here. "

John exchanged a sharp look with Elena. "So was it an enemy, or was it just some cosmic event—maybe a rogue asteroid or gamma burst? What made the crater on the planet?"

BETR's metal shoulders sagged. "I wish I could recall precisely. The station was hit—orbital bombardments, social collapse, everything at once… I don't know. What I returned to find was the signs of utter chaos. Many died, some fled I suppose. I was off-world, doing tests near the star. When I got back, there was… nothing left but a few corpses and drifting debris. I was alone. I searched the station, went down and searched the planet, but everyone I'd ever known was gone. They just vanished. I've always just figured the rumors turned out to be true and one side or the other decided to shut down the colony to deny energy resources to the other, but I didn't see it and I do not know what actually happened."

A hush fell. Only the station's hum underfoot and a distant crackle of overhead wiring interrupted the silence. In that lull, the crew weighed the gravity of each word—bombardments, social collapse, war, external threat. So many incomplete pieces of a puzzle that explained why they'd found an empty station in orbit around a ruined planet.

Amir set down his camera, voice trembling with empathy. "So you found no survivors?"

"Not… exactly," BETR admitted, breath rattling with a mechanical undertone. "I found others—like me—who clung to life through… harsh means. Experimental implants. AI-run surgeries. Over time, we grew apart, lost track. And I—" It stopped, brow furrowing.

Riley broke the quiet with a gentle tone. "You what?"

"I put myself in stasis. Floating deep in space, near that star, to wait. I woke every decade or so and checked on experiments, investigated to see if anything had changed. When my ship detected what I assume was your entry into the system and the station's beacon flared, I awoke. It's been centuries, I think. My sense of time is… broken. Hell of a noisy entrance by the way, but I suppose given your origins and lack of experience with the Alcubierre fields and Park drive systems, that would explain a lot. That would mean you are The Aurora, the only one to ever use that technology for relativistic flight…" he turned and gave a searching glance at Elena to find her intently staring at him with wide eyes.

Captain Morrow pinched the bridge of her nose, eyes closed briefly. "So there might be more like you out there?"

"Possibly," BETR said, the word weighted with sorrow. "Or they might have succumbed to the some fate. When I put myself in stasis, it was after most of the survivors decided to self terminate. The rest had some plan for leaving. I chose to stay and finish my research. I haven't detected any other signals in decades. My craft was specially designed, based on the latest stealth technology to shield me against solar radiation and heat dissipation the likes of which I'm sure you've never seen. It allowed me to remain hidden by the solar interferences within close proximity to the star as the years passed. Others would not have had such respite. If there are any more survivors, I'd imagine they are deep underground now on the planet or are long gone."

Elena took a step closer, examining the readouts on her portable scanner. "You said you could fill in some blanks the station AI can't. Do you remember anything about how the station's final shutdown began? We found some references to sabotage, or a misfired weapon, or an attempt to harness negative energy."

A flash of pain crossed BETR's face. "We tried to harness something we barely understood. Perhaps it was that. It's hard to say what fragment you were looking at. It all blurs—my memory's fractured by centuries of partial power. It's quite different, though it feels a lot like I remember as a human… the brain fog when you first wake up and haven't had your coffee yet. But I was the one who shut down the station's power and put it in a minimal power mode. I returned every decade or so to ensure it remained in orbit, but once I had completed my augmeta, I was done with it."

The juxtaposition of the machine in front of him acting so human made John uneasy. His voice sliced through the haze. "We're trying to decide how to move forward. We have colonists in stasis, half this station is offline, and we're dangerously low on resources. We can't risk the same downfall."

BETR's dark eyes flicked over John. "If you intend to stay, you'll need to fully repair the station. There are hidden sub-systems we once built—defenses, scanning arrays. I can help." He paused. "But I must warn you: if the threat that destroyed us is still lurking—I don't know what happened here or what to tell you. I can give you no words of encouragement or better understanding than I have. All I can do is help you with your efforts."

"That's exactly why we need you," Morrow interjected softly. "Answers, guidance, anything. We'll decide if it's safe to remain."

Silence settled again. Riley glanced at each face, feeling the oppressive weight of so many unknowns. Walters shifted awkwardly. Vogel turned to examine a battered console where the station's AI flickered on a side panel, perhaps eavesdropping on this extraordinary exchange.

Eventually, Morrow stood. "All right. We'll accept your help, on a probationary basis. Riley and Elena will run more scans and tests of your systems if they see fit and ensure that you're not hiding anything dangerous. I expect you to work with them, not just be a subject or patient. This is a first opportunity to help bridge a gap in knowledge of your technology and ours."

BETR offered a slow nod of assent. "That's fair."

She turned to Elena. "Get an engineering team to coordinate with… him. See if we can access those hidden subsystems and piece together more logs." Morrow shook her head, "we really need a better name for you. I'm not calling you BETR. Such an arrogant implication."

Elena pursed her lips. "We'll need resources from the colony ship too—more power cells, better insulation. And the supply situation—"

Morrow closed her eyes a moment, torn. "We'll start rationing. Riley, spread the word. That means more of those damned energy bars for daily meals. Keep the real food in reserve for evening meals until we stabilize. The rest of our colonists remain in stasis until further notice."

Serena and Han, standing near the door, exchanged resigned looks. John crossed his arms, his expression caught between relief at a potential ally and deep suspicion of so many unanswered questions.

At length, Captain Morrow leaned in closer to BETR. Her posture softened, but her gaze remained cool, guarded. "Let's find a path forward—together. For now, you get to remain on the station, under supervision. We'll see how your story checks out. You'll forgive me for not blindly trusting you right away?"

BETR bowed its head in agreement, shoulders slumping as if a great burden had briefly lifted. "Thank you. I… I don't want to see this place remain a tomb."

An awkward silence and pause filled the room, so John spoke up to ask the question on the back of everyone's mind, "I'm almost afraid to ask, I think everyone is… what of Sol?"

The almost alien robot face turned to look at John, sending a chill down his spine. "I waited for a long time. Weeks turned into months, then years. I waited for the next merchant ship, cargo transport or maybe a scout from Sol or another system. I was sure when our FTL comms went silent, someone would come. You're the first to arrive. If my history is correct and given the age of your ship and level of ignorance," he turned to look at Captain Morrow, "you are The first colony vessel that left Sol over a millennia ago aren't you?"

Captain morrow was frozen for a moment, the weight of the statements sinking in before she registered the question at the end. "Yes. That's correct."

"Then, there is much you don't know indeed. I will try to help, but I'm not a historian or an AI, though I share more similarities with an AI than a historian now."

Riley placed a gentile hand on BETR's shoulder and spoke softly in his bedside manner, "Come on Bet, lets head to medical for a bit and give you a full checkup. Elena, swing by engineering and grab some kit? I think we're going to need a bit more than just biological tools."

"Sure thing, see you there." Elena said over her shoulder as she practically jogged from the room.

Captain morrow gave a waving motion at John. "Get that suit off and store the craft. Han, go with Riley as our diplomat of peace." She delivered this last statement with a sharp look directed at John. He got the message loud and clear.

"Yes Captain." John's noticed his reply was almost as robotic as Bet's. Bet, that's what Riley had called him. The thought echoed in John's head as they walked down the corridor toward the medical bay, thoughts swirling in his head about earth, a multi system economy, FTL… It was like the future had come and gone and they'd missed it. He felt as if he was lost in a galactic apocalypse and they had only one bet to place. John shook his head, so lost in his thoughts he outwardly expressed them. The realization of which shocked him back to focusing on what was in front of him.

26

The medical bay's lights pulsed to life as Riley swept in, guided by the subtle overhead glow that illuminated rows of storage lockers and a few mostly intact diagnostic tables. The space smelled faintly of antiseptics, even though centuries had passed since anyone had last occupied it. Part of the station's automated cleaning routines, perhaps —strange holdovers from a brighter era. Now, it felt almost clinical in its emptiness.

BETR—or Bet, as Riley had taken to calling him—stood in the center of the medical bay patient area, gaze traveling the walls with a mixture of distant nostalgia and caution. Positioned adjacent to the hangar bay, presumably for quick access when bringing in casualties, the medical bay was an adaptable area that could be screened off into sections for privacy or isolation depending on the needs at the time. Currently, the entryway appeared to be part office and part waiting room. Offering ample seating with a console that could have been used for research or reception. At the rear, an adaptable wall partition which could be removed or relocated was a door that lead to the patient area. John, pistol holstered, hovered near the door—more out of instinct than suspicion now. He couldn't quite decide if this strange half-human was still a threat. But Captain Morrow's sharp instruction to remain diplomatic echoed in his mind.

John said nothing as Bet stood in the center of the large open area, surrounded by a mix of equipment and patient beds around the perimeter of the oddly shaped area. Narrower at the entrance, the medical bay occupied the entire area between the inner corridor that stretched like a loop around the inner portion of the station and the outer hull giving it a somewhat trapezoidal shape that curved along the outermost bulkhead. Along the side walls were what appeared to John to be different stations, presumably for different medical functions. Each station apparently could close itself in with wall sections that extended from the deck, bulkheads and from overhead in some cases. One such area was closed in this way to create an isolation chamber of sorts. With the rest of the area open, it gave John a sense of something more like a factory than a medical facility.

Elena arrived moments later, breathless from jogging through the station's winding corridors, arms laden with a small crate of diagnostic equipment. The box clattered onto the nearest table, scattering a few tools across the smooth metal surface. "Sorry," she said. "Didn't think we'd need all this so soon, but I figured better safe than sorry."

Riley gave her a quick nod, then turned to Bet. "Alright, let's get started. First off: a baseline scan, see what we're dealing with biologically, then we'll move on to the… ah, mechanical side."

Bet inclined his head. The mechanical plating along his collar and jaw shifted with a soft almost inaudible whirr, revealing faint seams of artificial muscle beneath synthetic flesh. The odd mix of metal and patchy synthetic flesh was a bit unsettling to John, but Elena and Riley seemed too preoccupied with a facisnation for the technology than the unseemly appearance of Bet's synthetic form. "I'll cooperate. Hopefully we can answer each other's questions."

John stepped closer, folding his arms, eyes lingering on the unusual mix of metallic and organic tissue at Bet's joints. So this is what a 'synthorganic human' looks like, he thought. Thinking of how easily it would allow adaptation to any environment, presumably without having to torture himself in a gym everyday he could was quite appealing to his desires. "You said the station's technology allowed you to become this," he said, tone carefully neutral. "I didn't realize we had such a… sophisticated med bay."

A faint echo of a smile tugged at Bet's mouth. "It's not just this bay —back then, we had entire wings dedicated to augmeta and biotech. This room you see? It's only a fraction of what we once possessed. This was more of a triage ward, meant to receive patients from the flight deck. It's quite well provisioned though and suited most every need when there was not a crisis to attend to." His dark eyes flickered over the diagnostic tables, the empty shelves. "We had smaller surgical pods, advanced gene-labs. Some of it might still be hidden deeper in the station."

Elena's eyes brightened with scientific curiosity. "Are you saying there could be a lab dedicated to these augmentations... umm I think you called them augmeta? Working condition or no, we could possibly salvage data or equipment?"

Bet's shoulders lifted in a metallic shrug. "It's possible. Many systems sealed when the station alarms triggered. If they survived the damage, you might find entire wings still locked down." He glanced at Riley's diagnostic wand, which hummed as it swept from head to waist. "The question is: how much damage remains and what condition much of it is in after centuries of disrepair and abandonment?"

Riley tapped through the first set of readings. "Vitals are... well, unique," he muttered, arching a brow. "Heartbeat's an engineered fusion. The implants are directing blood flow and oxygen. Your body is more mechanical than organic, yet somehow the organic bits have adapted to it. Honestly, I'm not even sure what we should classify you as medically."

Bet offered a hollow chuckle. "I often wonder that myself. I notice that you're using your own tools. That's not from the station."

"I've had a lot of trouble understanding the station equipment. There seems to be a great lack of controls, displays or anything useful to most things around here. It makes it hard to tell what something is or can do when I can't even figure out how to turn it on," Riley said.

Bet nodded. "That's understandable, here allow me." Bet placed a hand on a console next to the exam table they were congregating around. A drawer along the wall next to them slid open revealing an assortment of devices. "Here, try this one."

Elena placed a small sensor array near Bet's arm, watching as the station's advanced scanning interface glowed to life. "I'd kill to learn how these implants were made," she said under her breath. "Back on Earth, we had next-gen prosthetics, but nothing like this. It's so integrated—like you were built for deep-space survival."

Bet's expression darkened for a moment. "Built is a strong word. It was... forced, in many ways to adapt. Survival overshadowed ethics at the end. I assure you, I was not built like some machine. I was born, same as you.." He gazed at the device reading his bio-signs, mechanical face tinged with regret. "We were losing too many people, space and time manipulations were harder on the human anatomy than we anticipated and the lines between man and machine blurred out of desperation. Planets like this one presented simple challenges different from our evolutionary origins that simple genetics might overcome. We weren't adapted for the gravity difference here for instance, but most of space wasn't so accommodating as this world. We moved out into the galaxy faster than evolution could keep up with the changes we were pressing upon ourselves, so we began with forced mutations… gene therapy in an old term, to attempt to advance ourselves. The human race began to diverge, those who remained in space or at the outer reaches of systems grew taller and thinner, 'heavy miners'-those who mined larger rocky planets with increased gravity compared to Earth, grew shorter and developed greater bone and muscle density. Our attempts to control evolution was being fought by it. Flip a switch in a lab and nature flips five more to do what it wants. There was no way to simply avoid all natural born to precisely control the genetic evolutionary changes that would occur. Then humanity started to blend man and machine. I don't imagine you would have recognized society or humans had they been here when you arrived. To me, you all appear as much like I'd imagine a museum's example of prehistoric humans would look to you. As pure and weak as newborns, or some of the isolated pockets of 'Creationists'. Before you ask, as I assume that means nothing to you, Creationists were a religious based sect within galactic society that felt the need to remain unaltered by augmeta or even gene therapy. They were somewhat radical in their views and referred to the rest of humanity as 'Homo Nex'. They believed we were no longer the same species."

John noticed Elena's shoulders stiffen. A pang of sympathy ran through him—he realized that for as fascinating as this was, it was also a testament to unimaginable trauma. Clearing his throat, he asked, "These augmeta… if the station still holds that technology, could any of us benefit? Our colonists received gene therapy while in stasis to assist with adapting to what we could anticipate for this world. I'd imagine the technology here would be more capable than our own."

Elena blinked at John, surprised by the question, then glanced at Bet, a cautious eagerness shining in her eyes. "He's right. We've all felt the glare from the star. And some of our gear isn't specialized for these intensities. Those of us who crewed the ship haven't received the same benefits as those in stasis. If we can replicate your gene enhancements, it might help us adapt to the environment."

Bet studied John a moment, the mechanical side of his features whirring faintly. "Yes… in theory. We had advanced corneal overlays, neural calibration for IR or UV spectrums. Some of that might still be on file in the station's archives. Provided the… events that terminated this entire settlement didn't corrupt everything. My final adaptions were made here in this very bay, after the end. Some of that still exists in this very room. Other resources may be found on the planet and around." He motioned at the far side of the medical suite where new and strange equipment remained untouched.

A spark of intrigue settled into John's mind—part practical need, part curiosity. He knew how unpredictable this was: letting an unknown synthorganic cyberneticus entity guide them toward potentially irreversible surgeries. But imagine not being blinded by star flares, stumbling in the dark corridors, or feeling the effects of crushing gravity he mused.

Riley dipped his head in agreement, scanning Bet's torso next. "You see that?" he pointed at the display, showing interwoven synthetic fibers around Bet's ribcage. "This is basically internal body armor. Good for radiation shielding, maybe ballistic protection as well?"

Bet nodded.

Elena let out a low whistle. "I had no idea you could blend that so seamlessly with organic tissue. It's—both horrifying and brilliant."

Bet's lips curled in a rueful smile. "Hardly seamless. You're seeing me centuries after the surgeries. The first years…" He trailed off, voice trembling slightly. "It wasn't pretty. I'm also not a physician either. I'm afraid I've turned myself into a bit of Dr. Frankenstein's monster. The typical application of all this would have been quite elegant and beautiful. Aside from very few external attachments and augmeta, you likely would not have been able to tell that most individuals had augmeta. A cranial interface at the temple was typically the only visible change… although you may have noticed that vanity had gotten the better of us. I dare say, John here would have stood out quite sharply in a crowd. I've never seen such a square jawline in my life. Rather brutish looking, compared to… apologies, I don't mean any offense to you, perhaps to humanities warped sense of vanity though."

A respectful silence followed. They all sensed the underlying tragedy behind the technology. For Bet, survival had demanded a terrifying metamorphosis. For the station's lost colonists, it signaled a desperate gamble that ultimately failed to save them and what about the rest of humanity? Was there even a rest of humanity left anywhere in the galaxy?

John carefully unlatched the retention straps of the pistol holster at his thigh, letting the sidearm rest gently at his side. He slid it around toward the rear of his thigh, still in reach, but at an awkward stretch rather than in plain sight. Making the adjustment appear for his own comfort, he intended it to demonstrate a growing comfort more than purely physical. A small gesture of trust. "Well," he said quietly, "I'd be lying if I said I wasn't interested in a few… improvements. But we're not turning ourselves into beauty-centric synthorganic cyborgs tomorrow. We just need help with small modifications to make life easier here, if that's even possible."

Bet nodded, glancing at Elena. "It might be, if the station labs are intact enough. But I'll warn you—it's a slippery slope. Once you start, you may find other changes appealing. That's how we, that is to say, how humanity got here in the first place."

John exchanged a look with Elena, who shrugged thoughtfully. "We don't have the luxury of being squeamish if it helps us survive. But caution is wise."

Riley powered down the final phase of the scanner, drawing a breath. "Alright, no major red flags besides the obvious. I'd like to run some deeper analyses—maybe scan your neural interface. But physically, you appear stable enough."

27

Captain Morrow's voice crackled over John's comm. "Everything alright in there?"

"Yes, Captain," John replied. "No issues. We're just having an interesting chat and gossiping. I might put on a pot of tea."

"Good to hear," Morrow said. "We'll convene shortly to decide our next moves, and bring me a cup. Two sugars and a pinch of citric acid."

John chuckled to himself at the exchange, but then very much wanted that tea. He decided he was going to indulge the Captain's request. With a sudden thought, John turned to Bet and asked, "would you like some tea as well? I'm sure it's been a long time." John was curious how Bet would react and answer.

Bet's dark eyes flicked toward John, and for a moment, the being seemed taken aback—an ancient memory stirring behind that half-metal visage. Something like an awkward, but sincere gratitude softened the lines of his foreign features. John imagined this is what a toaster would look like if it could show emotions.

"Tea," he repeated quietly, as if the word itself might be unfamiliar after centuries adrift. "I'd nearly forgotten the taste of anything… real. They still grow tea leaves on Earth? Oh, well you wouldn't know now would you. I apologize, it's rather inconsiderate of me to keep forgetting the time dilation you all experienced."

Elena snorted softly, pushing a lock of hair behind her ear. "We manage. The fresh leaves we have now are genetically modified strains, grown in hydroponics, but they're close enough to the real deal from Old Earth. I think we have some dried leaves from Earth still though, if you don't mind them being a millennia and a half old at this point." She gave Bet a wink at the mention of time.

A trace of a smile pulled at Bet's lip. "Then yes—my system can still handle it, I'd like to try." He paused, as if searching for the right words. "It's been so long since I enjoyed something… human. I still require a basic nutrition to support what remains organic, however that has just been a fabricated mix of organic compounds to satisfy my system's needs."

John's grin was unexpected, even to himself. Since Bet's arrival he'd been poised on the edge of suspicion, but the idea of sharing a simple cup of tea with this half-cyborg survivor struck him as both surreal and oddly comforting. He raised an eyebrow at Riley.

Riley shrugged, flashing that reassuring smile which reflected a bedside manner he'd honed over years of medical work. "I can't see why not, so long as his system can still process something a little less purposeful than a tailor made body fuel." He gave Bet a once-over. "If something goes haywire, we'll know fast."

Bet dipped his head. "Then I accept."

The idea of breaking the tension with an ordinary ritual—tea—made even Elena chuckle softly under her breath. She began packing up the diagnostic tools, eyes darting now and then at the far corner of the med bay, where advanced, half-forgotten biotech units rested amid dust and gloom. One problem at a time, she reminded herself.

John keyed his comm again. "Captain, where would you like to have your tea?"

Morrow's reply crackled back, laced with mild amusement. "I'll meet you in the rec lounge in twenty minutes. We'll plan our next steps."

Riley gently placed the last scanning module into its holder. "All right, Bet, if you can walk, we'll head to a small kitchenette we've set up near the hydroponics deck. We keep the real tea leaves for special occasions—though 'special' is kind of an understatement right now."

Bet glanced down at his leg, testing the weight on it. A soft squeak of servo accompanied the motion. "I think I remember the way, but why don't you show me instead.. but, if you don't mind," Bet reached out and touched the console, then stretched out on the exam table. "My ship's been a bit cramped and it's been quite some time since I was able to make some repairs."

As he spoke, panels rose slightly at the edge of the table. Mechanical arms descended from above and the equipment went to work. In only a minute or so, all the motion and activity stopped and in a reverse of how it all started, everything went back to the way it was. Bet spun around to a seated position and then stood. There was no sound to his motions anymore. "Ahh, that's much better. Sometimes the Tin-man just needs a spot of oil I suppose."

Riley gave Bet a puzzled look. "That's quite the ancient reference. I wouldn't even have known what it was from if our resident historian hadn't educated us so thoroughly on our journey."

"Ahh, yes. Well, when you have nothing but time on your hands and a few centuries to pass, you tend to find entertainment where you can I suppose. Shall we?"

"Yes, but you're going to have to show me how you did that. I can't even get the stuff to respond and with a touch, you just executed a rather complicated set of instructions. It might be routine enough I suppose, but that was a bit more than just turning things on." Riley said.

"I'd be happy to, but we shouldn't keep the Captain waiting for intellectual black holes. I promise to show you everything I know." Bet assured him.

Elena tapped a panel at the med bay's door, and it hissed open, letting in a draft of cooler air from the corridor. "We'll keep this suite offline for now," she told John quietly. "Until we're sure about how to proceed with… augmentations, or any other medical repairs. It's kind of wild isn't it? Feels a bit unreal to me."

John nodded, stepping aside so Bet could pass. A swirl of conflicting thoughts tugged at him: curiosity about these surgeries that might help them survive Kepler-452's harsh environment, wariness at the cost that had clearly claimed many colonists' lives, and empathy for a being who still clung to bits of humanity in a post-human shell. Suddenly, a question occurred to him. "Bet, was there a proper name given to this system or the planet? I keep using the catalogue designation in my head."

They moved out into the corridor in a loose procession—Elena and Riley bracketing Bet in the middle, John trailing with his sidearm slung low, a show of caution and pragmatism rather than immediate suspicion. The hallway lights still flickered in a lazy pattern, as if uncertain whether to fully commit to brilliance.

"Enera was the name we gave the star. Aurion was the planet's name. The system has been called a number of things. Some preferred to call it Solivara, others called it Nevara. We just called it Home."

Bet's mechanical footsteps echoed in the following silence. "It feels… comforting, and strange." he admitted in a low voice. "These familiar corridors, the faint hum of life support… It's like coming home to a house you never expected to see again, only someone else lives there now."

No one contradicted him. They all sensed the thread of loss woven into his words: this station was indeed a broken home, filled with ghosts and half-remembered wonders they knew very little about. And now, perhaps for the first time in centuries, it had guests who might remake it—or discover the final secrets that had destroyed it, but they had indeed moved in.

Filing into the rec room, John made straight for the kitchenette and placed a bag of water in the heater. Reaching for a cabinet door to grab the tea and teapot, he felt a strange unease about how relaxed he was. How was it that he was comfortably making tea with a new and unknown potential threat at his back? It struck him as slightly unusual for him to be so quick to relax and accept anyone so new and different in such a trusting manner. At first thinking to himself that it was simply because he believed what Bet had said and that he was no threat, John suddenly realized his logic was flawed. Bet was unarmed, but that didn't mean he was no threat. He was mostly machine and well adapted to a planet with twice the gravity John was accustomed to. Surely he could be a threat, capable of causing any one of them great harm even without a weapon. He in fact had no logical reason to not still classify Bet as a potential threat.

"Elena, would you mind taking over for me please? I need to talk to Riley for a moment."

With a nod, Elena made for the kitchenette to take over the tea prep. John motioned Riley to a far corner, hoping for a bit of privacy, but not truly sure if Bet could overhear them. His augmeta might give him incredible hearing as well, he would have to choose his words carefully.

"Hey, I'm sure it's just… well that was a lot in the last couple hours. I'm sure it's just that I'm in a little shock over it, probably all of us are. Would you mind giving me a quick scan, see if anything's off? I don't quite feel myself right now." Meeting Riley's eyes, John tried to convey his fears almost telepathically. "I don't seem to be thinking as clearly right now."

Riley's eyebrows nearly climbed off the top of his forehead as he kept eye contact with John and reached for the medical scanner at his hip. Removing a small stylus looking instrument from the back case of the scanner, Riley pricked John's fingertip with it. The holographic display flickered to life, displaying results of John's blood chemistry analysis.

At first, the results didn't look out of the ordinary, but Riley's brow began to furrow as he noticed small discrepancies.

"A touch of elevated blood pressure, that is unsurprising. Slightly higher adrenaline levels, that is absolutely expected. Mild dehydration, looks like you need that tea more than you thought."

Riley continued evaluating the results, zooming in on a set of markers in John's endocrine profile.

"Cortisol is low," he muttered. "That's odd… you should be practically oozing stress hormones given everything that's happened - lack of sleep, near-combat readiness, the shock of meeting…"

John shifted uneasily, "So you're saying I'm too calm, too relaxed?"

Riley nodded. "Exactly. Your brain's running at a subdued fight-or-flight baseline. It's almost as though something's…" his words trailed off as they made eye contact.

He tapped another icon, analyzing a subset of neurochemicals. A secondary scan displayed faint but measurable traces of an unusual compound. "I'm seeing micro-lactones—complex molecules that don't typically show up in the human bloodstream. They're reminiscent of certain pheromones some animals produce, known to reduce aggression or anxiety in group settings."

John exhaled slowly, eyes narrowing. "Could Bet be… causing this?"

"Possibly," Riley admitted. "If Bet's augmentations included something like a modified version of sweat glands, or a bio-nanite system that could disperse calming agents, these micro-lactones might be saturating the immediate environment. You inhale or absorb them, and your stress response is suppressed."

A subtle chill settled in John's posture. "That's not comforting. You're telling me I'm basically being chemically nudged to trust him."

Riley pricked his own finger and found the similar results in his own blood sample.

"Inadvertently or otherwise," Riley confirmed, frowning at the data. "I'm not seeing any immediate harm—your, I mean… our vital signs are stable, it's more like a mild sedation. But it definitely explains why you feel so relaxed."

He clicked the scanner off and folded his arms. "We'll need to talk to Bet about this, see if it's intentional or just a leftover adaptation from centuries of survival…" his words trailed off as Bet approached.

In a blur of motion that bordered on reflex, John unholstered his sidearm and pointed it directly at Bet's face. Bet stopped moving. A stillness that reminded John of turning off a maintenance bot.

"I do not mean to alarm you. My augments do include an improved auditory sensor array. Not only could I hear your words, but I could hear your heart rates as they elevated from across the room. Your body temperatures fluctuated by a fraction of a degree and I note a galvanic skin response. I certainly appreciate the emotional response this has caused and I come to explain myself."

"You'd better have a damned good explanation for this," John growled.

"I do."

Bet actually sighed and his posture relaxed a bit as he took a half step backwards. John's critical eye did not miss the posture shift, the potentially intentional body language meant to convey ease and perhaps a slight submissiveness. Just how much of this human was left in there? Was it ever human? Was this all a ruse?

"If I take a few steps back, will you lower your weapon? I'll explain, but it may be a bit of a story. I'd like to give you enough background to understand me, but I'd rather not do it while your emotionally triggered finger is poised to end me before I can get it out."

John slowly nodded and as Bet took a couple steps back, he removed his finger from the trigger and brought the pistol in slightly closer to his body relaxing his aim, but still keeping it pointed in Bet's direction.

Bet nodded as if in appreciation. "Thank you. I was a bit of a nerd, a scientist and engineer. I was always more comfortable playing with antimatter than I was around other people. It wasn't until…"

Bet's posture seemed to slump a tad more as he paused. When he spoke again, his words were more full of emotion than anyone in the room might have expected from what appeared to them as a robot.

"Until I was alone that I realized how much being around people mattered, even if I had no previous desire to interact with them directly. No matter how much my body has been altered or how little of me is left biologically, who I was is still who I am. I have not changed in my mind. At least, as best as I can tell with the obvious observation bias. I'm not entirely sure I would know if I have changed and there's nobody around to tell me. There's been nobody for so long…"

"I'm aware of your sob story, get on with it." John cut in sharply.

"I'm still socially awkward. I'm still terrified of interacting with people, but I had to. I have to. I don't want to be alone anymore. I believe what you are experiencing is a direct result of me adjusting my own body chemistry to ease what's left of my biology. This bit of brain left in me that responds to these chemical signals.. I've given myself a calming dose to help me not be so frightened and awkward. That is, if such a thing were even possible. I crawl out of that coffin of a ship and am greeted by weapons, mech suits and an abundance of caution... all of which is perfectly understandable though! From your perspective. I mean, I wouldn't expect any less if I were in your situation. I did not want to be too nervous or scare anyone... I was, am terrified of all of you. So I calmed myself, by signaling my augmeta to alter my own personal chemistry and apparently I emitted a chemical signal that many other augmented humans would once have simply interpreted similar to how you interpret body language. Another augmented human would not have been affected. Everyone in my time had control over their own systems and would have been immune to any effects. I didn't think about how it might affect your millennia old un-augmented genetic composition. I've never been around anyone who had no augmeta before. I couldn't have known."

John, suddenly taken with empathetic emotions put the safety on his weapon, but did not lower it further. Unsure if it was still chemical manipulation or if he actually believed this being, he remembered the Captain's words. Diplomacy. He would offer Bet diplomacy but he would remain cautious.

"You will cease whatever chemical form of communication you are accustomed to at once. Until we understand it better... understand each other better, turn it off if you are going to remain aboard my ship. If that prevents you from calming yourself in the same way, then you will have to deal with that. We will certainly take your situation into account and would not judge you for being socially awkward. But, If I feel you are intentionally manipulating or are a threat to my crew, I will toss your metal ass out of an airlock without a moments hesitation. Am I clear?" Captain Morrow's voice almost boomed from the doorway, startling everyone and making John grateful he'd safetied his weapon already.

"Absolutely clear Captain. I truly meant no harm, this situation is just as bizarre and unexpected for me as it is for you." Bet replied, looking the Captain directly in the eyes as he did. Turning back to John, "John, I apologize to you specifically, but also to the rest of the crew as well," he said with a glance at Riley. "It won't happen again, and if I may…" Bet indicated the scanner in Riley's hand.

"May what?" Riley said.

Bet extended a finger toward the scanner, "I would like to transfer some data to your unit. All the information to answer all your questions about what is going on Dr."

Riley gave John a quick glance as John glanced at Captain Morrow. Riley shot her a look and received a curt nod in reply. With a bit of a mental chuckle at how they all exchanged glances, he held the scanner out at arms length, cautious and not wanting to leave John's side. Bet hesitated just a moment, then seemed to resolve himself and took a couple steps forward to place his finger atop the scanner. In a flash, a wall of data, chemical equations, molecular models and such started to display on the scanner's holoscreen. An entire library of information almost instantly available to him.

Riley gasped, "wow. It's going to take me days to sort through all this… fascinating."

"Fascinating indeed", John said as he brought the pistol up slightly, a motion intended to get Bet's attention. It apparently did as he immediately took a couple steps back.

"We need to have a long talk now," Captain Morrow said as she took a seat and motioned for everyone to join her.

Elena, silent and perfectly still through all of this, started gathering cups and delivering the tea. Riley and Bet joined the Captain, but John remained still, keeping his pistol pointed in Bet's direction.

28

As Elena served the tea and took her seat, she placed another cup in front of an empty seat for John.

"John?" Captain Morrow dipped her head at a seat opposite of Bet. "How about you enjoy this tea that was your bright idea and let us all talk like civilized humans. Put the sidearm away. That's my decision."

Bet paused his motions and glanced at the Captain. With a slow nod in her direction, Captain Morrow got the impression that if Bet still had biological eyes, they might be a little wet at that moment. Having chosen her words carefully, she was unsurprised to see Bet's reaction to being included as a civilized human being.

"Thank you Captain. I'm touched by your words. What questions can I answer first?"

"For starters, that thing you did with Riley's scanner. Have you been messing with the AI, the stations computers in similar manner?"

"No Captain. To answer the spirit of your question, I have not been 'messing' with anything. That said, I have been interacting with them. The same way Riley's use of his scanner is not 'messing' with it, but an appropriate interaction with the device's intended use. There are some, what society used to consider, basic implants that everyone gets. Before we even learned to talk, as children we received some basic neurological interfaces that allowed for basic daily interaction with technology and each other simpler. It was used to open doors, both physically and metaphorically, adjust the temperature in a room, dim the lights… that sort of thing.

This ability to naturally interface with the technology around us is why Riley is having great difficulty getting anything in the medical bay to function. Why I'm surprised John and his team were even able to operate any of the craft or equipment. So much of this station and the world around you is simply inaccessible to you.

As we got older, we would upgrade or update these implants for expanded interactions with our equipment, computers and each other. Parents, for instance could unlock or lock certain features for their children. A toddler should probably not be able to operate heavy machinery with a thought after all, or access sensitive knowledge far beyond their developmental years. For everyone, the general population that is, the basic transmission and communication protocols and abilities are there, but are far more limited in… shall we say, bandwidth and protocols. One might interface with a holoscreen to make selections or input simple data like Riley does with his fingers on his med scanner, but with a thought instead of the slower mechanical means of touching an input device.

Sending commands to the many devices that allow it without physical contact is one thing, but to read the output from a device like Riley's scanner in my mind's eye though, I would need to be holding the device. The lack of displays on consoles is because we would be in direct contact with them, thereby authorizing the bidirectional communication and giving us the display similar to what you might call a HUD. As I have not molested any of your equipment, save for one medical station I operated under the oversight of your team. Done simply to make some basic maintenance repairs to my limbs, you can rest assured I have made no file or data exchanges of any significance other than with Riley's device.

And yes, before you ask me to clarify that ambiguously phrased admission, I have silently interacted with the AI without your awareness. In what once would have been a standard practice of what you might call a handshake or greeting. I alerted the AI to my presence aboard the ship and transmitted my identification codes. The AI was of course already aware of my presence, so this is something of a standard formality when entering a station, building… pretty much anywhere that would have a central AI for the operation of the facility. These codes allow the ships system to locate me anywhere aboard and track my movements, activities and life signs. It's like… checking in with a receptionist and getting a visitors badge with a location beacon on it, but perhaps a little bit more advanced than that. Basic stuff when this station was operational and how accountability was kept for everyone aboard.

With this action, the station AI flooded me with questions

essentially. To the station, you and your crew are like ghosts. It can't see you and track you like it does me. I'm a part of its world, but it can only see the impact you have on the environment around you. It's mostly blind to you, but it knows you're there based on the body heat you emit, the changes in CO2 levels in a given area, that sort of thing. You are all just a shadow of environmental anomalies to it. Apparently, you gave it quite a fright when you came aboard. It ran a considerable number of systems checks and thought it was... well, I believe it phrased it as something like a 'cascading fault in logic and perception that required immediate maintenance or termination.' Fortunately, before the station terminated itself, it discovered patterns in some auditory sensors that were anomalous to any kind of issues it monitored them for. Basically, it started listening to and translating your speech with sensors intended for maintaining the station. Until I was able to assure it that you did in fact exist, the AI was still operating under the assumption that it may have been going insane. Like an AI version of schizophrenia."

"You've..." Captain Morrow sipped her tea and let out a small sigh. "I don't want to say 'poisoned' but I'm at a loss for words at the moment. Forgive me the accusatory nature of the word. You've... chemically altered my crew and transferred data in a way that to us appears as magic. Since we've just landed recently in a world a millennia more advanced than the one we left, just over a year ago from our perspective, we are at quite the disadvantage here. So what else don't I know? Don't WE know? I don't want any more frightening surprises."

Bet seemed to think for a moment and then something seemed to catch his eye about the captain's chair. "Don't be alarmed Captain, I'm about to activate a holoscreen."

Captain Morrow gave him a nod. With her permission granted, a holoscreen popped out of the armrest of the Captain's chair. Bet reached over and touched the other arm rest nearest him. The display began showing a 3D rendering of Bet. Slowly rotating around, limbs spread slightly. Lists and menus of data populated off to one side with properties and details showing up at the bottom of the display. Bet sat back. As he did so, a tablet like device rose out of the outside of the armrest he had just been touching.

"This," he said, indicating the display, "is me. All of my augmentations, abilities and details. There's a lot to list and I'm not sure what you would find important to mention now or not, and I imagine Elena and Riley will be most anxious to sort through it all. The device at your left is a 'tab" or, that's what we used to call them. It's part ships interface, part personal computer, capable of comms..." he looked at John. "I believe what you might refer to as C3. Command, control and communication. With proper authorization, it has full capabilities there. While it was often easier when we were alone to just do everything in our heads, it was hard to carry on a conversation or walk around when your entire field of view was occluded by data. It was also easier to collaborate with a physical device. Humanity never did quite let go of its affection for physical objects and gadgets. It contains all of this information and more. This data is also now available from any interface on the ship. This tab has been unlocked for you Captain. Authorization and credentials were managed by our neurological implants as they were as unique as a fingerprint, only harder to forge. As you do not have this ability, authorization will remain unlocked on that tab for your use, but I caution you. Anyone with physical access to that tab will have full administrative authority over the station. Will that satisfy your question Captain?"

"I believe it may. That will take some time to process and digest though. What else can you tell me now?"

"Along with my personal file, I've also transferred all data I have related to the station and status of the planet current to about 4 months before..." his words trailed off.

"Before you lost everyone?" Riley offered.

Bet nodded in agreement. "There are also tabs located at many of the consoles. There were personal devices, but it was not something we carried around everywhere. Each console station has a similar docking port as the one here in your chair. This allowed us to extract a portable version of what we were working on to travel with or to discuss with others, without having to sync through the greater network. It was a convenience thing."

One armrest of the chairs opened up and proffered a tab to its occupant. Everyone except John's. Bet obtained a tab from his own chair and slowly passed it to John. "Your chair appears to have already given up its tab to a previous occupant. Please, take this one. I've unlocked this tab for you and given it the same authorization the head of security would have had. Riley, you've got full access as our highest ranked medical personnel. Elena, same for you as head of engineering and systems. If I've assumed your rank and positions incorrectly, please note that you may pass them to any who should hold such authority."

Bet turned to face Captain Morrow directly. "If you would like any other such devices for key personnel, I will be more than happy to assist you with that. For now though, let's use the systems engineer tab. Elena, if you would hold that a little closer please… thank you. There you go, I've accessed the slightly obscure sub menu of a sub menu within the command structure. If you note the option flag in the code there which indicates the default state of access panels for these tabs. You would simply…" Bet had touched Elena's tab but now seemed to just stare at it with some concern as his words trailed off.

"Captain, I'm afraid my magic trick is a bit underwhelming. You see, I've forgotten that you would have no way to interface with these tabs. Simply providing them by bringing their existence to your attention was one thing, but I'm afraid now I must 'mess' with them. Do I have your permission to make attempts to alter station parameters to allow for physical interactive input? It would make far more of the station accessible to you and make these tabs far more useful than just pretty gadgets" Bet inquired.

Captain Morrow gave her assent and bet placed his hand palm down on his arm rest, his body went very still. The holographic display on each of the tabs shifted slightly to give a slight bubble impression which glowed around key points. New bubbles and cubes began to show up on the displays that somehow implied some intuitive notion of an ability to interact with them. John reached out and touched one of the floating cubes at the top of the display and a menu of options dropped out the bottom of it like a banner. He read over the menu noting keywords such as communications, personnel, station defenses and more. He touched the station defenses bubble. His holoscreen shifted and another series of boxes showed up above a long list of sorted sensors and weapons.

Elena looking over as John played with his tab chuckled. "It took me an hour to get my wrist comp to be able to navigate to that display on the command deck."

"You probably never would have gotten there if it weren't for the station AI assisting your attempts. It had already created much of this new interface system based on old maintenance routines, a bit of archaic code and such. Apparently it perfected a bit of it while working with a member of your crew who seemed quite interested in reviewing archives of logs and records. I'm still not sure how you all were able to bypass authorization though." Bet mused. The AI seems to be a bit…

reluctant to explain that to me now. Anyway, touch that bit of code there for the default state… yes, like that and you'll get a menu for available arguments. You'll have to forgive me, but that portion of the interface is something the AI and I were able to slap together by blending the access levels of certain elements a technician might be granted with a sort of physical interface system. Without the intended way to interface with these, I'm afraid you won't be rewriting any station code for a while, but perhaps best you get a bit more oriented with things first anyway."

Elena selected the option for the tab storage covers to default in an open state. The covers on every chair opened. Glancing around, there were a few opened ports around the rest of the kitchenette as well.

"The station is yours Captain. These tabs may help bridge the gap to many of its secrets and features which have been hidden to you."

"Thank you Bet, I'm sure this will be a great help. You speak as if you're in constant communication with the AI. How is that?" Morrow asked.

"Through my neural interface of course. You're still a ghost to it. As I said, it thought and still acknowledges the possibility that you are simply an artifact of degraded systems and essentially a figment of its imagination, so to speak. It doesn't really have any imagination at all."

"Can we interact with it better without implants?"

"Somewhat, Captain, through the tabs. However, it's of great difficulty to the AI to interface that way. It's not that intelligent or interesting as far as AI goes. It's really intended to be more of an interface for the neurological augmeta." Bet explained.

<h1 style="text-align:center">29</h1>

Aurion Station's corridors thrummed with a resurgence of life—an eerie echo of its prime centuries ago. Even just the name for the planet and star given to them from Bet, the awkward synthorganic colonist, seemed to make everything feel more comfortable and homely to the crew. Lights glowed steady where they once flickered, and the air smelled crisper from newly activated or serviced filtration units, each whirring to cycle out residual staleness. Even so, sections of corridors remained scarred by past destruction—sealed bulkheads and collapsed passageways where the incident had ravaged everything beyond hope of repair.

Yet for all its battered edges and missing sections, the station was stirring. Captain Morrow could feel it in the subtle hum beneath her feet, a sign that power grids had been reconnected, thrusting the old star-fortress into a hesitant rebirth.

Holographic readouts that once blinked only sporadically now displayed a patchwork of data: stable environmental controls for half the station, partial scanning arrays, and the barest flicker of a defense grid. Captain Morrow stood at the central console, coffee mug in hand —an indulgence she'd rarely permitted herself since resources were at a premium. But today, a sip of something strong felt earned.

Around her, consoles flickered with system status updates—some lines in crisp English, others in more advanced text reminiscent of Bet's time. Elena Park scrolled through the labyrinth of menus, guiding the station's AI through reinitializations that were long overdue.

"It's responding quicker now," Elena said, fingers dancing across a holo-keyboard, an addition she had worked with Bet to aid interaction with the station's systems. The holographic keyboard was very useful when working with numbers and code where their new voice recognition system was not as accurate or effective. "We can't bring every module online, but the central ring is stable, life support's at seventy percent in occupied zones. Weapons remain questionable. The event must've fried half the arrays." Still unsure of what exactly happened to the station, planet and its citizens, they had started simply referring to it as 'the event'.

Morrow set her coffee down, scanning a schematic. "Focus on scanning first. We don't want any surprises sneaking up on us. And if we can patch through exterior visual feeds, let's confirm that stealth satelite is parked where Bet said it would be."

Elena nodded. "Working on it."

Morrow's comm alerted her to an incoming request from Riley.

"Riley, what's new? How are the latest colonists?"

"All good Captain. No issues so far, everyone's in excellent health and ready to get to work."

"That's great news. How many more left to wake?"

"That's why I'm calling Captain. The initial colonial workforce is awake now. Give these latest additions a day or so to adjust and we can start sending them down to the planet anytime you're ready."

"We'll keep them up here working on the station for now. I want a ground team to investigate a bit before I start sending everyone down at once."

"Whenever you're ready Captain."

Further below, in the station's engineering sections, a coalition of newly awakened crew and Bet himself worked under dim, resurrected floodlights. The clang of metal, hiss of plasma torches, and hum of maintenance drones filled the air. Patches and bypass circuits covered old event damage, and portable tool kits from the colony ship mingled with strange hybrid gear left behind by the advanced colonists.

John stepped carefully through a half-collapsed corridor, his posture guarded. He found Bet crouched beside a mess of cables, splicing them into a console once used to regulate thermal distribution.

"You sure that's the right circuit?" John asked, noticing Bet's inhuman hand deftly twisting wires and fusing fiber optic lines far more nimbly than any normal human could.

Bet glanced up, mechanical eyes reflecting the flicker of sparks from the work going on around him. "If we don't reconnect these lines, the station's cooling loop can't reroute overflow heat. We'll have power surges every time we spool up more generators. Trust me on this."

John exhaled, crossing arms over his chest. "I suppose I have to."

John seemed to be warming up to Bet as time passed. His knowledge and skills far surpassed anyone else. Aside from being astoundingly brilliant, Bet was also exceedingly helpful with a work ethic that would have exhausted John. Bet never seemed to stop and rest. It seemed he didn't have any need for sleep. Occasionally, Bet would stop for a short time for what John thought looked like meditation, but would then get right back to work in short order.

Around them, Amir seemed to float around on the outskirts of all activity as he documented everything—holorecording the half-repaired corridor, the flaking station walls covered in advanced signage, the scuffed logos of a colony lost to time. Vogel and Walters, carried fresh power cells from the colony ship—lugging them to reinforce the station's battered core.

"We'll have the new cells installed soon," Walters said, wiping sweat from his brow. "Then the station can handle more than just partial lighting and full station gravity. Maybe even the habitation ring next."

Bet twisted the final wire, reattaching a panel. "Not too quickly. We need a safe ramp-up or we'll blow half the nodes."

John quirked a brow. "You seem to know this station's system architecture inside out—makes sense, if you grew up here."

The synthorganic gave a short nod, an edge of sadness in his voice. "I sort of did. I spent my first twenty years or so on the surface, but haven't gone back too often since then. It's been so many years... yet it's like muscle memory. I remember how she breathes, even though her voice has changed."

No one replied. They all felt it—a faint ache for the ghosts that once walked these corridors.

After waking the last of the initial colonial settlement wave, Riley supervised the activation of a few more med pods they'd unearthed in another sealed compartment of the station. Basic stasis chambers, different from the ship's old capsules. These were more modern capsules built for medical use with far more features to treat a patient than the crude long term sleep chambers aboard their ship. Clara, brought in to assist with the station's biological systems, squinted at the readouts.

"These pods are older than I expected," Clara murmured, brushing dust off a console. "But the hardware is advanced in ways that ours aren't—modular designs, specialized for quick surgeries, augmentation procedures." She cast a thoughtful look at Elena's notes.

"If we get these working, we might have a way to offer the colonists some better options than the basic gene therapy they got on the way here."

Clara paused at a battered interface, glancing at logs. "Though it'll take a lot of time and resources to make them usable again. Last thing we need is to toss a crew member in and have the pod short out mid-procedure."

Riley offered an encouraging smile. "One step at a time. At least we have something to work with."

Back on the Command Deck, Captain Morrow surveyed a newly consolidated schematic: sections in green meant stable corridors and modules, yellow for partial atmospheric or structural compromise, and red for sealed or collapsed areas. Her expression softened—only a fraction of the station lit up green, but it was progress. Months ago (subjectively, for them), it had all been silent, derelict.

Bet's mechanical voice crackled through the overhead speakers: "Captain, the engineering deck is reconnected to the main distribution grid. Cooling loop stable. Recommend we spin up primary life support units four and five to reduce load on the backups."

She tapped the console to confirm. "Acknowledged. Elena, bring them online carefully. Let's avoid blowing anything."

Elena's voice piped in, "Understood, Captain. Initiating start-up... now."

A muted rumble vibrated through the station's core. Displays winked off momentarily, then stabilized, and the overhead lights brightened a notch. The screens flickered to life with new data feeds: temperatures, radiation levels, system logs. Morrow let out a breath she didn't know she'd been holding. Step by step, they were bringing the station back.

30

Over the course of a few weeks, the station began to come back to life. Newly awake colonists began to fill the corridors and areas of the station with life as they worked about in their areas of profession and worked to learn the inherited technology now available to them. Even as things continued to improve for the time traveling colonial mission, tensions lingered. John's private wariness about Bet's inadvertent chemical influence on the crew still weighed on him—though Bet swore he'd "turned it off." John had forgiven Bet for the incident, but it punctuated just how out of place they were in this new world. There was also the knowledge that entire sections of the station might contain similar secrets or traps. Unavoidable consequences of differences between the society that built the station and the complete lack of augmeta in the new colonists. Outside of the immediate issues that bothered John, If the unknown threat that ravaged the colony truly remained out there, each new corridor they opened could lead to old nightmares. The irritation of seeing a threat around every corner grated on John's mood as he struggled to accept this mission would not be the peaceful retirement from danger he had hoped it would be.

Captain Morrow glanced over her shoulder at Amir, who'd just appeared in the doorway, note-taker in hand. "How's morale?" she asked quietly, aware that a large chunk of the crew—those from stasis —no longer remained asleep to preserve resources. Ration bars and nutrient packs were fairly standard issue most meals as they tended the hydroponics bay and waited for the initial cycles to reach maturity and begin producing sustainable food sources.

Amir shrugged. "Better than you'd think. The ones awake are excited to see progress, to have real work. The new technology and space station is a fun puzzle for most of them. Having such a head start on, well everything isn't missed in their considerations. And Bet's presence, while… complicated, has given us hope we might truly understand how all this works if not what happened." He offered a small, rueful smile. "Maybe even recover enough that colonizing this system is not such a pioneer's struggle."

Morrow gave a slow nod. "Keep an ear out for any sign of discontent or fear. We're juggling a lot of unknowns. If the station is mostly functional, that just raises the question of what else might be hidden."

With the power grids shored up and vital systems humming, the station entered a new phase of its improbable resurrection. Each green icon on Morrow's console represented a small victory—a hallway cleared of debris, another airlock back in service, an ancient data node reinitialized. Yet for every success, a dozen questions remained.

Questions in mind, Captain Morrow came to a decision and touched her comms panel. "John, ready your team. Elena and Bet, join John in the hangar deck. I want a preliminary recon of the surface."

John seated himself in the pilot seat of the station's transport shuttle as Han strapped into the copilot seat. The rest were still putting on their suits and strapping in to the crew section in the rear of the shuttle. Bet leaned in between John and Han briefly as he passed, touching the console. The navigation windows populated and a preflight checklist popped up in front of John who huffed at the sudden help. Han turned to look at Bet who was already headed to his seat in the rear.

"Bet," Han called after him. "Thanks. You're going to have to teach me to do that sometime soon."

Bet nodded at her and said, "Sure. As soon as we can get some basic augments done. All this technology will work so much better for you once you've got a neural interface."

The flight down to the planet was uneventful. The shuttle craft descended smoothly and transitioned to atmospheric flight with almost no perceptible changes. John and Han leveraged their tabs and some additional interface improvements that allowed some compatibility with their wrist computers. Bet, positioned himself just behind the pilot's seat, ready to assist if there was any trouble, but otherwise content to let them get used to the craft. The first destination was a flyover to conduct a more detailed scan of the impact sight northwest of the city. Once Han indicated the data had been collected,

John turned the ship toward the city. Han aided as they both viewed the navigation window, following the course Bet had suggested. They eased the ship down to land in what appeared to have once been a beautiful park in a southeast corner of the city. Although it was a largely overgrown field, John was struck by the absence of trees on the planet.

Despite the absence of taller vegetation, the team found mobility difficult as they exited the shuttle. The shorter grass equivalent and strange shrubs, vines and various other plants grew in a dense mat of vegetation about waste deep. Serena took the lead, pulling a vibrosword from her tool belt.The thick handled cylinder, just long enough to grip with two hands in a suit, thrummed to life with a flick of her thumb. From the end shot out a narrow bar that had a white sheen over a metallic core. Almost instantly the edges of the bar began to emit a soft glow and a slight humm could be heard. As Serena slashed at the dense overgrowth, the blade seemed to pass through vines as big as her wrist as if they weren't even there. The ultrasonic vibrations of the blade destabilizing the cellular structure of the plants while an electromagnetic field contained the super heated cutting edge. The Vibrosword cut through just about any organic matter like a plasma torch with a razor's edge. The path ahead would become far easier to navigate after that.

Casting a sidelong glance at John, Serena said wryly, "it's not exactly a machete, but it seems to work pretty well." and gave a slight shrug.

"Better than a machete," he replied, stepping back and motioning everyone else to give her some room as well. "Ok landscaper, you should have the waypoint in your HUD. Looks like we're headed for that first tall building dead ahead, show us the way. Han, you're covering Serena. I'll bring up the rear." John announced over comms, more for Captain Morrow's benefit than anyone on the planet. Everyone was already moving with a purpose. "Captain, we are moving toward objective Bravo, how copy? over."

"Loud and clear John. Stay safe down there and bring back some good news."

The captain's calm and casual tone helped ease John's mind slightly. It made the mission not feel so much like an all too familiar military operation. As he walked, pausing every step or two while Serena cut the path forward, John scanned the area around him. He could feel the strain of the increased gravity on him. Every step felt so much harder. His suit felt like it weighed a ton and if it didn't have a built in mechanical assist system, he would find even walking to be a laborious chore. The augments the rest of his team received in stasis must have given them a huge advantage over him. Laboriously, he turned his head to gaze in every direction. The dense vegetation spread far and wide, covering the ground like a plush carpet. The sun was so bright, he found himself squinting even with the shading turned up to maximum on his visor. John wasn't entirely sure, but he could swear the sky was a different shade of blue than he'd ever seen in his time on Earth. It almost reminded him of a much brighter weird jungle version of his home on Mars.

"Bet, do you know if they ever managed to terraform Mars?" John radioed, to satisfy his curiosity and to kill the silence that would keep everyone tense. The slight strain in his voice betrayed his physical struggles.

"There were many attempts over the years. Most failed and the minor successes had little impact overall, but it was the source of so much knowledge. It's my understanding that politics got in the way and terraforming experiments moved to other systems. I don't believe the Mars atmosphere was ever restored to a 'habitable' state. There were large domed cities there at one point. Vast areas of open air under sealed domes that supposedly felt pretty close to having an atmosphere and being outside. Perhaps that was just compared to a space station though. I'm not sure. I wish I'd gotten a chance to visit Sol. That would have been nice to see."

John didn't respond straight away, absorbing Bet's words. He wasn't sure why they jarred him; maybe it was the reminder that back home —or what used to be home—things didn't always go according to plan, either. His visor's HUD showed Serena's progress cutting through the dense mat of vegetation. The broad shapes of ruined buildings loomed in the distance, their surfaces scorched and collapsed in places. If he looked carefully, he could almost see faint scorch marks and splintered alloy beams—testaments to whatever catastrophe had struck.

A rustle from up ahead and to John's left made him tense for a split second—just a patch of vines swaying and getting tugged as Bet passed by. The synthorganic's steps were nearly soundless otherwise, mechanical joints moving with practiced ease. More unnerving than the lack of noise he was accustomed to Bet making on the station was the near-glow Bet gave off in bright sunlight, the solar rays glinting off patches of metallic plating.

"You alright?" Han asked softly over a direct comm channel, noticing John had hesitated.

John cleared his throat. "Yeah. All good." He forced a reassuring nod and resumed scanning their surroundings. The day's warmth—if that was what it could be called—felt thicker and more humid than anything John was used to from lunar or Martian cold climates. The environment demanded adaptation, but at least the suits had decent environmental controls to keep him from overheating.

The group advanced another dozen meters. Vines parted smoothly under Serena's vibrosword, leaving behind stems that hissed and curled where the blade seared them. Occasionally, she had to shake off coils of the vegetation that wrapped around her arm or legs, determined not to be slowed down.

"Captain," John called over the main channel. "We're about two hundred meters from the large structure we identified as a primary target. Looks like a tower or maybe a multi-level building, possibly four stories tall, no more. We should get eyes on the interior soon."

"Copy," Morrow's voice replied. "We're picking up your helmet cams. Marcus has a great link established now. Great resolution. The vantage looks… well, I can't say pleasant, but it's progress. Any sign of local wildlife the feeds missed?"

John gave a minimal grunt. "None so far. Just an overgrown field. Still no trees, either. Strange place, Captain—like the forest never got past the underbrush stage. Probably for the same reason I don't see any buildings taller than four stories. Most are single story and appear to take up a larger footprint rather than using vertical space. The gravity down here is quite noticeable."

A momentary pause crackled over the comm. Then Morrow responded, "Keep me posted. If there's anything alive, it might not appreciate visitors. Clara cautions that wildlife may be much smaller with an increase in density to compensate for the environment. I think we're all looking forward to encountering alien life, just be safe about it. Morrow, out."

Han adjusted the brightness in her visor, swiping a finger along the inside edge of her helmet. "Is it just me, or is this star about to scorch my retinas out?" she muttered.

John chuckled grimly. "You're not alone. Bet, your eyes do better in this glare, right?"

Bet nodded. "They were modified for high-radiation zones. I'm experiencing no discomfort from the light, if that's what you're asking.

Coming from space and artificial lighting you can set to your own comforts, I'm not at all surprised you find this to be so bright. You'd probably feel the same way on any planet around a similar g-type star right now."

From the front, Serena paused, glancing over her shoulder. "We can trade if you want, John. You lead with your fancy ocular implant buddy, give my arm a break. Besides, aren't you missing your cardio today?"

John shook his head. "No thanks. I'm getting plenty of exercise back here. I didn't get a year's worth of relaxed gene therapy like you did, so don't you go falling out on me now. Let's just keep pressing—there's only so much day left before we consider heading back, and you can't seriously convince me you're getting the least bit fatigued yet. "

Bet let his gaze wander across the horizon, as though searching for something. "If the city structure is still partially intact, there might be an entrance not far from here. Possibly underground levels, too—we built subterranean power grids and research stations for environmental control. If the event didn't flood them with radiation, that could be a treasure trove of data."

John grunted. "We'll see about that." He motioned for Serena to continue, and the group trudged forward through another stretch of dense vegetation. The thick, vine-like growth and wide, leafy shrubs slapped against their suits with each step."Besides, if the damage down here were due to some sort of nuclear event, we'd be seeing radiation spikes still. I'm not showing any residual radiation."

Bet grunted acknowledgement. John thought nothing of it, but Bet was struggling not to correct him. The details of accuracy and possibilities that troubled his mind were those of a scientist and not particularly relevant at the moment as long as there was still no radiation being detected. They would simply find out soon enough, besides, it wasn't like it was going to affect him like it would these ancient historical humans who obviously had no idea about the many other things which could cause radiological issues within confined spaces. He was on an expedition with such fragile humans and their antiquated ignorance, if only he'd been a zeno-archaeologist like his mother had wanted.

At last, the looming structure rose directly before them—a massive edifice of fused alloys and polyglass. Chunks of upper floors had collapsed, leaving exposed beams jutting out like broken ribs. The surrounding debris left scattered piles of rubble half-hidden beneath layers of vines which extended dozens of meters up the sides of the tall structures.

Serena tested the ground with a cautious step. "Watch your footing. There's a dip here, maybe an old walkway or crater." She slashed another patch of stubborn growth. "We've come this far; we might as well see what's inside, right?"

John consulted his HUD, verifying minimal radiation readings—safe enough for exposure. "Agreed," he said, then keyed his mic. "Captain, we've reached the building. No immediate sign of structural hazards, other than missing a chuck of the top floors, but we'll proceed carefully. Main floor looks intact."

"Copy," Morrow answered. "If it looks too unstable, don't risk it. We can always explore another sector."

Vogel, who hadn't said a word up until this point, keyed her mic, "good, get me out of this fucking kudzu! I haven't seen it this bad since I was a kid running around my grandpa's farm in GA."

John looked closer at the vines. It was kudzu. He'd seen it grown in some hydro-farms for food, fuel, medicine and rapid growing compostable material to enrich soil on Mars. But this did not look like any version of kudzu he was familiar with. For one, he'd never seen kudzu with such thick vines and stalks before.

Han stepped alongside Serena to help clear rubble, gripping a portable sensor drone from his pack. "We can run a quick structural check. If it's passable, we find an entry point. If not..." He shrugged, giving John a pointed look. "We haul ourselves back to the shuttle."

"Bet, any idea if this was a commercial district, residential, or something else?" Elena asked.

Bet cocked his head, as though recalling an ancient mental map. "I believe it was a research ward, possibly a data archiving facility upstairs. If so, the ground floor might hold labs or offices. There were some vertical gardens around here too. They were beautiful, not like this."

A brief hush followed as they took in the battered façade. Serena deactivated her vibrosword momentarily, letting the humming blade retract into its cylindrical handle. Seeing no indication of trouble from Han's drone, she spoke up. "We're close to the door—well, whatever's left of it. Let's do this."

She advanced, the team fanning out behind her. Han snatching her returning drone from the air as she walked. Overhead, the glaring star beamed down mercilessly, highlighting the unnatural emptiness of the surrounding field. John paused to sweep the horizon once more. The imposing silence unsettled him—no rustle of animals, no insect hum, only the faint whirr of suits and the hiss of the gentle breeze across vine-laden rubble.

"It's… too quiet," he muttered softly. "Let's stay on guard."

He resumed forward steps. Beneath them, the ground sloped downward, revealing a jagged entryway. Twisted metal doors lay half-buried in a mound of rubble and vines. A faint breeze drifted from the opening, carrying a stale, musty odor that spoke of centuries of abandonment.

Yet through it all, the station's away team persisted—pushing deeper into a city that once thrived and now stood in silent ruin. Above them, in orbit, Aurion Station and Captain Morrow watched, ready to offer guidance or call them back if the unknown hazards proved too great.

With Serena's vibrosword leading the way, they stepped into the threshold of lost knowledge and a possible new future.

31

The team descended a once grand staircase entry, now overgrown to the point of being a gentle sloped ramp toward the entrance of the beat up building and in through the broken doors. As they passed over the threshold, they walked out of the bright daylight on Aurion and into a dark cavernous tomb. The old entry floor was covered in a thick layer of dirt that thinned the farther in it went until fading into a fine silt dust that seemed to cover everything. The open area felt pitch black after being out in the bright sun. Once lined with tinted windows, every pane of polyglass that formed 3 of the walls was now covered with vegetation so thick that no light could shine through. One by one, the automated lights turned on each of the team's helmets. Illuminated strips down arms and legs began to softly glow, giving each member of the team a slightly illuminated outline. The suits did not emit enough light to do much more than give each other a sense of position and movement for the rest of the team. Serena, being the first one through the door, immediately switched on her helmet's advanced imaging system. The helmet used multiple ranges of infrared, low light amplification and lidar like systems to overlay an enhanced image in the visor. Serena dimmed the brightness of the overlay to a comfortable shadow, allowing the flashlight illuminated area to be clearly visible through it, but not so dim the details it provided for the shadows were lost.

"Every time I use this night vision, I feel like I'm in a video game," Serena said.

"I never was able to get used to this system," John spoke up. "The thing just makes my eyes want to go back and forth between whats on the visor and what's out there."

"Oh, you're one of those?" Han spoke up. "You ever try the eye dominance settings?"

John grimaced, "That crap's even worse. Doesn't matter if I kept the overlay on one side or the other, that just makes me go cross eyed."

Serena laughingly said, "well, that explains your aim."

"He does favor that antique on his hip. I always thought it was because he wanted to be some sort of cowboy from an old flic or book or something. A real romantic for the Western's" Han prodded.

"You see anything about me that says cowboy?"

"Well, now that you mention it," Vogel joined in, "you've about got that Maverick attitude down, like you're ready to ride out into a sunset alone. Bit of a hero complex too."

"You're all real damn funny." John rolled his eyes, secretly enjoying the camaraderie.

"You favor that relic of a rock thrower on your hip because you can't focus on the visor's targeting system with newer weapons." Bet stated, though it had a slight uptake in pitch at the end to almost imply a question.

"I do just fine with the visor's targeting system, I just prefer my rocks to have their own sights. My pointy sticks too. I've seen energy weapons blocked or disabled. Sometimes you just need to go kinetic. Nobody expects it anymore."

"There's a good reason nobody expects it anymore. As for the focus thing, I think I can help you with that when we get back to the station, if you'd like."

"How are you going to do that?" John asked, "I've already spent hundreds of hours getting as used to this as I'm going to get."

"I'm going to give you what you want. Remove the distance issue from the layers in your visor that causes your focus issues and put the image directly into your optic nerve." Bet offered.

"Well you can count me right out of that party," Vogel said, "nobody's poking at my optic nerve or eyeballs. Just thinking about that shit makes me twitch!"

John contemplated this for a moment. "So that's the neural interface you were talking about?"

"Yes." Bet replied, "that's one of the things it does. It interfaces with your tools and equipment. You'd be holding your weapon, and the targeting system would show up in your minds perception of what you see, just as if it were on the vizor or in front of you. A full customizable HUD designed specifically for you show up with a thought with perfect clarity and it lets you send commands too."

Bet walked over to a desk centered along the back wall in this open entryway. He touched the desk and a holodisplay came to life on the wall behind the desk, listing several key features and tenants of the building and presumably the floor and office numbers where they could be found.

"Now that's handy!" Serena said as she walked up to the desk. "I'd have never known there was any tech in this desk."

"Still not touching my eyes." Vogel mumbled.

"Most of those names mean nothing to me, but look at that one there." Han said as she pointed at a line toward the bottom of the list. "Biotechnical. I wonder if it's just office and administrative crap or if there's a lab in there."

Bet scrolled the list down farther, revealing several subterranean levels for laboratories, datacenter and an engineering firm. "These were why I brought you to this building. I'd expect this will be essential for re-establishing a presence here on the planet and maybe bringing some of you into this millennium."

John shot him a look he figured would be lost in the dark, but he saw Bet's synthetic skin form something like a smirk in reply. Before he could say anything, Captain Morrow's voice came over the comms, "Bet, can you get a floor plan or any more information to bring back?"

"I've already obtained it Captain, though it was as accurate as a blueprint in its time, we can't trust that everything is going to be in good order. I've also queried the building's status. The power has been gone for a long time, only a few stations like this one will have their own backup power sources. The building as a whole is offline. We'll need to provide power somehow if we want to be able to open doors and explore with some illumination."

"Excellent work. Proceed to objective Charlie and then get back up here. I don't want you camping out like a bunch of scouts on a weekend trip yet."

John put his hand in the air and rotated it slightly, indicating to his team it was time to move. "Aye Captain. We'll head to Han's toy store now."

Once back out in the sun, each of the team disabled their visual overlay as the visors dimmed automatically, except Serena. Instead, she lowered a complete blackout visor and turned up the illumination of her overlay.

"Going full gamer mode?" Han asked with a slight tap to the back of her helmet.

"Well, unless you've got some welding goggles, I can't take much more of this bright sun today, and now we're walking right into it as it sets."

Bet tapped her on the shoulder and populated her visor with a map overlay.

"I'm not sure i'll ever get used to that either." She muttered mostly to herself. "Thanks though."

Taking point again, Serena lead the team down what remained of once paved walkways and roads. She thought it was odd to have roads, but no parking lots. Patches of paved areas were broken up by sections where the vines had broken through, eventually turning most of the road to gravel and making a river of growth over the road they had to climb over and cut through. After only a block or two, Han caught sight of an odd bulge in the vines and moved to investigate.

"Han, what are you up to?" John asked.

"There's something over here, I want to check it out."

Han removed her vibrosword and began to surgically remove a mat of vines to reveal what was creating the bulge beneath them. Once she got a bit of a look at what it was, her work intensified significantly, pulling vines away in a hurry like a child unwrapping a present.

"What is it?" Vogel asked.

"You're not going to believe this shit!" Han gasped out in clipped breaths as she worked feverishly to remove the vines. With a couple more whacks, she rolled back the vines like a carpet to reveal what was underneath. "Bet, is this what I think it is?"

"If you were thinking that is a Galactic Harley Anti-gravitational Personal Transport system for single occupant, then yes."

"A flying motorcycle! You've got to be kidding me! Folks used to zoom around on these?" Han asked as she looked at Bet, eyes as big as saucers behind her visor.

"A number of personal transport systems were used here. Many were single occupant such as this. Most were a bit more stable though. The models known as Flying Carpets were quite popular as personal transports." Bet offered.

"Ok kids, enough with the toys, we've got some walking to do here and John looks like he's struggling." Serena said.

John tried to shoot her a look or voice an argument to the teasing, but quickly discovered he had none to offer. He settled on an acknowledging grunt instead. The difference between their genetic modifications and his gym strength was wearing him out. For all the extra strength his muscles provided, the additional weight they created seemed to thwart entirely. John was feeling rather weak and he was not at all happy about it.

Han was poking at the bike, trying to understand the controls. Bet reached out and laid a finger on it. Suddenly a small holographic display emerged signaling a red indicator in what appeared to be a universal dead battery symbol. Han's shoulder's slumped when she saw this.

"You couldn't possibly have thought you were going to ride that thing did you?" Serena said.

"You'd look like the dumb soldier dressed in a white plastic shipping container that flew his speeder into the tree… you remember, the one in that ancient film Amir picked for movie nights. The one with the magicians that fought with glow sticks." Vogel said.

John couldn't help but laugh at the thought and slapped Han on the back. "Come on crazy, we'll find you some safer toys to play with soon. On the bright side, at least there's no trees here for you to run into."

Before they left, Han marked the location on the team map. A location marker she named 'Master Han's speeder, get your own.' Seeing the indicator pop up on their maps as the helmet visors updated each other, a chorus of chuckles ensued and a few heads shook. The team made their way toward the edge of the city where they found the large lot of construction equipment they had seen from the station's scans. Han was excited at all the equipment and Vogel seemed oddly taken with what appeared to be some form of tractor. Once again, none of the controls seemed to be available to the team until Bet touched them.

"Ok, that is getting really old." Han said.

"Like I've said before, every human in the galaxy had the appropriate interface for this. Just because you come from a time barely after humanity climbed out of the trees, doesn't change the facts. This is old and basic technology, as standard as your rocks, sticks and loin clothes." Bet retorted.

"Well you don't have to be a dick about it," Han huffed.

"Calm down you two. I'm sure Elena can figure something out if nothing else," John said, interrupting any further comments.

Marcus's voice came through the comms, "Ground crew, Alvarez has informed me of an increase in solar activity. The Captain has requested immediate return to the station. How copy? Over."

"Loud and clear Marcus. How much time have we got?" John replied.

Alvarez came on channel, "You're going to have a bumpy ride even if you dusted off now. The first flairs will be passing by in about eight minutes. You can't beat it back, you're going to have to surf some solar winds on the way up. I can't be absolutely sure, but it looks like this will be getting worse though, so the Captain said get your asses back up here ASAP. I'm already sending the data we have to the shuttle for navigation."

Bet looked toward the sun with a curious look. "We'd better go."

That was all the encouragement anyone needed. The team practically ran the many km back to the shuttle. When they got there, Serena said between gasps for breath, "Han, I'm now of the opinion you need to get that bike working, and Bet, I hope you know where the dealership is."

John had to stop twice to throw up along the way. Completely spent of all energy, his muscles were screaming in agony as he sat down in the pilot seat. He chuckled to himself as he strapped in and began preflight startup and checks. The attention to his task was the only thing keeping his mind off the way Bet seemed to have a magical touch with the equipment and what he had said about the visual overlays. While those were all well and good, the gravity was going to be his weakness unless there was something Bet could do to help with that. With the last of the checks done and green lights across the board, they took off and headed back to the station.

32

Elena was seated at a console in engineering browsing through the station's library of information. After several hours of studying briefs, journals and every other resource she could find on the advancements made to her reactor and drive designs, she came across a brief that made her jaw drop. As Elena stared at the holoscreen, her heart thumped hard in her chest, leaving something close to pain as if it had actually skipped a beat. There on the screen was her name in a brief she'd found in a communications log. The idea that her work was referenced so many centuries after she essentially vanished from humanity the day the colony ship departed made her mouth dry and goose bumps form on her skin. An electric feeling shot pleasantly up her spine and massaged the inside of her scalp with the validation. Even with as good as it made her feel, she still found it as unsettling as discovering her own in memoriam marker.

Engineering Brief: Integrated Particle Harvesting, Magnetic Reconnection Acceleration, and Zero-Point Energy Antimatter Production System

Presenter: Dr. Morales, Chief Engineer, Stellar Energy Systems Division
   Audience: Lead Scientist, Antimatter Research Initiative

Introduction:
   Dr. Elena Park's groundbreaking work in antimatter production and artificial magnetic reconnection laid the foundation for our latest advancements in large-scale antimatter synthesis and energy harvesting. Building upon her principles, we've developed an

integrated system that combines solar wind particle harvesting, magnetic reconnection acceleration, and quantum vacuum energy storage to enable continuous antimatter production for energy applications. This briefing outlines the engineering framework of the system.

1. High-Energy Particle Harvesting from Solar Winds

Concept:
We start by capitalizing on the vast and abundant energy of the solar wind. Charged particles (primarily protons and electrons) streaming from the Sun are collected using a magnetic funnel system.

Key Components:
- Magnetic Funnel Array: A large-scale magnetic field generator captures solar wind particles. The fields are configured as a wide-mouth cone that focuses charged particles into an electrostatic storage grid.
- Dynamic Field Orientation: Leveraging Dr. Park's work on magnetic reconnection, the funnel fields adjust dynamically to optimize particle collection based on solar activity and magnetic flux density in the solar wind.

Output:
Collected particles are funneled into electrostatic grids, where they are slowed, separated, and stored. These grids maintain a charged environment to ensure particle containment without excessive energy dissipation.

2. Magnetic Reconnection Acceleration

Concept:
To achieve the energy levels necessary for antimatter generation, we accelerate the stored particles using artificial magnetic reconnection events.

Key Processes:
- Magnetic Reconnection Chambers: Particles from the electrostatic grids are fed into controlled magnetic reconnection zones. These chambers replicate astrophysical reconnection events but on a

contained, industrial scale.

- Particle Energization: During reconnection, the magnetic fields release stored energy in bursts, accelerating particles to relativistic speeds. This process follows Dr. Park's model of wave-particle interaction in collisionless plasmas.

Engineering Note:

We've implemented gradient field stabilizers to regulate particle acceleration and prevent energy losses. This ensures that a significant percentage of the particles reach the target energy range for quantum phenomena induction.

3. Quantum Vacuum Energy Storage

Concept:

Once the particles achieve sufficient energy, they are released into a quantum vacuum reactor where their kinetic energy is used to induce zero-point energy fluctuations.

Mechanism:

- High-Energy Particle Interactions: The accelerated particles collide in a vacuum chamber designed to exploit quantum field polarization effects. These interactions amplify quantum fluctuations, allowing us to "tap" into the vacuum energy field.

- Energy Harvesting: Specialized converters transform the amplified zero-point energy into a usable form. This energy is used to power the antimatter synthesis system.

Advancement:

Dr. Park's original theories on quantum field manipulation provided the basis for our vacuum polarization methods. By controlling the spacetime environment within the reactor, we've maximized energy yields with minimal input losses.

4. Antimatter Production

Concept:

The zero-point energy harvested from the quantum vacuum reactor powers an advanced particle collider to produce antimatter on an industrial scale.

* * *

Production Process:

- Positron and Antiproton Creation: High-energy collisions of protons and electrons (derived from the harvested solar wind particles) generate positrons and antiprotons.

- Magnetic Antimatter Traps: Newly created antimatter particles are captured in Penning traps and stored in magnetic containment fields. Cryogenic systems ensure stability over extended durations.

Efficiency Breakthrough:

By integrating zero-point energy as the primary power source, we've reduced the net energy cost of antimatter production by over 80% compared to initial systems that relied on fusion or conventional power generation.

5. Scalable Applications

System Benefits:

- Continuous Operation: The integration of solar wind harvesting with zero-point energy reactors enables a self-sustaining energy cycle. The antimatter produced not only fuels propulsion systems but also powers the entire harvesting and production operation.

- Massive Yield: Using this system, a single large-scale facility located in high solar wind activity regions (e.g., near the heliosphere) can produce grams of antimatter annually—a dramatic leap compared to laboratory-scale outputs.

Future Development:

- Space-Based Harvesting: Positioning these facilities in orbit or at Lagrange points near the Sun would significantly enhance collection efficiency and scalability.

- Refinement of Quantum Energy Interfaces: Continued optimization of the vacuum reactors could further amplify zero-point energy yields, enabling even greater antimatter production.

Conclusion

Dr. Park's contributions to magnetic reconnection and antimatter production gave us the tools to engineer a system capable of reshaping energy generation and propulsion technologies. By combining particle harvesting, magnetic acceleration, and quantum energy conversion, we've created a self-sustaining, scalable process that brings humanity closer to mastering the antimatter economy.

We are seeking feedback on potential refinements to the reconnection chambers and quantum vacuum interfaces which would be invaluable as we finalize the next generation of this system. Together, we're not just harnessing the power of the cosmos—we're redefining it.

End of Brief

Elena sat at the futuristic space station console stunned, just staring at the holoscreen. *Unbelievable,* she thought. They had actually done it. As the implications began to flood through her thoughts, she came to a startling realization. If this colony had been a waypoint or even an endpoint for humanity's intergalactic travels, there must be an energy source in system. A galactic gas station of sorts. Hadn't Bet said he was working near the sun when the colony ending event happened? Why would he have been in that part of space if there weren't some destination? His ship alone did not have sensors and scientific equipment enough to substantiate his claims for data collection and scientific research as he had implied. Could that be why so many of his adaptations or modifications were centered around being able to better handle the increased radiation levels and environment such as one would encounter at a facility so close to the star?

Elena jumped out of her seat so fast she nearly lost control of her body in the station's lower gravity. Mag-boots engaged and she managed to catch herself with a grip at the edge of the console. It was all that saved her from plummeting face first into the deck of the station. Collecting herself, she decided to walk instead of run to... *'where?'* She thought.

She addressed the station's ai instead. "AI, what is the location of Bet?"

"I'm sorry, I do not have a crew member named Bet."

"BETR, Elmo, the only crew member you can track."

"Dr. Morales is currently on the flight deck with 3 other anomalies I believe are individuals."

"Excellent, thanks." Elena automatically replied, and then she stopped dead in her tracks. *'Dr. Morales? Wasn't that...?'* She mumbled to herself as she turned back to look at the display and the brief she had just read. There it was, right there at the top. Dr. Morales.

"Dr. Morales… is Bet!?" She pondered to herself. Now she was running to the flight deck. Bracing herself against the bulkhead as she rounded the curve of the stations passageways with a stiff arm, placed against the bulkhead every few paces. She reached the flight deck completely out of breath. As she stumbled through the entry, she leaned over and placed her hands on her knees, panting and right in front of John, Marcus, Riley and Bet. Startled by her sudden arrival and obvious haste, Riley rushed to her side with concern for her wellbeing. As he reached for his medical scanner, Elena waved him away, managing to get out a breathy "I'm fine."

"Good, then would you mind telling us what the hell is going on here?" John inquired, a hint of irritation and concern in his voice.

"I need… to talk… to Bet." Elena gasped as she struggled to catch her breath. "There's no emergency. It's just really important to me."

John gave a harumph in reply. Riley muttered something about her needing a bit more cardio in her routine as well.

"What can I help you with Elena?" Bet asked as he moved closer to her.

"Are you Dr. Morales?" Elena asked after a few more deep breaths and straightening up, regaining her composure, mostly.

"I am, or rather… I was. I'm curious how you made this connection though. Care to explain?"

Elena looked him dead in the ocular inputs, "Bet, I've been reading about this new process you've developed, something about integrating particle harvesting, magnetic reconnection, and quantum vacuum reactors? Sounds like you're pushing my old theories to their limits. What's going on?"

"Ahh. You must have read one of my papers then. Yes, and I'm familiar with your work as well. You gave us the foundation, and we've been pushing forward with it ever since. The process is a bit of a beast, but at the core of it, we've combined solar wind harvesting, artificial magnetic reconnection for particle acceleration, and quantum vacuum energy to create a self-sustaining antimatter production system. It's massive, scalable, and efficient."

"Solar wind harvesting? That's ambitious. How are you managing to collect and store particles at a large enough scale to matter?"

"We're using a magnetic funnel system—a dynamic magnetic cone. It captures charged particles, mainly electrons and protons, from the solar wind and funnels them into electrostatic storage grids. The grids keep them contained and charged while we prep them for acceleration. It's all based on dynamic field alignment. Your work on magnetic reconnection made us realize we could direct those same principles toward capturing particles efficiently in the first place."

"Ah, I see. So you're storing these particles in electrostatic grids. And then what? Just dumping them into a reactor? That seems... chaotic."

"Not quite. The stored particles are fed into magnetic reconnection chambers—and here's where your research really shines. We've created controlled reconnection zones to mimic astrophysical events like those you modeled in your earlier work. By inducing reconnection, we're able to accelerate the particles to near-relativistic speeds. The chambers are finely tuned with gradient field stabilizers to avoid energy losses, and the particles leave the process supercharged."

"Impressive. But acceleration alone doesn't get you to antimatter. What are you doing with these high-energy particles after the reconnection phase?"

"That's where it gets interesting. After acceleration, the particles are directed into a quantum vacuum reactor. We designed this reactor to induce quantum field interactions—basically creating spacetime distortions by using the kinetic energy of the particles to amplify zero-point energy fluctuations. Your early work on vacuum polarization effects was instrumental here."

"You're manipulating the quantum vacuum... to extract zero-point energy? And this powers the antimatter production?"

"Exactly! The energy harvested from the quantum vacuum reactor drives the antimatter synthesis process. We use this energy to power a high-energy particle collider where we generate antimatter—positrons and antiprotons primarily. The collider is energy-hungry, of course, but with the zero-point energy reactor feeding it, we've eliminated the need for external power sources. It took a while to get there, but eventually the sigmoidal growth pattern took off once "

"That's... extraordinary. How are you handling the antimatter? Storage must still be a nightmare, especially at these scales."

"It's tricky, but we've adapted your Penning trap designs for large-scale applications. We use cryogenically cooled magnetic containment systems to store the antimatter safely. The traps are independently stable for months at a time now, which is a huge improvement over earlier designs. With appropriate external power and support systems, we can keep the antimatter stored indefinitely."

"And you're producing this at scale? What kind of yields are we talking?"

"With the operations before the colony fell, we were generating grams of antimatter monthly. The real breakthrough is that the process is now self-sustaining. Proximity to the sun makes solar power quite efficient. This powers the magnetic field generator we use to collect the particles in solar wind. Solar wind particles feed the system, the reconnection chambers energize them, the vacuum reactor amplifies that energy, and it all loops back to support antimatter production."

"A closed-loop system for antimatter production that bridges the efficiency gap with solar power. You've done what I never thought possible. And this all hinges on my old magnetic reconnection research?"

"That was the spark. Without your equations, we wouldn't have figured out how to make the reconnection process stable enough for controlled acceleration. It's like you gave us the blueprint for the universe's most efficient energy transfer system. We just scaled it up and found ways to apply it to particle harvesting and antimatter creation."

"Bet, this is incredible. We were only able to produce micrograms per year when I built the drive in the colony ship. It took a couple years and cost more than the entire rest of the ship and its contents combined just to get the fuel we used to get here. The implications for propulsion, energy generation, even terraforming—it's limitless. But you're sure the quantum vacuum reactor is stable? Tapping zero-point energy on this scale feels like playing with fire."

Bet nodded, "It's a valid concern. Stability was our biggest hurdle, but we've implemented multiple safeguards. The reactor's energy output is capped by feedback controls, and any fluctuation outside the expected range automatically shuts down the particle feed. So far, we've had zero incidents, even at full power."

"Good. The last thing we need is a runaway quantum fluctuation tearing a hole in spacetime." Elena Chuckled, "Well, Bet, I'll admit, this surpasses my wildest dreams. You've taken my ideas and turned them into something… revolutionary."

"Thank you. We couldn't have done it without your pioneering work."

The three men were standing around them, jaws dropped. Riley was the first to shake the shock over what he'd just overheard and came to the same realization Elena had. "That explains your advanced radiation shielding and some of the other choices in your adaptations."

"Yes," Bet turned to look at Riley, "It was essential for my work in the Lagrange points of Enera. Even with some rather advanced shielding, the conditions were hardly what one would consider ideal."

Marcus spoke up. "So, if I'm understanding all that correctly, and I'm sure I don't have but the slightest clue what you two just said, there's a chance we could go back to Sol?"

Bet grimaced slightly, a look the crew still found strange on his partially metallic face. "A chance, yes. But it's not that simple. I was near the facility when the colony was hit. I can confirm the energy collector is intact, and there is a very large amount of antimatter there as well. Perhaps a couple hectograms now. Enough to… well, it's more than we'll ever need if we had a whole fleet of ships capable of FTL. But that's the problem, we don't even have FTL capable ships."

Elena seemed lost in thought all of a sudden. Noticing, John asked her, "what's on your mind? I know that look… what crazy idea do you have now"

"I want to make the Aurora FTL capable," Elena replied.

Bet paused, seeming to stare at Elena for a moment. "Perhaps you'd like to review the reconnection chamber specs and quantum vacuum models—your insight could be what we need to convert your drive to a full fledged FTL drive. We'll have to fabricate a lot of components, but I'm happy to assist you in locating everything you need."

Marcus shook his head and pinched the bridge of his nose. "Before you start designing a new drive and making plans to rip apart the only working ship we have currently, the one sustaining an entire colony worth of people who currently have no idea what is going on I might add… You need to talk to the Captain. I like the idea of having the option to make it back to SOL in our lifetime and possibly without playing time traveler again, but we need to bring the Captain up to speed and probably the rest of the crew. There's still the debate over what to do with the colonists. We're in a giant space bus here."

Elena gave him a quick nod, then grinned from ear to ear. With an almost girlish glee on her face, she turned and started jogging down the corridor, shouting back over her shoulder as she left, "Thanks Doc!"

"Well at least she's going to get that cardio in at this rate," Riley said, mostly to himself.

John turned to Bet. "So… were you going to tell us just how big a deal you were around here?"

Bet looked a little chagrined at John's question. A look John appreciated at that moment. "Actually, I was hoping it wouldn't come up, but I suppose it was inevitable given the circumstances."

"Why's that?" Riley asked.

"I don't like the attention," Bet replied.

"Great, we get an introverted cyborg full of mystery and poor taste. This is what all of humanity is counting on now?" Marcus muttered as he left to follow Elena.

Bet hung his head. "Come on pall, time to get some attention from the Captain," John said as he slapped Bet on the back and started walking toward the bridge.

Bet looked up and found Riley staring at him. He stared back, unsure what would come next.

"When all this is over, their questions and the questions those questions raise… come find me in medical. I'll see that it's quiet for a while so you can relax in peace, then I want you to show me the equipment and run me through the procedure for the neuro-interface augment that's so infamously standard. Sound good to you?"

Bet nodded. "Thanks. The quiet sounds nice. I got a lot of that, centuries worth… I thought I'd had enough of it, but now I kind of miss it."

"Makes sense. It's a lot, after all you've been through. You've got to pace yourself, emotionally… just do it far better than Elena does physically and you'll be fine," Riley said as he motioned toward the passageway. "After you."

As Bet walked onto the bridge, he saw Captain Morrow massaging her temples as Elena was still explaining all that she'd learned in a rather fast and excited speech. When she finished, Captain Morrow took a deep breath and held it, then slowly let it out. Taking another breath, she spoke.

"So, let me see if I understand this right. We've got more antimatter than was previously made in all of human history, relatively speaking… before we left Sol… Oh this is giving me a headache trying to keep a timeline straight in my head. Ok, so… a bunch of antimatter, but if I remember correctly from my physics lessons, that's not even a percent of what we would need to get home in 120 years, which would not be relative time, but actual time… or is that relative… Uhh, it doesn't matter because we don't have the antimatter to do it anyway. So other than way more than we need to fuel this ship for dozens of trips, which would put us so far into the future we may witness the heat death of the universe by the time we arrive… Why is this so exciting? Seems to me all we've done is solve the energy needs for the colony and space station for generations, forever… I don't know." Captain Morrow plopped down in her chair and looked between Elena and Bet. "I need you to explain this to me in Captain terms, not your science talk."

Elena seemed deflated. Unable to come up with what to say, Bet spoke up. "Because Captain, you don't fuel the ship with antimatter the whole way, like you did to get here. The warp bubble requires a huge burst of energy to create, but not to sustain. To sustain the travel, we would supply it with a far more steady supply of energy."

"Exactly! Basically the antimatter is the capacitor that gets the motor turning, and once it's moving we use ZPE's to keep it going. Zero-Point energy modules, which the antimatter generation fills as part of the process. Antimatter just gets us going, so we only need grams at a time. We can still use antimatter for thrust, but we won't need thrust to get anywhere." Elena blurted out, excited to have found an explanation.

"Antimatter may also be necessary if we need to stabilize the warp field along the way," Bet added. "It's the kickstart when we need a massive amount of energy really really fast, but the ZPE's provide near limitless power in a steady stream. In order to control the output and for redundancy sake, we would use several ZPE's on a FTL ship. But to put it another way, one of the ZPE's could provide a near limitless amount of energy for a whole planet indefinitely. The trick is regulating how much energy output it produces, so it doesn't animate everything in a singularity event, which I'm speculating would be the result of a worst case scenario because I've never seen one do that."

Captain morrow just stared at Bet. The silence began to grow uncomfortable and Elena began to fidget. Bet stood completely motionless. When he couldn't take it anymore, John cleared his throat. Having no effect, he did it again. Captain Morrow blinked slowly.

"Captain. We've got some difficult decisions to make here. We've got the intel on from the first planet side recon. The infrastructure appears to be intact for many of the subterranean structures. There is farm and heavy equipment available, but it requires an implant or some sort of interface for us analogue humans to use them…" John trailed off as Captain Morrow's gaze slowly crept in his direction, landing with a cold, hard stare.

Captain morrow took another deep breath, closed her eyes and exhaled slowly.

"For the year we were traveling and even before that, I played out a million scenarios in my head. We really had no idea what we might find here. Never in my wildest dreams did I even imagine anything close to this. I've got nearly an entire colony on ice, a food shortage issue… it's a shame we don't run on batteries, apparently we can keep them charged until the universe dies." Captain Morrow rolled her eyes, took another breath and continued.

"The station we're on is barely functional and roughly half of it is still inaccessible or missing completely. Truth is, I'm not even sure how it's still in orbit… ehhh!" She raised a finger to forestall any explanation from the scientists.

"I don't want to get into the details, it isn't relevant at the moment. You can explain the orbital mechanics and whatever flavor of that magic Bet used to keep it available to me later, once we've got every other problem on the triage list solved. Now, Elena, before you even think one more thought about this crazy notion of converting this space bus into an FTL magical speed demon, you need to come up with some way for us to adapt the equipment for the colonists to use it. No way in hell am I thawing out an entire colony and dictating to them they must receive implants. The wrist comp interface still has compatibility issues and I don't want to rely on them as a mandatory means of operation. Make an interface that can be used to provide missing controls on each piece of equipment. Bet, I trust you will render her some assistance on this. John, ready a shuttle, you're taking Clara and Amir to the planet. Both have questions and Clara wants samples. While you're down there, have your team scout for foraging opportunities to boost food rations in the immediate. Bet has provided some documentation on local flora and fauna, Clara will bring you up to speed on the compatibility list and what to look for. You've all got a lot of work to do, so go get to it."

John and Elena gave verbal acknowledgment. Bet just nodded. The three of them left at once without another word. Captain Morrow let out a heavy sigh and slumped back in her chair, completely ignoring posture and decorum as she thumbed her comm panel for the medical bay.

"Riley, Captain Morrow. You there?"

"Yes Captain. What can I do for you?"

"Got any good whiskey?"

Riley chuckled, "Yes Captain, and I'm saving it for a more special occasion. But, I think I've got just what you need."

A few minutes later, Riley showed up on the bridge carrying a sandwich.

33

Captain Morrow sat slumped in the command chair, eyes half-lidded, temples throbbing. The overhead lights hummed with an incessant drone, a signal that the station's newly revived systems never slept—constantly demanding a thousand decisions from her. Half a console away, a status board flashed with green and yellow readouts, each pulsing for attention. She longed for a break but couldn't slow down; the colony needed her to stay present, steady, unshaken. She had her mission and now more than ever, the weight of all humanity rested squarely on her shoulders.

"Captain?" Riley's soft voice cut through her spiraling thoughts. She blinked and turned, catching sight of the medical officer standing in the threshold, a small tray in his hands—and a sandwich perched neatly atop it. He wore a sympathetic smile that radiated his usual warmth and a kind of quiet confidence.

"Riley." Morrow forced her posture straighter. "Am I glad to see you."

"You look like absolute shit, Captain."

"Gee, thanks a lot. Not as happy to see you anymore."

"Here, I brought you something. Eat."

"We're up to our elbows in half a dozen crises: the planet-based expansion, sustaining food production, getting the colony established… We can't afford to lose momentum." Her tone was tense but laced with exhaustion.

"But you still have to take time to eat. You called me up here, well Doctor's orders. You sit there, you eat your sandwich and you don't think about any of the other stuff until it's gone, and if I see you cram it in your cheeks I'm going to squeeze your face like a pimple. I mean it. Here," Riley thrust the sandwich into Captain Morrow's hands. "Eat."

Riley saw the exhaustion in her eyes, the dark circles forming heavy atop her almost gaunt cheek bones. The extra wrinkles around here eyes and forehead. He placed the tray on a side console. "A quick bite won't fix everything," he admitted gently, "but it might keep you from crashing. Figuratively or literally."

She eyed the sandwich in her hands, realized she couldn't even recall her last proper meal. "We have rations, you know. Didn't realize we had actual bread to spare," she teased, voice drained but calmer.

"We had a small stock leftover from the hydroponics deck experiments. Not exactly fresh-out-of-the-oven, but it beats nutrient bars. Take a breather, Captain. Those nutrient bars might keep your body alive, but they are crap for the soul."

"Are you calling this soul food?" She gave him a raised eyebrow.

Riley almost belly laughed at that comment. "Absolutely not! Nowhere close! But it's a hell of a lot closer than those sawdust flavored bricks you've been eating."

Morrow lowered her gaze to the sandwich, a flicker of gratitude tempered by guilt. "We're still rationing. Are you sure this is okay?"

Riley raised a brow. "I double-checked inventory. It's fine." Then, in a quieter voice, he added, "Look, the crew can sense when you're at your wit's end. Holding the entire station together is tough, but if you run yourself ragged… well, that's no help to anyone. So there's my justification, and if you need my permission… don't make me repeat myself." He caught her eye and gave her a wink with a half cocked grin, almost a smirk on his face.

She let out a slow breath, feeling tension in her shoulders she hadn't realized was there. "Alright. Fine. Just… don't expect me to chatter about my feelings."

He smirked softly. "I wouldn't dream of it, Captain." He took the liberty of the seat next to hers. "Just a quick bite. Then you can get back to all those urgent tasks. But in the mean time, since you've got me hungry for it now, I'm going to tease your appetite with a little story about some soul food."

"My favorite meal back on the lunar base, back when I was still just a trauma nurse, was a special crawfish something. There was a guy that worked in the lab, said he was from Louisiana. Now about 12 hours or more before we were expecting a resupply shuttle, he would start working on something in the lab. It didn't take long and you could smell it everywhere. First time he did it, he tried to cook it in some beakers. Just a small meal for himself, but by the time that day was over, everyone on station knew all about it. He couldn't keep the smell from filling the whole station. It got everyone hungry. From then on, he'd work up a giant pot in the back of the lab. Stirred it all day and talked real funny to it. When the supply shuttle arrived, that man was part ninja. Nobody ever saw him leave that cook pot. All we saw was a big wooden spoon laying across the top and he had magically teleported to the airlock and back. He had fresh crawfish, I think they are tiny lobsters or something. Look like lobsters, he called them 'bugs' but I swear they look like lobsters. Anyway, he'd add that delicate little lobster meat to this pot he'd been working all day. Captain, never in my life have I ever tasted such a thing! It was so creamy in my mouth and the flavors! It had layers, so many layers. First it was a little bit of silky tomato sauce, and a bit of that little lobster meat, then some seasoning would start marching in. Right about the time you wanna say mmmm, BAM! The heat got ya and took that mmm right out of your mouth."

"You know all too well, when you spend enough time in space, you're going to eat bugs. Actual bugs. This was 5 star dining and I don't care what he said, they were not bugs. If I even knew what the hell I was talking about, I might could find a recipe for you, but I don't have a smuggler's connection for some weird Earth lobster bugs and well…I can't cook. But, I can make you a sandwich." Riley seemed lost in another world as he rambled on and on about some meal he'd eaten back on the moon over Earth.

Morrow nodded. Taking the sandwich in hand as Riley talked, she bit down. The slightly stale but distinct taste of real wheat-based bread hit her tongue—far better than the synthetic paste dough the station tried to pass off as "bread." A wave of relief washed over her, an odd sense of normalcy she rarely felt nowadays. She didn't have the foggiest idea what Riley was talking about, but he seemed to be happy remembering it. Watching him, half listening while she chewed on her sandwich, brought a warmth to her heart she didn't realize she'd been missing.

"It's… good," she admitted, chewing thoughtfully. After a few moments, she set the half-eaten sandwich back on the tray and exhaled. "Thanks, Riley."

Riley offered a small grin. "Glad to help." He paused, as though weighing his next words. "You know, if you need more than just a sandwich, you can come by the med bay. Even if all you want is quiet for ten minutes. Seems to be my most common treatment lately… sometimes stepping away is the best remedy for stress. The one thing you can get in the med bay you can't hardly get anywhere else, is a quiet place to be left alone for a bit."

Morrow massaged her temples, nodding without meeting his eyes. "I might do that. Eventually." She straightened, renewing some of her composure. "But for now… I have a station to oversee."

Riley inclined his head, understanding. "Then I'll leave you to it." He cast one more glance around the bridge, noting the swirling data on the consoles and the holographic feed of planet-side progress. "We're in good shape, Captain. The crew's morale is better than you think. it's you I have my eye on."

With that, he exited, the hatch sliding shut behind him. Morrow watched him go, then let out a long sigh. Somehow, just a bit of real food and a reminder that someone cared had pulled her back from the brink of a stress induced meltdown. She flexed her hands, rolling her shoulders. The headache still throbbed, but it was more manageable now. Then the image of Riley rambling on about some crazy Louisiana Earth bugs he ate in a lab on the moon hit her. Captain Morrow, alone on the bridge, allowed herself to laugh, just a little. Trying to stifle it made her snort. That threw her into a giggle fit like she was a little girl again. Out in the hall, just outside the hatch, Riley smiled and pulled his toe out from the hatch so it could close the rest of the way.

She picked up the sandwich again, took another bite, then pressed the comm panel to resume her duties. Maybe, after this crisis or the next, she'd take Riley up on that quiet time in the med bay.

34

Riley returned to the medical bay, the door whooshing shut behind him with a soft hiss. He expected the place to be empty, but instead found Bet stretched out on a diagnostic bed near the far wall. The overhead lights gave Bet's metal plates a ghostly sheen.

Riley smiled faintly. "Getting comfortable, huh?" he asked, walking up to the console. It felt like a gentle admonishment, but his tone was kind. "You alright? Any issues?"

Bet opened his eyes, mechanical irises adjusting to focus on Riley. "No issues. You promised me a quiet place to clear my mind—this seemed suitable."

"By all means, stay as long as you like. Or at least until we need that bed for a real patient," Riley replied lightly, settling at the console to pick through the backlog of device calibrations and new biotech references Bet had provided.

He paused, casting a glance back at Bet. "Thanks again for the sandwich tip, by the way. The Captain is calmer now—I think."

Bet gave a small nod. "Good. Calmness is a precious resource around here."

Riley let out a gentle chuckle. "Ain't that the truth." He turned his attention to the console, scanning lines of advanced text describing neurointerfaces and specialized procedures. The complexity made his head swim, but it also excited him. "We'll figure this out, step by step," he murmured to himself trying not to disturb Bet.

Bet sat up, swinging his legs off the bed. "If you have questions, I can walk you through some of it. I only remember partial details, but I'm sure we can fill in gaps with the data we've got."

Riley beamed. "I'd appreciate that. Let's take a look, shall we?"

And with that, the med bay's hush was replaced by the quiet murmur of two minds—one synthorganic, one thoroughly human—working together in pursuit of knowledge. The day's stresses receded, replaced by the promise of what they might accomplish together.

At one point, between topics, Bet stopped and turned to face Riley directly, "Thank you, Riley. For not treating me differently than anyone else, I mean."

"I don't understand, is the crew treating you poorly?"

"No. Nothing like that. John has his trust issues, understandably, but he and several others… When they look at me, all they see is the machine. It's just nice to be treated like the human I am inside… well, what's left of him anyway."

"What does it mean to be human?" Riley asked.

Bet sat there, motionless for a moment. "I've never thought about it quite so directly as that actually. I always asked myself if I was still human."

Riley inclined his head, "I don't know if I could accurately find the words to express what it means to be human. I can tell you what a human is, but so can my med scanner. In most cases, I could tell you what isn't human. The med scanner appears to always know. Does that make the med scanner smarter?"

"Now you're just playing word games with me."

"Isn't that something humans do?"

"I'm not sure I like this game." Ever so slightly, Bet squirmed in his seat.

"That, right there. What was that?"

Bet looked very confused. "I have no idea what you are talking about. Have you hit your head recently?" Bet leaned forward, reaching for the med scanner. "Maybe I should ask the med scanner, not you."

"Just a moment ago, when you said you weren't sure you liked this game, you moved."

"So moving is human? You don't make any sense at all."

Riley rolled his eyes, "no, WHY did you move? You don't have the same nerves in your lower extremities anymore that cause your legs to start going numb if you sit too long in one place, you don't get the hot spots that remind you to move so you don't create pressure wounds. You could sit there all day as still as that med scanner and I bet if you had a mind to, you could sit so still you'd appear to be just a part of that chair."

"So, you made me uncomfortable on purpose?"

"Sure did. It was the easiest emotion I could illicit a response with that wouldn't have been totally cruel... except, I'm not kissing you, so that left one option," Riley let out a soft sigh. "The point is, that's an emotion. If you were robot, machine or med scanner, you wouldn't have FELT anything. You wouldn't have been uncomfortable and therefore you would not have twitched as you did in that human mannerism. It's a lot harder to see it in your facial expressions and I do believe you've got a poker face on most of the time, but it's there. It doesn't matter how much of you is machine or tech. What matters is how and what you process. You feel things just as you did when you were human. That's proof that it's not all just some neurological chemical soup. True feelings, that comes from somewhere deeper. I'm not sure what it means to be human, but I can assure you... that's a really really big part of it. And that's what matters. I won't say that's all that matters to me, but I already told you. I'm not kissing you."

"You are a very strange individual, Riley. But thank you. Again, I guess. When you're lost inside your own head for so long, it's hard to see past the spirals we make in there sometimes. If I thought I was awkward and didn't know how to interact with people before, well that was a walk in the park compared to now. And now you're doing a good job of convincing me I'm not the only awkward one around here."

"Ehhh, you're doing just fine. Hey, all that reading and research you did waiting out there... do you know anything about Earth cuisine? Specifically, crawfish? Its some sort of, umm muddy bug lobster thing."

Bet just stared at Riley with a perfectly still unblinking face. When Riley made eye contact, Bet let his lower mandible drop slightly and caused a portion of his synthetic skin to contract above his left eye. Riley understood what look Bet was trying to make, but it just looked so awkward on the rigid metal of his face. Despite having so many moving parts, it just lacked the softness that made extra wrinkles and endearing qualities to facial expressions. Riley burst out laughing.

"Never mind, I don't even know why I thought you might know something about it. You've spent your entire life here, haven't you? I guess I'm just making your point about awkward now..."

"Earth people eat muddy bugs?" Bet didn't even have to try now, the look of pure bewilderment on his face was so obvious, it caused Riley to burst with laughter again.

"Sure do. I've had it myself. I just can't remember what it's called.

Crawfish something or another."

Riley's laughter was becoming infectious. After their talk, to sit here having such a normal conversation filled Bet with a sense of compassion he had not felt in centuries. Then, he released the tight grip he had on his body's system and felt the 'chemical soup' as Riley had put it, for the first time in so long, he could not remember. Then, a noise escaped him. It sounded like a metallic bark. The noise, so weird, startled Riley and Bet. Bet began to squirm a lot, nervous and ready to run for the door.

"Did… did you just laugh?" Riley asked.

Riley's eyes were growing so large, Bet thought they might pop out of the man's face. The expression Riley was giving him caused it again, but this time, more followed as he shook his head. Riley almost fell out of his chair he was laughing so hard. Tears were rolling down his face and he held his belly as the laughter that was so contagious was surely hurting his abdominal muscles. For the first time and about two centuries, Bet remembered what it felt like to laugh and in that moment, he knew exactly what Riley meant. There aren't words to express what it means to be human at all. It was something you just… felt.

Moments after Riley started holding his belly, the ridiculousness settled down and Riley fought hard to regain his composure. He wiped his face, took deep breaths and occasionally fought the urge to start back up again. Bet watched all this and remembered, pulling up long buried memories from so long ago, back when he had working lungs and vocal cords. Fully wrapping himself in his moment of being human, but the the advanced processing abilities inside him was busy at work. As Bet stood up, he nodded at Riley and locked eyes. As they looked at each other, the human side of him felt that unspoken communication and smiled slightly, but the mechanical arm reached out and touched Riley's console. The movement was so subtle and so sincere was the gaze between them, it went completely unnoticed. Bet nodded slightly again, and made for the exit.

"Bet, come back anytime buddy," Riley called after him.

"Will do." Was the reply that came from the corridor outside the med bay.

Riley sat back up thinking about that very strange and yet amazing interaction with Bet. His concern for the Captain started to slide back into his mind and the reality of everything crept back in, slowly melting the smile off of his face. Riley made a motion to dismiss the

document he and Bet were previously looking at, but when it vanished there was something else on his display. Several files were open and one of them, was a picture of his lobster bug. Riley's butt hit his chair with a loud thump and his jaw nearly hit the console with the same force. Another open file caught his attention.
*****

Crayfish see also, "Crawfish"
Crayfish are freshwater crustaceans belonging to the infraorder Astacidea, which also contains lobsters.

…

The file went on, but Riley was smiling so big his cheeks were burning. "I knew it! I knew they were lobsters! … Bugs, HAH!"

The third file open on his terminal caused tears to pour down Riley's face. Barely able to read the text through the tears welling in his yes, he didn't notice Bet peaking around the corner just long enough to see Riley reach for an absorbent towel to wipe his face and blow his nose. Bet nodded to himself and walked silently down the corridor. If anyone else was around, they may have wondered where the soft whistling tune was coming from. Bet had made a friend and he let the chemical soup flood his brain, completely unrestricted, and he enjoyed it.

ARCHIVE FILE: CRW-ETOUF.ARC
Recovered by: Dr. 'Bet' Morales
Origin: Ancestral Louisiana, Earth (Cajun/Creole tradition)
A classic dish believed to have emerged from the French-inspired "stewing" methods of southwestern Louisiana. Its name, "étouffée," means "smothered," reflecting how shellfish is gently cooked in a rich, roux-based sauce.

Crawfish Étouffée
Serves: 4–6
Ingredients
1 lb (450 g) peeled crawfish tails (fresh or thawed)
4 tbsp unsalted butter (or cooking oil)
1 small onion, finely chopped
1 stalk celery, finely chopped
1/2 green bell pepper, finely chopped
2 cloves garlic, minced
2 tbsp all-purpose flour (for a light roux)
2 cups seafood or crawfish stock (substitute chicken stock if needed)
1 tsp Cajun seasoning (or to taste)

1/2 tsp dried thyme
Pinch cayenne pepper (optional, for heat)
Salt & black pepper to taste
1 tbsp chopped fresh parsley (optional garnish)
Steamed rice for serving
Instructions

1. Roux Base:
- In a medium saucepan or skillet over medium heat, melt the butter.
- Stir in the flour gradually to form a roux, whisking continuously until it's a light caramel color—about 5 minutes. Watch carefully to avoid burning.

1. Sauté Vegetables:
- Add the chopped onion, celery, and bell pepper to the roux. Sauté for 3–5 minutes or until they soften. Stir in minced garlic for the last minute.

1. Build the Sauce:
- Slowly pour in the stock while stirring, ensuring no lumps remain.
- Season with Cajun seasoning, thyme, cayenne (if desired), plus salt and black pepper to taste.
- Reduce heat to low and simmer 10 minutes, letting flavors meld.

1. Add Crawfish:
- Gently stir in crawfish tails. Simmer 5–7 minutes more, or until tails are heated through. Avoid overcooking—crawfish can turn rubbery if left too long.

1. Taste & Adjust:
- Sample the sauce; tweak seasonings if necessary. It should be savory, slightly spicy, and richly flavorful.

1. Serve Hot:
- Ladle the étouffée over steamed rice. Garnish with parsley if you like.

End of File

Bet's note to Riley: "Crawfish may be scarce here, but perhaps you can adapt with local crustaceans—or genetically engineered stand-ins. I trust your taste buds—and your memories—will find comfort in this revived culinary classic."

35

John stood in the station's main hangar bay, arms folded across his chest, scrutinizing a trio of bulky equipment pods lined up near the shuttle's open loading ramp. Stenciled across their sides were hasty scrawling indicating experimental gear the crew hoped would make their planet-side tasks less grueling. On this trip, though, they had an additional toy to test—a "prototype device" that Elena and Riley had cobbled together to interface with some of the planet's leftover machinery. If Elena got this right, the prototype should allow an un-augmented human to interface with the heavy equipment which apparently required a neurol-interface in order to operate.

John synced his wrist comp to his utility suit as he eyed his ragtag group—Han, Vogel, Doc, Clara, Amir, and Serena. Each was geared up for the planet's harsh daylight and dense overgrowth, though their expressions ranged from eager (Han) to resigned (Serena). Vogel wore a half-smirk, evidently ready for another chance to drive heavy equipment. Amir hovered near the back, fiddling with a handheld camera rig he intended to use for "cultural documentation," while Clara lugged a sampling kit almost bigger than she was. On this trip, they would be utilizing mechanical assistance gear to help negate some of the effects of gravity on the planet.

"All right," John said, raising his voice over the low roar of thrusters warming in the shuttle's underbelly. "We get down there, test this new device on the leftover colony equipment. Elena—" he gestured to the topmost crate, "—says it should pair with the site's old control modules. If we've guessed right. If it fails, record what data you can and pass it to Elena, then fall in with one of the other teams."

"I'm calling it an older sister of the neural interface," Vogel joked, giving the crate a pat, "but it's basically a converter for those who don't want—" she clamped her mouth shut as she caught Serena's glare. Neural interfaces were a hot topic. "—um, sorry."

Han stepped between them, grinning. "Relax. We'll be lucky if it boots up anything at all." She reached into her suit's thigh pocket and pulled out a fist, which she placed in her other palm with her thumb up. She wiggled her eyebrows mischievously at Vogel. "Ready to settle this?"

A faint chuckle rippled in the group. Serena rolled her eyes, while Amir—camera rig in hand—turned it on them. Vogel shrugged and accepted the challenge. "All right, Winner gets to pick." They each said the age-old line: "Rock, paper, scissors—shoot!" The mid-air gestures ended in Vogel's scissor shape getting promptly smashed by Han's rock.

"Tractor's mine," Han sang out, broad grin on her face. "Finally get to test that beast. I can't wait to flatten some vines."

Vogel chuckled. "Suit yourself, but if that hunk of metal's battery is dead, don't blame me."

John cleared his throat. "Clara, you'll handle your samples from near the landing site and wherever we end up clearing. It's mostly kudzu down there, but we did see some variety that wasn't completely choked out yet a bit farther to the east of where we put down. Amir, you get your video logs or whatever it is you're after. Serena, keep watch for wildlife. If there's anything bigger than a cricket out there, we need to know what it is and how it tastes. Oh and Riley wants any shelled creatures you find if you're near water and see some. Something about testing toxicity levels in the water." John tossed her a waterproof pouch. "Here, he sent sample bags. Said he didn't want your gear getting all messy."

Serena gave a confident nod, caught the bags and went back to checking the charge on her vibrosword's handle. "I'm on it."

Clara pushed her sampling kit aboard, glancing nervously at the group. "I'll be quick, I promise. Mostly want soil and plant specimens. The new equipment can wait until I at least figure out if we can cultivate some of these alien plants back in the hydro-labs."

John waved them up the ramp. "Let's load in."

The shuttle's engines purred as it glided through atmosphere, descending onto the same broad clearing the crew had scouted on the previous trip. Han, seated at the co-pilot console, was practically vibrating with excitement. The moment the thrusters dusted the ground, she slapped the harness release and leapt to her feet. Serena, more calmly, stood, double-checking her gear. Vogel cast a longing gaze at the equipment crate as if it were an old friend.

Within minutes, they fanned out under the glare of Enera's ultra-bright glair. John had hovered just above the ground briefly before landing to burn away the vegetation in the area. The vegetation beyond the scorched area surrounding the shuttle still reached waist height, though not quite as thick as the kudzu they had seen in the city proper. With a faint whine, the shuttle's cargo ramp lowered, revealing the crates of experimental gear. A mechanical lifter extended, depositing them gently on the uneven dirt, assisting them with much of the labor.

The crew began working on one of the crates labeled "experimental." After executing a few commands with her wrist comp, Han touched a section of the crate that had begun emitting a soft glow. Everyone took a step backward as the crate began to hiss and move. Sides of the crate began to extend, fold in on themselves and rotate. Before long, the crate had transformed into a strange cart looking rover with a bit of the outer crate having formed a trailer behind it. John thought the thing looked like some weird robotic bug. After placing the remaining crates and gear on the trailer section, Han took a seat on top of one of the plastic shelled containers and started controlling the new device with a holographic joystick projected from her wrist. The machine started to move forward at a normal walking pace. The addition of a few plasma torches on the front of the unit cleared out everything in its path, leaving a scorched soot covered path for the cart to follow. Some piece of equipment underneath the cart worked the soil into an easy to use walking path for the crew. John was particularly impressed at how the machine was not only clearing away the foliage and flattening the surface, but it also seemed to be compacting it in a way that felt almost like ceramic. They left no footprints or marks of any kind in the ash colored path as they made their way toward the edge of town and in particular, the heavy equipment.

"Let's fire this up," John said, punching commands into his wrist console. The protective shell of the crate Han had used as a driver's seat hissed open, revealing a squat, metal console with a small holographic projection pad. It looked underwhelming, but this was Elena's best guess at bridging old colony tech with the technology of the neural interface system—something to let them operate leftover tractors and excavators the old fashioned way if the neural interface wasn't an option.

Han marched up, stuffed a small power cell into a docking slot, then flicked a switch. A subdued hum rose from the device, lights blinking across its panel. "We have liftoff," she murmured, grinning. A holoscreen projected from the top, giving a custom set of controls, allowing the operator to direct the equipment with hand gestures and holographic controls. The device was functioning as expected so far, but they still had to get it installed on some of the equipment in order to test it.

36

Within the next hour, they'd managed to coax an ancient tractor-like vehicle from its resting spot in the weeds. The hull bore faded logos, dented panels, and strangling vines around its treads. Han crouched near a half-buried diagnostics port, the new device perched next to her like a helpful little droid.

"Here goes," Han said, attaching a thick cable from the device to the tractor's side. The console's holo-projection flickered, reading strings of data in garbled script. "It's... trying to parse the system."

"Bet said these machines ran on localized AI," Vogel noted, stepping up to watch. "If the memory banks and neural net are intact, it might just power up."

Han poked a holographic icon, scanning the holo readout. "We're getting partial boot. Possibly the battery's not completely shot. Let's see... oh, it's responding!"

A dull hum emanated from the tractor's engine compartment as parts began moving, and a pair of headlights flickered on and off, then glowed steadily in some sort of systems check. Han whooped in victory, ignoring Serena's unimpressed smirk. With a squeal of metal on metal, the tractor's large wheels twitched, dislodging a mass of vines.

John raised an eyebrow. "Just don't drive it into a sinkhole or something crazy you can't see below the overgrowth. We're here to test, not bury you alive."

Han gave a mock salute, hopped onto the driver's platform, placing her hands on the holographic controls and carefully advanced the throttle. The ancient machine lurched forward, flattening alien vegetation. "Yes!" she exclaimed over comms. "Running on new old

201

tech, but it's working! We need to do something about the visuals though. Its so bright out here the holographic display is kind of washed out and hard to read."

As Han moved forward, the excitement of operating equipment that was futuristic from her perspective showed in the joy on her face. It made her chuckle to think this equipment was essentially an old abandoned relic at this point. The weird situation just made her laugh as she marveled at just how screwed up any sense of time or normalcy had become. She was quite sure she was on a very unique adventure and she was about to 'tractor the hell out of an alien field'. Without a clue what she was actually doing, she tried to remember the summer at her grandparents farm, when she rode in the tractor with her grandfather as they prepared the fields. She might not know the first thing about farming, but she was certain about one thing. The overgrowth and vines had to go before they could do anything.

Han was about to set out across the field when she realized the tractor didn't seem to have any tools for dealing with the vegetation. With a frantic look around the lot, she spotted some attachments. One looked a bit like a plow, but with a round bulge at the bottom where she was certain her grandfather's tractor used a blade. Driving over to the corner where the attachments were lined up, Han got out and started investigating each of them, trying to determine what each attachment did. She decided there was only one way to find out on a few of them.

Han toggled her comm system. "Bet, can you see my helmet feed?"

"Yes, Han. How can I help?"

"What am I looking at here?"

"That, is what you might know as a cultipacker. That will smooth things out and prepare it for seed."

"What do I need to clear out all these vines?"

"You see that box attachment for the front there, just to the right of the cultipacker?"

"This one? With the bulge at the bottom?"

"Yes. Put that on the front, so you don't get tangled. That should slice and chop them up a bit. Then you'll want that large disk shaped attachment for the back."

Bet continued to help Han get everything hooked up and functioning, occasionally having to pause and search archives for manuals and notes with aid from the station's AI. Between the two of them, it took just over an hour to get the attachments cleared from the vines and positioned on the tractor with everything functional. Once that was done, Han tore off into the field, exuberantly tearing into the thick vegetation and mulching it into the soil as green compost.

Amid the noisy hum of the tractor and the loud clangs, bangs and sounds of thick vines getting chopped and turned into tiny bits, Clara set up a tiny pop-up lab on the shuttle's cargo ramp. At the edge of the scorched landing zone, she knelt down to carefully slice away topsoil layers and bag them in labeled pouches. Another kit handled leaf cuttings from the weird undergrowth and fibrous vines that choked the old farmland.

She occasionally muttered notes to herself: "Strange chlorophyll variants... possibly chlorophyll-d or some analog... root structure dense... maybe forced adaptation..."

Serena strolled by, vibrosword inactive but ready, scanning the horizon for signs of movement. "Find anything edible?" she asked in passing.

Clara shrugged. "Not sure yet. That's for the labs. But I see promise in these broad leaves—maybe we can cross-pollinate them with Earth strains. We need new crops. And this kudzu looks way too close to some earth varieties to be coincidental."

"Good luck," Serena said, then tilted her head, noticing a small swirl in the distance—dust or perhaps an animal. She tensed, but it faded. "Guess I'll keep looking. I'm going to cut a path to the east. I'll let you know if I note significant changes in what's growing."

While Serena sliced a path to the east, Amir was exploring to the west closer to the edge of the city ruins. Standing near a twisted metal signpost half-buried in the dirt, Amir raised his old-but-trusty camera rig, panning slowly across the scene: Han on the tractor clearing vines, Clara stooped over soil samples, Serena trailblazing with her glowing blade in hand, and Vogel fiddling with a second piece of equipment from the lot where many were stored.

"Day... what is it... day 68? 69? Hard to keep track," Amir muttered into the microphone. "Here we stand on Kepler-452b. Aurion I suppose it is called now, in what appears to have been farmland and some sort of industrial zone near the old city perimeter. Tractor number one is operational—miraculously—thanks to a bridging console designed by Dr. Park. The planet remains eerily quiet, no fauna spotted beyond minor insects so far. No trees or very tall structures, but from the effect of what this stronger-than-Earth gravity is doing to me, that makes a lot of sense."

He zoomed in on a battered structure in the distance, half-collapsed. "In another era, that might have been a barn or storage facility… or so we speculate. Hard to tell. The overgrowth here is formidable, kudzu-like in thickness. Yet, hope stirs among the crew—progress is tangible."

Lowering the camera, Amir sighed, thinking of the many back on the station who still slept in stasis. "We do this for them. I just hope they aren't all that's left." he whispered to no one in particular.

Farther to the east, Serena ventured behind a low hill, vibrosword reactivated and humming faintly. She'd seen a flicker of motion earlier. *Probably nothing,* she thought but she wanted to be sure.

Picking and cutting her way through tall, wiry stalks of grass, she paused. A distinct rustling came from a clump of vegetation a few meters away. Slowly, she raised the vibrosword. "Easy," she whispered, heart pounding.

A sudden burst of movement parted the grass—two large rodent-like creatures, stalky-limbed with broad ears and a back covered in a scaly bald skin, darted out. They froze upon seeing her, black eyes reflecting the sword's glow. Serena's breath caught. Finally, signs of actual fauna…

She approached carefully, switching from a lethal stance to a more curious posture. One creature bolted, skittering away in a zig-zag sprint. The other stared, trembling. Serena clicked the recorder on her suit. "Animal life confirmed," she spoke softly. "Rodent analog, about half a meter in length, large ears, skittish— Short stalky legs, runs kind of funny."

At that, the second rodent squeaked and vanished into the underbrush, leaving only crushed grass in its wake. Serena exhaled in relief. "Guess you're as scared of me as I am relieved to see you."

A grin spread across her face. We're not alone, after all. She tapped her comm. "Hey, folks, we have live animals here. Just saw two… rodent-lizard-things. Seems harmless."

John's voice crackled back. "Copy that, good news. Means the ecosystem's robust enough to support them. Keep an eye out in case there are bigger predators."

"Will do," Serena answered, scanning the grass. "But I have a feeling I'm the scariest predator around right now."

Now that she had identified a life form, Serena removed a sphere from a pouch at her side. About the size of an apple, she brought it over to her left wrist where her wrist console sprang to life. The sphere began to vibrate and Serena tossed it up into the air. After a brief arch, the ball suddenly stopped and hovered in place, as if it had just gotten stuck on something. Returning her gaze to her wrist, Serena touched the holodisplay a few times and the sphere shot off. An image projected above her wrist, with a bright spot in the center that moved toward the bottom as the sphere flew off in the direction the animals had gone.

With advanced imaging, the sphere was able to track the path of the animals by the body heat they left behind as they brushed against the tall grass and their feet warmed the soil with every step. Following the glowing path, Serena was able to locate the two animals as their paths began to converge on what appeared to be some sort of den. Serena marked the location on the map and began searching the area in a spiral manner away from the den, looking for more signs of life.

With the drone set to run an automated search pattern and alert her if it found anything, she began cutting a trail toward the nearest water in the area, a small river or large stream that flowed many kilometers to the large body of water that lie far to the east of the settlement. Remembering Riley's request to look for any sort of shellfish or filter feeder in the water, she set off to attempt to see what she could find. Apparently, Riley needed these to conduct some sort of tests for toxins in the area. The ground runoff would end up in the stream and these creatures, if there were any, would hold within them many clues as to what was in the water and soil around the area.

Han had been busy on the tractor. Soon, the tractor had cleared a broad swath of ground, enough for Clara to gather ample soil and for Vogel to test a second vehicle—a rusted excavator with minimal success. Vogel made many notes about the issues driving the excavator and the need for additional controls with which to operate the many functions of which it was capable.. Amir, enthralled by the day's progress, captured footage of each small victory. Serena roamed the perimeter, quietly contenting herself on finding harmless local fauna and searched the waters edge for more, laughing at herself as she chased small creatures in the water with an improvised net.

Serena looked down into the water, carefully trying to focus on what she thought might be some sort of life form. She thought the slight discoloration in the soil may have been one of the creatures she had seen several times, but had not been able to catch yet. The things were fast! Discarding the improvised net on a stick, which hadn't done her much good yet, she retrieved a small tool from her belt. Typically used for diagnostics, she carefully extracted a couple of wires and placed them gently touching the water's edge on either side of the spot she thought was one of those creatures she had been chasing. With a satisfied smirk on her face, she activated the device, sending a potent but relatively harmless electric shock into the water. She was completely satisfied with herself as the darker colored spot in the stream bed began to thrash briefly and float to the surface. Scooping it with the net, she placed it in one of Riley's sample bags along with some water. Holding it up to get a better look, she saw the collection she had gathered of shellfish like creatures Riley had described wanting. Gooey squishy animals within a hard coin like shell, and the new find. It was the strangest looking thing she had ever seen. It had a body about the size of her fist and a thick tail about half the length of her forearm. It appeared as if it had a hundred legs under its main body, long stiff antennas and dark black orbs protruding from either side of what she assumed was its head. At the back, a webbed tail like appendage seemed to be protruding from under the slightly darker than soil colored leathery back of the creature.

As she stared at the strange alien life through the clear walls of her sample container, she thought she might understand a bit better what it was that excited Clara about dirt so much, or Han about the new technology she was finding and driving around. Why Riley and all of the science oriented crew could seem so fascinated by what she previously thought was boring and trivial. As she walked back toward Clara and the shuttle, there was a lot of movement and she could feel the weight shift in the sample container she carried. The creature she had stunned was awake now and frantically trying to swim away. As she approached the rear of the craft, she stopped and watched as the webbed protrusion at its rear was pulled back into its body, only to snap back outward again, like a large funnel to push against the water. When it reached its full extent, it collapsed in on itself, giving another push before it sucked back under the leather back of the creature as a thin slimy looking string. She could see how the creatures were able to get such fast movements, shooting away from her attempts to snare them in her net. The mechanics of its movement were perfect for such fast actions. The black orbs must be some sort of visual organ, like eyes but maybe adapted for this planet.

As she stood there, watching in amazed rapture at the creature, she almost didn't notice Clara walking up to her.

"It's amazing isn't it? Discovering something new, learning how it works and right now, you're probably the universe's greatest authority of knowledge on that creature."

"Is that why you do it? You want to be the smartest person in the universe?" Serena replied with a smirk, "seems a little… egotistical, doesn't it?"

Clara laughed, "Egotistical is the first requirement to being a scientist, didn't you know?"

Serena shook her head and offered Clara a look at the sample container.

"No, it's the fascination with discovery. It's seeing something new that nobody else has ever seen and wondering why? How? And figuring it out. It's like a puzzle, if you're lucky enough to get one so new as us… here, on a new world." Clara looked around, and got a somber look on her face. "We may not be the first to see this, but we're the only ones here now. I expected a new planet… not one previously inhabited, but we work with what we have I suppose."

"So life is just one big puzzle for you?"

"Pretty much. You look at something new and have to unravel its mysteries, or you look at the same things everyone else is looking at and you see them in a way that nobody else has or ask a question nobody else asked before. Everything has so much to teach us. Take this creature for instance. Fascinating isn't it? What have you figured out, staring at it like you were you must have learned something?"

"The way it moves. I had such trouble catching them. They'd always evade the net at the last moment, accelerating away at lightning fast speeds."

"Then how'd you catch this one?"

Serena held up her diagnostics device and the wires hanging from it. "I tried something a little different. Shockingly, it worked."

Clara laughed again, a broad smile forming on her face. "So you've learned all about its locomotion, it's got some sense for motion or threat and very quick reflexes. It's also vulnerable to electricity. Bravo, you've uncovered a lot… but what does it eat?"

Serena just stared at Clara, slowly shaking her head. "I haven't a clue."

"See, always another question to answer. One big puzzle. Now, can you give me a hand packing the rest of these samples, we'll need to get back before your new pet starves to death."

Serena nodded, holding the sample container up for one last look before she placed it in one of the open crates alongside Clara's samples and closed the lid.

John, overseeing it all, allowed himself a moment of satisfaction. The prototype bridging console functioned better than expected. Maybe Elena really was onto something, but he'd rather the convenience of using this technology the way it was intended. In the distance, the sun hung lower in the sky, still blazing but edging toward the horizon. He toggled his comm. "Team, wrap up in the next half-hour. Let's pack out and head back before nightfall. Elena and Riley will want to get to work with what we bring them. Good work, everyone. We'll be back soon."

With that, the day's trials ended on a note of cautious optimism. The dusty tractor, humming away at half power, symbolized the possibility of reclaiming lost technology—of forging a new life from the ruins of a forgotten civilization. And as they prepared to depart, each member felt it: a rare sense of hope that maybe—just maybe—they were one step closer to making Aurion truly theirs.

After arriving back on the station, Serena walked into the medical ward with the sample container held proudly in front of her. When she walked in, she called out, "Riley! I got your alien fish tank here."

Riley pulled back a curtain. "Wonderful! Please, place it down right there."

"Sure thing. That all? I need to grab a bit to eat, I'm almost hungry enough to eat your fish."

Riley tried to hide a sheepish look as he cleared his throat. "I need those for testing."

"Riley! You're not actually considering…" Serena gasped.

"No no… these are for testing. … but if the tests go well, maybe you could catch a bunch more?" Riley gave her a hopeful look.

Serena shot a look at the container and what looked like a wave of nausea crossed her face. "I can catch your critters Riley, but I don't think I'll be putting one of those things in my mouth."

Riley shrugged, "well then I suppose it'll just be more for me."

"You can't be serious! You'd actually eat those things?" Serena looked genuinely appalled.

"I don't know." Riley picked up the container and then pulled up the image of a crayfish on his console. "It looks kinda like an Earth crustacean that was popular in the southern US, by the Mississippi River. I think they called it cajun food."

Serena looked back and forth between the creature and the image on the projection. "Riley, you're really starting to worry me. You sure you're ok? Do you need Doc to replace you? Are you sick… like in the head or something?"

Riley chuckled, "I'm perfectly fine Serena, I really do need these for testing. If there's anything serious going on with the water down there, these guys should tell us a lot about it. Did you get the scans I asked for too?"

Serena pulled out a portable scanner and handed it to Riley. "Sure did. I copied all the drone data over too. Found a couple land creatures, some rodent analogue perhaps, but quite large. Thought you might be interested in seeing that stuff too."

"Excellent! Thank you."

"I suppose i'll leave the mad scientist here to his alien fish experiments… or dinner. I'm going to go grab a wonderful nutrition bar." Serena smirked at Riley.

Riley waved her off, already preparing to run samples through some machine Serena didn't recognize.

37

Riley was perched at a compact diagnostics station, intently studying the readouts from the newly captured alien "crayfish." The med bay was quiet as usual—only the soft hum of machinery and the occasional beep of an automated analyzer intruded on the stillness. He caught himself nodding in mounting excitement at the scanning results. "This is fascinating," he mumbled under his breath. "Similar to Earth crustaceans, but with a few wild differences in the exoskeleton's composition..."

Before he could muse further, the hiss of the automatic door announced another arrival. Bet—towering, metallic plating glinting under the med bay's fluorescent lights—entered with that careful, half-awkward stride Riley had grown to recognize as Bet's attempt at a casual approach.

"Riley," Bet said softly, inclining his head in greeting. "I came to see how your tests were progressing."

Riley's face broke into an immediate grin. "Bet! Perfect timing. Was just about to run a final toxicology profile on this guy"—he tapped the transparent container that housed the alien crayfish—"and see if we can replicate an old Earth recipe."

At that, Bet's mechanical brow quirked. "Another Earth dish? Like the sandwich from earlier?"

Riley chuckled. "Not quite. Something a bit more... exotic. I owe you a huge thanks for digging up that file on crawfish étouffée, by the way. It's stirring up memories I thought I'd lost. I can't say we'll find the same spices or replicate the flavors, but if these samples prove safe..." He trailed off, a hopeful glint in his eye.

Bet gave a minuscule nod, the hint of a smile playing across the half of his mouth that remained organic. "I'm glad to help. A small gesture, but I recall you wanting to connect with your past—some sense of normalcy. Food can do that."

Riley fiddled with a sensor module, then put it aside. "Exactly. You did me a kindness, Bet. Anyway,"—he flicked open a holo-screen showing the results of the crayfish's exoskeleton analysis—"I'm about done here. The real reason I called you down is... well..." He hesitated, voice quieter. "The next step we discussed? The neural interface for me. I'd like to move forward with it."

Bet studied him thoughtfully, mechanical eyes adjusting focus. "You're sure? It's... a big step."

"I'm sure," Riley affirmed, squaring his shoulders. "I've gone as far as I can with these standard terminals. The med bay's advanced functionalities—hell, half the station's features—are locked away behind subroutines designed for neural input. I can't keep half-stepping if I want to treat patients properly."

Bet nodded once, gravely. "Then we'd better speak with the Captain, your 'Doc' Walters, and Elena. Clara, too, though I know she's... uneasy about augmentations. She'll insist on verifying the procedure's impact on your biology."

As if summoned by mention, the door slid open to reveal Captain Morrow, "Doc" Walters, Elena, and Clara all converging on the med bay. Captain Morrow wore an uncertain look, though her posture was steady; Doc looked freshly awakened but resolute, stethoscope draped around his neck, ready to reclaim some measure of his professional domain. Elena was, as always, brimming with technical excitement at a chance to push boundaries. And Clara... Clara's expression was a blend of curiosity and reluctance, arms folded over her chest.

"I already anticipated as much," Riley said as he shot Bet a wink.

Morrow wasted no time in getting right to her thoughts. "Riley, are you absolutely certain about this? I don't need to remind you of the risks. If something goes wrong—"

Riley turned to face them, posture confident despite the weight of the moment. "I understand, Captain. My oath is to preserve life, and ironically, it's this technology that can help me do it better. I won't be forced into it, but I choose it. Besides, the chances of something going wrong are quite minimal."

"That might be worse," Captain Morrow said. "Next thing you know, this will be a conveyor line for everyone wanting mods."

Elena stepped forward, eyes glowing with possibility. "I've been scanning these protocols, cross-referencing with Bet's partial archives. The neural interface procedure is relatively simple in this era's standards—but it's still major for us. That said, we have the hardware. Doc Walters can assist from the medical side, Bet has the data, and I can handle the technical integration. Clara, we'll need your expertise with the biological components and aiding Doc with the procedure."

Clara gave a small sigh, looking between Riley and Elena. "I'm not thrilled about these augmentations yet, but if it's you, Riley... you're the heart of this place—everyone loves you. I'm not about to stand in your way. Just promise not to lose yourself in it."

Bet gave Clara a curious look.

"Sorry Bet, but as common as this is to you, we still don't have the first clue what to expect yet. You are our only experience with all this fancy augmeta and that hardly offers any meaningful baseline or comparison from our perspective. I hope you can understand that."

Bet nodded. Clara had a point, a good point. It was so commonplace in society and happened at such a young age there was no comparison. He determined her points and concerns were quite valid and not at all insulting.

Doc Walters cleared his throat. "Well, I'm up for it—especially if you need a second pair of hands to keep an eye on vitals."

Captain Morrow took a slow breath. "Then I'll authorize it, with one condition: if any sign of complication arises, we stop immediately. Understood?"

Riley bobbed his head. "Understood. Thank you, Captain."

"Riley, please come see me as soon as you're back on your feet," Captain Morrow addressed him directly, with a slight tone in her voice that caught Riley and Bet's attention. It did not go unnoticed to either of them, the small tear starting to form in each of her eyes.

Deliberately avoiding the urge to look at Bet, Riley could see him studying the Captain out of the corner of his eye. "Sure thing Captain. I'm sure it won't take any time at all. I'll be better than new in no time."

Captain Morrow started to say something, but just closed her mouth and nodded. Bet bowed slightly. "Let's prepare, then. We'll set up in the med bay's sterile suite, coordinate the procedure. Elena, if you'd queue the station's older surgical instructions from my database—"

"Already done," Elena interjected, a faint, triumphant smile brushing her lips. "I can't wait to see how these advanced protocols differ from ours."

Clara rolled her eyes at Elena's enthusiasm but nodded agreement, stepping aside so the group could shift into action. Doc Walters began pulling instrument trays from the storage cabinets, rummaging for anything that might approximate the recommended gear. Morrow lingered at the doorway, a final protective look in her eye as she watched Riley strip off extraneous gear and settle onto a patient chair with surprising calm. The hint of worry still in her eyes, the weight of the galaxy seeming to rest on her shoulders. With a final look, she returned to the bridge, wishing she would be alone but also welcoming the knowledge that Marcus and Alvarez would be there waiting on her, ready to go over logs and plan the next steps.

The Captain's departure wasn't even noticed as everyone started getting busy. Bet instructed and educated as they worked.

"All right," Doc Walters said, rolling up the sleeves of his freshly laundered scrubs, "everyone knows their part?"

Bet, Elena, and Clara each answered in unison, "Yes, Doc," prompting a faint grin from the security detail's physician.

Riley stretched out on the bed, letting out a measured breath. "No time like the present."

And so, the unlikely quartet—synthorganic Bet, engineer Elena, "Doc" Walters, and reluctant scientist Clara—converged around Riley, each focusing on their role. The lights overhead dimmed, replaced by directed surgical spots that cast sharp beams onto the specific area around Riley's head and neck where they would be working. Elena keyed in the station's advanced interface, summoning a silent swirl of holographic readouts. Clara prepped a series of biological stabilizers, injection ampoules bristling with nano-bonding agents. Doc Walters performed final scans and shaved a small patch of hair at the base of Riley's skull. Meanwhile, Bet hovered with unwavering attention, providing real-time data from the old colony archives. Holographic images began to float and swirl around Riley, displaying vitals, visual representations of the inside of his skull, spine and neck. It was a fascinating dance of light, the likes of which none of them, except for Bet, had seen before. Activated by Bet's neuro-interface, a holographic menu surfaced in front of Doc. Highlighted on it in a procedure list, was the neuro-interface procedure itself.

To Riley's surprise, and everyone else's, the whole procedure took only a few minutes—just a series of numbness flooding the back of his neck, delicate robotic arms whirring quietly as they inserted an implant the size of a fingernail. The station's ancient protocols guided them in precise, fluid movements, almost as if it had been done a thousand times before on this very table. The entire thing was so fully automated and quick, everyone just stared at each other in dumbfounded shock.

"I told you, this was as common as being born," Bet said. "This really was as routine as getting a checkup for society in my time."

When the final beep signaled completion, Riley blinked, feeling a subtle pressure in his scull and a new presence growing at the edge of his consciousness—like a door opening to a softly lit corridor. He didn't move, waiting for permission. Riley watched as the implant in the holographic display in front of him appeared to dissolve slowly and reform as ultra-thin wires touching almost every part of his brain. He couldn't feel it, but there was a sort of sensation almost like the echo or hint of a scalp massage.

"Neural interface is integrated," Elena announced, voice trembling with excitement. "Vitals stable. Brain activity… normal, with an extra spark." She let out a breathy laugh. "You're good, Riley. You notice anything yet?"

The metaphoric door in Riley's head flew open. He closed his eyes for a few moments. Elena and Doc watched as his heart rate increased. Doc opened another panel showing more information about Riley's shifting body chemistry and examined it nervously. Bet placed a gentile hand hon his shoulder and spoke quietly.

"Just give him a moment to adjust. His interface and brain are getting to know each other right now and he's probably got quite the adventure going on in his head right now. This is normal, all this is well within expectations."

Slowly, Riley opened his eyes and turned his head, focusing on a random piece of equipment across the room. Almost instantly, a faint overlay flickered in his vision—tiny data tags labeling the device's operational status, battery level, and internal pressure readings. He gasped. "That's… oh wow."

Clara exhaled relief, stepping back to let Doc Walters approach. He quickly performed a follow-up scan, verifying no internal hemorrhages or neural misfires. Fingering the comm system in his wrist comp, he called the command deck. "He's all good, Captain."

"Already?" Captain Morrow responded, walking back into the medical bay.

"Yes Captain. I've seen more involved sutures. It really was nothing."

"Must have been, I wouldn't have even made it back to the command deck. I got curious and turned around to come back and missed everything."

Morrow watched Riley's wide-eyed wonder, a smile forming. "Guess it's official. You're part machine now."

Riley laughed, voice thick with emotion. "I'm still me… but yeah, this is… incredible." He paused, glancing at Bet. "Thank you. All of you."

Bet inclined his head, another slight twitch of a grin. "Welcome to the new frontier, Doctor Thompson." As Riley glanced over at Bet, there was something different about him. He couldn't quite figure out why, but Bet somehow seemed more complete when Riley looked at him. Almost intuitively, Riley knew Bet was excited. How had he known that? It was intuitive, like reading a facial expression, but Bet had no facial expression. He had no body language, nothing to give Riley such a strong understanding of how Bet felt. As this started to puzzle Riley, Bet winked at him. Riley's eyebrows shot off the top of his forehead.

And with that, the med bay lights rose again, the surgical arms all retracting into overhead panels. Captain Morrow let out a quiet sigh of contentment, nodding to Elena, Doc, and Clara in silent thanks. They'd just taken a monumental step—further bridging the divide between old Earth and the advanced technology of this lost colony. "Riley, are you ok?"

"Yes Captain," Riley said, reluctantly shifting his gaze from Bet to the Captain. "I'm better than new already. I'm sure this will take a little time to get used to and there's a lot Bet will have to show me, but I'm just fine. Better than fine."

Riley, fresh from the operating chair, couldn't resist testing his new mental link, flicking invisible commands that made the overhead monitors display patient logs and scanning subroutines. The entire med bay responded to his unspoken prompts, as if an extension of his body now. He beamed at them, tears threatening his composure.

"Brace yourselves," he said, eyes bright. "We're about to cure more than just alien crayfish allergies with this."

"Riley, give it a few days before anyone else gets the procedure. I want you to be fully acclimatized before anyone else gets implanted. Understood?" Captain Morrow shot Elena a glance.

Elena and Riley nodded. "Yes Captain."

"Excellent, Now I think all of you should get back to other projects, I need to have a talk with Riley in private if you please."

As everyone said goodbye and left, there was a lot of curiosity and many questions for Riley, but it would have to wait. Once they were alone, Captain Morrow's facade cracked.

"What's going on Captain?" Riley asked, offering her a seat on an adjacent exam table.

"I'm hoping that's what you can help me understand. I, uh… something's not right," she admitted, quietly enough that her voice almost disappeared under the hum of the station's air circulation.

Riley set a soft glow on the alcove's overhead lights, approached her with gentle caution. "What symptoms are you experiencing?" he asked, calmly but with building concern.

A tension band tightened around Morrow's brow. "Headaches… bone aches, too, especially at my shoulders. Fatigue that doesn't ease with rest. I can't seem to shake them, no matter how much I sleep." She opened her hand, showing how it trembled slightly in the subdued light. "And I've been more irritable than usual, as you've probably noticed."

He studied her trembling hand with a critical eye, then her posture —shoulders hunched in a subtle way that belied constant pain. "Captain, you've been pushing yourself for weeks. Stress alone can do a number, but your reference to bone pain…" He trailed off, flexing his new neural interface to bring a diagnostic panel up on the exam suite's overhead monitor. "Let's run a quick check. Have a seat on the bed and lie back, if you please."

Morrow grimaced but complied, sliding onto the crisp white sheets. She watched as a series of slender scanner arms unfolded from the bed's chassis, humming softly. Her face held that steely determination she'd used a thousand times in crisis—but now it was turned inward, bracing for news. Riley mentally instructed the scanner to begin a full-spectrum sweep. Data began streaming into his field of vision, lines of text and images only he could see as well as holographic details floating above the captain.

Her expression shifted from guarded to worried as she noticed his frown deepen. "What do you see?"

"A lot. Forgive me, this is going to take some getting used to. It's like having a holoscreen on the entire world only I can see, like a HUD… this… I have't had a lot of time to adjust to the visual overload Captain, but this is really truly something. Please, give me a minute to sort through this, and I apologize if my bedside manner is suffering as a result."

Riley chewed the inside of his lip, focusing on the swirling lines of data. He recognized an irregular pattern in her cellular structure, something reminiscent of radiation scarring, but more advanced. The final readouts made his stomach lurch: abnormal cell growth in key areas, a pattern that had no business being there unless…

"Captain…" he began, voice soft, eyes flicking up from the invisible text only he could see. "You appear to have a rare kind of malignant growth. The station's best guess and my professional opinion, is that it's linked to cumulative radiation exposure." He swallowed, letting the diagnosis land. "Radiation's always a risk out here, but you've seen a lot—multiple EVA missions, high-energy anomalies. It might have built up silently even before we left Sol."

Morrow's shoulders stiffened, her jaw set. But she forced herself to remain calm. "I see. So, what are our treatment options?"

Riley felt a surge of relief that she wasn't panicking or lashing out. Calm and rational was normal for her. "We have advanced surgical procedures," he said carefully, "especially now that I can better interface with the station's old medical gear. We could attempt gene therapy or advanced regeneration—maybe Bet's knowledge can help." He hesitated, seeing the flicker of fear in her eyes. "You still want to keep this under wraps?"

She exhaled slowly, pressing her fingertips to her brow. "I don't want the crew panicking, not when morale's so fragile. We'll handle it quietly. If treatment works, nobody has to know."

"Captain, with all due respect, you matter a lot to these people. If your condition worsens—"

She shot him a look that reminded him exactly who was in command. "No. I'm not letting this overshadow everything else. If we can treat it discreetly and swiftly, that's what we'll do. Don't make me pull rank on you, Doctor."

Riley closed his eyes briefly. "Understood," he said, though his voice trembled with conflict. "But I'll need at least one more set of hands. Doc Walters may be a trauma specialist with the security detail, but he's fully qualified for surgeries and might notice I'm… hiding something. And Bet…" He swallowed. "He's got historical data and I suspect personal experience with advanced cancer treatments—he might be essential. I'll also point out that in matters of your health, you cannot pull rank on me. In that, it's quite clear in regulations that I outrank you. So don't make me pull rank, which I will absolutely do if

I believe for one second that your judgment and the safety of this crew and colony are in any way compromised. I'll respect your wishes to the limits I am able to still do my job, but we're going to beat this and I'm going to need some help to ensure that's a fact."

Morrow's gaze flicked away, eyes fixed on the sterile floor. "Then bring them in, if you must. But only them. The rest of the crew remains in the dark. Agreed?"

Riley's chest felt tight, but he gave a tense nod. "Agreed. Only who is necessary for your care." He paused, letting the hush settle between them. "We should start soon. The scans suggest it's at a stage we can manage if we move fast, and that's by the standards from when we left Sol."

She inhaled a shaky breath. "Then let's do it. Quickly. Before it becomes something I can't hide."

He placed a reassuring hand on her arm, scanning her face. "I promise, Captain," he said quietly. "We'll treat this, and you'll be fine."

Morrow forced a small smile, but the fear behind her eyes was unmistakable. She rose from the bed, squaring her shoulders. "Time is short. If you need me for any more scans, let me know. Otherwise, keep me posted on the plan."

"Will do," Riley said, letting his sympathy show just enough in his voice. "Until I have a chance to cross reference a treatment plan with supplies inventory, let me offer you a bit of relief. For the moment, we can treat the symptoms and slow the progression," he said as he obtained an odd device and ampule from a cabinet in the wall. Returning with the strange device, he administered a dose of the oddly metallic looking liquid.

"There, you'll start feeling a lot less fatigue and a bit more your old self again shortly. Remember, this hasn't changed anything, it's just buying some time and giving you your power back." He walked her to the suite door. As it slid open, she turned for a moment, meeting his gaze with unwavering resolve.

"Thank you, Doctor Thompson," she said, voice barely above a whisper. "But no pity, okay? I'm still the Captain."

Riley managed a subdued grin. "Understood, Captain. No pity— just solutions."

With that, she slipped out, leaving the med bay as poised as ever. But for Riley, the heaviness of the diagnosis weighed like an anchor. He glanced back at the still-lingering scan results floating in his augmented field of view, then gently closed them with a mental flick.

Taking in a measured breath, he mentally tasked the station's system to pull every fragment of relevant data the archives might hold.

"All right," he murmured. "We handle this, quietly and fast."

It didn't take long to locate references to the Captain's specific type of cancer in the archives. There was even a cure for it. Of course they had cured cancer in the future, or his future, their past… As Riley struggled to control his thoughts, he tried to locate the resources required to implement the cure. Traversing the archives was both easier and exhausting with the new interface. With his hand still resting on his console, his mind began to drift again. This time, it was to Bet and wondering how he seemed to find everything so easily. Moments later, Bet walked through the door.

"Hey, I was just thinking about you," Riley quipped.

"I know," Bet said.

This took Riley by surprise and he pulled his hand from the console, staring at Bet. "What do you mean, you know?"

"I mean, we're both connected through this station now. That interface reads your mind. You were connected to the archives, essentially interfacing in a very crude way with the station's AI. It alerted me once you accessed records, because I asked it to after your implant procedure."

"Wow, ok. This is really a lot."

"And that's why I'm here. You can't teach a cave man to fly a ship just by putting him in a cockpit."

Riley let out a laugh at Bet's attempt at humor, but then he stopped short. "That's the second time I somehow just knew something about you without any reason. It's like I knew that was an attempt at humor, not just in context… I can't explain it, I just knew. And earlier, when you winked at me…"

"Yes. Do you remember when I first came aboard and John had the reaction to calming pheromones my systems were emitting?"

"Sure, but you said you'd keep them off…"

"And I have. This is another piece of a set of nonverbal communication protocols that was a part of. It was a whole series of communication protocols that allowed us to communicate on a deeper level much like you pick up context clues in body language, only this requires no translation or interpretation, there's no room for misinterpretation."

"I see. I'd love to explore that deeper with you later on and find out how that works, but right now, I need you to show me how you do the magic finger file transfer. I've got some scans from Captain Morrow. This is not to be shared outside of you, me and Doc Walters, understand?"

Bet nodded. "Just locate the data in your mind, then touch the console and 'push' it. The interface with handle the rest."

"You mean the thoughts? Or the memory?"

"No, the data. But, I suppose thinking about doing the scan may help you find it. I've never had to think about how I do it before and you won't either really soon. It'll be as natural as breathing."

Riley was skeptical, but attempted to do just that. To his surprise, it worked flawlessly. As he thought about conducting the scan, he could feel the data in his mind. As his mental focus shifted to it, it felt like a very odd way of recalling a memory. With a thought and a mental flex, he pushed the data out. Bet started looking over the data and nodded. He touched the console and began pulling up the inventory records Riley had been attempting to make sense of, going almost right to the entry they needed.

"How do you do that so easily and fast?" Riley asked.

"I told you, you're now interfacing with the station and thus the AI more directly. Ask it to do the work. It's far faster than you. You're still trying to sort through files like you would if they were physical copies. Instead, let your mind flow like normal thoughts, but include the station. It will take direction and assist you with your goals." Bet gave Riley a small grin and stepped aside, gesturing for him to try.

Riley placed his hand on the console and thought 'uhh Ai, umm station, I need to locate a specific medicine…"

"What you need is not specifically medicine, but the resources for the medical equipment to administer a cure. Unfortunately, that inventory was kept in a special wing of the station that is no longer available. It was destroyed in the disaster." The AI's response came quickly and through a speaker at the console Riley was touching as well as in Riley's head. Riley shot Bet a wide eyed surprised look of astonishment.

"What the actual fuck was that?" Riley exclaimed in a very uncharacteristic manner that made Bet chuckle. It wasn't actually audible, but rather it was as if Riley could feel it in his head.

Riley fell back in his chair and closed his eyes, taking a deep breath.

"That, is the station's AI," Bet offered. "I said let your mind flow like thoughts through the data giving it direction. You must have directed a thought or instruction to it conversationally. It responded."

"Why has it not been talking to us before now? That's just…"

"Because, until now, the only individual aboard the station I could communicate with was Bet. You may be humans, but I cannot see you or interact with you. The times I've tried to communicate with you on the bridge were difficult. I've been having to rewrite subroutines and attempt to pick up and translate vocal language through station sensors. The way your thoughts are transmitted to me from the neural interface are not as crude as the auditory vibrations you use to communicate with each other. I've also been quite damaged, and only recently been able to sustain a more full function thanks to Bet," the AI replied.

"Ok, I have so many questions not the least of which why an AI can't understand speech, but they will have to wait. So there's no cure for the Captain?" Riley asked.

"I did not say that. I said it was not aboard the station. I do not know the status of supplies on the planet." There was a hint of irritation in the AI's response.

Bet stepped in, vocalizing his request for Riley's benefit, "Display the last known locations and inventory status, if available, for possibly obtaining these supplies on the planet."

"This is all I could find. I estimate an 86% probability of this medical facility surviving the destruction on the planet and still having the resources in a viable state. Many of the resources there could have been lost if the backup power was unable to sustain storage conditions however. I have no data on which to provide any probability of backup power loss to the storage facility," the AI replied, displaying a map and lists of details.

Bet turned to Riley, "You should probably get some rest. You've got a lot to learn and that's best done with a fresh mind. I'll get this information to Doc and head to the planet with him on John's next trip. For now, you should get some sleep."

Riley nodded, feeling absolutely exhausted all of a sudden, both mentally and physically.

38

Elena approached the rear of the drop ship with several cargo crates in tow. Gliding almost weightless on transport carriers, the 4 cargo crates contained two dozen new interfaces for equipment. Based on the previous success and feedback with the two prototypes, she had worked with the station's fabrication equipment to manufacture new smaller units that should be far more durable and easy to use. As she approached, John walked out the rear loading ramp.

"Those the new interfaces?" John asked as she approached.

"They are indeed. Should be a lot easier to install, just plug and go. Smaller, more efficient, an improved magnetic clamping system for installation and I've included an additional power source in case any of the equipment needs an extra boost. Did you get the spare power cells I sent down earlier?"

"Already loaded and ready to go. We're going to have more equipment than we have bodies to operate here soon."

"I think that's the idea, isn't it? Having as much ready for the colonists as possible?"

John nodded in agreement, "thats the idea. I hear the Captain is wanting to send down the first wave soon. We're scouting potential residences this trip. If we find something suitable, we may have a semi-permanent crew on the surface after today. Serena's quite eager to get settled down there."

"That's progress. You need anything else from me?"

John shook his head, "not right now. You can leave those there. I'll get them loaded up and strapped down."

"Thanks, safe trip."

John nodded in appreciation and waved goodbye as he grabbed

another crate to load. By the time he had the crate secured and turned to grab another, Han and Vogel were coming up the ramp, each bringing another crate. With the three of them working together, the rest of the cargo loaded quickly. With a bit of time to spare before daybreak on the planet's surface, John called for everyone to muster on the command deck to go over the mission details. With the crew on deck, Captain Morrow addressed everyone.

"We've made a lot of progress. The addition of the equipment you're able to get operational on the planet is a huge bonus. Instead of having to deploy the colonists and depend entirely on the equipment we've brought, we've been able to stretch out our food reserves longer and get a huge head start for them. Once we've got a stable food source available, I plan to start waking the colony and sending them planet side. It's the same deployment plan as it always was, just accelerated with the details of the present situation. This makes getting the fields prepped and the crops going a high priority. We will also need someplace to put the colonists. The hab shelters we brought can be a backup, but I'm sure everyone would rather have fancy apartments in the existing structures with all the amenities. That will free up the hab shelters for storage, additional labs and whatever else we need, as well as expansion and emergency backup. That assumes we can establish some recover of the power grid and locate a power source as well. For the immediate, we have enough solar and powered generators to make do initially. It appears that hunting will be sparse near by the settlement, but station scans of the surface indicate far better options to the north and to the south. Clara, I saw your report from the last trip. Would you give us a brief description of what you found?"

Clara cleared her throat and straightened her posture a bit. "Sure. The soil samples indicate a rich lively soil, full of all the biology we need for healthy crops. The soil composition is highly compatible with earth crops. It appears the previous colony has modified the soil a bit for better compatibility, although the native soil and biology shouldn't pose any problems with larger scale agriculture. The truly interesting thing is the kudzu. The vines are in fact a mutated form of Earth origin kudzu. After searching through old logs we've recovered, it appears that a genetically modified version of kudzu was farmed here for several purposes. Although edible, the nutrient value is low. Using it as a food source would require considerable processing and the result would be similar to the nutrient bars we all love so much. The fibrous vines do offer plenty of options for industrial applications, however the primary use would be for rapid production of compost. The kudzu in the fields is nitrogen affixing, so the soils are very rich in nitrogen, too high in fact for some of our crops. This is very good news for the staples however. Our first crops should be heavily focused in corn, wheat and potatoes. These crops will benefit from the higher nitrogen content and will help balance the soil for future rotations while providing everything we need to start a basic agricultural infrastructure. Later in the season we will be adding Broccoli and lettuces to the mix. I think I have also identified a solid place a bit farther south for a citrus orchard. There's just one problem with immediate agricultural needs. The kudzu has taken over the fields we need to cultivate. Simply mowing them down and tilling them in will not remove them. They will come back and completely overtake the crops, choking them out. Unfortunately, our options are limited. The surest way to remove them would be to eliminate any nodules, seeds and live roots in the soil with the use of the stations point defense battery; lasers and masers with some modifications to account for atmosphere. The drawback is that it will kill everything in the soil and it would take the rest of the growing season to replenish what is lost. It would set us back too far to be a viable option."

Captain Morrow nodded along. When Clara finally paused, she interjected, "and you have another solution?"

Clara sighed softly and continued, "I do, but I don't like it. The kudzu has become a highly invasive species here. While I don't like the idea, we have little choice at this point if we're going to get enough food production on time. Ideally, we can get at least one of the cities old vertical farms operational again. Then we can utilize the kudzu as a nutrient base for feeding the vertical farms. But, we can't put all our eggs in this one basket, so I have created an herbicide that I believe will only target the genetics of the kudzu. Being of earth origin, it's different enough from the samples of native flora I collected, I don't anticipate any unexpected fallout, but I simply have not had enough time to properly test or gather enough data to know how safe it will be. To avoid as much possible issue with unexpected results, it will have to be applied by hand. Limited quantities force this as well. This means we will only be able to expand our farmable land a bit at a time."

Han, listening intently, gave Vogel a nudge and a wink. "Looks like we're going to have lots of fun on those tractors for a while. We're farmers now."

Vogel rolled her eyes at Han and simply nodded. Han noted the barest hint of a smile on her face though and knew Vogel was just as excited as she was to have an important role, and to play with the heavy equipment of course.

"Excellent. John, you and Doc will be working with Bet to scout buildings. You'll be scanning for structural integrity and locating the most suitable living areas first, then you will be searching for supplies in the laboratories. I want you to keep an eye out for any form of access to the underground infrastructure. From what data we have on the colony, there was a massive underground network of facilities and tunnels. We need to know as much as we can about what we don't know," Captain morrow paused and looked at the assembled crew one by one. "We've been given a huge head start here, but there's also the unexpected complications that came with it. I just wanted to say thank you to each one of you for the incredible job you've done so far. We've been met with extraordinary situations none of us predicted. You've all been adaptable and brilliant thus far. Keep up the good work."

Elena spoke up, "Captain, I would like to take a shuttle to the inner system to collect antimatter and ZPE modules. I know you've got Bet on the ground team, but I think it would be best if he were to assist me on this. Nobody knows the inner system's facilities better than him and I doubt I could get it done without him."

Captain Morrow pinched the bridge of her nose and grimaced. "We need him to help locate the resources we need from the medical labs. That mission is just going to have to wait."

Bet, who had been perfectly still the entire time, shifted slightly in his stance. "Captain, Elena's right. We're going to need power for the planet. I can give John and Doc everything I know about the city, in fact I've already given you most everything I know. I didn't spend a lot of time on the planet, at least not in the facilities they will be exploring. I'm not sure what use I will be there, now that they've got Elena's interface devices, it's the next best thing to a neural interface now. I'd be far more useful retrieving power supplies."

Captain Morrow let out a heavy sigh as she thought. "Alright. Just be careful!"

"Thank you Captain," Elena said with a large grin.

"Any more curveballs anyone wants to throw at me?" Captain Morrow said as she scanned the whole assembled crew with a gaze. "No, ok then. Let's build a colony."

Within the hour, two ships launched from the station. One headed for the planet and the other in toward the inner system. On the station bridge, Captain Morrow watched the holographic projection of each and their flight path with intensity. Jason was coordinating telemetry and corrections with both flights simultaneously while Marcus ensured constant communications and adjusted the sensor feeds to keep track of the missions.

Han, in the co-pilot seat confirmed a safe landing with Marcus before jumping up and bolting for the rear of the craft, eager to unload and get to work. As Han and Vogel took off for the heavy equipment with several crates of gear and new interfaces, Serena went south, searching for more suitable game to hunt and to scout out the proposed citrus farm. John and Doc set off for the inner city.

It took little time for Han and Vogel to get all the equipment fitted with the new control interfaces and begin testing each. A few started right up without issues, a few others with the aid of the power boost Elena provided in the new units. Most however, were non-functional. Using some of the equipment that was functional, they managed to pull several others into a large maintenance warehouse beside the lot. They spent the next few hours restoring function to most of the maintenance equipment with the remaining interfaces and spare parts they located in the facility.

"This would be a lot easier with one of those implants," Han commented after a particularly frustrating attempt to get a hoist operational.

"I'm still not sure I like the idea." Vogel replied as she was sorting through the many cabinets of parts and tools, taking inventory of what they had available to work with. "Now this, I can support." Vogel pulled a large speaker system out of a storage closet and started tinkering with it.

"Is that really the highest priority right now?" Han asked with an overly dramatic eye roll.

"Absolutely," Vogel replied with a huge grin as the system powered up. After a few more minutes working out a connection between her wrist console and the speaker array, Vogel let out a shout of victory as ancient Earth heavy metal blasted from the speakers. The sudden volume made Han jump and bang her head on the support beam she was working underneath. Rubbing her head, she couldn't help but laugh as Vogel closed her eyes and began twitching and moving in a way Han thought looked like she might be having a seizure. Han never understood the peculiar dance moves, but I had to admit the music was rather energizing.

A couple blocks away John and Doc could hear the music while they were investigating a residential building. With a couple of drones circling the building they quickly had a pretty good scan of the building with no obvious issues to the structural integrity. They sent the drones flying through the building and followed on foot with handheld scanners in roughly 30 minutes time they were confident the building had no structural damage and were able to identify a list of repairs that would be required to the electrical and plumbing systems. The building was three stories tall and contained 120 individual housing units, most capable of supporting a small family.

Having identified more than suitable housing on their first attempt, John and Doc were feeling lucky. John sent the scan results and report back to the station and they began their search for medical supplies and underground access. Returning to the building they scouted briefly on their first trip, John and Doc made their way through the dark to the rear of the building where they found a staircase. Once they had reached the door, two floors down, John pulled out one of the fancy new interface devices. Hoping the door, which did not appear to have any physical latch or access panel still had enough power to open, he was very pleased when the holo display in his hand gave him a simple green button that said 'OPEN'. John pushed the button and the door slid quietly open. Sharing a look with Doc, they stepped inside. At first, it didn't look like much, just a dark hallway, but as they walked farther in, overhead lighting began to illuminate the space ahead as if reacting to their presence, or perhaps the presence of the interface in John's hand. It seemed this facility still had a reserve power. Slowly, the entire basement floor began to come to life. Offices to either side of the hallway lit up, a dim glow behind tinted glass. John could see individual consoles, desks and the occasional personal effects of its prior occupants. They kept walking until they came to a large polyglass doorway. Again, using the 'OPEN' button on the interface, John opened the doors. Inside was a vast open area full of lab equipment. One wall was lined with cabinets of what John assumed was computers and data storage. Along another wall, were cabinets, storage lockers and elaborate storage vessels of many types. Some appeared to be glass with a vented hood on top, others appeared to be cryogenic storage pods. A few colored cabinets indicated they contained strong acids or reagents. Doc was looking around, jaw agape as he took it all in.

John swept a beam of light along the nearest row of lab benches, eyes skimming across the clutter of beakers, half-buried data tabs, and archaic glass tubing twisted into improbable shapes. The overhead lights had come on—dim but enough to show he and Doc the chaotic sprawl of a once-bustling research facility.

"What do you think they did here?" John murmured, stepping around a toppled stool. Glowing readouts blinked in the distance, as if the lab itself was waking from a long slumber.

Doc chuckled, kneeling beside a counter to inspect a transparent cylinder. Inside was a jelly-like substance, shimmering faintly. "Something advanced, that's for sure." He tapped the container with a gloved finger. "Or maybe they were making some sort of kids toy slime," he mused. "Interesting. These labels are in some advanced notation. I can't read half of them."

John approached, pulling one of Elena's new interface devices from his belt. He let it hover over a particularly complex label. The device's holo-display flickered, parsing text in erratic bursts. "Magnetic recon… negative energy? Some references to gene editing…" He frowned, shifting the angle to pick up more text. "We must be in a bio-molecular engineering lab and that sounds extra particularly nasty. I'd say it's fifty fifty that either kills you instantly or gives you super powers."

They exchanged glances—exactly the kind of place that might hold what both of them quietly sought. For John, a chance at augmentations—optical enhancements, body chemistry controls, maybe even some form of the mythical rapid cell regeneration. For Doc Walters, crucial resources to tackle the Captain's cancer. Neither had openly admitted their motives yet, but the tension was there, unspoken.

John cleared his throat. "Well, let's keep scanning. Bet said the colony used labs like these for everything from AI neuro-interfaces to advanced immunotherapies. There's gotta be something we can use."

Doc nodded, trying to maintain a neutral tone. "Agreed. Let's start from left to right, see what's stored in these big cabinets along the wall." He pointed toward a series of tall, sealed compartments embedded with digital locks. At one point, they might've glowed bright with easy, daily access—now, each panel displayed flickering text and half-functional lights.

Approaching the first compartment, John held the interface close. The lock beeped uncertainly, an amber glow sputtering across its surface. "Give me a second," he muttered, cycling through the console's rudimentary hacking suite and access code library. A flash of green signaled success, and the door slid open with a reluctant groan.

Inside: racks of small, sleek canisters labeled with a futuristic script. One row glowed softly, a faint coolant aura wafting out as the door's seal broke. Another row seemed inert, the canisters coated in dust.

Doc leaned in, visor lights throwing reflections around the tall cabinet. "Bio-suspension mediums… Some references to advanced polyclonal therapies. Interesting." He plucked one canister from a rack, turning it over in his hands. "These could be used for cellular reprogramming—like advanced gene therapy. A chunk of the label says something about tissue regeneration markers."

John stiffened. Regeneration? That sounded mighty close to what he wanted—body repairs that extended well beyond normal healing. "Let's stash a few," he said, trying to sound casual. "Could be valuable for… well, injuries." He paused, then added, "And maybe other uses."

Doc, still scanning the text, only half-heard him. "Sure. We'll bring them. Might help treat difficult conditions."

They moved on, opening another door. This one displayed shelves of sealed vials, a swirling array of dark fluids with "NRL-OPT" scrawled across the front. John tapped the console's translator. Neural-Optical Protocol? The readout flickered, offering partial results:

"… recommended for advanced ocular implants… wave-lens calibration… caution: must be administered with correct synergy facto…" the rest of the words cut off.

John's heart picked up. "Doc, this looks like something for optical augmentation. Maybe it's the calibrant you'd need for advanced eye enhancements." He tried to sound nonchalant, but a hint of excitement bled through.

Doc raised an eyebrow. "You eyeing fancy retinas, Ferris?"

John forced a half-laugh. "Maybe. And if it means fewer suits and less squinting at that damn bright sun, all the better, right?" He quickly grabbed a couple of vials, tucking them in a protective case. "You and Riley can test it later."

Doc said nothing, but an amused smirk played on his lips—he suspected John's deeper motives ran beyond simple brightness comfort. But who was he to judge? They all had their reasons.

A few cabinets down, they stumbled onto something big. A large metal trunk, the size of a traditional footlocker, with a partially lit screen on top that read: RAD-RES Protocol. John's device beeped as it tried to interpret the text.

Doc's breath caught. "RAD-RES. Radiation resistance? This might be exactly what the Captain needs for her… " He crouched, carefully prying open the trunk. A wave of cold air escaped, and rows of carefully labeled injector kits glinted under the overhead lights.

"'Radiation Tolerance/Rapid Cell Repair Serum'," Doc read aloud, eyes wide. "This… if it's still viable, might be what we need."

John mustered feigned innocence. "Captain's definitely had some radiation exposure over the years. Are you saying there's something wrong with her? I figured it was just stress, but that would explain a lot."

Doc's expression turned guarded—he obviously knew more about the Captain's situation than he was letting on. "Right," he said softly. "Let's hope it's not too degraded after all this time." He picked one kit up, scanning it with a portable analyzer. "The readout suggests partial stasis is intact. Some vials might be stable. Look, I can't hide what I'm obviously after here and you're going to draw your own conclusions, but know that I'm under strict orders from the Captain and Riley not to discuss… anything about anything or that there is even anything at all. So whatever conclusions you draw on your own about me trying to locate a cancer treatment, you'd best keep entirely to yourself. Understand?"

"I know and see nothing," John replied. "Just as you don't see me looking for specific augments… anything that might help me do my job…"

Doc fixed his glare on John for a brief moment, then nodded. "I'll keep an eye out for something like that too."

"Thanks Doc and don't worry, I don't want to get you in trouble with mommy and daddy either."

They loaded a few of the kits into a sturdy container, storing them carefully—Doc's practiced hands ensuring each injector was cushioned. He tried not to reveal his relief at finding a possible lead for Morrow's secret cancer cure. For a moment, a flicker of hope illuminated the dusty gloom of the lab.

One final cabinet bore a curious symbol—a stylized double helix. Inside, shimmering containers labeled "CellChem Master Synth" lined the shelves. John recognized half a word on the translator: "body chemistry controls." Something about advanced endocrine regulation. This set off alarm bells of excitement in his mind—exactly the type of thing he'd wanted for controlling adrenaline, boosting strength, or maybe augmenting stamina. He didn't hesitate, sliding a few into his own supply case. Doc watched with polite curiosity, but said nothing.

They spent the next half hour rummaging deeper into the lab, carefully cataloging anything that seemed potentially relevant—some partial data on advanced neural frameworks, incomplete records of an "implant suite." The place had likely been half-evacuated at the time of the colony's fall, so many items were missing or simply not present. But the haul they'd collected was a promising start, for both of their covert missions.

At last, they reached an imposing set of locked doors near the far corner of the lab, leading into what looked like a sealed corridor that descended further underground. The interface console displayed a flurry of errors, refusing to open it. John growled in frustration, punching a final override. Still no response. "Power must be cut or the system's locked," he grumbled.

Doc eyed the corridor beyond. "I'm guessing that leads to the bigger facilities. We'll need Bet's guidance or maybe the girl's hacking skills. For now, guess we're out of luck."

"Yeah," John muttered, turning away reluctantly. "Han would probably take it personal until she beat it. Vogel would have it singing and dancing in a day. Better load up what we've got. We can return once we've got more tools or… help." A pang of dissatisfaction gnawed at him—there might be an entire hidden wing of augmentation tech behind that door. But he knew their personal agendas would have to wait.

They retraced their steps, guiding the crates of found supplies back toward daylight. At each step, leftover lights flickered off behind them, as if the lab was sinking back into its century-long sleep. Outside, the bright afternoon sun made John's eyes ache. He clutched the vials of possible ocular enhancements, longing for the day he wouldn't have to squint anymore and could see better in the dark.

Doc gave him a sidelong glance, noticing the tension in John's jaw. "You all right?"

"Just the glare," John replied, half-truthfully. The suit's visor tinted automatically, but it still didn't help the underlying frustration. He forced a grin. "Let's get these goodies back to the ship. The Captain will be thrilled."

They trudged to the waiting cargo-lift, crates in tow, dusty footprints trailing behind. As the automated loader rumbled, lifting the crates aboard their transport, John inhaled the planet's humid air. Overhead, the sky hung a hazy, alien blue, reminding him how far from Earth they truly were.

"We've still got plenty more time," John said. "We had such quick luck in the first two buildings, let's check out another one of the points of interest."

Doc nodded, casting another glance at the cargo as the loading ramp closed. "Looks like we can scan a couple more buildings along the way if we head for this one," he said as he indicated a glowing arrow on the holographic map hovering above his wrist.

"It's a plan, lets get it done."

39

The two set off for another trip into the city. After walking a couple of kilometers, they found their path was blocked by extremely dense kudzu growth which seemed to be pouring out of what remained of an old vertical garden.

"Looks like we're taking the scenic route," John said, indicating the dense growth.

"If we go back a block, maybe we can cut over there." Dock manipulated and tried to make sense of the holographic map. "There's just so many shadows the station can't see and areas that haven't been scanned yet. It's hard to tell, but it looks like it connects back a few blocks over, right next to the residential building."

John nodded agreement and started backtracking to the previous intersection. They found the path mostly clear, though John did have to clear a bit of vines with his vibrosword a few times. When they reached the residential building, they sent the drones flying for exterior scans and updating their map. Seeing only minimal damage and nothing blatantly obvious, they went inside for more detailed scans of the interior structure.

"Let's keep scanning," Doc said, stepping carefully around another thick snarl of kudzu at the building's entrance. The structure loomed overhead—less battered than many they'd seen, but still riddled with cracks and creeping vines. Most of the windows were missing or shattered, the holes covered in thick walls of kudzu leaving the interior dark despite the planet's fierce midday sun.

John flexed his sore shoulders, holstering his vibrosword after clearing a trail. "Agreed. The drone suggests minimal structural damage from the outside, but the place is old—let's stay alert."

They pressed inside through an arched doorway, dust drifting in lazy motes under the faint overhead glow that flickered to life at their approach. Debris littered the corridor: bits of collapsed ceiling, broken furniture, clumps of dried vines. Every footstep seemed to echo ominously in the hush.

Doc checked his wrist console. "Han and Vogel are a couple blocks away, testing that excavator. Maybe we should just have them demolish this one."

John nodded. "Oh, I'm sure they would love that." He gestured for Doc to follow deeper in, stepping around an overturned cabinet. "Let's see if we can reach the upper floors or a basement, see if we can get a good read on the primary support structure or see if there's anything worth salvaging."

Doc was half-absorbed in reading the holo feeds from his scanner when a subtle groan reverberated through the floor. John froze, spotting a jagged fissure near Doc's feet. He tried to react and get Doc's attention but he was too late. Doc took one more step just as his holodisplay started to alert him to discrepancies in the density scanning and the ground gave way with a horrifying crack. Doc's foot plunged through crumbling concrete, and a split-second later, an entire support column toppled inward, pinning Doc beneath it.

"Doc, watch out—!" John lunged forward, but the column crashed down with a deafening crunch, pinning Doc's legs against the fallen chunks of cement. A plume of dust and debris engulfed them, and the building groaned as if exhaling centuries of tension.

When the dust settled, John found Doc pinned beneath the tilted column, half-hidden by rubble. Adrenaline spiked in John's veins. "Doc!" He scrambled over fractured slabs of concrete and chunks of rubble, hooking an arm around Doc's torso, trying to shift the beam. It refused to budge, grinding stone against stone in a sickening scrape. John adjusted his approach and positioned himself beside Doc in an attempt to get better leverage on the support beam. John struggled against the weight, pushing his power assist apparatus to its limits. Applying all of his strength and that of the mechanical arms and legs in his suit, he managed only to shift the beam slightly. The mechanical assist gave out and so did John's strength. The Beam shifted back in place and threatened to shift further.

Doc's face was contorted in pain, breath ragged. "I—I can't feel my legs," he managed, voice tight with shock. Blood soaked the ruined fabric of his suit near his thighs. "John... you gotta get me out—"

"I'm on it," John said with forced calm. "Don't move. Let me see if I can wedge something under this."

"Right, like I'm going anywhere," Doc replied through gritted teeth.

John pried a piece of rebar free and tried to lever the column, muscles straining. The beam shifted a centimeter before locking again and the metal bar bent under John's force. Not enough to free Doc.

Defeated, John toggled comms. "Han, Vogel—emergency. We're in the second building to the east. Structural collapse pinned Doc's legs. I can't free him alone."

A burst of static preceded Han's urgent reply. "Copy that, John. On our way. Vogel's grabbing the portable lifters—sit tight."

John closed the connection, heart hammering. He turned his attention back to Doc, pressing gloved hands to the wound sites. Doc's suit had auto-tourniquets engaged, slowing the bleeding, but the sight was still grim. "Hang in there, Doc. Help is coming."

Doc's breathing hitched as a wave of pain crested. He managed a weak smirk. "Never a dull moment, huh?" He tried to shift, but the crushing weight made him groan. "Augh… God… I'm used to being on the other side of this. I think it's worse, knowing what's going on and how bad it really is."

"Quiet," John murmured, scanning the debris overhead. The last thing he needed was more collapses. The entire corridor looked precarious, new cracks forming across the ceiling. A few more beams hung at odd angles, threatening to follow the first if disturbed.

Only a couple minutes later—though it felt like an hour—Han's voice crackled again over comms: "John, we're at your building. Activate your location beacon, send a pulse."

John tapped his wrist console to broadcast his exact position. A tremor reverberated through the floor, sending dust trickling from above. "Hurry," he muttered into the mic.

Clank—Clank. Footsteps in the rubble signaled arrivals. The corridor behind them lit with flashlights, Vogel's calm voice cutting in: "John, you good?"

"Over here," John called. "Watch for cracks in the floor—about half the hallway's compromised."

Vogel emerged first, hefting a portable hydraulic cutter and a mechanical jack sling. Han followed with a second kit, eyes wide at the sight of Doc pinned under the column. "Damn," she breathed. "Let's do this quick and careful."

"Yeah," Vogel said tersely, dropping to one knee near the beam. "I'll rig the lifter on that side, you handle the tension cables, Han. John, you just keep Doc stable. The last thing we want is the column shifting the wrong way. Be ready to pull him free."

John steadied Doc, offering what reassurance he could. Doc clenched his jaw, trying to stay silent, but occasional groans betrayed the agony he was in. "We'll have you free soon," John promised, meeting Doc's pained eyes.

Vogel slammed the portable lifter's base onto a stable patch of flooring. With practiced efficiency, she extended the mechanical arms under the beam. Clank—whir. Gears and hydraulics engaged. Han linked the tension cables to an overhead brace, mindful not to jostle the precarious support.

"All set," Vogel said, voice tight. "John, on my mark, pull Doc clear if it lifts enough. Go."

She activated the lifter. With a grinding squeal, the beam shifted, rising a fraction. Dust rained down in a choking cloud. John, coughing, reached under the gap, hooking his arms around Doc's shoulders. "I've got you—pulling now!" he yelled.

Doc stifled a scream as his crushed legs slid out from beneath the beam. Dragging lifeless behind them, Doc's legs left blood smeared streaks and drag marks in the fallen dust.The moment John had him free, Vogel deactivated the lifter. The column sank back in a cascade of broken concrete with an echoing thud. For a breathless second, none of them moved—unsure if the building would hold. Then silence.

Doc's face was ashen, breath shallow. John and Han quickly dragged him to a safer patch of floor. "We need to get him to the shuttle. Now," John said, checking the vitals on his wrist console. "Those legs..." he trailed off, not wanting to finish the thought. The suit's auto-tourniquets were the only thing preventing catastrophic blood loss. "My suit's busted, faster if you carry him."

Vogel nodded. "I'll help carry him. Han, secure this hallway so we don't trip another collapse."

Han, exhaling sharply, swiftly scouted the corridor. "We can exit two rooms over," she said, scanning the walls. "That's the route we came in. Let's do it fast."

Supporting Doc between them, John and Vogel half-lifted, half-dragged him away from the debris. Pain etched itself across Doc's features, but he didn't complain—just tightened his grip on John's shoulder, drawing on every reserve of grit. They inched their way out of the building, dust swirling around them like a ghostly shroud.

Outside, the planet's glare assaulted their visors, but John only had eyes for the wounded man leaning against him. "Hang in there," he repeated, voice thick. Vogel hailed the station, alerting Riley to prepare for their arrival. "Han, take over for me."

Han took John's place to carry Doc between her and Vogel. John managed to get the shuttle's doors open and the initial pre-flight startup sequence going from his wriest comp. Without the aid of the mechanical assistive device, John struggled not only to carry his own weight, but fought against the tight joints of the broken and bent equipment contained in his suit.

"Serena, how far out are you?" John panted into his mic.

"Too far, don't wait on me. I'm good. Just get Doc to the station," Serena's reply held no hesitation or doubt.

Together they carried Doc onto the shuttle's loading ramp, laying him on a medical pallet. The engines roared as the ramp sealed shut behind them, and John collapsed beside Doc, breath ragged. Vogel strapped in the copilot seat, adrenaline pulsing.

Han jumped to the cockpit, spooling the engines for a swift launch. "Station, we're inbound, medical emergency—Doc was pinned under a collapsed building, crushed legs." She shot John a fierce glance. "Stay with him, John. We can get him to Riley in time."

John nodded, pressing a hand to Doc's shoulder. "You heard her, Doc. This is just a bump in the road, right?"

Doc's eyes fluttered, pain-laced, but he forced a tight-lipped smirk. "Some… bump."

The shuttle lifted off, leaving behind the building that nearly claimed one of their own. As they hurtled toward orbit, John silently prayed the station's advanced med bay would be able to patch Doc up. Meanwhile, standing over a large animal she'd shot for dinner, Serena watched the shuttle take off and head for the station. The previous excitement of a surprise BBQ with everyone had completely vanished as she worried about Doc. With nothing to be done about it, she knelt down and began dressing her kill. She was on her own, an entire planet to herself until Doc was taken care of and they could come back for her.

40

As soon as the shuttle craft touched down in the station, Riley, Marcus and Jason were ready with an emergency gurney. The device was not just a portable bed to transport Doc, it had its own set of triage equipment. John and Vogel were already carrying Doc down the ramp before it was even halfway open. They tried to place him down as gently as possible, but they were more concerned about getting help started than his comfort. As soon as Doc was stretched out on the gurney, Riley saw a data readout provided to him by the gurney via his neuro-interface. Reviewing Doc's vitals as they moved to the nearby medical bay, Riley began running scans. Semi-circular sensor arrays began rotating out from under the gurney and over Doc as they rushed to the medical bay. With the sensors online, the bed was able to give him a complete picture of the damage before they even got to the better equipped medical suite. When they arrived in the medical bay, the bed itself slid its entire surface over relocating Doc to the actual exam table. Having already assessed Doc's injuries, Riley was working on stabilizing Doc's vitals, closing severed arteries and veins before he was fully in position.

The rest of the crew stood back, trying to give Riley space to do what he needed to do. What they saw as they watched on was a brilliant choreography of lights and machines. Holographic displays floating around over Doc and the bed as Riley issued commands and manipulated the holographic interface like a conductor performing his greatest symphony. Mechanical arms and medical devices moved from the ceiling above, the wall beside and a few rose from the floor. To watch him work, it was hard to imagine he had not had much experience with the neuro-interface yet. Mechanical arms moved around, almost mimicking Riley's arm gestures, but working with an autonomous purpose once his commands were given.

Amid the occasional flashing lights and lasers. Riley was single handedly doing everything that used to require a dozen people to accomplish. As beautiful and amazing as this image was to watch, the entire crew seemed to be holding their breath, hoping that Doc would pull through. A breath that seemed to become a collective gasp when Riley waved a hand over his head and a privacy curtain flew out around the entire scene, blocking their view.

Captain Morrow, taking the hint, was the first to speak. "Let's let Riley work. He'll let us know when there's news. Come on."

She ushered everyone back out the door and toward the shuttle bay next door where there was a room large enough for all of them to wait. There was little fear that Riley wouldn't know where to find them, because John would not stop pacing near the passageway door. Captain Morrow understood. Doc was part of John's team. Hell, she wanted to join him. Instead, she caught his eye for a brief moment and simply gave him an understanding nod. He blinked and returned it. A silent understanding passed between them, one any tested leader understands. Morrow went to sit with the rest of the crew, not as the Captain, but as one of them. She sat down next to Han and Vogel and in short order, the three were all leaning against one another in comfort, waiting for news.

When Riley did come, John stood motionless in the door, frozen with fear as he tried to read Riley's face.

"Where's the rest of the crew?" Riley asked in a quiet professional manner that gave nothing away.

John nodded toward the ready room. "In there."

"Come on then, best I say it once and answer any questions eh?" Riley motioned toward the door and John walked in.

Still unable to sit, John stood like a statue by the door as Riley moved to the center of the room. All eyes on him, he cleared his throat.

"He's fine. He's stable. He's going to live. That's the good news. Now, the bad. Due to age and loss of station resources, there just wasn't enough of the right treatments and supplies available to save his legs, so he's sedated for the time being. There should be no problem fitting him with prosthetics although I am planning to wait for Bet's return. He has the most experience with that sort of procedure and I'll need his help to use the fabrication and technology this station has to offer. We do want to give Doc the best we can after all. For now

Doc is sedated, so it's probably best to get back to doing what you would normally do and let this play out. He will be just fine, but he won't be awake anytime soon."

There seemed to be a collective sigh in the room as tension was relieved. Even John relaxed a little, although not much.

"Thank you Riley. What we did see in there… that was incredible. You're incredible. We appreciate you very much," Captain Morrow said as she moved to give Riley a very uncharacteristic hug. The act startled Riley at first, but as soon as he returned the gesture, the entire mood shifted in the room. Tightly held emotions began to slip for some, others simply relaxed physically but remained somber, quiet and still. Han and Vogel Joined the Captain and Riley found himself in the center of a very awkward group hug.

Riley stood at the room's center, cheeks coloring from the lingering group hug. The Captain had broken from the huddle first, clearing her throat as if to restore some composure. Vogel and Han stepped back, too, letting their arms fall as they exchanged comforting glances with John. The moment of intimacy felt both alien and necessary—a shared vulnerability they rarely allowed themselves in this harsh new reality.

John inhaled and exhaled deeply, as though a weight lifted from his chest, but tension still etched across his brow. "He was… I—Doc means a lot to me," he managed, voice low. "We've watched each other's backs through so much. Knowing he's going to live is… a relief."

Captain Morrow rested a hand on his shoulder. "He's strong. He'll bounce back." She nodded at Riley. "Thank you. For everything." Her gaze flicked to the door that led toward the med bay. "You said you want to wait for Bet's return to handle prosthetics?"

Riley bobbed his head. "Bet has some… specialized knowledge. If we use the old colony's advanced prosthetic solutions, it could mean a near-seamless integration—like limbs they used to attach with neural interfacing. I'd prefer that over patchwork Earth designs we have in stasis cargo." He hesitated, pressing lips tight. "Doc deserves the best shot at a normal life, especially with all he's contributed. What the station could offer would cut months, possibly years off of his rehabilitation and give him improved function over his old legs in this environment."

A quiet came over them again. Eventually, Captain Morrow patted him gently on the arm, then turned to John. "Serena is down on the planet. She asked me for an update earlier, so I let her know we'd call once you had definite news. She's… on a personal errand, apparently. I can handle it if you'd rather—"

John squared his jaw. "No, I got it." He knew he owed it to Serena to speak with her directly. Doc was part of their crew, the old security detail who'd survived many scrapes before. John suspected Serena would want to hear the full story firsthand.

"Thanks," Morrow murmured, then exhaled slowly, scanning the rest of the group. "Han, Vogel—any immediate tasks you've left undone?"

"Loads," Han said, "but nothing that can't wait a day or two."

"I'd really like to get back down there soon though. I wasn't planning on being back up here so soon and I'd like to go apartment shopping," Vogel added.

Marcus and Jason had stayed behind, letting the others take the lead. Marcus adjusted his wrist console and offered in a calm voice, "We'll keep an ear out for any planetary developments or calls from Elena and Bet. The last we heard, their shuttle was half-way to the inner system."

Captain Morrow nodded, then turned her attention back to Riley. "All right. You, Doc, and whomever else you need—take the time required. If you need me, I'll be on the bridge." She hesitated, eyes flicking to John with concern. "Let me know if you need anything and don't keep Serena waiting."

"Understood," John said, standing a little straighter. "I'll contact her now."

Without further ceremony, the small crowd dispersed. Some left for the hangar, a few back to the bridge, and Captain Morrow quietly strode away with Marcus and Jason, presumably for a briefing about the next planet-side steps. That left John and Riley alone at the threshold of the med bay.

Riley checked his wrist console, scanning the feed from inside the suite. "Vitals are stable, sedation levels normal," he reported softly. "He's got enough medical nanites to keep him from feeling much pain until we can do the real work. You can see him if you want, but… he's out cold."

John paused, hovering in the door, remembering how fragile Doc had looked under that privacy curtain. "Maybe later," he mumbled, voice thick. "Not sure I can stomach seeing him that way right now."

Riley offered a gentle nod. "Take your time. He'd want you to keep forging ahead with the mission anyway."

"Speaking of which," John paused, "I'll have Han and Vogel bring you the recovered gear while I contact Serena?"

Riley gave John a puzzled look.

"We were able to recover some interesting supplies from one of the labs before investigating the residential building that fell on him," John explained. "I almost forgot all about it."

"Well, I can't wait to see what you've found," Riley said.

John got a bit of a sheepish look on his face. "Actually, I'm hoping you can make sense out of some of it for a few… augments I'd like to do. I've been feeling a bit disadvantaged here and today really punctuated that for me. I'll take any advantage I can get." John shrugged. "If I can better do my job, with advantages like you've gotten… If I could prevent something like what happened to Doc…" his words trailed off.

Riley nodded in understanding.

John swallowed hard, nodding once more before turning to leave. "Take care of him," he said, glancing back just before the door sealed. "We need him back."

Riley watched him go, a swirl of conflicting emotions in his chest: pride at preserving a life, worry for the deeper issues—like the Captain's hidden cancer, or the colony's uncertain future. With a weary sigh, he refocused on the med suite monitors. One step at a time, he reminded himself. One crisis at a time.

41

Han and Vogel arrived at the med bay's main entrance pushing a small transport sled piled with carefully secured crates. The plastic-and-alloy containers rattled quietly over the deck plating, each labeled in a hodgepodge of old colony notation and fresh color-coded tags. The hum of station air recyclers provided a steady backdrop as they drew near Riley's domain.

At the threshold, they paused; inside, Riley stood at a side console scanning the feeds from Doc's sedation chamber. The sight still awed Han, who couldn't help but recall how not long ago, Riley had been a standard med officer—now he looked more like a magician, communicating with and moving things using just his thoughts and a wave of his hand.

"Riley," Vogel announced gently, drawing his attention. "Brought the supplies from John's run."

Riley blinked as if snapping out of a trance. "Perfect timing," he said, stepping toward them. He offered a tired smile, motioning them deeper inside. "Let's see what we have."

Han keyed the sled's locking mechanism, opening the top crate. Inside were rows of vials, canisters, and ampules. Many of the supplies and materials John and Doc had collected in hopes it was still viable for use.

"All from that lab they found before the building collapse," Vogel explained, shifting her weight. She eyed the containers warily. "John said some of this might be… well, pretty out-there stuff."

Riley took a deep breath, then activated his holo-display. With a flick of his fingers, he beckoned the station's AI subroutine to connect. Inside his mind, courtesy of the neural interface, a calm monotone presence materialized—an echo of the station's partial AI, still incomplete but enough to parse advanced colony text. The sensation had become strangely normal to him, a personal translator whispering in the back of his consciousness allowing him to understand the labels.

Riley's eyes glazed over for a second as lines of data scrolled across his mental HUD. Out loud, he murmured, "Okay, item one: 'CRISPRex G-Sequence Reformat.' Looks like… advanced gene editing cocktails for organ or tissue growth. Some morphological expansions possible…" He paused, heart pounding slightly at the possibilities— these might even be used for building specialized organs or advanced healing solutions.

Vogel frowned. "Gene editing… that's a loaded phrase. Is it stable? Safe?"

Riley gave a half-shrug, half-nod. "In theory, these colonists had it down to a science. Jokes aside, we'd need serious caution, especially without Bet's direct guidance. At least until I can get up to speed on all that's new since our time. In a lot of ways, I feel like I've gone back to med school." His mind flicked to Captain Morrow's hidden condition, wondering if something like this might help.

Han gestured to a second box. "These are those ocular boosters, right? 'NRL-OPT'? John was hoping you'd have answers. He's pretty dead set on wanting augmeta now. Inferiority complex or something."

Riley tapped that label with a pointer finger. The station AI flooded his mind with chemical structures and usage guidelines. "Yes… neural-optic calibrators. They can reinforce or reprogram retinas, potentially tying them to a neural interface for real-time adaptive vision." He inhaled slowly. John's going to be thrilled. "But the synergy factor's tricky. If done incorrectly, it could cause severe migraines or even permanent sight damage."

Vogel gave a grim snort. "He wants to see better, not go blind. So we wait for Bet's final word on that, too. I'm noticing a trend here."

"Agreed." Riley motioned them to open the next crate. Inside, a row of injector kits sat braced in foam. "That's… interesting." He brushed dust from the label. "Says 'ZC-FRegen'—some sort of advanced cell regeneration formula."

Han's eyes widened. "Could that help with Doc's missing leg?"

Riley's breath caught. "Potentially… or at least accelerate prosthetic integration. Might not regrow the entire limb, but it could fuse nerve endings. This is—this is big." He lifted one injector kit, scanning it with a small handheld device. "Eighty percent stable, says the system. We'd need to refine a catalyst for it, but it's workable."

He placed it aside, continuing the inventory. The med bay's overhead lights glowed a touch brighter and several cabinets opened as the station recognized new materials needing regulated storage. Some of the lesser items were standard triage expansions—wound sealants or antibiotic analogs. But near the bottom of the last crate, a squat black container stood out: RAD-RES Protocol—the radiation tolerance solutions Doc and John had discovered earlier.

Riley's pulse quickened. Captain Morrow's potential cure. "Han, Vogel… thanks for bringing these in. I'll be analyzing them further and get them in appropriate storage until Bet returns." He tried not to let his excitement show too plainly. He reminded himself how much he had to learn just to catch up to Bet's basic general knowledge. Once again, the realization of just how far medicine had advanced left his mind staggered in awe.

Vogel rolled her shoulders, tension easing. "Sure. Anything else we can do here?"

Riley shook his head. "Not right now. I'll let you know if I need help transferring them to a cryo-chamber or something." His interface flickered again as the AI fed him more instructions for correct storage temperatures. He raised his voice absentmindedly rambling as he investigated more of the collected resources. "Temperature's recommended at minus 30 degrees for stable shelf life… and this one is minus 28 for some reason. Strange tolerance windows. Hmm, that must be why that one cold storage locker had so many individual compartments and settings. Yes, yes of course. Oh and the auto-feed carousels too-anyway, I'll handle it."

Han and Vogel exchanged an amused glance at Riley basically talking to himself. But they recognized that the neural link was part of his new normal. "Okay then," Han said gently. "We'll head back, see if John needs a hand or if the Captain wants us planet-side again."

As they moved to leave, Vogel hesitated. "Riley—Doc's… safe, right? If he wakes up early, let me know?"

A small, reassuring smile touched Riley's lips. "I promise. He's stable, and sedation is set carefully. I won't let him suffer and he's not waking up until we're ready for him to. He's as comfortable as being in stasis now."

Vogel nodded once, then exited with Han, the double doors sliding shut behind them.

Alone in the med bay, Riley took a long, steadying breath. He turned to the crates arrayed around him. "We have everything we need for Morrow's cure," he murmured, voice tinged with relief. "And more than John bargained for on the augmentation front." He paused, letting the AI feed him deeper analysis: instructions for splicing gene therapies, recommended synergy for optical implants, and yes—the entire regimen for advanced radiation purging if used in tandem with certain quantum Zeno surgeries. A sense of guarded hope flared in his chest.

He crossed to Doc's sedation chamber, peering through the observation window. The younger man's face was peaceful in unconsciousness, though lines of strain still haunted his features. "Hang in there kid," Riley whispered. "One crisis at a time. We'll get you those new legs—no, better than that. We'll make you unstoppable."

With a final wave of his hand, he summoned an overhead holo listing everything to be sorted. The mechanical arms around the room stirred to life, ready to store each precious find in the correct temperature-locked cabinets. Watching everything moving at his will gave him a thrill, it was like he had discovered magical powers, and he allowed himself a sly grin and the thought. 'Dr. Wizard.' This was it— the nexus of their colony's future, bridging lost technology with raw human will. If it all worked, they might cure the Captain, repair Doc's injury, and grant John the enhancements he craved. But if something misfired… he pushed the thought aside. No place for doubts now.

Quietly, he began the cataloging process, orchestrating data, ensuring no mislabeled vial threatened any more heartbreak. The lights hummed, the station's AI guiding him at every step, the neural link forging a fluid dance of mind and machine.

Riley worked quickly, methodically transferring each vial and injector kit to its assigned place in the med bay's refrigerated cabinets. The silent mechanical arms followed his mental commands, guided by the station's partial AI whispering instructions into his neural link. Every so often, he'd nod or mutter a confirmation out loud, the habit of speaking to a partner only he could hear. If anyone walked in, they'd see him orchestrating an invisible dance—hands gesturing with no external console in sight.

At last, he stood back, satisfied. "All labeled, all stored," he exhaled, mind drifting to the newly discovered wonders: advanced CRISPR cocktails, ocular calibrators, cell regenerators, and—most crucially— RAD-RES vials that might cure cancer. A swell of excitement warred with caution in his chest. These cures were far from guaranteed, and he wouldn't breathe easy until Bet returned with the knowledge to apply them safely. Meanwhile, he continued reading, learning and pushing his knowledge forward with help from the station AI and the database of records, scientific papers, reports and experiment results. The gaps in his knowledge felt endless at times, but he was fascinated with it all and eager to learn everything he could. Then he had a thought. Centuries old relics of Sci-Fi tickling his curiosity…

AI, must I read all this information and digest it like I did before the interface or is there a better way?

Responding in his mind directly, the AI answered. *I'm not sure I understand the question. I believe you are asking if I can provide a memory or knowledge transfer via the interface. Is this correct?*

Yes, something like that. Can I just… download the knowledge of medical advancements over the last millennia?

In a way, yes. However, for something of this nature it will require a more physical interface for appropriate access and bandwidth. Security protocols do not allow access to alter your memories without a physical connection.

A file appeared on Riley's mental HUD with a model and description of the piece of technology required. *This piece of equipment was designed for just such a thing, however there are some issues. For one, that piece of technology is in a portion of the station that is still under vacuum and lacking proper life support to sustain you through the procedure. The other issues are potential side effects and outcomes. Although it will be possible to implant the memories, it will take quite some time and a lot of interaction for your mind to incorporate the knowledge within those memories into your consciousness. You may approach a new piece of equipment and it will trigger a dormant memory. You'll feel like you suddenly remember how to use a piece of technology you have never seen before. The latent memories will only be triggered in such a fashion, so you will have to discover and learn by actively using the memory implants.*

He turned, glancing through the med bay's observation window into the recovery suite. Doc lay motionless beyond the glass, the gentle beep of monitors confirming sedation. Riley pressed a palm to the cool surface, whispering, "Well that could save a lot of time."

42

A hiss at the doorway signaled John stepping inside the medical bay. John's eyes flicked to the carefully stocked cabinets, then to Riley, lips pulling into a half-smile. "That's a lot of gear. Good finds, huh?"

Riley nodded, looking quite distracted as he was obviously pushing aside heavier thoughts. "Better than I expected. Some of it is unbelievably advanced. We'll need Bet, though. We can't just guess at procedures we only half-understand. Unless…"

John grunted agreement. "Figured as much. We're not about to risk half-baked implants that might blow up in our faces. Unless what? What are you thinking?"

"Well, there are additional medical suites that are still under vacuum. They, or the technology within may yet be recovered. Some of it might be of great importance."

John gave Riley a curious look. "Do we know the condition of these medical suites?"

"Not yet. Perhaps you could fly by and take a look from the outside on your next trip?"

"Sure, just send me the locations you want me to check out. I'll see if there's any obvious hull damage or something. Perhaps the shuttle's sensors can get us some more details," John eagerly replied. His gaze strayed toward Doc's sedation chamber, brow furrowing. "How's he doing?"

"Stable," Riley confirmed softly. "Just waiting. First I cure my ignorance, then I cure… whatever I must."

A moment's silence stretched between them, heavy with unspoken worries. Then John cleared his throat, shifting focus. "I, uh, also wanted to let you know I got ahold of Serena. She's… well, she's not taking it lightly. She's not saying much, but I can tell it's getting to her."

Riley's eyes flicked up. "She doin' okay down there on her own?"

John shrugged, shoulders tense. "Hard to say. She's 'Serena.' Tried to play it off casual, but I know she cares about Doc like the rest of us. She's probably out there stabbing vines until her arms go numb just to blow off steam or something. Being alone is nothing new for her. "

Riley smiled, picturing Serena hacking away at the seemingly endless kudzu, but the humor faded quickly. "She's strong. Still, you might check on her personally once she's back."

"I will," John said. His gaze dropped to a particular locked cabinet, the one with "NRL-OPT" stenciled on it. A flicker of anticipation crossed his face. "So… you can confirm that stuff's safe?"

Riley pursed his lips, following John's line of sight. "Safe enough with the right synergy factor. But do you want to wait for Bet to help us finalize it?"

John swallowed, arms crossing. "I'm not… patient," he admitted, almost laughing at himself. "But yeah, I'll wait for some of it if that's best. I don't fancy going blind. I would like the nuro-interface though. And if you can help catch me up to the gene therapy the rest of my team received, that would be fantastic."

"Smart call." Riley stepped to a nearby console, gave it a light tap, and brought up a subdued holoscreen. "We can certainly prep your body in the meantime—some baseline scans, a minor immuno-boost and a neuro-interface. That'll speed up integration once we start with anything else if that's what you want."

The flicker of doubt on John's face vanished, replaced with firm resolve. "I do," he said simply. "Being stuck squinting around this place doesn't help anyone. And if Doc's accident taught me anything, it's that we need every edge we can get in this… frontier."

Riley dipped his head in agreement, flipping the console closed. "All right. We'll get started soon. I'll just be cautious about crossing lines with the Captain. She's… still on the fence about so many augmentations, but these preliminaries shouldn't be a problem."

John nodded. "I respect her concerns. But she's seen how it saved Doc's life, seeing how you operate now. Maybe that's softened her stance a little. I'd like her approval, but I really don't need it."

A thoughtful hum escaped Riley as he mulled over that notion. If anything, the Captain's hidden illness might push her to accept advanced procedures—once she couldn't hide it anymore. But he kept that to himself, not wanting to betray her confidence.

"Philosophically I would love to agree with you, however I'm not really sure who the supplies belong to. We are in a very unique situation we weren't prepared for and the Captain is essentially our governing body. If I or we collectively own all this, then I have no objections in terms of ethics… but the way we've been operating, resource allocation is up to the Captain and just as on the ship, she is my boss unless it pertains to a medical decision for life and safety-you know the rules. And that's an important and functional system at this point I'm not prepared to rebel against." Riley's gaze was firm as he expressed himself to John who simply nodded, accepting Riley's wisdom and perspective.

Suddenly, the overhead comm beeped. Marcus's voice came through, calm but urgent: "Riley, John—report to the command deck, please. Captain's requesting an update on planet-side progress and the medical shipments. Over."

John and Riley exchanged a look. "She's not letting up even with half the crew battered," John muttered with a rueful twist of his mouth.

"She can't," Riley said, powering down the med bay's main holograms. "We still have a colony to build. Come on, let's go see what new crisis awaits."

As they hurried down the corridor, the station lights guiding their path, Riley's mind raced with a swirl of possibilities. In his mental overlay, the advanced therapies called to him like an unfinished jigsaw puzzle. Captain's cure. John's augments. Doc's new legs. So many lives hinged on these new technologies. And if they succeeded, maybe—just maybe—they'd prove that this old station and its lost civilization weren't just ghosts, but a bridge to a better future.

As John and Riley entered the command deck, Captain Morrow turned from the glowing system map, her gaze calm but searching as Riley and John stepped onto the bridge. The overhead lights shimmered across the wraparound consoles, and in the center, the holographic display of the whole system slowly rotated—Elena and Bet's shuttle a faint dot on a wide, arcing path toward the inner star. A hum of background chatter from various station modules accompanied the scene, indicating the never-ending demands of life aboard the orbital station.

"You rang, Captain?" Riley said with a respectful but easy tone. He couldn't help noticing the flicker of tension around her eyes—there and gone in a heartbeat.

Morrow acknowledged them with a brisk nod. "Marcus told me you have updates about the new medical supplies, plus your next moves planet-side." Her gaze danced between the two men.

John cleared his throat, taking a step forward. "Yes, ma'am. As you know, Riley has Doc stable. The supplies from that old lab are stored and inventoried. Han and Vogel are working with some of the awakened colonists to get more of the station accessible and functional. Looks like we'll have some heavy-lifting technology for advanced procedures if Bet's knowledge can fill in some missing pieces."

Morrow's eyes flicked to Riley for confirmation. "And the condition of those… materials? Are they safe to use?"

Riley dipped his head in a calm gesture. "They're in better shape than I'd expected. Energy does not seem to have been any struggle for this colony and apparently even the cryogenically stored items were kept viable with a backup energy source on the lab. I'm not sure how that works, but I'm sure Elena has some fancy word soup for an explanation. Anyway, Some items appear geared toward neural augmentation, advanced gene therapies. Lots of supplies for synthesizing medications, " He held her gaze meaningfully with a grin and gave her a slight nod—just the smallest hint that some of what they'd recovered might be relevant for her personal crisis. "Let's just say we can accomplish a lot with what they found and a lot more once we have the right environment and instructions in place."

A flicker of understanding passed between them. Morrow glanced away, keeping her voice neutral. "Good. For now, we keep that gear under wraps. No reason to stir up the entire colony on potential augmentations that we don't fully grasp yet."

"Understood," Riley said softly. "I'll keep it discreet."

Captain Morrow's attention shifted to John. "And you're heading back planet-side?"

"Yes, ma'am. I want to drop Han and Vogel, so they can continue farmland prep and building clearance. Then I need to catch up with Serena—she's out near that orchard site, possibly expanding territory or just whacking vines with a vibrosword." He cracked a faint grin. "She's worried about Doc as much as any of us."

Morrow nodded. "She'll probably want to see him once she's done down there." Her expression softened. "I suspect she's taking it harder than she'll admit."

John exhaled slowly, recalling how Serena hated losing any comrade to injury. "We found some advanced cell regenerators that might speed up his recovery—she'll be glad to hear we're not just leaving him in stasis."

Riley cleared his throat gently, stepping back into the conversation. "Something else you should be aware of, Captain, there's… another small matter…" He paused, trying to gauge who else might be listening. Jason stood at a corner console, seemingly engrossed in flight telemetry, and Marcus was quietly adjusting a sensor feed near the main holomap. It was hardly the environment for a private chat—but perhaps enough for a cryptic hint.

Morrow inclined her head. "Go on."

Riley let the hush stretch a moment. Then he spoke with careful, measured words. "Some of those recovered items could be extremely helpful for… certain high-exposure conditions. I'm concerned about Elena's potential radiation exposure on her trip, I'll be sure to conduct a proper checkup when she returns. If there were any, radiation related issues… I don't believe it would be any problem to treat now. Everything we have now, makes the medicine I used to practice seem like poultices and herbal teas by comparison."

A glimmer of relief flashed in Morrow's eyes, so brief John might not have noticed. She gave a slight nod. "Good. That's some great news and a welcome relief. This crew is up against enough challenges as it is, it's comforting to know that we will have such an advantage." Turning slightly, she aimed her voice at the others. "Marcus, note in the station logs that we're storing newly recovered medical assets in med bay four. Category M. Keep it secure please. Link it to any updates from Riley's notes for need to know access. I want any inventory details secured just like the medical data. Don't need some tech savvy know it all poking around and finding something they have no business finding and starting a riot or something."

"Yes, Captain," Marcus said, swiftly updating a console. "Logged and locked."

Morrow turned back, posture poised. "All right. John, take your shuttle. Get planet-side as soon as you're ready. I want a full report on that orchard region—plus any trouble with the wildlife. The last thing we need is a field of rodent-lizards of unusual size devouring newly planted crops."

John offered a crisp nod. "I'll keep in close contact. We'll do recon on the RLOUS's and update you within a few hours." He glanced at Riley. "Before I go, I intend to have Riley assist me with a neuro-interface and some other minor treatments. Using the hacked together hardware Elena made is functional, but less than ideal. I'm not saying I need to be on Bet's level down there pillaging in a lab, but I need to be a lot closer to do my job properly. This last trip has punctuated the need to take advantage of opportunity there."

Riley gave him a reassuring smile. "We were discussing this when you summoned us Captain. John's pretty adamant on this subject. If I have your permission, It is my suggestion and desire to proceed with his ill spoken request." He shot John a sideways glance with his final words.

Captain Morrow studied them both intently. After a moment, she gave a brief and curt nod. It was obvious she was uncomfortable with the idea, but failed to settle on a suitable objection.

"Thank you Captain," John replied quiet and with a tone of grateful respect.

"One last thing Captain, sorry. I almost forgot." Riley injected.

"Go on."

"I have discovered record of some advanced equipment in a medical specialty area that appears to be intact, but still under vacuum. I need to pressurize that area or salvage anything that remains there," Riley stated.

"I don't exactly have the bodies for something like that. The teams are working on accessing higher priority areas currently. It's going to have to wait," the Captain said, shaking her head.

"Actually Captain, I'd be happy to give it an attempt myself, if John can provide me active sensor feeds on his next flight So I can verify the data I'm seeing is accurate and there's no hull damage in that section. Or we could wake a couple more of the colonists with some specific skills for the purpose." Riley stared at Captain Morrow with a rare intensity. Something in his look unsettled her.

"Rations are still tightly budgeted. We really need to establish a better food supply before we start waking colonists at will. While we might be good for now, I do not want to get into a bind later on. I don't like risking you either Dr. Thompson. As our only medical professional capable of fixing the other half of our entire medical staff, you're putting me in a tough spot here. What is so important?"

"I wouldn't push the issue if it wasn't important Captain, but without this equipment I'm at... we are all at the mercy of Bet's limited knowledge. Right now, his understanding of the technology and some basics bridge a gap between my medical knowledge as a physician and the tools. And that's not enough anymore. There are huge gaps... a millennia of gaps in my knowledge. I only know what everything we just obtained is capable of in theory and by the explanation of the AI. If you want me to actually practice medicine with all the fancy new stuff sometime this century, I need access to that other facility at the very least. What you saw me do for Doc may have looked like magic, but that doesn't magically give me the knowledge of 1,400 years of clinical trials and laboratory research. That's what is in there Captain. Not just a fancy new toy, knowledge." Riley explained.

"Not just..." Captain Morrow caught his careful choice of words.

"Of course. Some of the equipment would be quite exciting indeed, but that's hardly the point of predominant priority. I'm researching constantly, even now I'm organizing the queries for more research I will run on my walk back to medical. I can't absorb it fast enough this way to be relevant."

"And something in that section will help you what? Learn faster?"

"Something like that."

Captain Morrow shot Riley an irritated glare. "How?"

Riley took a deep breath before he spoke again. "There's a direct interface system for the neural link that will allow for unrestricted access and bypass security protocols. It wouldn't be very safe to have a computer in your head if it were easy to hack now would it? In order to access, program, update, modify... a specific piece of equipment is required."

"You're not making me any more comfortable with the idea of augmeta Dr. Thompson. What sort of access is it that would allow you to learn faster?"

"Direct memory implant."

"Excuse me? You want a machine that can alter memories? Well, I don't see any down side to that at all!"

"I'm sure it is quite safe Captain."

"I'm not so sure at all. That sounds like the sort of device that nightmares are made of."

"Right now, that's a device that could save lives. I'm not asking for permission, I'm asking for assistance." Riley was starting to show signs of irritation.

Captain Morrow shook her head, "No, Dr. Thompson. Your insubordination is a cause for great concern here and I do not appreciate the position you're putting me in. I don't want a mind control device on my station and you are not putting yourself and by proxy what is possibly all that remains of the human race in jeopardy. Do you understand?"

"Captain, if you can find someone else with the skills and knowledge to utilize the equipment and treatments we now have at hand, someone with the skillset and knowledge to conduct micro surgeries using quantum fields to treat, remove, modify, or isolate in time at a molecular level then I would be more than happy to transfer your and anyone else's medical file to them while I continue practicing medicine with herbal teas. Because currently that's where it feels like my knowledge is at by comparison to what I don't know."

It seemed clear to the Captain that stress was simply getting the better of him. Doc's accident must have put as much fear in Riley as it did in John, but for different reasons.

Captain Morrow's tone softened as she attempted to sooth him. "Riley, You're doing amazing. We've all been under a lot of stress since we arrived and you've had more than your fair share of it. What you've done for Doc already is nothing short of magic by our old standards. That's hardly herbal teas and poultices. But a machine like that is just too dangerous to prioritize. As long as it's inaccessible in vacuum, it can't be used for harm. And that doesn't even begin to cover my concern for your safety in an attempt to use such a thing."

John who had been silent through this exchange clearly saw the issue in communication and attempted to help. "Really, Captin, it's not a big deal. I'm happy to help and it won't take much of our time."

"I appreciate your eagerness John, but I don't believe I want such a thing on my station or even to exist."

"Then maybe you two would like to discuss the matter in private?" John attempted.

"I hardly see the need for that. Thank you for letting me know such a potentially evil thing exists, but for now the mind control device can stay in vacuum until I'm ready to launch it into the star." Captain Morrow was looking rather frustrated. Her last statement causing John to take a step back from Riley as if to say 'you're on your own with this one'.

Riley's words were clipped and terse. His frustration getting the better of his always calm bedside manner. "I understand your fears with the equipment, Captain, which is all the more reason to obtain it understand it and implement appropriate safety and security protocols. A lack of knowledge and understanding has been a basis of fear since the birth of humanity. But there is a bigger argument than your fear here that I need you to understand. I need you to listen very carefully and set your damn arguments aside for a moment."

This got everyone's attention. John took another step back from Riley. The outburst was so out of character, he hadn't even thought Riley was capable of such hostility. Riley took a deep breath, closed his eyes and slowly let it out. When he continued, it was with much more control. It was also obvious to everyone that the control was forced and there was still a hint of irritation to his tone.

"There are just some things, some ailments which were not curable in our time. If something like that were to come up it will remain incurable unless I can update my knowledge before something like that were to progress and become a time sensitive issue. If such a thing were a problem, I do not believe I have enough time to bridge the gaps in my knowledge. Worse yet, not knowing what I don't know could make me more dangerous than doing nothing about an ailment that comes with a death sentence. I hope now I'm making myself perfectly clear on the importance of this matter to you, Captain. Or do I need break confidentiality some more to spell it out? Captain."

Captain morrow slowly took a look around the command deck and noticed Marcus and Jason had slipped out at some point. They hadn't overheard.

John spoke soft and quiet. "Captain, I know I'm just the muscle around here, but you know damn well I'm not stupid. I saw what Doc was prioritizing down there and connected the dots. Riley is trying to help you, not fight you. You know he would never use such a thing to hurt someone deliberately, but if there's a machine that can pour more than a thousand years worth of knowledge into his head, that sounds like a pretty high priority to me. If it saves your life, it's at the top of my priority list too. Also, I wouldn't mind being able to download some extra knowledge myself. That sounds like a huge advantage. Imagine waking up and suddenly having a whole subject in your head? Would make cross training quite easy. Let us do this. I will personally ensure the security of such a device ensures that it won't be used for evil."

Captain Morrow plopped down in her chair, defeated and completely exhausted.

"Very well then. Do what you must, but if there's any issue I'm taking it out of your hide first. I'm holding you entirely responsible here."

"Understood Captain." Riley gave a deep slow nod that may have even been taken for a slight bow. "I'm sorry for my insubordination. I should have approached that completely differently."

"Riley, just get your equipment and fix my damn body so I can feel like myself again, and we'll call it even. Ok?"

"Of course Captain, I'd like nothing more."

"I'm sorry too Riley. You were trying to tell me without telling me and I got a little thick headed, didn't I?"

"Mmmmhmmmm. Real thick Captain," John interjected, earning himself a scowl from the Captain.

"Fine, back to work the both of you. And if you see Marcus or Jason on the way out, please let them know its safe to return."

43

Riley strolled down the slowly curved corridor toward the medical bay, his mind brimming with data to analyze, vials to double-check, and a thousand swirling questions about expediting his learning. The station AI's mental echo tantalized him with glimpses of specialized equipment and memory-transfer technology. However, his immediate priority was to return to the medical bay and conduct tests while simultaneously conducting research. Forced learning through practical application and necessity. One crisis at a time, Mr. Wizard.

Returning to the medical bay, Riley was deep in thought, engrossed in a conversation with himself. John walked in, and it took Riley a moment to notice him. Clearly, John was eager to undergo his treatments and get back to the surface.

"well I suppose we'll get to it then, just have a seat here," Riley said as he indicated to a medical chair. The very same one in which he received his neuro-interface.

John sat down and with hardly another word, Riley got to work. And what seemed like only moments later, John's neuro-interface was beginning to make its connections.

"Take it a bit slow at first, it can be a bit overwhelming if you try to do too much at once, it's going to wear you out very quickly until you get used to it." With that, Riley transferred the recommended recovery and adaptation procedures he had meticulously crafted based on his experiences the day after getting his implant to John.

The sudden appearance of a text file in his vision shocked John. "Holy shit! What the Fu…"

Riley chuckled, "I think I'm going to make that a standard practice from now on. I don't see that ever getting old."

John glared at him, but couldn't help but cracking a smile.

"Welcome to the club," Riley said. "Now, if you want some real fun, try talking to the ship's AI."

"That dumb ass computer hasn't been worth much this entire time. Why would I want to talk to it?" John asked.

"It's not dumb. It lacks any sort of rudimentary interfaces like would be required to interact with us. Remember what Bet said, everybody got these interfaces as children. It was assumed that everyone had them. They built much of their technology with that assumption and some very basic things we would assume to exist were simply not included. You know programmers and their updates. I think he's been working on improving it too, but that's neither here nor there right now. Try it, you'll see. Just think about talking to it. The interface will do the rest."

Reluctantly, John gave it a test. *hello AI are you there?*

"I'm here John, What can I help you with?" The AI's voice seemed to come from within John's head, causing him to jump in surprise.

"Told you." Riley joked as he poked John with an elbow.

"Ummm… what is the status of my shuttle?" John asked the AI.

"shuttle PC22 is currently classified non flight worthy. Shuttle PC22 is low on fuel. Would you like me to fuel the craft and prepare it for launch?"

"YES! … umm sorry, yes please."

"Shuttle PC22 will be ready for flight in 94.5 minutes."

John turned to Riley with wide eyes, his eyebrows raised so high that they smoothed out some wrinkles and gave him a couple of years of more youthful appearance. Riley met his gaze with a wide grin.

"Cool, isn't it?" Riley asked.

"Uhhh yeah. So all this time…"

"We've been missing out on more than you can imagine," Riley finished his sentence. "Just wait until you talk with Bet again… That's going to be an interesting experience for you."

"How so?"

"You'll see. This makes up for everything he lacks in body language and more. You'll actually see more of him that's inside that overly utilitarian shell of his. For now, you'll need to know that this has the ability to broadcast a supplemental communication based on your genuine emotional state, or something like that. I'm not sure I understand it fully myself yet. Essentially, the gap between where we were and what you've just unlocked seems to be similar to the gap in what we realize now and what these interfaces can possibly do. Based on the research I've been able to do so far, the interface units we have here, the ones you and I have that is, were something more advanced than the typical units everyone received. It would seem, we're left with the remnants of the latest and greatest that were available in their time. I don't believe everyone would have had access to..." Riley became aware he was rambling as he thought aloud and stopped talking.

John just sat there for a moment, taking it all in. Small shimmers of light sparkled in his vision. He focused on one and he saw basic information in his view about a scanner Riley was holding. What was weirder was that as he read the information window, he realized he didn't need to. He already knew the information. When he looked again, the sparkle that was previously on the scanner was gone. "Weird." The word escaped John's lips.

"What's weird?" Riley asked.

"Well, I saw this sparkle of light on some things. Like your scanner there. When I focused on it, it showed me a basic information window, but it was like I'd already read it and remembered it as I was reading it. Now it's gone."

"That is interesting indeed. AI, Can you explain why John is having this phenomena that I did not experience?"

The AI's voice spoke in both of their heads as if having a conversation with them. "Certainly." Just then, a realistic image of the AI appeared in their vision, standing between them as if a 3rd party in the room and conversation. "Since Dr. Morales, whom you know as Bet arrived, many repairs have been made to my neural network. My status has improved much and based on our previous conversation about knowledge transfer in the form of implanted memories, I was able to deduce a significant lack of knowledge. From the interactions and data I have been able to analyze since your arrival, I also come to the conclusion that you are out of your time line. As such deductions indicated a certain baseline of knowledge would be lacking, I took the liberty of pre-loading some helpful guidance basics into the available units. What he is experiencing is a visual clue presented by the neuro-interface to one of the memories I have included within its pre-loaded memory. I believe that is how you might understand the concept at this point anyway. This is just as I explained to you earlier how a knowledge transfer works, it will require interaction in order to recall and integrate the knowledge and memories into your conscious mind. While the interface may contain vast amounts of data within itself, the knowledge you require to make decisions must be organically linked within your human brain. I've also taken the liberty of including as advanced a set as I could for authorization codes and what amounts to a dictionary or translation software to help John understand the world he is looking at. The information windows contain text, but when you simply focus on them the right way, you should just recall the information see the text. This is how children learn about the world around them before they are capable of reading. With enough interaction, a child gains the ability to read as the link between the text and the absorption of their meaning are linked within the neural pathways of their minds."

John and Riley just stared at the AI in utter shock. Slowly, a huge grin started to grow on John's face. The future, was everything he hoped it would be… and more.

"That's it. You're all set. Welcome to the new world and read those instructions I gave you or maybe just focus on it and you can absorb it… They are based on my experience and not just some standard form I dug up."

John nodded, "Thank you. What about the immune boost and scans you mentioned?"

"Already done. Go, Your shuttle will be ready soon and you've got work to do. Just don't overdo it the first day, ok?"

"You sure I'm going to be safe to fly?"

"Nope. You are fine, but I have no idea what that shuttle is going to do to you. My first experience in here was rough. You'll have to be the judge of that, but I'd suggest you let your copilot know what's going on…"

"What do you mean what it will do to me?"

Riley gave a light sigh. "Touch this console here, the one for your bed."

John did as Riley said and a wall of holographic views popped into existence in his vision. John took a step back, releasing his touch on the console. His vision cleared.

"Woahhhh" You think I'll get something like that in the shuttle too?

"I'd count on it." Riley said with a knowing grin. "This is about to be the wildest flight you've ever made, and likely the most exhausting too. Mentally, your first experience or two is going to wear you out in a way you've never felt before. It's different, there's a hell of a lot more data available to you, but unlike the world we were used to, you can't simply ignore it. It's all there, all at once and you have to learn a new way of focus. It can get mentally exhausting at first. And here, keep these in your pocket," Riley said as he handed John two pills. "Thats for the headache when you land. I'd suggest you take them before you leave, give them time to kick in and reduce the knife through your eyes feeling you're going to get."

"Oh, sounds lovely."

"Nothing in this world or the last is free John. Remember that."

And with that final statement, Riley motioned toward the door. John got an uneasy feeling he intuitively understood Riley wanted him to leave, like a sixth sense he was impatient. *'Weird'* he thought to himself. In the back of his mind, he was also wondering what the AI was doing with his shuttle.

"The shuttle is almost ready. The maintenance bots are 76.3% done with their inspections. Two minor repairs must be done, but will cause no delay in readiness estimates. Fuel is prepared and will be loaded once the maintenance is complete. You really shouldn't have flown so many times before doing the routine maintenance John. You called me while you were having that other thought, so that came through the connection as well. it's not weird at all. That is a basic form of communication protocols built into the neuro-interface which you seem to have no control over. You will learn to withhold thoughts and emotions in time. Your age and established perception of reality are the hindering factors, but these communication enhancements encouraged far better comprehension and reduced incidents due to misinterpretation of spoken words by 78.6%. To put it crudely, far less drama to cause delays in efficiency. A most practical solution for such an emotional species as humans." The AI spoke in Johns head.

"You ok?" Riley asked.

John, just realizing he hadn't yet moved, gave Riley a forlorn look. "Yeah... Does the AI seem a bit... I don't know, arrogant to you?"

Riley laughed. "Oh, for sure. Just wait. The more it wakes up, the worse it gets. It changes in knowledge and personality with every bit of the station that's recovered and brought online."

"Well, can we turn it off?" John asked hopefully.

The AI popped back into their vision as if it were a real and tangible being, giving an overly offended look. "Hey, I'll have you know..."

Riley swiped a backhand through the AI's image.

"HEY! I asked you not to do that!"

John watched the interaction amazed, and wondering if he'd just gone crazy.

"Just ignore him, and if he gives you too much crap, use him as a sparring partner. He loves that!" Riley gave John a wink. "His lack of ability for physical interaction breaks the illusion in your minds eye. Apparently it hits him with a ton of error messages to contend with. I call it negative feedback training."

The AI gave them both an angry glare and vanished. John, stood, shook his head and rubbed his hands down his face, making an exasperated sound.

"So, the rumors are true. You have gone off the deep end," John said.

"Just a bit." Riley shrugged. "Welcome to the party my friend. Now, about you getting out of my office and back to work. I've got 1,000 years of research to do and I'm not even exaggerating. If anything, I'm understating it. Don't forget my scans on your way out."

44

Captain Morrow stood quietly in the sterile hush of the infirmary, the soft hum of the environment blending with her own steady breathing. She touched the small spot at the base of her skull, concealed beneath her short hair, where the neuro-interface implant had been carefully embedded just hours earlier in preparation for her upcoming procedure. Its subtle presence was both comforting and disconcerting, a tangible reminder of how deeply this advanced technology would intertwine with her own biology.

As she watched Riley receive his knowledge implants, a quiet unease stirred within her. She contemplated the implications of such profound integration between human minds and machinery—where the line between individual understanding and artificial augmentation blurred into uncertainty. Yet the potential was undeniable. This technology represented survival, healing, perhaps even evolution. But at what cost, she wondered, would humanity retain its essence when knowledge could be downloaded as simply as updating software? Could memories be rewritten to change a person? Could memories be extracted? The potential for evil in this technology still frightened her to her core, but as she watched over Riley, she could no longer deny the potential benefits.

Riley's eyelids fluttered as the neuro-mapper finished the knowledge transfer, its intricate array of circuits dimming as the session concluded. A gentle hum faded into silence as the delicate device connected to the back of his head ceased its operation. His fingers brushed the edge of the helmet-like interface, releasing a slow breath, the weight of newfound understanding settling within him like a tangible force.

"You alright, Riley?" the captain asked softly, concern threading her words.

"Yeah, Captain," Riley responded, voice steady despite the wave of information still coalescing in his mind. He carefully removed the helmet-like apparatus, placing it gently on the console next to him. "It's quite an experience—like having an entire medical library downloaded straight into my neurons. It's a very odd feeling. I know it's all there, like additional weight in my head. But it's like… it's like those crates over there. If you try to lift it, you know it's full, but you don't know what's inside until you reach in and pull something out. It feels like that. It's a very odd sensation."

He stood, testing his balance briefly, then moved confidently toward the newly acquired surgical suite. The slender rods, interwoven with intricate waveguides and quantum stabilizers, awaited his touch. He grasped one, observing the subtle resonance that pulsed gently in response.

Captain Morrow hovered near the observation window of the secondary infirmary, her gaze fixed on Riley as he prepped the newly acquired surgical suite. Outside the sealed hatch, two station drones carried additional crates of medical apparatus—tools that hummed softly with the promise of healing.

"It's strange, isn't it?" she remarked quietly, almost to herself. "The boundary between human and machine—it's becoming thinner."

Riley decided to pretend he hadn't heard her remark as he worked on laying out all the tools and preparing for the procedure. As he worked, he began to explain the tools and procedure to the captain. Talking it out seemed to help him organize the implanted memories that were streaming into his consciousness as he made connection to them with each interaction and thought. While it helped him to process the new knowledge, it also helped ease the captain's anxiety.

"These waveguides will let me isolate malignant growths at the quantum level—well, theoretically," Riley admitted, looking up to meet her eyes. "The knowledge implant provided by the station's AI filled in the gaps. Now it feels like second nature."

She raised an eyebrow, arms crossed carefully over her ribs—still stiff from the radiation damage that plagued her. "Quantum surgery through instant knowledge implants? That's quite the leap, even for us."

He nodded, conviction shining in his eyes. "This technology isn't just advanced—it's intuitive, tailored specifically to the human brain. It leverages observation at a quantum level to halt and remove malignancy without traditional surgery."

Captain Morrow sighed lightly, uncertainty and hope battling in her expression. Her eyes flicked once more to the holographic display depicting the disease within her own body, clearly marked with luminous, pulsing overlays. "Then by all means, Riley, let's proceed."

He stepped forward, helmet-like neuro-mapper now removed and placed carefully aside. "Let's rewrite the rules, Captain."

Riley tapped one of the rods with gloved fingers, voice low but clear. "These waveguides will let me isolate malignant growths at the quantum level," he explained. He glanced back at Captain Morrow, who was studying him with equal parts trust and unease. "With this we can hold cancerous cells in a sort of suspended state and literally nudge them toward self-annihilation. It's all anchored in quantum Zeno effects… it's like stopping an arrow in mid-flight by watching it too closely."

She raised an eyebrow, arms crossed carefully over her ribs—still stiff from the radiation damage that plagued her. "You're telling me you can stall the disease just by… observing it?"

Riley nodded, setting the rod down gently. "That's the bones of it, yes. Properly harnessed observation exerts enough of an effect to arrest the malignant spread, while we phase in targeted interventions." He stopped, letting a shy grin cross his face. "Look, Captain, I know it sounds like hand-waving sci-fi. But we've got the proof-of-concept right here." He patted a narrow console flickering with the station's signature advanced code.

The captain's gaze shifted to the console. It displayed layered holograms of human cellular structures—her own, in fact—recorded from earlier scans. She could see the malignant clusters, identified with discrete color overlays. Riley's proposed plan had them pinned, unchanging in the sim. "And you think you can do this?"

"Not alone," he said, shrugging off the self-consciousness. "But with these new instruments… yes. The AI walked me through the calibration. We'll start small, localize the effect on your bone marrow first, then scale up if it holds. The station's technology is leaps beyond anything we had back in Sol."

She watched him connect one last set of cables: impossibly thin threads that fed into a control panel at the table's edge. Each connection glowed, the color shifting from dull gold to a crisp, iridescent white. With a thought, he brought up the next batch of quantum operation parameters. The overhead lights cast shifting reflections off the waveguides, each strobing in a delicate dance of advanced optics. It might have been beautiful if it weren't so critical.

With everything set up, Riley invited Morrow to get into the surgical pod. Standing next to the pod, Morrow let the medical gown she wore drop to the deck at her feet. Standing there, completely nude, Riley observed her gaunt physique with a clinical eye. The cancer had taken its toll on her body and it pained him to see her in such shape. Gently, he helped her onto the operating table of the pod.

Captain Morrow lay suspended in the sterile, softly illuminated surgical pod as the procedure began. Around her, advanced nanobots and automated RAD-RES injectors whirred to life, their precision honed by centuries of scientific study and engineering. In a display that blended hard science with a touch of magic, a series of quantum isolation modules activated along the afflicted tissue. These modules projected a chronotactic field—a localized temporal stasis—effectively "freezing" segments of her cells in time, inspired by the quantum Zeno effect.

Within this isolated window, the tissue's natural decay was halted, allowing the station's AI-guided CellChem Master Synth to meticulously excise the malignant clusters. As if in a choreographed ballet, streams of nano-scalpel beams and repair nanobots danced around the frozen tissue, reassembling her cellular structure with unprecedented precision. Each quantum pause created a brief, but infinitely repeatable, moment of surgical clarity—time itself held hostage so that damage could be undone and vitality restored.

The procedure was a marvel of both technology and theoretical physics: while the rest of her body remained alert, these isolated sections were impervious to the passage of time, allowing for extraction, repair, and reintegration on a molecular level. The entire process, echoing the principles of quantum measurement, continuously reset any aberrant pathways before they could evolve further—a self-correcting mechanism that promised not only to halt her disease but to reverse its progress.

In the quiet hum of the operating chamber, the interplay of advanced robotics, temporal engineering, and bio-regenerative science painted a picture of radical healing—a moment when science fiction transcended into a tangible, life-saving reality. As minutes turned to hours, a quiet metamorphosis took hold. The Captain's once-hidden pain seemed to ebb away, replaced by a soft radiance that hinted at renewed vigor. Her posture straightened imperceptibly, and even the relentless tide of her internal ache softened, as if the very fabric of her being was being rewritten.

When the procedure was completed, Riley helped her put the surgical gown back on and escorted her to a more comfortable bed in a private recovery room. Captain Morrow concluded her day with a log entry. 'Today, we have not only defied the perils of deep space but also the ravages of time upon our very flesh. We move forward—not as victims of our past, but as pioneers of our future.' With a final thought, she shared the log entry with Amir and stretched out in her bed to sleep, feeling capable of relaxing for the first time since before they arrived in system.

45

The hum of the shuttle's engines filled the cabin with a constant, steady vibration. Outside the reinforced viewport, the star blazed in sharp relief against the emptiness of space, its radiation filtered through the ship's protective shielding. Their trajectory carried them deeper into the system, toward the heart of what had once been the colony's energy network.

Elena sat with her legs stretched out in front of her, absently scrolling through data on her tab. Across from her, Bet remained motionless, his form reclined slightly against the seat, eyes closed but no doubt processing endless streams of information in that hybrid mind of his. He had been silent for the better part of an hour, leaving Elena to her own thoughts.

She studied him subtly, noting the way the artificial components blended with what little organic tissue remained. He was more machine than man now—his limbs sleek with metallic plating, neural interfaces integrated directly into his skull, his voice carrying an ever-so-slight synthetic undertone. And yet, there were moments—small ones—where something deeply human still lingered beneath the surface.

It had been gnawing at her for a while now, the questions she hadn't yet asked. How did he end up this way? Who had he been before?

"So," she said, breaking the long silence. "I realize I don't know much about you, Bet. Not really."

His eyes flickered open, their irises briefly flashing with an artificial sheen before settling into a dull, almost weary glow. "That's mutual," he said. "We've worked together, but we've never really talked."

She hesitated before asking, "You weren't always like this. The enhancements, the machine parts… it's not just some personal choice, is it?"

Bet exhaled slowly, as if weighing his response. For a moment, she thought he might deflect, might tell her it didn't matter. But then he leaned forward slightly, his fingers interlocking.

"No," he said, his voice quieter than usual. "It wasn't a choice. It was survival."

Elena frowned. "What happened?"

Bet's gaze shifted to the viewport, his expression unreadable. "It was… a long time ago," he started. "I was one of the lead engineers overseeing the construction of the energy facility we're heading to now. Back then, it was meant to be the pinnacle of human ingenuity— mass-scale antimatter production, energy harvesting systems that could sustain entire worlds. We were on the cutting edge of everything. I was proud of it. I poured years of my life into it."

Elena said nothing, sensing he needed to tell this at his own pace.

He continued, his voice tight. "We were in the final stages of testing a new quantum containment grid—one that would allow us to store vast amounts of energy with near-zero loss. The calculations were sound. The simulations were perfect. But reality… doesn't always follow the models."

His metal fingers curled into a fist. "There was a containment breach. A failure no one saw coming. A cascading collapse of the magnetic fields… The entire sector went up in an instant."

Elena's breath caught. "You were caught in it."

Bet gave a single nod. "I don't remember much. Just pain. My body… most of it was gone before they even pulled me out. Radiation, plasma burns, complete cellular failure. The doctors—if you could even call them that—told me I wouldn't survive another day." He let out a short, humorless chuckle. "They gave me a choice, . Die, or let them replace what was lost."

Elena's fingers tightened around the edge of her tablet. "And you chose to live."

Bet turned his gaze to her, something unreadable flickering in his expression. "It wasn't really a choice. It was desperation. I didn't want to die. But I also didn't realize what I would become. That's not something you can really prepare for or comprehend in such a situation."

Unable to utilize warp field technology inside the system, the trip took about a month. Over that time, Elena and Bet got to know each other a lot better. They spent days discussing scientific theories and advancements between Elena's time and Bet's. They also spent a lot of time sharing stories of their past, what life was like for each of them before they became disconnected from the rest of humanity. Elena told Bet what Sol was like before they left and Bet described the colony, galactic economy and some of the stories others had shared when traveling through the system.

After weeks of travel and discussions, their destination came into view—a vast structure suspended in the gravitational stillness of a Lagrange point. At first, it appeared to be a very large asteroid. But as they drew closer, details began to emerge.

Bet's voice was calm, but tinged with something resembling pride. "We captured an asteroid and moved it into place," he explained. "Hollowed it out and built the facility inside. It was one of the most ambitious engineering feats ever attempted here, but it saved us massive amounts of time and resources. A lot of the materials we excavated during the hollowing process were used in its construction —iron for steel, rare elements for specialized alloys, and exotic materials fabricated for extreme conditions. The materials were separated and purified for use in an auto-factory."

Elena's gaze flickered across the surface of the asteroid. "You still needed to bring in more resources though."

Bet nodded. "From the planet, from other mining operations. We mined a great many asteroids in the process. It was a logistical nightmare, but it worked. Fortunately, automated mining drones were able to do much of the work. Operations scaled rapidly after we spent the first year just building more mining drones. Eventually, we had a steady enough flow of resources we could keep a constant production going. When we were done, we pushed the resources back to the planet to build the station and much of the city. Eventually, most of the drones were decommissioned."

As they got closer, Elena's eyes narrowed at something on the asteroid's surface. "There's equipment down there. And—" She leaned in, her voice dropping. "The side facing away from the star… it's crawling."

Bet adjusted the sensors, enhancing their view. Dozens, possibly hundreds of machines and bots moved in coordinated activity, like an overturned ant hill. Everything moved with a clear, singular purpose— efficient, precise, relentless.

"The rest of them that weren't decommissioned never stopped

working," Bet murmured, his voice unreadable. "Even after all this time."

Elena stared in awe. "I can see why you said this was an engineering marvel."

Bet exhaled. "It was more than that. This method of asteroid hollowing was so efficient that it became the basis for constructing entire ships. We built vessels out of these rocks, massive ones, capable of traveling between systems. The adaptability was unmatched—you could carve them for just about any purpose."

Elena considered that. "Still, it must have been incredible to see them in action."

Bet nodded, his expression distant. "It was. And now, we're about to walk into one of the last of them still functioning."

As the shuttle made its final approach, the massive asteroid-turned-facility loomed before them. The docking bay gaped open, welcoming them into Bet's past and Elena's future..

As their shuttle approached the massive asteroid facility, it became clear that docking would not be a simple task. The bay was nearly filled to capacity with enormous modular containers, each stacked in orderly rows, their sheer scale dwarfing the small vessel. The facility itself was a marvel of engineering, its hollowed-out core bustling with automated activity, as if the place had never truly been abandoned.

Bet surveyed the scene, his expression unreadable. "Modular transports," he muttered. "A standard we created. They're designed to link together for transport like the old Earth train cars. Each one capable of refueling an interstellar vessel."

Elena stared at the seemingly endless expanse of energy modules, her mind struggling to comprehend the staggering power contained within. "Each of these... can fully power a starship?"

Bet nodded. "Not just refueling. Each module is a self-contained reactor, complete with everything needed to sustain and power a ship. They were built to be adaptable—self-sufficient energy cores that could be swapped out instead of requiring lengthy overhauls. Instead of ships becoming obsolete, their fuel sources advanced with each iteration."

Elena shook her head in awe. "This place... this entire asteroid... it holds enough energy to sustain fleets for centuries."

Bet's gaze remained fixed on the facility. "That was the idea. Maintenance downtime was one of the greatest limitations to interstellar expansion once we satisfied the energy requirements. These modules changed that. Ships didn't have to wait in drydock for months. Instead, they just swapped fuel pods, ensuring peak efficiency at all times. The bots here would refurbish them, upgrade them, and keep them at full capacity."

Elena watched as the automated machines moved with synchronized purpose, carrying out repairs and adjustments with mechanical precision. The entire place still functioned like a beating heart, sustaining itself long after its creators had vanished.

Bet exhaled slowly. "Like I said, we even used this method for ship construction itself. Some of the most massive interstellar vessels weren't built in traditional yards—they were carved from asteroids, hollowed out just like this one. The rock served as natural armor against radiation and micrometeoroid impacts. It saved an unfathomable amount of resources. Ghastly things."

Elena turned to him. "You don't seem particularly fond of them."

Bet let out a quiet chuckle. "I never liked them much. They always felt like caves to me. Unlike traditional ships, most of their interiors weren't sleek or refined—just smoothed-out stone corridors, remnants of the lasers used to carve them. Living inside one always felt primitive, no matter how advanced the technology running it was."

She could see it in his expression—a mixture of nostalgia, pride, and perhaps even a lingering discomfort. This place wasn't just a marvel of engineering. It was a relic of an era where innovation had pushed the boundaries of human potential.

As their shuttle maneuvered toward an open docking point, Elena took one last look at the whole of the enormous facility, a testament to humanity's ambition.

"This place still runs," she said softly. "Even after everything and all these years."

Bet nodded. "Because that's what it was designed to do. And now, we're about to put it back to use."

46

Elena and Bet stood near the observation window of their shuttle, watching as the station's automated systems activated. Massive mechanical arms, guided by legions of maintenance drones, maneuvered the modular containers into position, linking them to their ship with smooth precision. The process was seamless, an elegant ballet of machinery that spoke to the efficiency of the station's design.

Bet crossed his arms and nodded in satisfaction. "They'll handle the loading. These bots were designed for self-sufficiency, and they'll be faster than we ever could be."

Elena glanced at the growing train of modular containers, each one a fully self-contained energy system capable of fueling an interstellar vessel. The sheer amount of energy contained within the asteroid was staggering. "So… what do we do while they work?" she asked.

Bet gave her a sideways glance, his cybernetic eyes flickering with interest. "Ever wanted a tour of the largest solar research facility humanity ever built?"

She raised a brow. "That depends. Are we going to be floating the whole time?"

Bet chuckled. "The artificial gravity will be shut down here in the shuttle bay to make attachment easier. But inside the station? We'll take the transport system. It's a smooth ride."

She hesitated for only a moment before nodding. "Alright. Show me what we built."

As they left the shuttle bay, the transition into the asteroid's interior was seamless. The corridors were vast, far larger than she had expected, lined with sleek, low-energy lighting. Within minutes, they reached a transport hub—an enclosed rail system that stretched deep into the heart of the station.

They stepped into a transport pod, a streamlined capsule designed for high-speed travel. Bet entered a destination on the console, and within moments, they were gliding through a vast tunnel system, accelerating smoothly into the asteroid's depths.

Elena leaned back, looking out of the observation panels. The tunnel walls were lined with reinforced alloys, a subtle reminder that while they were deep within the rock, this was no crude mining facility—it was a high-functioning scientific and industrial hub.

"How big is this place?" she asked.

Bet gestured out at the tunnel walls as they rushed past. "Fifty kilometers in length. And thick enough that we left over twenty kilometers of mass as shielding from the star's heat and radiation." He tapped the console, bringing up a holographic projection of the facility. "We added several layers of additional shielding on the star-facing side, but we also left sections with retractable shielding and direct tunnels facing the sun. That allowed for research into solar dynamics, energy extraction, and even high-energy particle physics."

Elena's eyes widened as she studied the map. "So, this wasn't just an energy station—it was a full-scale star research lab?"

Bet nodded. "The largest ever built. We used those tunnels to observe solar plasma flows, magnetic field interactions, and radiation patterns at a scale never before possible. Scientists studied everything from coronal mass ejections to antimatter formation in solar flares. Some even theorized we could directly harness exotic particles for experimental propulsion systems."

Elena shook her head in amazement. "And all of that was happening right here?"

Bet chuckled. "Not just here. Some sections of the station were entirely dedicated to gravitational wave studies. The proximity to the star allowed researchers to observe how the sun's gravity distorted space-time, gathering data that couldn't be collected from any planetary observatory. There were even tests on how stellar mass could be used as a lens for deep-space observations—imagine using a sun as a telescope."

She stared out the window in awe. "I had no idea we'd built something like this. And now it's just… abandoned."

Bet exhaled slowly. "Not abandoned. Dormant. Waiting." He turned to her. "Everything here was built to last. It just needed people to return."

They continued gliding deeper into the station, passing junctions where the transport system branched into different sectors. The sheer scale of it was overwhelming—laboratories, reactor chambers, observation decks, all buried within the asteroid's massive form. The deeper they went, the more Elena realized just how much humanity had once achieved here, and how much had been lost to time.

She turned back to Bet, eyes sharp with curiosity. "So where are we heading first?"

Bet gave a small, knowing smile. "The core research labs. I think you'll find what they left behind very interesting."

Elena studied the holographic model of the facility intently as they traveled. Suddenly, something caught her attention and caused an involuntary gasp. "You have an entire production and fabrication facility here? 3D printers, automated foundries... what..."

"Those were essential in building this facility. It was the first stage. Essentially creating the means to build itself, or be self replicating."

"Is it still functional?"

"Of course. Maintenance would need to be done. Parts replaced, etc. Once, this was a hub of science, new experiments had new requirements. We built what we needed right here on sight. As long as we have the resources needed, we could build the most intricate sensors and instruments imaginable, atom by atom if we needed to."

Elena was dumbstruck. The possibilities ran through her mind. She was still lost in thought, daydreaming of all the experiments she could conduct, the equipment she could never even dream of before, when the transport came to a stop.

The transport pod gradually slowed as it approached one of the facility's primary research sectors. The doors hissed open, revealing a cavernous hall stretching before them. Unlike the corridors they had seen earlier, this space was more refined, its walls reinforced with composite alloys and embedded with intricate arrays of sensors and equipment.

Elena stepped out, her boots making a soft sound against the smooth flooring. "What exactly did they study in this section?"

Bet gestured toward a massive, transparent window lining one side of the hall. Beyond it, a heavily shielded chamber housed a complex assembly of machinery—toroidal containment rings, electromagnetic stabilizers, and a network of intricate conduits that pulsed with dormant energy.

"This was one of the primary plasma acceleration testbeds," Bet explained. "They experimented with high-energy plasma confinement —seeing if they could control and direct charged solar material for artificial star creation."

Elena blinked. "Wait… you mean controlled fusion?"

"More than that," Bet said. "They were testing ways to create and stabilize miniature stars. Theoretically, they could have been used as sustained energy sources for long-term interstellar travel. Imagine a ship that carried its own artificial star—no fuel limitations, no reactor wear. Just a stable fusion source capable of lasting for centuries."

Elena walked closer to the window, her mind reeling. "Did it work?"

Bet's expression darkened slightly. "Not… entirely. They came close. But controlling that level of energy proved unpredictable. There were… incidents."

A chill ran down her spine. "What kind of incidents?"

He turned toward her. "The kind that left parts of this facility permanently sealed off."

She exhaled slowly, glancing back at the vast, silent chamber beyond the glass. Whatever had happened here, it had pushed the limits of what was possible. And now, after so many years, those secrets were waiting to be uncovered.

Bet placed a hand on a nearby console, activating it with a flicker of light. "Come on," he said. "Let's see what else they left behind."

The air inside the research lab was cold, sterile, untouched for decades. Soft emergency lighting illuminated the vast chamber, casting long shadows against the reinforced walls. The room was silent, save for the low hum of the transport pod as it docked behind them.

Elena stepped forward cautiously, her eyes scanning the towering columns of dormant machinery, arrays of intricate wiring suspended along the walls like veins in an enormous, slumbering beast. The ceiling stretched high above them, dotted with thick conduits that had once pulsed with unimaginable energy. She exhaled, feeling the weight of history press down upon her.

"This place," she murmured, "it's like walking into a time capsule."

Bet moved beside her, his cybernetic eyes flickering as he interfaced with a nearby console. The screen crackled to life, displaying fragmented logs and incomplete datasets. "More than a time capsule," he corrected. "This station wasn't just about energy production—it was an evolving hub of experimentation. What was built here wasn't meant to be static. It adapted, changed, reshaped itself with each new breakthrough."

Elena watched as Bet scrolled through encrypted files, unlocking long-sealed research notes and schematics. "You said earlier that some experiments didn't go as planned," she said carefully. "Just how dangerous were these projects?"

Bet hesitated before answering. "Some of them were revolutionary. Others... well, let's just say there's a reason no one ever came back here."

A shiver ran down Elena's spine. She glanced toward a row of thick, reinforced doors on the far end of the chamber. Each was marked with warning symbols, some of which she didn't even recognize. "What exactly did they leave behind?"

Bet turned his gaze toward the sealed containment units. "Prototypes," he said. "Failed constructs. Unstable energy matrices. Experimental propulsion cores that never made it past theoretical stages." He motioned for her to follow. "Come on. If we're going to get a better understanding of what happened here, we need to go deeper."

They moved toward an auxiliary corridor, stepping past long-dormant workstations and abandoned equipment. The deeper they went, the more signs of sudden departure they found—half-finished assembly units, disconnected power conduits, shattered display panels. Whatever had caused the station to be abandoned, it had been swift and absolute.

As they reached another section of the facility, Bet activated a secondary power relay. A deep mechanical groan echoed through the corridor as old systems flickered to life. A soft blue glow pulsed along the walls, illuminating the passage ahead. Elena turned to Bet. "What did you just turn on?"

Bet glanced at the readings on his interface. "Looks like... an active research archive. Data storage for classified projects. If we can access it, we might find out what the final days of this station looked like."

Elena took a deep breath and nodded. "Let's do it."

As they approached the archive chamber, a door hissed open, revealing a massive circular room lined with data cores. Some were intact, others flickered with corrupted files. In the center of the chamber stood a large, inactive holoprojector. Bet moved toward it, fingers skimming over the control panel.

"If this still works," he said, "we're about to learn exactly what they were working on."

Elena braced herself as Bet initiated the system, and the chamber came alive with the echoes of forgotten knowledge.

The holoprojector hummed, flickering to life with cascading streams of data. Holographic schematics, old research logs, and mission reports scrolled through the air in front of them. The station's final recorded moments were stored in fragmented logs, buried beneath layers of security encryptions that even Bet struggled to bypass.

"This encryption is heavy," Bet muttered, his cybernetic interface flickering as he attempted to break through. "They didn't want just anyone looking at this."

Elena frowned. "Who exactly was running this place?"

Bet's fingers paused over the controls as he scanned the data. "A coalition of private and government-funded research teams. But some of these security measures… they look military."

Elena's eyes widened. "Military? I thought this was just an energy and research station."

Bet's expression darkened. "That's what it was supposed to be."

The projector flickered again, shifting through logs until a grainy video feed stabilized in front of them. A scientist, weary and disheveled, stared into the camera.

"This is Dr. Conrad Leto," the recording began. "Date: final cycle before containment shutdown. If you're seeing this, then we failed to stop it."

Elena tensed as the man continued.

"The singularity project was supposed to change everything. A stable artificial gravity well, a controlled singularity we could harness for limitless energy. We built the core deep within the station, shielded it under kilometers of rock and alloy." He exhaled sharply. "But something went wrong."

Bet narrowed his eyes. "Singularity project?"

Dr. Leto's voice wavered. "The simulations said it would hold, but the energy fluctuations became unstable. We lost control. The event horizon began expanding beyond its containment field, pulling mass into itself. The emergency protocols failed, and we had no way to neutralize the reaction."

Elena's heart pounded. "They created a miniature black hole?"

Bet nodded grimly. "And they couldn't contain it."

The scientist in the recording looked over his shoulder, as if hearing something. "We initiated full station lockdown, sealed off the core chamber, but it may not be enough. If you find this—if you have the means—do not open the containment doors." His voice dropped to a whisper. "It's still in there."

The recording cut out.

Silence filled the chamber.

Elena turned to Bet. "Tell me we're not going anywhere near that containment chamber."

Bet's face was unreadable. "That depends," he said. "If the singularity is still active… then this station isn't just a relic. It's a ticking time bomb."

Elena's breath came in slow, measured intakes as the weight of the revelation settled upon her. The holographic recording had long since ended, leaving only silence and the ghostly glow of flickering status lights in the archive chamber.

Bet was already scanning the remaining data logs, his cybernetic fingers moving rapidly across the console. "The core chamber is still sealed," he muttered. "Multiple failsafe layers intact. If that singularity is still inside, it hasn't consumed the station yet."

"That's not exactly reassuring," Elena shot back, pacing as she tried to process what they had just learned. "There's an uncontrolled black hole contained inside an abandoned asteroid station, and we're walking around like it's just another workday."

Bet's eyes flickered toward her, a subtle shimmer in their mechanical depths. "It's not active," he said, his tone measured. "If it were still growing, we wouldn't be standing here. The station would have collapsed into it long ago. But that doesn't mean it's safe either."

Elena stopped pacing. "You think it stabilized?"

He hesitated, then nodded. "Possibly. If it collapsed into a microstate equilibrium, the event horizon could be contained within its original boundaries. That's assuming the failsafe mechanisms held."

Elena exhaled sharply. "And if they didn't?"

Bet's fingers stilled on the console. "Then this station could be on borrowed time."

She swallowed hard, then straightened her shoulders. "So, what's our next step?"

Bet tapped into the control panel, bringing up a new section of the station's schematics. "We need to verify the containment integrity. The singularity's chamber is in a secured vault deep in the core. We'll need to navigate through several security layers to access it."

Elena eyed the map warily. "You're suggesting we get closer to the thing that shut this place down?"

He smirked faintly. "I'd rather know for certain than guess."

"Fine," she sighed, rubbing her temples. "Lead the way."

The corridor leading to the containment sector was unnervingly silent. The deeper they moved, the more it became apparent that the station had been hastily abandoned—emergency shutdowns, power reroutes, and doors locked in place, frozen in time. Some areas bore signs of structural strain, the metal warped in places where gravitational anomalies had likely twisted reality itself.

Elena kept close to Bet as they entered a reinforced transit chamber. A manual override was required to access the next sector, and Bet's mechanical interface quickly bypassed the ancient security codes.

The doors groaned open, revealing the central containment facility.

A massive observation chamber loomed before them, ringed with thick transparent panels that offered a glimpse into the depths below. At the center of the room, an enormous fusion of alloy and energy shielding pulsed faintly, layers of hardened material encasing the singularity's last known location.

Elena stepped forward cautiously. "Is it still in there?"

Bet's sensors whirred. "Scans show minimal energy leakage. The event horizon is still present, but stable. Whatever happened here, they managed to freeze it in place."

Elena's eyes narrowed as she stared through the glass, past the multiple reinforcement layers. The space beyond seemed distorted, subtly wrong, as if light itself hesitated before passing through. The gravity fluctuations were barely perceptible, but they were there, a lingering sign of the anomaly's presence.

"Can we shut it down?" she asked.

Bet's expression hardened. "I don't know if we should."

Elena turned sharply. "What do you mean?"

"This singularity could be a hazard, yes," Bet admitted, his voice calm but firm. "But if it's stable, if it's contained, then it's also something else."

Her heart pounded. "A power source."

He nodded. "The potential here is immense. If we understand how they stabilized it, we might be able to harness it instead of destroying it."

Elena shook her head in disbelief. "You want to experiment with a black hole?"

Bet met her gaze evenly. "I want to know what we're dealing with before we make a decision."

She exhaled, glancing back toward the core. The sheer scale of it, the implications of what lay behind those barriers—it was too much to ignore. But every instinct in her screamed that tampering with it could be catastrophic.

Bet turned back to the control interface. "We need more information."

Elena crossed her arms. "Then let's get it. But if that thing so much as twitches, we run."

Bet's smirk returned. "Deal."

With a deep breath, he activated the system's diagnostic mode, and the station's forgotten secrets began to unfold.

47

Bet moved quickly, his cybernetic fingers dancing over the ancient console as he extracted every scrap of data from the station's archives. The terminal pulsed with flickering light as information streamed into a compact, crystalline storage device that shimmered with a strange internal glow. He disconnected it with a practiced motion and turned toward Elena, holding it up between them.

Elena eyed the cube with curiosity. "That's not like any storage device I've seen before."

Bet smirked, tossing it lightly in his hand. "This is a high-density quantum lattice drive. It's more than just storage—it restructures and optimizes data at the quantum level. You could fit entire planetary archives in this thing, and it would still have space left over."

Elena took a cautious step closer, watching the shifting glow within the cube. "And how exactly do I access it?"

Bet's expression shifted to something between amusement and condescension. "Well, you don't. Not in your current state."

She frowned. "My 'current state'?"

Bet tucked the device away and gestured for her to follow as they exited the chamber. "You're still running on biological limitations, Elena. Your mind is fast, but it can't process this level of data in real time. You'd need a neural interface—something that allows direct interaction with quantum-encoded information."

Elena glanced back toward the containment chamber, giving the singularity one last, lingering look. The enormity of what they had just uncovered sat heavy in her mind, but there was something exhilarating about it too. They weren't just retrieving forgotten knowledge—they were stepping into a new era of science, and she wasn't sure she wanted to do it from the sidelines.

As they moved through the dim corridors, Bet veered toward a storage alcove and keyed in an access code. A recessed panel slid open, revealing a collection of old but functional hardware. He grabbed a sleek, wrist-mounted device and held it out to her. "This will let you read some of the data on our way back. Limited access, but enough to start making sense of things."

She took it, feeling the surprising weight of the device. "And if I want full access?"

Bet shot her a knowing look. "Then you'll need modifications."

They reached the shuttle bay, where the automated loaders had finished securing their initial cargo. Bet checked the status readouts and frowned. "We've still got room for more." He tapped into the station's logistics system and issued a command. "I'm requesting additional pods and extra ZPMs. No sense leaving resources behind."

Elena watched as the station's AI acknowledged the request and redirected more supply units toward their ship. "How long will that take?"

"Not long," Bet said. "And since we have some extra time..." He turned toward her, arms crossed. "You serious about those modifications?"

Elena hesitated for only a moment before nodding. "Yeah. If we're going to keep doing this—if I'm going to keep up—I need the upgrades."

Bet's expression was unreadable for a moment, then he nodded. "Alright. Let's get started."

The modification chamber was unlike anything Elena had ever seen. It made Riley and John's previous enhancements look primitive by comparison. Whereas their upgrades had been designed to fit specific roles—Riley's medical-matrix augmentations and John's high-speed neural optimization—what Elena was about to receive was something entirely different.

This was the bleeding edge of human scientific achievement, crafted in one of the most advanced research stations ever built. It wasn't just an interface for data—it was an evolution of thought itself.

She sat in the examination pod as Bet prepared the systems. Soft blue light pulsed in rhythmic intervals as robotic arms adjusted their positions. A high-frequency hum resonated through the room, filling the air with an almost tangible energy.

"This isn't just an implant," Bet explained as he brought up a detailed schematic of the device. "This is a quantum neurological network. It's not just interfacing with your brain—it's expanding it."

Elena's pulse quickened. "Expanding?"

Bet nodded. "Riley's surgical prowess and machine interface? Child's play. John's advanced computation? Useful, but linear. This is something else entirely. Your neurons won't just process information faster—they'll operate on multiple layers of quantum entanglement. You'll think in higher-dimensional space. Pattern recognition, memory recall, abstract reasoning—it will all happen simultaneously."

Elena swallowed. "Will I still be… me?"

Bet's expression softened. "If you truly meant that I'm still me, then you'll still be you, but… more. The way you experience time, logic, and even creativity will shift. You'll see connections you never saw before."

She closed her eyes for a moment, weighing the decision. The risks, the unknowns. And then she opened them. "Do it."

Something in Bet's posture shifted ever so slightly. Unexpressed, was the relief he found in this. Elena's choice here, helped ease his doubts. Left alone in his mind for so long, her assurances and belief was a comfort to him. He was grateful she accepted, because the outcome would help him accept or reject that he was still himself.

The process began with a cooling sensation at the base of her skull, followed by an overwhelming flood of sensory input. It was as if every cell in her body had suddenly woken up at once, every nerve alive with electric clarity. The world around her seemed to sharpen, its edges more defined, its sounds richer, deeper.

Then came the flood of knowledge. Quantum mechanics, general relativity, theoretical constructs she had once struggled with now fit together with effortless cohesion. Formulas unfolded in her mind like music, concepts expanding outward in perfect synchronization. She gasped, her hands gripping the sides of the pod as her thoughts raced beyond anything she had ever known.

Bet was watching her closely. "Breathe. Let it settle."

She did as he said, her mind gradually adjusting to its new capacity. She could feel the quantum lattice integrating with her consciousness, weaving itself seamlessly into her cognition. The barriers between thought and action had dissolved—understanding was immediate, intuitive.

Before her minds eye, a kaleidoscope of colors and fractals seemed to swirl, each one bringing to life a new thought and concept. Every bit of knowledge she fought so hard to gain in her past now felt like minuscule and insignificant bolts in a much larger framework. Her mind began to connect gravity, time, mass and energy into beautiful new shapes that all seemed to blend together, as if in a unified theory. It felt as if she were floating through space and time as an outside observer with every grasp and concept she ever imagined right there in front of her, but just out of reach. Everything made sense, she understood how everything was connected. Her life, consciousness, space, time and down to every atom in her body... everything was all connected and she could see it, but just as clear as it was in that moment, her grasp on it faded. She fought to regain the knowledge she felt like she was losing. She struggled to remember what she had seen. Slowly, she became more aware of her own body, sweating and laying flat on an unfamiliar table. To her mind, she felt as if she had just been teleported through all knowledge and back into her mortal and limited body.

When she finally met Bet's gaze, she wasn't the same person who had stepped into the chamber. "This is..." She searched for the words, but nothing felt sufficient.

Bet simply nodded. "I know."

She exhaled, steady and sure. "Let's finish loading the ship. We have a lot of work ahead of us."

With the most advanced modifications ever conceived now a part of her, Elena had taken the final step into the unknown. She spun on the table, letting her feet hang over the edge. As she stood up, the weight of her body felt foreign to her. Her feet more solid, but her control over her body unsure. She stood there, contemplating the feelings within her body, the sensations that seemed to be different. Her arms felt like long strings until she focused on them, then as if just by looking at them they took a familiar form. Likewise, her legs seemed to stretch wildly. She suddenly felt like she was many times her height, but once again, when she looked at her feet they suddenly took a familiar form. Her whole body snapped back into focus and she tried to take that first step.

What felt like many minutes to Elena, flashed in barely a second real time. Bet, reached out to steady her, but by the time his arm reached hers she had steadied. As their eyes met, an understanding passed between them. Bet, already familiar with the sensation, seemed to be reading her mind.

"Just breathe. Focus on me and take a deep breath. Do you feel me now?"

Somehow, Elena knew he didn't mean the sensation of his touch on her arm. She could feel him. Not his thoughts, but his emotions. Like body language, but telepathic and clearer. She nodded slowly, eyebrows trying to climb off her forehead and eyes growing wide as it all started to gain focus. She started to look around and felt a pinch on her elbow.

"No, look at me." Bet said sharp and quick.

Her eyes flicked back to his, questioning. Confusion passing between them via the neural interfaces.

"Just give it a second more. If you look around right now, you'll likely pass out or have a massive anxiety attack due to the overload of input on your senses. You just found your hands and feet again, didn't you?"

"Yes." she whispered.

"I told you, it's a whole new way of thinking. Give your mind a moment to adjust. The interface will settle down in a moment, once it finds an equilibrium with your mind. Over time, you will grow into it and evolve."

Elena slowly nodded, never taking her eyes off his. A slight hint of fear started to pass between them.

"It's ok. This is normal. I could not explain it to you anymore than you can explain it now. You'll feel like yourself again in a second or two. Now, slowly take a look around."

As Elena's gaze drifted from Bet's eyes to the laboratory around them, more information than she ever imagined could exist was showing up like holographic projections in her mind, in her view. As every machine, every device and every console tried to flood her mind with all of its data at once, she stumbled. Bet, anticipating this, maintained his grip on her arm and held her steady.

"Think about it being clear. Think about muting anything you're not actively looking at. Imagine it as you saw it before in your mind." Bet's voice was coaching, comforting and had a depth she never noticed before.

She did as he said and slowly the intrusions in her mind and visual perception began to fade as if she were turning the volume down on an antique speaker. With a little work, she began to feel more like herself again, more in control and able to function.

"That was... Holy shit! I have never... I mean, it's just so... " her words trailed off time and time again as she struggled to explain what she felt.

"I know," Bet said calmly. "And now you understand why I couldn't even try to prepare you for that? There's just no way to describe it is there?"

"wow," was all Elena could muster at the moment.

Bet's laugh came through her ears and her mind at the same time. No longer the slightly mechanical and awkward sounding event it was before, she could feel the warmth and depth of his laugh. The understanding of a mutual experience, just as she might a best friend. No longer was he so mechanical and monotone to her mind.

The ship's engines hummed with a steady resonance as Elena and Bet secured themselves in the cockpit. The cargo was loaded, their mission complete, and now it was time to return to the station. But everything felt different.

Elena sat back, feeling the weight—or perhaps the lack of it—of her new mind. Her vision seemed clearer, her perception broader. It was as if an entire universe of knowledge had been unlocked within her, and yet, it was still settling, still expanding. She turned her head, and the motion felt smoother, as if the delay between thought and action had vanished entirely.

Bet activated the ship's autopilot before turning to her. "You're processing at a higher level now," he said, watching her closely. "That's good. But you need to learn how to filter."

She blinked, aware now of a million microdetails rushing through her awareness—subtle shifts in the ship's pressure, minuscule fluctuations in the fusion drive's output, distant electromagnetic waves from the station they were returning to. It was overwhelming, like standing in the center of a storm made of information.

Bet smirked as he saw the realization settle in. "You're hearing everything at once, aren't you?"

Elena exhaled sharply. "Yes. It's… a lot."

"That's normal," he reassured her. "Your brain is adapting. You need to compartmentalize—focus only on what matters. The interface is designed to prioritize what you need, but you have to guide it."

She closed her eyes and concentrated, visualizing the overwhelming flood of data as streams of light, twisting and converging in a chaotic pattern. With a thought, she willed them into order, focusing only on the ship's systems and their flight path. The other noise faded into the background, still there, still present, but no longer drowning her.

She opened her eyes, steady now. "Better."

Bet nodded. "Good. Now, let's try something more advanced." He reached to his side and produced the quantum lattice storage device he had taken from the station. "I want you to interface with this."

Elena hesitated for only a moment before focusing on the cube. At once, she felt the surge of stored data, a vast network of compressed knowledge stretching into her consciousness like an unfolding fractal. It wasn't just information—it was experience, equations, theories, entire research projects suspended in quantum code. Almost reflexively she put up mental walls, providing resistance to the flow of information, slowing it down from a flood to a trickle at a time. As her mind adapted to the sensation, she found that she could control the flow more easily, grabbing only bits and pieces at a time. She could focus on entire swaths of data, or one line from a single report.

She gasped. "This... I can see it all."

Bet leaned back, watching her carefully. "Don't just see it. Control it."

Elena willed herself deeper into the interface, reaching for specific patterns, isolating them, analyzing them at speeds she would have thought impossible only hours ago. Ignoring experimental reports and data, she focused on gaps in her knowledge. Equations from long-lost scientists scrolled past her awareness, quantum theories so advanced they almost felt like living things.

She pulled herself back, severing the link. Her breath came quickly, but her mind was calm.

Bet raised an eyebrow. "You're adapting fast."

Elena smiled, exhilarated. "It feels... natural."

Bet chuckled. "That's the point."

The ship's nav systems chimed, signaling their approach to the station. Elena looked out at the approaching structure, a vast testament to the past, and now, perhaps, the future.

She flexed her fingers, feeling the new power humming beneath the surface of her thoughts.

"Let's see what else I can do."

48

The docking clamps locked into place with a dull, mechanical thud. The hum of the ship's systems dimmed as the station's atmosphere took over, filling the air with the familiar sterile scent of processed oxygen. Elena exhaled slowly, steadying herself as the reality of what they had accomplished settled in. They had returned with more energy than anyone in their crew had ever seen in their lives.

Bet was already moving, checking the manifest one last time as the station's personnel prepared for cargo transfer. Through the viewport, Elena could see a flurry of activity. John stood waiting at the docking bay doors, his stance tense but eager. Riley was beside him, conversing rapidly with an unfamiliar tech, his excitement barely contained.

The airlock cycled, and the doors hissed open. John stepped forward first, clapping a hand on Bet's shoulder. "You sure took your time," he said, but there was no annoyance in his voice—just relief.

Bet smirked. "I see you've had some work done."

John's excitement was evident. "Got a lot to catch you up on. We've been busy while you were gone. A few others did too. Riley's been busy."

"You still seem very much the soldier. Expecting trouble?"

"Expecting? No. Better to be prepared and not need than to need and be ill-prepared."

Bet nodded slightly. "That's not a bad policy. Still, what use is a soldier with nobody to fight?"

"There's always something to fight. The star's brightness, radiation, darkness and challenges in the ruins. No settlement of humans has ever existed without controversy. It's a matter of time before I have to play sheriff."

"There's been a lot of changes around here." Bet said as he looked around the bay, taking note of the new faces.

A transport crew was already moving to offload the modular power cells. The station's AI-directed drones hovered in synchronized formation, scanning and logging the cargo. At the center of it all was the prize: a pristine Zero Point Energy Module, glowing faintly with untapped energy.

Elena watched as the crew carefully maneuvered the ZPE onto a reinforced hover platform. The sheer amount of power contained within it was staggering. If successfully integrated, it could power the entire colony below.

Elena glanced toward Riley, watching the way he moved, the subtle precision in his stance. "The interface," she asked, "how different does it feel?"

Riley smirked. "It's like waking up after years of being half-asleep. The connections between knowledge and instinct—they're instant now. I don't just understand complex procedures—I see them happening before I even begin."

Elena nodded slowly. She could relate. The overwhelming flood of awareness had been terrifying at first, but now, she found herself eager to push the boundaries of what she could do. "And the crew?"

John stepped in. "Most of them took minor neural enhancements—reflex upgrades, data-processing accelerators. Enough to make a difference." He hesitated before adding, "I went a little further."

Elena's eyes narrowed. "How far?"

John shrugged, but there was a new sharpness in his gaze. "Cognitive enhancement, tactical overlays, accelerated regeneration and some predictive modeling systems. I needed something to keep up."

Bet gave him an approving nod. "Smart move. We can't afford to fall behind."

The last of the cargo was being secured, and the hum of the ship's power cycle echoed through the bay. The transport crew moved with methodical efficiency, aware of the importance of their payload. The weight of responsibility hung over them all—what they were carrying could alter the course of the colony's future.

Elena took a deep breath, the magnitude of the moment settling in. They had left this station as one version of themselves, but now, every single one of them had changed. The modifications, the knowledge, the sheer scope of what they had recovered—it was a transformation not just for individuals, but for their entire species. She contemplated Bet's fears of being more computer than human.

John stepped beside her, following her gaze. "Feels like we're on the edge of something big."

Elena nodded. "We are."

Bet exhaled, his voice calm but resolute. "Then let's not waste any more time standing around feeling like giants while there's so much work to punctuate how small we are."

Elena and John both turned to glare at Bet, but instead they caught the humor in his words like never before. Marveling at the complexity and personality of a being they once thought to be a monotone machine, Elena and John exchanged a look and both burst out laughing. There was so much truth in Bet's words though. It was easy to feel like giants. A subtle reminder of humility was a good thing.

Captain Morrow walked up just as they were regaining their composure. "Elena, Bet. Welcome back. How was the trip?"

"Thank you Captain. It was everything I thought it would be and more. The facility isn't just an energy plant, it's a massive scientific research facility the size of a small city and carved out of an asteroid. Kind of reminds me of an evil scientist secret lair... and now that I think about it," Elena turned and looked at Bet. "That would make you the..."

"The evil scientist? Not until I monologue about my evil plans." Bet teased back.

Captain Morrow and John exchanged an amused look. It seemed a couple of months with Elena had pulled some of Bet's personality out.

"Well, the evil scientist here was in charge of a lot of things. We're quite lucky to have him around. Right now, I've had a millennia of knowledge dumped into my head and it's been a long trip. I'm a bit eager to get started on some new projects." Elena's enthusiasm was shared with the rest of the crowd via neural interface. "But first, I need to get some rest."

49

Elena woke in an instant. Feeling wide awake and fully aware in an instant, she found the experience slightly disorienting, as if her brain had stood up abruptly. After the briefest of moments, the feeling eased and she was wide awake. Thinking to herself that might have been the best night sleep she could remember, she started her morning routine. She pulled on a fresh utility jumpsuit. The tough fabric was amazingly comfortable, despite being cut, tear and abrasive resistant. It was also quite thick due to the reinforced layers of the smart fabric. With the ability to constrict around her arms, legs and body in relation to additional g-forces in flight, the moisture wicking fabric pulled sweat away from her body, capturing and filtering the water. The jumpsuit also maintained body temperature, ensuring she stayed comfortable in nearly any environment. After closing the suit around her, it recognized her. The sleeve and leg lengths adjusted to a perfect fit by slightly contracting the fabric in areas between her joints and slightly around her wrists. Stepping into her boots, more smart tech, she felt them tighten snuggly around her ankles to her preset preference. The souls of the boots held a smart polymer gel that perfectly molded itself to her foot, ensuring perfect support and constantly measuring her pressure. The pressure sensing aided the flexible magnetic field that allowed her to walk on the metal deck of a ship or station in microgravity. With her own personal environment complete, her pants legs sealed themselves around the top of her boots as she stood on her toes and stretched. She enjoyed the feeling the suit gave her.

In the almost cramped quarters, she only had to turn her body to reach her locker, from which she removed her wrist computer and a small round box. She opened the box and retrieved a mouthpiece from within. Sliding it into position, she let it clean her teeth as she attached her computer to her arm. As she thought about turning it on to check function and power levels, the holographic detail sprung up above her forearm and the display of ship's time caused her breath to catch. Forgetting for a moment about the mouthpiece, she had a briefly uncomfortable moment where she felt the need to swallow and almost pushed the thing out of her mouth at the same time. She removed the device and placed it back in its container, took a deep breath and looked at the time again. Then she checked the date stamp. Sure there must be a problem, she verified it against the console station in the wall. She had only slept for half an hour. She had been exhausted when she laid down and was sure she had slept eight or maybe even twelve hours. It felt like she had anyway. She closed her eyes and thought in a flash, from the instant wake up to the short amount of time passing, this implant was going to take some getting used to, and her wrist computer had come on with a thought too hadn't it? Maybe she was imagining that. Shaking her head, she closed her locker and set out for the kitchen.

It was about halfway to the kitchen, lost in thoughts of energy and work the whole way, she stopped short. She couldn't remember the walk, but as soon as she had the thought a sensation like watching a memory in fast forward flashed through her conscious mind. Realizing she must look silly, she glanced around to make sure nobody else was in the corridor. Satisfied she was alone, she decided she didn't need caffeine anyway and would skip that part of her routine. There wouldn't be any anyway. Instead, she altered course and headed to the flight deck. As she passed the medical bay, she paused and decided to drop in on Riley. Hoping he was available and could reassure her that she wasn't crazy, she stepped into the medical bay. Riley was standing off to the side, hand lightly resting on a console and eyes closed.

"Hey Elena, give me just a second… I'm reviewing some samples from the planet."

Elena took a seat nearby, her mind racing.

Riley let out a deep sigh, "ok, this can wait. You, apparently cannot. Trouble adjusting to the new implant I take it?"

"Uh, I wasn't… I didn't… how'd you guess? I didn't say anything!"

"Yes, you did. You were practically shouting panic attack at me."

"I made no sound!"

Just then, Elena felt a very profound feeling of comfort and understanding wash over her like a wave, followed closely with a quieter, very subtle irritation.

"The implant," Elena muttered, eyes looking down.

"Yeah. You were projecting pretty intensely and of course I can't ignore it, so. Other than keeping control over your emotional projections, what is bothering you? Is it giving you any trouble?"

"No, at least… I don't think so. I woke up instantly after 30 minutes, but it felt like I'd slept for hours! Thoughts keep coming to me, like my brain is answering its own questions… I feel like I'm losing my mind!"

Riley smiled warmly and sat down across from her. Taking her hand in his, a tickle started to form in the base of her skull, like a fuzzy tickle in her brain. "It's normal. Remember, these were usually implanted at a strategic point during the developmental years. People would have grown up with these augments and worn them like a second skin. You, don't get that lifetime of years to adapt, you're having to do it in days and weeks. And while you were on mission I might add! Why in the hell did you and Bet think that was a good idea?"

Chagrined, Elena looked down at her hand in his and felt the tickle again. As she acknowledged it, a sensation snapped in her head, like her mind had just expanded. Riley jumped back, eyes bulging and she heard his voice in her head *'What the fuck was that?'*

'Holy shit, did he feel it to?'

'Your damn right I did…'

She looked up and locked eyes with Riley. His eyes looked like they would jump out of his head. The shocked look on his face seemed amusing to her for some reason and she tried to stifle a laugh and keep her face from betraying her amusement.

'Yeah, like that's going to work right now. I'm glad you're amused, but what in the hell? … there's nothing about this in my memory or research. It's not in any of the documentation, or any mention of it in the… query Thought projection'

Riley's gaze went distant for a moment. Elena thought *'he must be searching for an answer. Wonder if he always rambles this much in his head?'*

Elena looked up to see a smirk on Riley's face. *'No more than you it would seem.'*

Elena blinked and focused on closing the sensation in her mind. Picturing herself turning off a flashlight, for that was oddly the mental correlation that came to mind, the sensation ended and Riley was no longer in her head. *'Tell me if you can hear me now,'* she thought.

Riley just stared at her and blinked. "Well, that was novel."

"Didn't find anything in your query?"

"No, nor in the dozen I've run since then and no help from the station Ai either." Riley pinched the bridge of his nose, looking thoroughly confused. "I think I may have an idea what's going on here… and I think we need to talk to someone else too."

"Bet?" Elena nodded as she posed the statement as a question.

"Exactly. There were several versions of these implants. It would seem there was a basic version, kind of a general population type of deal. The kind of basic system one might give a child. They would unlock new capabilities with age and need, though some functions could be unlocked intentionally later on. I'm a little fuzzy on some of the details, but now I have many questions."

As Riley spoke, Elena was listening and thinking about Bet. As Riley finished his thought, she slowly lifted a finger and closed her eyes. Applying her full concentration on Bet, she started to feel the slightest hint of that tingle in her mind. She reached for it, but it was like a mental attempt to grip air. Just as she was about to give up, the tingle pulsed and then grew solid in her mind. Grabbing hold of it, she felt the connection open.

'*Well, that didn't take you long at all,*' a voice said in her mind. It was Bet's voice, but warmer. It was more human, without the mechanical lilt she was used to hearing.

'*Medical bay. Get your ass in here now. You've got some explaining to do.*' She thought, consciously pouring her emotional state through the link as well.

'*Under…*' Bet began replying, but she slammed the connection shut on him.

Elena opened her eyes and gave Riley a half smirk. "He'll be here shortly."

"You were able to reach him too?" Riley looked completely dumbfounded.

"Yes. And apparently I can hang up on him too."

This made Riley chuckle slightly as he shook his head. A few minutes later, Bet walked in with his hands raised and palms exposed, as if in surrender.

"Well?" Elena's clipped phrase was all the clue anyone needed as to her current emotional state. To be sure her message was clear, she consciously pushed her emotional feelings of confusion, anger and fear at Bet.

Bet flinched, dropped his hands and nodded. "Where would you like me to begin?"

"For starters, how about you explain what's in my head and fill in the gaps that Riley can't find any answers for, including why there's so much that seems to be missing from the information on this station, the data from the energy lab, hell we haven't even found so much as a math or history primer for children on the surface! There must have been schools! What the…" Elena closed her eyes, took a breath and continued, shutting off her emotional projection. "What is going on here?"

"For starters, why would you expect to find a detailed account of the capabilities for something that people were as familiar and comfortable with as their own hands?" Bet's voice was calm and a slight confusion ebbed from his projection with his words. He knew he was on thin ice.

"What you're discovering now, would have been like learning to walk as a child. It was an integrated part of identity and self before those things even had meaning for an individual."

Riley nodded, "I can see that, but how come there's no mention of this telepathy thing anywhere? It's not even in correspondence records or any of the text records that I can find. And there seem to be some considerable gaps in a lot of that data too."

Bet nodded at Riley. "Two main reasons to your first question and a couple points to your statements. First, much the same reason. That wasn't something worth mentioning anymore than you might feel the need to explain the difference between talking in person or through a comm link. A conversation is a conversation. A communication is a communication. What I expect you're curious about, is why there's no scientific, research or production data on these?"

Riley nodded. Bet continued, "These implants, the ones we've been using here, are all what you might have called 'State Secrets' in your time. I'm sure there are ample stocks of the common varieties on the surface, in fact I believe some have been recovered already and utilized. Those would have been common use and were not advanced or studied here. We had the ability to produce our own, but we were supposed to receive them all from Sol via routine supply drones. Kind of an interstellar freight solution. These advanced units that were made here in system represented some advancements that were made specifically for certain individuals in leadership, command or essential positions. We were a scientific minded society after all. For most jobs and folks, we could simply use the machine Riley recovered to unlock features or update the common systems. But, for a special upper class, in essence, a rather delicate and difficult process to replace the units was available. For most, it only required replacing that little hardware chip. For some though, the filaments that make contact throughout the brain was inadequate. These couldn't be easily removed, so an additional unit was added. What you have here, are the fully unlocked best there was, reserved for the upper limits of society. Our highest officials, our smartest scientists… and of course, our richest citizens as well. Therefore, none of the data you're looking for would have been generally accessible. Since I've been here on the station, I've been working with and working on the station Ai. The station's data is heavily corrupted. Large sections of storage were lost in the portions of the station that were lost. The station is all tied together and the Ai's matrix ran through the entire station. Losing chunks of the station had essentially lobotomized it."

Bet stopped talking. For once, Riley and Elena sat just as still as Bet.

Elena was the first to recover. "You built a cast system directly into the heads of the population?"

"Not exactly… but, I suppose from your time and perspective… it was more like…" Bet tried to explain. Obviously uncomfortable with the question.

Elena shot Riley a look and raised an eyebrow as Bet finished, "yes. I suppose that's exactly what we did… can we… this form of communication is so slow. With your permission…"

Riley and Elena felt the tickle in their minds. Both of them projected a mix of emotions at Bet, full of reluctance, distrust and irritation, yet they did allow the connection to open.

'Thank you. I understand your reluctance. Please also know that the only thing available through the connection is your surface thoughts. Your mind, your innermost thoughts, memories… non of that is able to be touched. That's why there is quiet in the connection, just like if we are having a conversation. Your brains aren't exactly quiet right now, but this isn't all of our thoughts constantly colliding and confusing everyone all at once. And as you can see, this is also a far faster way to communicate. For now, it will move at the speed of your thought, but as you're still thinking at the same speed you've always thought at, you're not going to get the full speed benefit of this form of communication without practice.' Bet's thoughts streamed through their consciousness in the blink of an eye.

Riley was absolutely amazed at all the implications and potential. The flood of thoughts that were running through his mind, but Bet was right. They didn't go through the connection, until he thought about the connection.

'Its amazing like all these thoughts but they don't go through the connection, oh wait… … did that go through?'

Elena was smiling at Riley as she nodded. She almost giggled as she heard Riley's thoughts slip through almost exactly matching her own.

'So. We can have entire conversations in the blink of an eye? At what range?' Elena thought.

'Typically, within the same room. Here on the station, the Ai system can actually assist. For instance, when you called me earlier. That was quite impressive. The station helped to amplify your signal, picking up on it and forwarding it along. I only knew it was you, well because that was the only logical explanation. Did you notice a difference this time when I initiated it?'

When Elena thought about it, she found that she could perfectly recall what it felt like. *'Yes, it felt like you. But, You're right here and I knew it was you.'*

'When you initiate it, for now think of it more like your standard comm unit. You think about who you're contacting, so push a mental self image with it. Kind of like announcing yourself on a comm, but you don't need to use a name. Just like you thought of me, simply include yourself. This will become second nature, and as your implant adapts to you, it will be able to assist with this. In time it will develop into your own mental fingerprint, for lack of a better description.' Bet explained.

'So we can have entire conversations with someone, in the blink of an eye, entirely in our own heads, in a crowded room… and nobody would know about it? I assume, as you said this was for leadership and the like, there's no way to intercept this communication? But you said the station picks it up and aids the connection…' Elena pondered openly.

'It's rather difficult to explain and I'm trying to not get stuck in the minutia of details, but think of it more like an amplifier… repeater perhaps… The station can't exactly pick up on the signals, but the same way you can communicate with the station, the Ai and the equipment, the station is so ingrained with this technology that it passes through the station, flows through it more like, less impeded. Instead of old world radio waves that were blocked by these bulkheads and the mass between, because of the technology so integrated in the station, it's more like we are standing farther apart in an open field with line of sight, to keep with the old radio analogy. The Ai is only included if you include it.'

Riley thought, *'I don't even want to think about what politics were like in your time. The side deals, scheming and plotting must have been thick and fast.'*

'It was. And if you think that was bad, try having a debate with a dozen scientists, each at the top of their respective fields of study in the system, some in the galaxy. When working together, it was incredible, but when there was a difference of opinion... so basically every other word in some cases,' Bet glanced at Elena who was nodding and chuckling at the thought. *'The conversations and debates could get quite heated. As fast as so much can be said, as intense as these debates could be... it was therefore considered good manners to keep your emotional projection in tight control when in group settings or public. Socially, that was considered an intimacy, although it was also used as punctuation. When it was used as punctuation, similar to how you projected at me when I entered, Elena, that was the social equivalent of foul language, and in some cases, could be taken for assault. The latter being quite specific to certain situations and social elements though. To most, it was just rude, or crass. For one to need such a demonstration, with this form of communication was seen to be as... well, as a commoner. A laborer. Lower class... we had our issues.'* Bet's thoughts trailed off with the barest hint of sorrow coming through with his final words.

'This is a lot, but this doesn't excuse you withholding knowledge from us. I wanted to trust you on our trip starward, but it really just uncovered a lot of questions that make me struggle with that.' Elena thought. She thought she might have picked up on the barest hint of sorrow coming from Bet's connection. *'You say it was rude to show emotion, but you use it. How is it that the one thing that makes you more human than your face can show was unacceptable?'* Elena definitely felt Bet's pain and regret at her thoughts.

'I said it was good manners to keep your emotional projection in tight control. I didn't say turn it off. Emotions can come across so loud, it's like shouting in a stasis chamber. It can overpower thoughts and could be construed as a domination or intimidation tactic. It was acceptable to include a thread, a quiet thread as a subtle suggestion. Those with the best control could wield it with the subtlety of body language, speaking more to a subconscious thought than a fully aware announcement. I'm sorry to have damaged our trust, Elena, but please consider my perspective for a moment. I've been putting myself through self stasis and floating in space for centuries. Occasionally, I would dock with the research station for sustenance and fuel, to look in on a couple projects. In the beginning, I tried to continue my research, but after a couple decades passed with nothing but dumb Ai and bots to talk to, I longed for human contact. When I approached the station, I could not communicate with any of you. It took me a great deal of effort to remember how to use such arcane means of communication, which I almost didn't do. If

*it weren't for the giant ship docked at the station, there was no indication anyone was here. *sorrow* I was so eager for human contact, and then I discover what *sorrow* well, what to me would be like you encountering a bunch of neanderthals. I'm sorry, but the time gap was vast. I didn't know what to share. I didn't know if I could trust you. From my perspective, you might as well have been alien invaders, scavengers or some weird remnant of humanity so isolated and separated that we come from different worlds, and in effect… it's not really much different from that. I found you just as scary and odd as you still find me.' *sadness** Bet's thoughts came through in a flash.

Elena could see what he meant about the subtle use of emotions now. It was just the lightest touch, a hint of emotion less intrusive than the look on someone's face, but clearer and easier to read. Bet was good at it, and the rest of his thoughts took just a second more to process.

Riley's thoughts came through, warm and comforting. *'Bet, we may be alien neanderthals to your perspective. We have come from over 1,000 years in the past. It's understandable that we look out of place, we feel out of place. When we left, less than two years ago by our experience, none of this existed. It's very much like we landed in an alternate universe when we arrived. I'm sure we have an exhausting number of questions, not the least of which probably seem like basics the youngest of children should know in your time. But, don't mistake our ignorance for incompetence. You must also understand that we share one huge question… what happened to the rest of humanity? Is there anything left of Sol? Is there anyone else out there? Where did all the people here go? What happened to all the bodies on this station for instance? They can't have all just… vanished.'*

*'They didn't.' *deep sorrow** two words in Bet's thought carried more weight and context than Elena or Riley ever imagined possible. Carried along with Bet's words, was a sadness as deep as space itself.

'What do you mean they didn't?' Riley asked.

*'They didn't all just disappear. When I returned from my experiments and observations, measuring solar activity on the other side of the star, I found them. So many dead. *lonely* *loss* The aftermath of a slaughter of this entire world *anger*… I gave them a solar funeral. *sadness* that's why you found no bodies here. I sent them to rest and gave their atoms back to the universe. I don't know what happened here. And I don't know what happened on the surface either. I went down there a few times. I only found a few hundreds of bodies. I don't know what happened to the rest. They did just vanish. For a while, I'd hoped they escaped underground, or to space. But no contact was*

ever made.'

Riley placed a hand on Bet's shoulder. Bet lifted his optical sensors to look at it and let out a mix of emotions so complex, it blended into something there was no word for. It was a feeling so strong, so layered that it was hard to understand and it left Riley and Elena feeling very uneasy.

'That must have been... I'm sorry for getting so angry with you earlier, Bet. I had no idea... but, that's also part of the problem. Communicate better with us, ok?' Elena thought.

Bet looked at her and just nodded.

50

John was loading the last of the supplies in the shuttle when his comm went off.

"John, it's Clara. You there?"

"I read you. How's the weather down there?"

"Beautiful and sunny today. But I'm sure you know that. I need a favor. Got a minute and a little room on your craft for me?"

John chuckled. Of course he knew the weather. He kept a close eye on it when he was flying. "That depends. I can make the time, but the shuttle has a mass limit. How can I help."

"I started some seed trays before I came down. It's a new hybrid I've been working on & I'd like to try them out down here. Do you make deliveries?"

"Well, I'll see what I can do. I assume you've got some details for me on which trays and how to pack them?"

"Already sent to your comp. Thank you. I owe you one."

John activated the holoscreen on his wrist computer and read her message. "Yeah, you're going to owe me two. You didn't mention the nutrients or the pumps. Conveniently slipped your mind?"

Clara's chuckles came through the comm, "not at all, it's just part of the advanced packing instructions you asked for."

"Hardly. I'll get that together. I'll be headed down as soon as Elena is ready. She was exhausted and Morrow ordered her to turn off alarms and light cycles and get rest. So, I'm at her mercy there. I'll see you when I see you."

"She's coming down too?"

"Yes, she's got some work to do. Apparently she can power a couple planets now, so hopefully you'll have something more reliable than those colony pack solar panels soon."

"Oh that will be nice! I'm good here, but it'll be nice to not feel like I'm on some weird camping expedition in the field. Hmmm. Maybe a hot bath, cold air… ahh some finer touches of civilization would be nice."

John shook his head as he walked toward the hydroponics bay. When he didn't reply, his comm went off again.

"John?"

"Yeah?"

"Stop trying to picture me in the tub and bring me some flowers first."

"I'm on my way. Quick as I can."

"See you soon. Safe flight." Clara cut the connection.

John, entered the hydroponics bay and began collecting everything on Clara's list and placing it gently in transportation totes. As he did so, he began humming, a melody he wasn't sure if he was remembering or just making up. While he studied Clara's meticulous labels, ensuring to grab exactly what she wanted, he reached up and scratched the back of his neck. Almost mindlessly, he realized he was still scratching, but it wasn't an itch… and it wasn't on his skin. Once it caught his attention, his thoughts seemed drawn to some part of his mind. It had a familiar feel to it. Almost as quickly as this registered in his mind, a strange feeling expanded through his mind. It briefly felt as if his head had grown too large for his body. Elena's voice seemed to come from inside his head.

"Hey John. You're not at the shuttle, just wanted to say thanks for loading all the gear. I'm ready when you are."

"What the fuck? How the fuck? Holy fuck! What are you… how are you… I'm losing my fucking mind!"

"Well, I hope your pilot skills are as sharp as your tongue. Relax, just discovered a new super power. I'll explain on the way down. You going to be here soon?"

"Oh shit. I'm losing my mind. I'm hearing voices… and I'm talking to them. Maybe I should go to medical, see Riley. I shouldn't be flying with hallucinations."

*"John! Relax *humor* you're not losing your mind. The implant. We have our own comms now."*

"Not cool. I would hear Elena's voice. I swear, if it adopts her attitude I'm going to jump out an airlock."

"Hey, you knuckle dragging ape! I can hear your thoughts you know. I

heard that!"

"Knuckle dragging? Oh this is weird. You're really talking in my head? I swear, one of us is about to go out an airlock."

**great humor* you just responded out loud and then thought the last bit about air locks in your head, didn't you?"*

"… lalalalalalalalalalalalalalalalala"

Elena cut the connection.

The sudden quiet and lack of feeling in his head left John standing in the hydroponics bay with his jaw open like a Venus flytrap. As the realization of what just happened started to sink in, he realized Elena had just had a good laugh at his expense. John wasn't sure how he felt about that. He was sure about one thing though. This was going to be a very weird flight.

As John approached the shuttle, pushing the maglev cart holding Clara's supplies, he saw Elena leaning against the rear ramp with a very snug look on her face and something he wasn't sure if he'd ever seen before. A smile.

"That was really you in my head then?"

"Yes, that was actually me. You're not going crazy, but you are going to need some practice separating your thoughts though. Do you always cuss like that in your head?"

"None of your fucking business."

Elena caught the humor in his voice and hinted in his projection.

"Your emotional projection is quite good. I think you'll get the hang of the communication quickly."

"Probably a lot easier if I'm not blindsided while lost on more pleasant thoughts than your voice in my head."

John felt the tickle in his mind again and focused on it. The connection opened and for a moment they just stared at each other.

'You know, I'd make a joke about how empty your head must be, but I already know better. No tirade of fucks this time?' Elena's thoughts entered his mind.

'No. What the hell is this?'

'I found out by mistake. I stopped by medical and when Riley and I touched, the connection opened. Scared the crap out of us too, so I had to have a little fun with you. I called Bet in and we asked some questions. Got some answers too. There's a lot to catch you up on, and this is far faster than talking, so get used to my voice in your head cowboy, I'm going to dump on you the whole way down.'

'Well that sounds just lovely. Load this up. I'm going to start preflight.'

John cut the connection, earning an admiring glance from Elena. He got the hang of that faster than she thought he would.

Once the preflight checks were done and flight clearance granted from the bridge, John and Elena made the trip to the surface. She explained all that she saw at the lab, her conversation with Bet and Riley, and even her experience waking after such a short nap and her reason for going to the medical bay in the first place.

51

As John piloted the ship through the atmosphere on final approach to land at the colony, he circled wide around the established area and the remaining city ruins to give Elena a better look at it all. Her focus shifted from getting John up to date on what she knew to her mission goals, establish a power grid for the colony. She carefully observed all that she could as John circumnavigated the city ruins, the impact crater and eventually the newly established colony on the southwest corner of the city. A few things stood out to her immediately, most concerning was a complete lack of above ground cables anywhere, even in the outskirts of the old city. She wondered just how long had humanity been in this system?

John's mind raced, trying to process everything Elena had just briefed him on while piloting the ship. As he approached the new dedicated landing zone, LZ1, for the colony proper, he noted a couple figures waiting at a safe distance off to the side. The ship touched down and John began the process of shutting it down. Elena extricated herself from the co-pilot seat, stretched and made her way to the rear of the ship as the loading ramp began its smooth opening motion to make a ramp to the newly made hard surface. 'Sure beats bushwhacking through thick vines,' he thought as he completed the shutdown procedures and made his way to the rear of the ship. By the time the loading ramp was settled on the landing pad, Serena, Vogel and Han were standing there ready to greet them, with a couple floating anti-gravity carts to help unload. John greeted them all with warm smiles and knocked forearms with each of them.

"Looks like you made it in one piece," Han jibed. "Even without a navigator."

"Elena did her best to distract me this time, but at least the weather's nice today," John replied. "Come to give us a hand with all this gear?"

"We've actually been exploring quite a bit lately. Figured we'd play tour guide too. I think we're all ready to get off power rations. The solar arrays we brought are fantastic, but we hadn't planned on having so much extra equipment and infrastructure when we got here. So we've been budgeting. There's so many comforts we could possibly use, if we had the power," Serena said.

John grinned. "Well, if you three are going to play escort, then that frees me up to make a delivery to Clara. She still in the greenhouse?"

"Always. She's been a one woman farming army ever since we got the kudzu cleared out."

Vogel interjected, "Well lets get busy. Lots to do and we're burning daylight."

"Most?" John gave her a puzzled look with a raised eyebrow.

Vogel had a huge smile on her face. "Oh, you'll see in a moment."

Once the carts were loaded up, the three women lead John and Elena to a small building next to the landing pad. The storage building, intended for shelter and staging supplies going to and coming from the space station, was three bays wide with a small office and seating room off to one side. A smaller room with a couple of cots beside that. As they entered the small warehouse portion of the building, parked in the center bay was what John interpreted as a truck. The thing looked like a collection of shipping containers and a portion of one habitation shelter were welded together in a collage of protruding boxy angles and placed on top of some sort of equipment chassis.

"What in the world is that?!" Elena asked with a hint of disgust in her voice.

Vogel's smile had grown. "Han and I scrounged up some spare materials and slapped this together in 2 days from what looked like a half built tractor. With a little work on the drive motors and frame, we were able to make a giant rolling toolbox transport vehicle. We've got some assorted gear in the front containers here," she gestured to some transport containers, "and we've got a large storage area in the back for recovered items. It's been a whole lot better than walking everywhere and having to carry anything of interest back from within the city. It will make your job a whole lot easier down here. There's a flat bed section there on the back corner and attachment points along the side to secure your larger equipment here. The flat bed section has extra vibration dampening beyond what the suspension has. It also articulates to ground level for loading particularly large and heavy items or accepting these grav-carts. Up front, you'll find a full navigation suite, sensor array and comms station. It may not be ugly as sin, but it's got everything a girl needs to get a job done."

Elena looked at the vehicle in a whole new perspective. She started to notice how everything about it served a purpose. Vogel and Han had put a lot of thought and effort into the machine, and in a very short amount of time. "That's actually quite impressive."

The weight of the compliment was not lost on the two women who beamed with pride.

"You haven't even seen the best part yet," Han said with an impish grin. "Lets get loaded up and take her for a spin, yeah?"

The crew had the vehicle loaded up very quickly. The way all the seemingly random and scavenged parts fit together and functioned made the job feel effortless. As they climbed up into the cab section, John and Elena were quite surprised at how spacious and comfortable the interior was. With large windows at the front, three swiveling chairs sat in a row behind a simple dashboard with a row of holoscreens. Along the rear of the cabin, was a couch.

John laughed mirthlessly, "Where the blazes did you find a couch?"

"Carried it back about 5 clicks on our shoulders from an excursion into the city a few days before we built this. Built the whole cabin around it," Vogel said.

Serena, Vogel and Han took their seats up front. John and Elena exchanged a glance then looked at the couch. John shrugged and made himself comfortable, stretching out as if he were in a spacious living area. Elena did much the same on the opposite side of the couch, albeit a bit less relaxed.

As the vehicle started up, holoscreens began displaying controls, maps, menus and communications status. The look and feel of it reminded John of transports they used in the outer system back in Sol. He knew exactly which ones they had gotten inspiration from as he thought about their old home. It felt like just yesterday since they left, but it also felt so long ago. Like it was another life before this one.

John was abruptly shaken from his thoughts as a large holoscreen appeared in front of the couch. A wild show of lights began to display, beams of light suddenly stretching out to fill the distance to the couch. Old earth music began to play loudly. Four hard long notes reverberated through the cabin before a slight pause and the beginning of a drum beat. The low notes came from vibrations in the couch itself and the sound was completely immersive as the display of light pulsed and danced to the beat of an electric guitar.

Serena began moving the vehicle slowly out of the bay as Vogel's head bobbed up and down to the beat. Han turned around to inform John and Elena, "Vogie here's been on a 20th century kick lately. Lots of Rage Against The Machine. She seems stuck in the 1990's this week. A huge improvement from her… V, what did you call it?"

"Disco."

"Yeah, Disco. Crazy here had a light shining on a ball of mirrors spinning around in the back. Talk about distracting! Took a whole two days before Serena attacked it," Han ended with a laugh.

The atmosphere and fun they were having had a smile on everyone's face, even Elena. John was smirking at her across the couch when she started singing along with the old song. John's eyebrows tried to climb back to the space station in surprise. Elena closed her eyes and moving her head up and down to the beat, sent her hair flying back and forth while holding a hand in the air and singing loudly. When the song ended and another did not begin, she opened her eyes and looked around to find the vehicle was no longer moving and everyone was staring at her, mouths agape. She started to shrink back into the couch, slightly embarrassed when Vogel shouted, "Fuck yeah!!! Rock on!!!"

Vogel spun around, swiped at the hollow screen and queued up a new playlist. Heavier and harder beats pounded as vocals began screaming and growling in almost unintelligible words to John's ears. Vogel got out of her seat and began tossing her hair around with her left hand in the air, moving back and forth perpendicular to her body as her right hand moved up and down in front, parallel to her torso. She leaned forward and back as she repeated these strange movements. Just as John was absolutely sure she had lost her mind, Elena got up and joined in. The holoscreen in front of the couch stopped displaying the light show and was now playing a flat recording, like the ones in the historical archives he'd seen, of some strangely dressed people with strange makeup and lots of metal spikes on their clothes. They were holding some sort of instrument and making similar movements. Understanding dawned on John what these two women were imitating in their jerky convulsions and strange behavior. Eyes bulging wide, he just stared and shook his head as he watched the incredibly odd spectacle.

As he watched the complete stranger that was wearing Elena's face dance and move until her cheeks turned red and a glistening of sweat started to form on her brow, John contemplated if he'd just completely misunderstood her all along, or if she was a completely different person now. Deciding this behavior and the knowledge of the music must have come from past experience, he started to picture the highly educated genius as a wild youth obsessed with the retro times. Picturing Elena as a counter-culture rebellious youth cast her in a completely new light in his mind and amused him greatly.

<h1 style="text-align:center">52</h1>

By the time the vehicle stopped in front of the tall clear structure of the vertical gardens Clara was tending, all five of the vehicles occupants were dancing. The vehicle had been driving itself for the last few songs and allowed the current song to finish before alerting its occupants to their arrival. By this point they were breathing a little heavy and laughing at themselves.

John struggled to stop laughing long enough to speak, but managed to address Elena, "I would have never guessed! I knew Vogel was a wild child in her youth, but I thought you were born with that chip on your shoulder." He gave her a wink for good measure.

Elena raised one eyebrow with a salacious gaze that looked John up and down. Shaking her head slightly. "Easy Cowboy. You'll have to keep dreaming. Not my type."

Elena gave John a wink and blew him a kiss with a little goodbye wave before she turned to speak to Vogel. "How big is that library? I've got a few suggestions for that playlist if you've got them. Check out this playlist..."

The two women moved to look at a holoscreen together as Elena's music collection showed up on the display.

John shook his head, as if to clear a thought and turned to Serena. "Y'all be safe. I'll check your location when i'm done here. If you're not too far, I may join you. Comm me if you need anything."

"Oh, don't worry about us John, I think we've got this. Oh yeah. I need you to drag Clara to the barbecue tonight. I've had a couple and she's always been too busy. Get her to come tonight, yeah?"

John gave her a nod and exited the cab. Once he'd gotten all the supplies Clara wanted off the vehicle, he slapped the cabin door with his palm twice and watched it slowly pull away. He marveled at how quiet it was with the door shut. The sound had been so immersive and clear in the cabin, like it was perfectly balanced in his head but never at an uncomfortable volume. It just felt loud inside, but outside the vehicle was practically silent as it pulled away. The loudest noise being the soft crunching of gravel under its weight as it rolled away. John didn't notice when the vehicle stopped after a short distance.

John was Just about to carry the first case through the door when Doc and Clara emerged from the building. Doc was walking sure footed and carrying a small case of his own.

"Doc! You're looking good man! I was going to come see you later. What are you doing here?" John said, still wearing the silly grin on his face that seemed to be stuck there after his ride from LZ1.

Doc glanced to his right and saw the vehicle on the street. "Ahh, I see you've gotten to ride in the party wagon. I'm just picking up some plant samples Riley and Clara want me to do some chemical analysis on. Ive got to get them back to the clinic now, but I'll see you at the BBQ tonight?"

John nodded, "Yeah, we'll be there," he said, with a nod in Clara's direction.

"Great! We'll catch up then." Doc said.

"Sorry Clara, but you had to know I'd bring in the big guns," Serena's voice almost right behind him startled John and nearly caused him to Jump. Serena didn't miss this and shot him a smirk.

"Speaking of, seems something's come up I need to attend to. Mind if I walk with you Doc?" Serena said, as the two began the short walk back towards the clinic.

John took a step and rotated around to stand beside Clara as he watched Doc and Serena walk away. "How's he doing?"

"He's fine. Better than you're going to be if you think you're taking the job of my secretary and managing my schedule now. Have you any idea..."

John's reply cut her off, "Nope! I don't want that job at all. It's not my doing... I was told we would be there and I'm pretty sure there was an implied threat to my skin staying in one piece if not directly assaulting my manhood. I'm quite attached to both actually, so I'm apparently robbed of getting to ask you to join me tonight."

"Serena. Ok, you're forgiven this time. She's been riding my case about it every time she catches one of those beasts anyway. Are those my seedlings?"

"Yup. Here, you take them, I'll grab the rest of your shopping list."

The two went inside, Clara explaining her latest experiments with genetics and what she had discovered from the plant life growing around them on the planet so far. John listened intently, admiring her passion and the clean smell of the vertical gardens. The first door lead to a large lobby area they crossed to another door. As they approached, the door beeped softly and opened for them with a silent movement. Clara's explanations began to include a tour of the facility as she mentioned which portions of experiments, research and propagation were going on behind each door as they walked a long corridor that curved around like the ones on the space station. To their left as they walked, Large glass windows provided a tranquil view of a large variety of trees, flowers and other plants that grew at ground level in something like a traditional garden and landscaping from back on earth. Walking paths wandered through the cultivated plants and occasionally a bench was positioned near a collection of one variety of plant or tree. In the center, a small pond and fountain sprayed in the bright light of the stars light as if under a spotlight. The mist from the fountain cast rainbows into the air around it. In the middle of Clara's sentence, John suddenly stopped, staring out into the garden. Noticing his attention, Clara followed his gaze and smiled.

"Oh, yeah. Some of the animals we brought in stasis were decanted last week. The bioreplication modules are functional now. The first round of embryonic and clones are progressing nicely. Beautiful aren't they?" Clara's voice was full of warmth and compassion.

"They are. What are they?"

"Butterflies from Earth. They're excellent pollinators. The only downfall is they spend the first stages of life attacking crops. We're testing varieties in several sections here to make sure there aren't any unexpected issues with the native flora, as best as we can. These observations will continue for quite some time and we will need to take many flights to collect plant samples from other areas of the continent as well. We can't release them outside yet because we don't fully understand the local flora and we don't want it trying to take over like the kudzu did."

"I've never seen them in person before," John said with a distant awe in his voice.

"Wait till you see what's on the 4th floor."

John turned and looked at her with a big smile. She thought he looked like a little kid being given treats on their birthday. Before she ushered him along, she noted there was still a slight tenseness around his eyes that remained. He was relaxed and happy, but something was on his mind.

"You look happy today, John."

"It's been a good day… and that wild pack of women I turned loose seems to be behaving like an invasive species."

Clara laughed at his joke and gave him a warm smile that went all the way to her eyes. "They're adapting. So much of this seems too good to be true, too easy. It's hard for people to accept sometimes, but those three have been down here the longest. They're good for moral of the colony as a whole. Everyone knows them. I think a bit of it is show though. They're convincing themselves as much as everyone else that everything is ok, to push on and focus on what we need to. What's on your mind John?"

John's smile faded a touch as he glanced over at her. Her warm patience and the slight upward tilt at the corners of her mouth soothed his nerves. "There's been a lot of new information since Elena and Bet returned, but all the answers just seem to bring more and bigger questions."

"we've all got a lot of questions and concerns John. Until last week, we'd not seen any physical remains of the previous colonists, other than Bet. Everyone wants to know what is going on… what happened, you know. It's too perfect of a situation here. We expected to rough it as scientists and pioneers, building from the ground up. Everything being so easy, so prepared for us to just take over with a head start of a hundred years sets off all the alarm bells…"

"You found remains? Why haven't I heard anything about this?"

"The report went straight to Morrow. She classified it. It wasn't pretty and she was concerned about how it might impact the colonists."

"How bad?"

"Well, let's get this to the lab and I'll show you."

"They're still there?"

"Here, actually… and you'll see why."

John wasn't sure what to expect, but trusted if there was something he needed to prepare himself for, Clara would tell him. The uneasy pit that formed in his stomach seemed to grow with every step though and the enjoyment from earlier seemed to fade quickly. He realized in an instant then, what Clara had meant by his team putting on a show. Their antics were a distraction. Temporary in nature, but somewhat essential to a positive mental health of the colony as a whole, and of course themselves. It was a coping mechanism for sure.

"Here we are," Clara said as she led John into her most recent lab.

The warm glow of panels above thousands of young plants gave a comforting feeling to a space that would otherwise just be rack after rack of pipes and tubs. Despite all the life in the large room, it felt clinical. A dramatic contrast to the garden he'd watched butterflies floating around in. It was space. The station and ship's hydroponics labs, but on the surface. It was familiar and unsettling at the same time. She showed John where to place his container and she moved to a barn shelf with the seedlings he brought down. It only took a couple minutes for the two of them to transfer the seedlings from their transport case to their new home here on the planet's newest nursery.

"It's amazing. They evolved and grew on earth. We moved them throughout the solar system and now, lightyears away… these are germinated in space and brought to an alien planet in hopes they will flourish. It's like our story, but it's easier to see when it's plants, you know. We aren't any different… but we don't necessarily see ourselves the same way day to day. These plants… they're kind of a reminder for how far we've come, individually and personally," John mused as he gently brushed his fingers over the tops of the new leaves.

Clara looked at John, a slight blush forming in her cheeks as his words resonated with her. "Magical aren't they?" Was all she could think to say.

"Yeah, all of it really is. And now, I've got tech in my head and we're forced to adapt… you said these are hybrids, right?" Clara gave him a nod so he continued, "I kind of feel like a hybrid now. Kind of like the genetics you've worked with here, but with the tech, the biomods… I feel like the plants here. Given the option and environmentally pressured to adapt to survive."

"You know, you should show that great brain of yours more often. You play the knuckle dragger 'Cowboy' routine well, but there's some really deep thoughts in that head of yours Mr. Ferris. You're right on the mark though. The sun is brighter here. While the solar radiation down here is approximate to that on Earth, the spectrum is slightly different and the star is much brighter than the Sun. These plants did not evolve for these conditions. As close as they may seem to us, they aren't the same as on Earth. In space, we use specific output of strategic portions of the spectrum to give them exactly what they need, but very little of the rest. Much of the white light in the growth is for our benefit actually, but these little guys needed a bit of assistance to not just survive, but to thrive here. I've been adjusting the lighting since we left, adjusting and incrementing them to the new conditions the whole time. After we got here and got more comprehensive data, I was able to finish the process. It took a lot of work and many generations to achieve. Plants live much faster lives though. We don't have generations ourselves to adapt, but generations before us did the work for us."

"So, you're ok with the mods?"

"My work is incremental. Such a leap forward is unsettling to me. The artificial aspect does not match the organic nature of my botanical passions, but yes. I'm ok with it… I just have my reservations still."

"I understand. I was so enamored with the advantages at first…" John trailed off. Clara patiently waited for him to finish. "I don't figure you can relate, but it's kind of like combat in a way. You don't really stop and take the time to analyze things, make pros and cons lists and weigh out your options. It relies on training, what's immediately in front of you, quick decisions and sticking to them or knowing when to abandon for a different approach. It's… intuitive. It's almost instinctual sometimes. I wanted the advantage. There's a massive impact crater, a missing colony… and there's just me and my team. We aren't a full military. We aren't even close to what I imagine a colony like this would have had, even in peacekeepers and lawmen alone. Its frightening to think about, so any advantage I could get… just seemed the instinctual right move based on my intuitive feelings and fears."

"That makes a lot of sense, but why do you sound like you're second guessing it now?"

John began to tell her all that Elena had told him, the weird conversation with Bet when he seemed to quiz John about his motives and desires for power, and the telepathy like communication he'd just learned about not even two hours ago. As he started talking, Clara listened intently. She didn't speak or interrupt, she just let him talk. John didn't recall when, but at some point, she had put her arm through his and started walking. Guiding him out of the lab, down the corridor and through an airlock type series of doors that moved so silently that it hardly registered to John as he spoke. He made sure to tell her everything, even his own private thoughts on the subjects. When he was done, he felt as if the tension in his shoulders had eased a considerable amount. He was looking into her eyes again, lost in her warmth and welcoming attention when he finished talking. His gaze shifted to the top of her head as he became consciously aware of his surroundings. A butterfly had landed atop her head. They were sitting on a bench in the inner terrarium.

Noticing his eyes move to the top of her head, Clara's smile grew and little delicate wrinkles formed beside her eyes. Slowly, she reached a hand up, laying it flat on her forehead, she moved it slowly back. It rubbed and messed up her hair, which seemed to flair away from her head in golden streaks capturing the light as her hand passed. Gently, going on feeling alone, she allowed the butterfly to walk onto her hand before she slowly lifted it away. As her hand came within her line of sight, she rotated it, allowing the butterfly to walk into her palm.

"Ahhh! Morpho peleides. The Blue Morpho butterfly. From South America, Earth." Clara giggled, "it still feels silly to me, adding Earth to the end of that now."

John stared at amazement as the large insect covered her entire palm and more. Its wings, he estimated, must have been about 18-20 cm across. A smile shape of a black line traced the bottom of its wings with linear patterns of white dots and dashes, but what captivated him most, was how the bright blue section over the majority of its wings were a bright iridescent blue that ranged from a slightly greenish teal color to a rich bright deeper blue. It was unlike anything he had seen in natural form before.

"Can I touch it?" John whispered?

"Here, hold your hand flat, next to mine and let it walk over if it wants, but don't touch the wings."

"Will it hurt it?"

"in a way, it can. Yes." Clara thought about how to reply as she held John's hand next to hers with her free hand. "You're familiar with camouflage in nature, right?"

"The concept, yes. Animals and even some plants I believe, adapt to blend in with their surroundings. The ones who do this best have the higher probability of survival and pass these traits on in reproduction. Over time some have become so adapted to their environment, they can be all but invisible."

"Exactly. Your textbook definition of evolution actually gets right to the point I am trying to make. The eye... it's all about the eyes with these amazing creatures."

John caught the amusement in her voice as she teased him, but he couldn't ignore the look in her eyes. She was pulling him in and he knew it. "Eyes you say?" He asked, his gaze never leaving hers.

"Yes, the eyes. Yours are playing tricks on you now. This butterfly is not blue. In fact, there's nothing blue at all on this butterfly."

John's gaze lingered briefly on her eyes before quickly moving back down to the butterfly, just as it flew off his hand. He watched it float along, as if weightless. "I'm afraid you're going to have to get to your point soon, or I'm going to get my eyes checked. I think these implants must be screwing with my vision, because that was a giant blue butterfly. You even called it a Blue… Blue Morpho, wasn't it?"

"Thats right, and there's nothing wrong with your eyes. It's an illusion actually."

Something seemed to catch her eye behind him. She stood up suddenly and took several steps past John before bending over to pick something up. When she returned, she held a much smaller dead butterfly, of some other species in her hand.

"This is the final stage of their lives. It's actually quite short for many, compared to the time they spend as larvae and pupa before this. In their adult stage, they develop these brightly colored wings. They are actually covered in really tiny scales, essentially. If you touch the wings, it rubs off like powder onto your fingers. But, if it were blue, then I should get a blue smudge on my fingers when I rub them, right?"

Clara gently rubbed her index finger across the back of the deceased butterfly wing. John could see the smudge it left behind. When she flipped her hand over to show him the tip of her finger, it had a black dust on it.

"Ok, that's weird. I'm going to need you to stop playing with me and tell me what witchcraft this is." John prodded her.

Clara let out something between a giggle and a chuckle that John adored. "The bright colors help to attract a mate, but you would think it might give their position away to predators, like birds for instance, right? Well, each of these scales doesn't hold any pigment. If you look at them under a really powerful microscope, you see that they have specific shapes, often with branches coming off of a central shaft. Each branch is perfectly spaced from one another to trap specific wavelengths of light. Instead of reflecting light, like pigments, they trap it, like using destructive interference, or wave inversion is used to cancel sound, but not really. It's just a good metaphor because light is hard to explain. Anyway, the scales are black or brown typically. The whole butterfly is typically black or brown. Because the frequency of light that isn't trapped by the wings is outside of what a bird can see visually, the butterfly makes itself virtually invisible to them. It's all an illusion of camouflage"

John was impressed. He watched the butterflies with a whole new appreciation. They were a curiosity, a colorful part of nature he had no memory of seeing before that appeared to float weightless. Now he saw them as brilliant tactical adaptations. They were like floating ninja ferries, invisible to anything that was a natural threat to them. That was something he could truly admire.

"Of all the things I've learned from you, that has got to be the absolute best brain nugget yet," John said.

Clara rewarded him with another of her laughs that delighted him so much. They sat there on the bench for a while longer in silence, watching the butterflies. Their hands still touching, softly holding one another's having barely moved since the butterfly flew off, except to rest gently atop their knees where their legs touched as well. Neither seemed to want to break the moment. It felt as fragile as the dust on a butterflies wings, yet just as beautiful and precious.

After a little while, Clara squeezed his hand. His attention hardly left the fact they were touching, but she brought his full attention to her.

"I'm sorry to spoil the mood, but there was something else I was going to show you." Clara's voice had changed. It was more businesslike now. He felt like she was consciously pushing any emotion out of it, trying to be neutral.

"The remains?" He asked. She nodded.

<h1 style="text-align:center">53</h1>

As the vehicle approached its first stop, a nearby sight Elena had visually identified as a potential distribution hub for the power grid, the four women were in great spirits. Laughing, dancing and singing had them all in a good mood, even if Serena and Han had no prior experience with the 20th century music genre Vogel called "metal." Next to the vehicle, Han opened one of the forward containers. Instead of just opening like a box, it hinged down and racks of tools and gear followed the lid out and down for an easy to reach, organized display. Selecting two spheres, big enough to fill her palm like a large fruit and on the verge of being too large to grip with one hand, Han activated the devices and allowed them to float into the air in front of her. Turning her back to them and facing the truck again, Vogel looked over her shoulder as a large holoscreen sprang to life deeper within the container.

"We've got a great visual by putting the larger screen back there, shielded from the star's glair. They can, of course, be used with wrist units away from the vehicle too," Vogel informed Elena as Han got the system operational.

"Very smart," Elena praised. "But, if I may, I'd like to try something with the second drone. I've got flight controls."

"Flight controls, yours." Han replied, falling back into her professional demeanor.

With a thought, Elena tried to connect to the drone directly, but wasn't able to establish any link. She reached out to touch the drone as it hovered, but still couldn't establish a link. "Well, I suppose it was too much to hope for some backwards compatibility with these implants."

Vogel snorted. Han suggested, "try using your wrist comp as an intermediary. Looks like you've got new tech upgrades there, should work."

Elena nodded and after establishing a link with her wrist comp, she was able to see the controls and visual image on her holoscreen. With a thought, she moved both to her mind. Han was still receiving the visual stream and sensor data on her display as Elena began to test her control over the drone. At one point, she opened her eyes. The overlay of the drone's visual feed with her own was so confusing and disorienting, she slammed them shut. That would not work if she had to walk around with her eyes shut the entire time. She began a mental exercise she had very little practice with. By imagining what she wanted, she gave the thoughts a mental nudge and let the technology in her head do the rest. After a bit of mental gymnastics, she was able to reduce the drone's visual feed to a smaller scale just on the edge of her peripheral vision to her right orientation, so that it remained in clear view without giving her the constant instinct to turn and look at it, but not in her direct line of sight. Sensor feeds in numbers and graphs were pushed into a column on the left side. Slowly, she opened her eyes and saw her very own personal HUD, very much like the one in her helmet's visor when she was wearing a full environmental suit. She played with the drone a few seconds more, flying circles around the vehicle, then under it, around Vogel and back over the top of the vehicle before coming to rest just over her right shoulder. It wiggled there for a moment or two before she was able to get a close approximation for sinking her line of site with that of the drone. After shaking her head back and forth slowly a few times, nodding and then turning around in circles, she had the drone's hover position matching not only her body movements, but her eye movements.

"If you're done with your Hokey Pokey dance, can we begin?" Han teased while tossing a third drone to Vogel.

"Oh yeah, I'm ready now… I think I've got the hang of this now." Elena said.

With that, three drones took off toward the building in front of them. Coordinating with each other, they each directed a drone in overlapping paths to scan the entire exterior of the structure. Finding no reason to worry, they sent the drones through the front door. Each one branching off to explore and map out all the equipment. Rows of large cabinets hosted many dozens of conduit lines. These all collected from behind each row, joining the others before it as they all ran through a trough in the floor until they disappeared underground at the rear of the facility. These seemed to run away from the impact zone, toward the southern portion of the city.

"If all those lines are output, does anyone see something from the northern or western side that looks like the line in?" Elena asked.

"I think I've got something here," Han spoke up after a short pause.

Elena took a glance over her shoulder to view her screen.

"That looks like what we need. I'm about done on the southeast side, I'll be there in a minute. Keep scanning the area. Getting a lot of good details here." Elena said.

"Uhh, I think you're going to want to take a look at this." Vogel's voice was monotone and cautious.

"What have you got?" Elena asked.

Vogel paused a moment, trying to get a closer look and switching back and forth between different sensors in an attempt to get a better view. "I think it's a hatch, but it's big. Big enough to get equipment through, but..."

"Service tunnel perhaps?" Han asked.

"That was my first thought, but this door doesn't look like the kind you would put on a maintenance tunnel. It looks more like a blast door," Vogel answered.

"Can you get it open?" Elena asked.

"No response at all." Vogel said.

"I'm going to look at it myself," Elena announced as she started walking for the door.

Han and Vogel exchanged a look and started opening other containers and grabbing gear. Vogel grabbed two bags, tossed one to Han then reached in for a third. She closed the lid on the container just in time to catch a smaller bag Han had tossed at her. With a practiced juggle of gear completed, they took off after Elena. Reaching her before she got to the entrance, Elena was halted when a bag was thrust at her from either side, blocking her path. She looked at Vogel on her right who just raised an eyebrow at her in response. Elena slung the proffered bag over her shoulders to carry on her back and looked at the smaller second bag Han was holding. Taking the bag, she saw Han give her a quick nod. Elena started to sling the second bag as Han and Vogel started walking ahead of her. Each of them walking in perfect step looked completely synchronized as they slung a left arm backward to tap the bottom of the backpacks before lifting their wrist comps in front of them. A second later, the backpacks on each of the two women expanded arms above each of their shoulders from the top of the bag. The straps automatically cinched around their hips and shoulders for a perfectly secured fit. Soft light began to glow from lines on the bag at the seams, straps and a few other places that must indicate purpose. Still in perfect sync, Both women removed a helmet from the smaller bag. With a well practiced ease, they doffed the helmets with their right hand while passing the storage bag it was in to the bottom of the backpacks with their left hands where they seemed to magically vanish into the backpack.

Elena was still standing there holding what she now knew to be a helmet in a bag as Han positioned herself at one side of the door and Vogel matched her position on the opposite side. Both women now stood there, visors and packs glowing and staring right at her.

Vogel started, "Well, this was your idea…"

"So are you coming, or what?" Han finished.

Shaking her head, Elena fumbled to repeat the movements she'd seen the two women so flamboyantly demonstrate for her.

"Yeah yeah, message received. This is your show and I'm the tourist here. Got it." Elena said with a laugh as her helmet adjusted its fit around her head and stepped inside the building between the two women while they grinned at her from ear to ear under glowing face masks.

"Seriously though, this is SOP for any new building. Since Doc's accident, we don't take needless chances here. Your pack is fitted with a wonderful sensor array that will record to your wrist comp. I'm sure you'll want to review it later in addition to the drone scans. You've got lidar up top, subsonic frequencies below, thermal imaging, temperature, moisture, air quality… it's a fully kitted portable environmental array, you'll see all that…"

Han picked up to finish Vogel's lecture, "… but do NOT ignore the density scans and structural analysis on the right side of your visor. You can rearrange the display all you want except for the bar at the top. If that sucker ever goes red, you freeze. Do not move until you evaluate what the pack is telling you. There's a pretty smart Ai in there analyzing every sensor and data feed in that pack real time…"

"… it will make noises, move and do things on its own to get the data it needs to be as aware of the environment as it can be. It can also control the utility suit your wearing. That compression that happens when you're pulling g's, it'll use that to set your legs rigid if you're about to take a wrong step…"

Han, "…it'll scare the shit out of you if it does go off, and your mobility will instantly decrease. It won't lock you stiff, we don't want you to fall over unpredictably and get yourself in more trouble, but if it goes off, you best stop what your'e doing real fast. Oh and it can also…"

Vogel, "… lock your mag boots to any metallic surface if it thinks that might help. Remember, this is safety equipment and is meant to prevent you being half robot like Doc because you decided to do something stupid and try to bring a building down on your head…"

Han, "… but in case you do, that's why you have the hardhat. Now, you remember the way to that door you wanted to see, or shall we take the lead?"

Elena burst out laughing. "How many times have you two practiced that routine?"

Han, "Oh, just about every time we enter a building, we go in like rock stars…"

Vogel, "but the safety brief, only about a half a dozen times."

Han, "maybe seven. Don't get too many tourists around here this time of year."

Vogel, "we're hoping once we can power the amusement park, business will pick up a bit."

Elena was still laughing as they made their way into the building.

Taking advantage of the pause in conversation, Vogel opened a comm link. She thought about it for a half second, and added John to the channel. "Station 1 please be advised, we are entering a building at this time. Elena wants to look at a door. Drone scans report a solid structure, no damage evident, should be a lovely casual stroll through another dark cave, Over."

The reply on Comms came from Marcus. "Got you loud and clear Vogel. I see four position beacons reading green. You're on the map. Receiving drone scans now for map update. Be safe in there. I'll make sure the Captain gets an update. This channel will remain open as usual. I'm getting a lot better bandwidth this time. Your data streams look great. Call us if you need us, but please don't call."

"What's the matter Marcus?" Han teased, "we too much for you to handle?"

"Always." The short reply came back.

In Vogel's comm view, a quick flash next to John's icon signaled he had received the message too. Then she saw a flash come from Doc's name. She thought to herself, 'Always good to know the boys are out there, but Marcus is right. I'd rather not have to call them for help today.'

As the three women worked their way through the utilitarian building, Elena stopped a couple of times to take a few notes about some equipment or check for details the drone scans wouldn't have provided. After answering some questions about the facility, Elena finally thought to ask a question that had been at the back of her mind since they entered the building.

"So, where did these packs come from? This is certainly not tech we brought, but it's not exactly colony tech either. I can't seem to interface with it like I can everything else colony tech."

Vogel answered, "Oh, it's colony tech all right. Several pieces. Took Han a week to hack it."

"It took me two days, and that's only because there were nearly a dozen pieces I had to crack and had to create a whole new interface to access the memory modules and the source code. It took me the rest of the time to rewrite all the code for everything to work together and train up the stupid Ai. Took you just as long to design the packs and get the build right."

"Well, that only took me two days as well." Vogel mocked.

"And you spent the rest of the time trying to stop the packs from strangling everyone that put them on." Han teased.

"Hmm, did we ever get them all patched? There was that one that kept flaking out, wasn't there?" Vogel asked, as if lost in thought.

"How many did you make?" Elena asked.

Han replied absentmindedly, "Oh, just three. But V and I have modified our own a bit here and there. You've got the spare."

Elena couldn't help but look down at the straps and check for some way to adjust them. She was just tracing the strap over her right shoulder down toward the waistband when she heard the other two stifling laughter.

"Oh, very funny you two. So just how much of that was bullshit?"

"Only the three packs bit. We made six initially, then six more as backups, but only eleven are operational. That was all the parts we had and the twelfth really does have some issues. Faulty hardware. It's rather fun to watch it try to strangle a chair though." Han answered. "But we did all twelve in a week."

"That's quite impressive, and a lot of tech to have recovered too. Did you find some old merchant's warehouse or something?"

"Something like that," Vogel explained. "We got kind of lucky and found a supply warehouse pretty quickly. Most of the stuff in there was junk, but there were a few treasures hiding in the dark corners."

"Yeah, but that's not the best part," Han added, leaving it hanging.

"Ok, I'll bite. Tell me tell me!" Elena played along, enjoying the banter.

Vogel and Han stopped. Turning around, they looked right at Elena. The illumination of all three vizor displays lighting up each face clearly. Elena could see huge grins on their faces.

"How do you recon all this tech and equipment got here? It's not like there's the massive industrial complex that was available back in Sol." Han asked.

Elena knew the answer though. "Did you find it then?"

The gleeful expression fell off their two women's faces. "No, not yet. Theres plenty of evidence for it though. How'd you know?" Vogel asked.

"Well, now it's my turn to have the upper hand here. You know that little cruise Bet and I just took? Well, there's a bit more out there than just an energy plant."

"Does it work?!" Han asked excitedly.

"Sure does. Bit low on resources at the moment though. It would take a considerable amount of work to get it operational, not to mention shuttling back and forth. It was really meant for supporting the laboratories and the energy farm, nothing on this scale."

"So, then there must be a big one hidden around here somewhere. Autofactories were just fiction stories, I never thought I'd actually see one. I wonder what all it can do!" Han said.

"Well, obviously we've seen what it can do," Vogel teased.

Han let out an exasperated sigh. "Not what I meant and you know it."

Vogel chuckled. The three women continued walking and talking about 3D printing, autofactories that could build atom by atom, all the mining and resources that would be required to run them. They were all quite enjoying the conversation so intently, it was almost sad when they reached the door and it was back to business.

The door was indeed built like a blast door. With a height of about 5 meters, it was nearly three times their height. It looked to be fairly square, about 5m in width as well, giving it almost a large vault like appearance.

54

Elena searched all over the door and the walls on either side of it for any sort of access panel or a clue for how to open it. Han and Vogel watched, with no small level of amusement, as Elena walked back and forth across the door. She ran her hands over every surface she could reach, talked to it like it was voice activated and finally just stood in front of it and stared at it. After what felt to Vogel like a rather lengthy amount of time to just stand there staring at a door she started to say something, but was quickly hushed by Han's quick and silent hand lightly thumping her shoulder. When she looked at Han, Han gave a slight shake of the head and placed a finger over her lips.

Han sent a text message to Vogel's visor that read, "Don't interrupt. I'm pretty sure she's trying to interface with it via implant. Probably some pretty good security on a door like this. Let her work."

Vogel nodded and replied back, "Shouldn't you be the one trying to breach security? She might be a genius and all, but this isn't her specialty."

The reply came back quickly, "And she's got rank. I'll do it when she gets bored and try not to show her up too bad."

Vogel tried and failed to stifle a laugh. It came out as more of a snort.

Elena let out a huge sigh and said, "Han, this thing's wrapped up tighter than it looks. Wanna give it a crack?"

"Thought you'd never ask. Can you patch your interface through your wrist comp? Perfect, yes. Just like that. Ok, on your holo, show me the interface… excellent. Thanks."

Han got to work on the door. As they all kept an eye on Elena's display, a bright light show was happening on Han's visor. Code and windows were flashing quickly across, casting an odd flickering of shadows across Han's face. Elena found the sight to be a little disturbing.

"Creepy isn't it?" Vogel asked.

"Yeah, she do this often?"

"Anytime we've got to crack open a new door or access some system on backup power… we've even had to bring our own power just to get into a few places. We've got big jumper cables on the truck for just that sort of thing. I'm pretty sure she turns up the brightness just for effect though. Such a showoff."

Han pretended to ignore them, but Elena was almost sure she saw the corner of Han's mouth twitch as the visor got just a little bit brighter. After a few minutes more, Han had displays on each of their wrist computers showing different data and was still working hard at getting the door open.

"It's never taken this long," Vogel teased. "Are you loosing your touch?"

"No way, this things locked down tighter than an ore miners airlock in pirate territory." Han replied. "This has more security than that insane lab we found last week."

Vogel let out a slow whistle in reply. "Damn. Considering all the treasure we've found once we got that one open, there must be something really good down there."

"Ok, I think I've got it… just one more…" Han was muttering to herself when all of a sudden all of their displays went blank. Standing at the end of a large pathway through a large building in front of a giant vault door, The weight of the darkness around them pressed at their fears. Only the dim soft glow of the illuminated stripes on their packs gave any light. There was utter silence, not even the sound of breathing.

"Yeah!" Elena's exclamation sliced through the air and caused Vogel and Han to both instinctively react, poised to defend themselves. The door began to move, slowly sliding inward, the centuries of dust and grime giving a faint grinding sound. In the low light, it was the only indication of movement.

Han started moving to unsling her pack when their lights and visors sprung back to life.

"That was weird. Did it kill the packs?" Vogel asked.

"Nah, I'm afraid that was my fault. I had to tap into the processing cores in each of them and re-task the neural nets just to get enough edge on that system. I… uhhh, kinda crashed them there at the end.

But hey, they rebooted and work fine and we're in, right? So… everything's fine. Big scary door is opening now… "

"Vogel, send the Captain an update." Elena ordered.

When Vogel pulled up her comms system and reported the status update, they all heard John's voice in reply.

"Hold location. Wait for backup. I repeat, do not proceed until we arrive. Not one foot through that door."

Elena was frustrated and her voice gave it away when she opened the channel and replied.

"It's just a big door in an electrical substation. It's probably just a maintenance shaft."

"Elena, I'm afraid that doesn't explain the insanity we just saw from your data feeds, or why it just cut off. We've regained access to your data feeds now, but mind telling me what is going on down there?" Captain Morrow's voice cut in.

"I got a little heavy handed with the gear Captain. The security on this one was different than we've seen before and I just needed a bigger hammer." Han replied.

The Captain's voice came back, "I could send Bet down with Marcus."

"Absolutely not necessary Captain. Serena and I are grabbing Doc now. We'll be there shortly. That's plenty enough." John replied.

Elena was getting a little frustrated and obviously wanted to see what was behind the door. It had finished sliding into the tunnel and was now sliding down into the floor beneath their feet. Over the top of the door, through the gap still way above their heads, a faint light was starting to flicker and shine through.

"Drives me crazy, we do all the work and he just swoops in and takes over like that?" Elena muttered without activating her comm channel.

"Well, that's kind of his job, isn't it?" Han replied.

Elena glanced over at her and Han just shrugged.

"Promise we won't get in the way of you doing your job." Vogel added.

Elena nodded and let out an exasperated breath.

"You're right. It's just so…"

In unison, Han and Vogel said, "we know."

Elena couldn't help but smile.

By the time the door completely opened, Han was preparing a drone to investigate. Just before she launched it, bright lights and a lot of noise coming down the passageway behind them. John, Serena and Doc pulled up in one of the smaller transport vehicles Han and Vogel had gotten working.

"I said not one foot, I didn't think I had to spell it out no drones either. Has anything crossed that threshold yet?" John barked at them as he marched out of the vehicle.

Han, sensing he was all business, accepted the rebuke. It suddenly dawned on her that something else must have happened to stir John up.

"No, Chief. I was just preparing for a little recon, same as we've always done. What's going on?" Han replied.

His team almost never called him Chief, a reference to his rank and position. The words caught John and he slowed his step and took a deep breath.

"Relax, just want to take every precaution with this one. There isn't anything 'normal' about this door is there?"

Han and Vogel exchanged a look and both gave John a shrug.

"Look, can we just get in there already? I seriously doubt there's anything more than some high voltage electrical systems and a bunch of wires down here. It's just a maintenance shaft and I need to get down there so I can devise a plan to get power up and running for the colony." Elena said in a rather exasperated tone as John walked up.

The lights on the vehicle dimmed as Serena and Doc stepped up behind John. Elena's eyes went wide when they each handed off an energy rifle to Han and Vogel. When Elena turned to launch into another argument with John, she found him thrusting an energy pistol at her. She looked down at the weapon, grip facing her, still in a holster with a belt and thigh strap dangling from it.

"I didn't come here to argue or tell you how to do your job. Just put this on and let me do mine, ok? Then we can go have some BBQ'd alien monster and laugh about how ridiculous the extra precautions were and how right you were... but if you're wrong..." John said, voice flat and even as he thrust the weapon in her direction again.

Elena rolled her eyes and took the proffered weapon. John looked them over. Han and Vogel were wide eyed and alert. He could tell they had questions and he admired their discipline in not asking.

"While you three were in here getting this big door open, Clara showed me the only remains we've found of the previous inhabitants here. We can go over the gory details later, but it raised a lot more questions than it gave answers, ok? I don't have anything to go on here except a gut feeling." John paused and glanced at Doc, "and I'm not about to risk any more accidents, good?"

John and Elena both noticed a slight tension release in Han and Vogel. To everyone else, it appeared as if Elena turned and stared at John for a brief moment. Then she nodded, he nodded back and they turned to face the open door. The action was so odd, Han and Vogel exchanged a look. Vogel mouthed "what the fuck?" And Han shrugged.

Inside the large opening was what appeared to be offices along the right side. On the left, were three stronger looking double wide doors that looked similar to a lift on a space ship or station.

Elena turned to John, "I suppose you want to investigate the offices first?"

John just nodded and started walking for the nearest door.

<h1 style="text-align:center">55</h1>

As John started walking for the first door, Han and Vogel fell into step behind him and off to either side. Doc walked up and motioned politely to Elena as if asking if he might formally escort her in some ceremony. The smile on his face and the kind act helped Elena relax and she joined him. Serena followed, bringing up the rear. Crossing the large area in what Elena noted was a military like formation, her unease began to grow again. She had exchanged a rapid and short conversation with John through their mental link before entering. The exchange had left her palms sweaty and her heart beat just a little bit faster. She felt Doc's light touch on her arm as they approached the first door, encouraging her to stop several meters back. They stood there and watched as John walked up and placed. His hand on the door. Han stood at an angle next to one side and Vogel on the other. As the door opened, Vogel stiffened and brought her rifle up a little bit higher. John's hand gently laid on top of it and slowly pushed it back down toward the ground in front of her. John stood there for a moment, then took a step back away from the door.

"Just like the other one. Have a look if you like." John said as he motioned toward the door.

Elena could feel a lump in her throat that made it hard to swallow. Her mouth was dry and her tongue seemed to be stuck to the roof of her mouth. She took a quick swig from the drinking tube at her right collar then stepped forward to take a look.

Inside was the half skeletal and half metal remains of a human, at least she thought it was human. It was hard to tell anymore. In its lap were unmistakably human hands at the end of arms. In the palm of one was a data core. In the other, a pistol. She could see a clear hole from one side of the skull through the other at a slight upward angle. She followed the angle up and saw another small hole and scorch marks high on the wall, just below the ceiling. Serena walked in and picked up the data core. After holding it in her palm for just a couple of seconds, she passed it to John. Her face revealed nothing, and her movements were smooth, fluid and purposeful as she walked back out of the office. As she did so, she unsheathed her vibrosword.

Elena turned back to John just in time to see him close his eyes and let out a soft sigh.

"Here. See for yourself."

He placed the data cube in Elena's hand. She saw in his face a deep sadness.

"What will I see?" She asked.

"Nothing good." Was all he replied as he stepped for the door.

Elena stared at the small blue almost opalescent cube in her palm for a moment, unsure if she wanted to see what was on it or not. Something had John shaken. The short answers, the all business attitude, the weapons and what was that look on his face? What did it mean? What happened to the rest of the colonists and why had this one barricaded themselves behind the blast door to end their life? Only one way to find out, she supposed. And with a deep breath, she mentally reached out to the data cube and connected her mind to it.

Overlayed in her vision, she could see one file and a locked folder. She focused on the file. In a flash, like recalling a memory that wasn't her own she watched in horror, the message this individual left.

She saw the colony full of life and people. Everyone was dressed a bit funny, some had small visible implants at their temples, but they all looked like normal people. The view panned and she realized she was watching from someone's personal perspective as a little girl ran from a beautiful woman, arms open and a huge smile on her face. She saw the girl jump and get caught in a hug.

"Daddy!" She said. "Mommy said we can go walk through the gardens today, are you coming too?"

Just then, pandemonium broke out. People started running everywhere, an alert came through what must have been an implant like a colony wide alert.

"Everyone report to your designated work areas or domicile meeting points. This is not a drill."

Fire erupted across the sky as if the clouds were on fire. The little girl was passed back to her mother. Quick words were exchanged and they ran in opposite directions. He stopped to turn and look back at them one last time. Then he ran for this building. She was heading northwest. A horrible feeling came over Elena as she realized the woman and child were heading straight for where she knew an impact crater lay. She saw the building she was in just up ahead, not but a few blocks away. Streaks of burning debris lit up the sky like a meteor shower in broad daylight. Confusion was everywhere as people were running in every direction at once. Taking a quick glance down a main pathway before he ran across, she saw billowing clouds of smoke, or ash… maybe water vapor. She watched it head directly for her briefly before sprinting. She heard the man cry out and lurch forward but he didn't stop. He looked over his shoulder and everything was gone. An energy weapon of some kind she realized. Not a laser though, maybe directed microwave or something like that? It had vaporized everyone that was on that path. She could hear the man's labored breathing as he ran harder, seeming to struggle with every step. There were people standing at the outside bay door, right next to where she had come in, they were waving at him to hurry as the door began to close. He ducked in and kept running until he was with a small group just outside the big door.

Then the image switched, he was looking out a front window as large mech suited individuals marched down the streets and wide paths between the buildings. They were herding people into large caged wagons. Then the impact came. The lights went out as a mushroom cloud of dirt and molten rock flew into the air. Someone grabbed his arm and began shouting at him to hurry. He was practically dragged through the big door. Two men stood just off to the side, hands on an access panel just inside the door, she'd missed that when they came in. They were shutting the door. She watched as it rose higher and higher before locking forward into place. Somehow, she knew that door had not opened until Han forced it open.

The scene changed again, they were moving into the doors on the opposite side from the office she was in now. A lift. It moved fast, plummeting so fast she could pick up on small signs in peoples hair and clothing that there was a reduced gravity in the lift. It seemed to go on for ages! Just how far down do those shafts go? The rate of descent began to slow and she saw the occupants struggle against the return of gravity and possibly even a little extra. The lift stopped and the doors opened. He walked through a lobby area at a quick pace, through a set of doors and into a large room full of holoscreens and at the very front, a huge 3D holographic view of the colony, the planet, all the way to the station and beyond. She could see small ships flying around the station. Most were no bigger than their shuttle craft she observed. Then a large mass began to enter into view. A massive ship, bigger than anything she had ever seen. The station was huge, the ship they had come here on was among the longest in existence when they left Sol. This ship was at least four times the size of their ship. She could see the view focus on the impact crater and the man dropped to his knees and wept.

The view started to change again, but she cut it off. Elena did not want to see anymore. She let her hand fall down to her side and closed her eyes. Slowly, she turned around and met John's gaze full on. She knew now what that look was on John's face. She knew he was looking at pure horror written all over her own face, and he felt it too. Seeing him wince slightly and Serena turn and glance in her direction, she quickly pulled back her emotions, keeping them all to herself now. John gave her a knowing nod. Slowly, she passed the data cube to Serena.

"4,500m down. A data vault. That's what the AI said when we first reached the station… That's what you've found here. Not a service tunnel." John's voice was neutral, completely void of any emotions. She felt him let his emotions show just enough to let her know he understood how she felt.

Epilogue

While Serena viewed the contents of the cube, John slowly walked back toward the large open door. Opening a comm link to the station, he reached Marcus first. He briefly relayed what they had discovered in very broad terms until Captain Morrow replied.

"John, what else is in there other than the one office and the lift?"

"I'm not sure yet Captain. I had to step back out the vault door to get a strong enough connection to the station. There's no chance we'll have comms while we're inside."

Captain Morrow didn't respond right away. After a few seconds of silence, she acknowledged his statement and started discussing the matter with Marcus. He wasn't sure if it was the Captain or Marcus that left the channel open, but he strained to hear what they were saying. Remembering he could turn the volume up, he did so just until he could hear the conversation. It would be loud if someone came back on the channel and he didn't want to blast his hearing in that event.

"Yes, I'm sure he'll check the entire level before proceeding, but what should we do with Bet in the mean time?" He heard the Captain's distant voice ask.

Marcus's reply was just as faint. "You want him down there for this?"

"I'm asking if you think I should detain him until we have more answers."

"Why would we do that? We have no reason to doubt him."

"We don't really have a real reason to trust him either, do we? For all we know, he could have been acting the entire time."

"Do you really believe that, Captain?"

"I don't know what to believe anymore Marcus."

"You're actually doubting the man who willingly gave us more energy than we've seen produced in our entire lives combined, basically the keys to this place… indirectly responsible … even still … alive. If he hadn't … Riley's implant … him establish link with the station AI, with the full authority the head of … entire previous colony held mind you… "

After struggling to hear what Marcus was saying, some of the sounds started to grow louder. Sensing the captain or Marcus was likely to get back on the comm, he turned the volume back down to a normal level.

"John?" Captain Morrow asked.

"Send him down here Captain. " John replied in answer.

"Excuse me?"

"I assume you left the comm channel open to indirectly involve me, meaning you either simply want me informed or you value my opinion as well. Send him down here. Don't tip him off that you're at all suspicious, because Marcus is right. You've got no reason to be."

"So you trust him then?"

"That's not what I said and that's irrelevant. If we do trust him, then we would absolutely want and possibly need his assistance with this. If he's been honest with us, then he has as much right if not more than us to know what we are finding down here."

"I hear a lot of 'if's' in your words John."

"Exactly. I'll handle any if's when and IF they come up. Until then, the man's got a right to know what happened to his friends and family." John's voice was stern and confident.

"Clear the rest of that level, find out what else is in there while you wait. I'll expect a full report before you go down that shaft John."

John turned around and found Serena standing just within hearing range behind him. He gave her a nod and watched as she turned and strode over to Elena, gesturing in his direction. With a flick of her head, Han, Vogel and Doc joined her and they started investigating the rest of the offices.

"The rest of the team is already on it, Captain." As Elena walked up, he added, "I'll work with Elena and try to transfer this file to you. Not sure if we can move it from the storage device to the wrist comp for transfer, but hopefully she's got an answer."

"Standing by. And John?"

"Yeah"

"Thanks."

"No, not yet. Don't do that yet." John said and cut the connection.

Elena held the data cube in her hand as she started messing with her wrist comp. After a few minutes of tinkering, he saw her turn and look toward the team. As they came out of another doorway, he spoke up to Elena. "Wait, not the time for surprises. Serena knows, contact her."

Elena turned to look at him. With an expressionless face, she simply nodded. John looked back toward his team and saw Serena turn around and bring them all to the large door entryway. As they arrived, he addressed Han and Vogel.

"I'm sorry you two won't get the entertaining initiation Elena started with me. You're about to feel something like a tickle in your mind. Focus on it. Implant has comms. Prepare yourself." John said as he initiated a connection with them.

'We'll work on the details later. Didn't want to shock you with this right now without warning.'

'Well, this changes everything!' Han thought.